Praise for *New York Times* bestselling author Lori Foster

"Readers will be thrilled with Foster's new sexy batch of fight club heroes and the women who love them."
—*Kirkus Reviews* on *No Limits*

"Storytelling at its best! Lori Foster should be on everyone's auto-buy list."
—#1 *New York Times* bestselling author Sherrilyn Kenyon on *No Limits*

"Foster's writing satisfies all appetites with plenty of searing sexual tension and page-turning action in this steamy, edgy, and surprisingly tender novel."
—*Publishers Weekly* on *Getting Rowdy*

"Foster hits every note (or power chord) of the true alpha male hero."
—*Publishers Weekly* on *Bare It All*

"A sexy, believable roller coaster of action and romance."
—*Kirkus Reviews* on *Run the Risk*

"Bestseller Foster...has an amazing ability to capture a man's emotions and lust with sizzling sex scenes and meld it with a strong woman's point of view."
—*Publishers Weekly* on *A Perfect Storm*

"Foster rounds out her searing trilogy with a story that tilts toward the sizzling and sexy side of the genre."
—*RT Book Reviews* on *Savor the Danger*

"The fast-paced thriller keeps these well-developed characters moving...Foster's series will continue to garner fans with this exciting installment."
—*Publishers Weekly* on *Trace of Fever*

"Steamy, edgy, and taut."
—*Library Journal* on *When You Dare*

LORI FOSTER

HOLDING STRONG

HQN™

ISBN-13: 978-0-373-77961-1

Recycling programs for this product may not exist in your area.

Holding Strong

Copyright © 2015 by Lori Foster

This edition published by arrangement with Harlequin Books S.A.

For questions and comments about the quality of this book, please contact us at CustomerService@Harlequin.com.

® and TM are trademarks of Harlequin Enterprises Limited or its corporate affiliates. Trademarks indicated with ® are registered in the United States Patent and Trademark Office, the Canadian Intellectual Property Office and in other countries.

www.HQNBooks.com

Printed in U.S.A.

Dear Reader,

My newest Ultimate series, with books that each stand alone but are connected by characters who know each other, involves mixed martial arts (MMA) fighters *and* falling in love. The books are not about fighting, but rather they are about high-level athletes fitting a monogamous, long-term relationship into the hectic schedule of training, travel, diet and competition.

The sport brings with it some hunky, capable alpha heroes so that all I need to do is add in the romance. Superfun for me and, given the reaction to the first two stories (*Hard Knocks*, an e-prequel novella, and *No Limits*, a novel), readers are enjoying them, too. I'm thrilled with the feedback I've gotten so far, and now I have my favorite couple yet!

Denver is big, strong, lethal in his skill, but he's no match for Cherry once she decides she wants him. As always, they have several things they need to work out—all while Denver keeps up with his training. This is one of my sexiest books ever, but that's because Denver is one of my sexiest heroes—something Cherry loves about him.

If you're not familiar with MMA, it is a full-contact, full-body combat sport allowing the use of strikes from hands, feet, elbows and knees, along with grappling techniques (think wrestling, but with submissions using manipulation of joints like elbows, knees and ankles), both standing and on the ground. The UFC—Ultimate Fighting Championship—is the best-known organization;

my fictional version is the SBC, or Supreme Battle Challenge. Many different disciplines are learned—Brazilian jujitsu, muay Thai, wrestling, boxing and kickboxing. You might read a term like a headlock, or an arm bar, or an ankle pick... just know that those are different terms used to describe the action, and given the scene, you should be able to get a visual. There won't be much of that, though, because as I said, the core of these stories is romance—sexy, fun, one-on-one romance.

After *No Limits* released, I got (happily!) bombarded with reader letters and emails asking which of the fighters would be next. Now you know it's Denver, and after him will be Stack. Armie, bless his kinky soul, will be last because let's face it, Armie has some things to work out before he plays the role of romantic hero. But if you'd like a sneak peek into the plans, check the back of this book for a special "bonus scene" from *No Limits* hero Cannon's point of view.

And of course, you are always welcome to reach out to me. I'm very active on most social media forums including Facebook, Twitter and Goodreads, and my email address is listed on my website at lorifoster.com.

I hope you continue to enjoy the Ultimate series. Do let me know!

Happy reading to all,

Lori Foster

HOLDING STRONG

CHAPTER ONE

WATCHING HER LAUGH, seeing her tease and flirt, burned his ass big-time. He loved when she laughed and teased with *him*—not so much when it was with other guys.

And therein lay the problem.

He had a near-savage lust for her. When he looked at her, when he heard that carefree laugh, he felt dangerously close to losing it.

Contemplating decisions and possible mistakes, Denver Lewis sipped his beer. He should look away from her but knew he wouldn't. She was all tits and ass and attitude in a petite frame, and God love the girl, she turned him on.

He'd avoided her, refused to be drawn in by her tempting smiles, and all in all given her the cold shoulder since determining they wouldn't suit. He had no right to judge her for having fun elsewhere.

But knowing and accepting that as true didn't talk him off the ledge. No, if anything it wound him tighter.

Damn, she looked good.

The shifting lights in the club played with her dark blond hair and the curves of her lush little body. His buddy Stack, another fighter, drew her into a fast dance. She didn't refuse. Ever.

Cherry Peyton was always the life of the party.

The loud music competed with the furious drumming of Denver's heart as he monitored her every move. The music's wild tempo kept her body from touching Stack's. They danced around each other and the rest of the crowd on the floor.

Every guy there made note of her, seeing her once and then taking a longer look. Her happiness, her laugh and that killer bod all combined for one hell of an impact on the male libido.

For over an hour, Denver watched her draw attention and smiles and, no doubt, sexual thoughts. He ignored other women who tried to get his attention, those who came up to him and propositioned him in modest and sometimes lewd ways.

Yeah, he wanted to get laid.

But he wanted Cherry, not anyone else.

It pissed him off that he couldn't get her out of his head. He should have had her before decreeing theirs an acquaintance-only relationship, then maybe he could have some perspective when it came to seeing her with other men.

Then again, maybe not—because days after meeting her, he'd known sex wasn't the only thing he wanted. He'd already begun to think of her as his, even though he hadn't even kissed her yet.

If only his territorial tendencies didn't clash so badly with her playful party-girl personality.

Seeing her accept her third glass of wine, he finished off his beer and called it quits.

At least on the alcohol.

He stewed while watching her indulge in several dances with too many different guys—never mind that they were all from their group, fighters that she, and he, knew well and trusted as friends. They'd all come down en masse to cheer on one of their own. Fighters from the rec center who sparred and coached together. Men he'd known forever.

Men who had befriended Cherry when she'd become roommates with Merissa, another fighter's sister.

She was well and truly enmeshed in his life, friends with his friends, a part of their inner group, and if he wasn't denying himself like a freaking masochist he'd be over there with them right now. She'd be laughing and joking with him. Dancing with him.

Treating him like everyone else.

That she was so well accepted in their circle made it even more impossible to stop thinking about her, because everywhere he went, he saw her.

Finally, after a robust dance that had her laughing aloud, Cherry began to fade. She dropped into a chair at a table with three other fighters and a few women.

Her gaze never once came his way—almost as if she knew where he was and avoided making eye contact with him.

Suited Denver fine. Mostly.

Damn it.

It wasn't easy, but he made himself look away.

Tonight had been an eventful one. They'd all gotten to the local fight venue early, some to grab a bite before the event, others just to ensure they got the best seats. They all enjoyed watching Armie Jacobson fight.

They'd enjoy it even more if Armie would accept the offers from the more elite, professional fight organization, the SBC, but for reasons of his own he dodged them, always insisting on sticking with the smaller, more local groups. It wasn't due to a lack of talent.

Cannon Colter was a star with the SBC, and both

Denver and Stack had recently signed with them. Since they each sparred with Armie, they knew firsthand that he was fast and deceptively strong, slick in a way that bespoke innate talent, something that couldn't be taught or learned but came naturally to a born athlete. Armie knew his shit.

If he accepted a contract with the SBC, he'd more than hold his own. Denver believed he would dominate there, as well.

But Armie blew them off every time.

Speak of the devil... When Denver saw Armie approaching him, he put his elbows back on the bar, glad to finally have a distraction. "How do you feel?"

"Whaddya mean?" Armie caught the bartender's eye and ordered a whiskey.

The competition had been done tournament style so that competitors had to win to advance, and had to fight multiple times. That arrangement wasn't common anymore, and wasn't the way the SBC did things. But the smaller events did what they could to highlight the fighters and drum up excitement.

Armie had knocked out his first guy, then submitted the next two—each in the first round. In the second fight, he'd locked in an arm bar so tightly that the other fighter had immediately tapped rather than risk injury. For the third, he'd submitted with a rear naked choke. Each time, he made it look effortless. Hell, he'd walked away with nothing more than a small bruise on his cheekbone and some mat burn on one elbow. That was it. No other injuries. He'd barely broken a sweat. Armie destroyed other fighters with disgusting ease.

Soon as the event had ended, most of the competitors and a lot of fans had converged on the nearby club for a promoted after-party. Armie, a fan favorite for the local organization, was sure to be the belle of the ball.

"You took that last guy apart. He was damn near knocked out when you decided on the arm bar."

Armie tossed back the whiskey and asked for another. "Yeah, he must've been new or something."

More like Armie was that good, but Denver knew he wouldn't admit it. For whatever reason, Armie shrugged off all opportunities to further his fight career. Because of that, Denver warned him, "Dean Connor was in the audience, scouting out the talent."

Only for a second did Armie react, but he shook off the stillness in less than a heartbeat. "Havoc was here?"

"One and the same." Dean "Havoc" Connor was a legend in the sport, and one of the most revered fighters ever. A while back, he'd switched gears from competing to training. Now, with another well-known veteran, Simon Evans, he ran one of the most successful and sought-after camps—the same camp where their buddy Cannon often trained.

And Cannon had an upcoming title fight for light heavyweight, so clearly they were doing something right.

Simon and Dean had the inside track with the SBC president and often recommended new recruits to bring under the SBC umbrella.

Brows drawn, Armie scoffed. "This gig wasn't exactly the upper echelon of talent. Why would Havoc waste his time with low-level competitions?"

Succinct, Denver told him, *"You."*

"Bullshit."

"He took a ton of notes while watching you, and as

soon as your fight ended he was on the phone making a call."

Armie flexed a shoulder. "He was probably here to see Cannon."

"He talked with Cannon. Merissa, too."

Armie almost fell off his stool. *"What?"* And then, with a quelling glare, "Why the hell would he talk to Rissy?"

"She was cheering for you like crazy and I guess that got his attention." Denver shrugged. Cannon's sister often accompanied him to the fights. No big deal with that. "Given she was with Cannon…"

"Yeah, maybe." Armie tossed back the second whiskey and ordered up a third.

Interesting. "Havoc's still here, but Cannon already took off with Yvette and Merissa." Since Denver hadn't yet convinced himself to leave the club, he ordered a glass of lemon water. In two and a half months he'd have his second fight with the SBC, so he'd started watching his diet already. Not that he ever got too far off weight, and not that he couldn't lose fifteen or even twenty pounds easily enough. But overall, he liked to stay healthy. He considered it part of his job requirements.

"I knew Cannon was booking. We'd already talked."

"He didn't mention Havoc?"

"No, and I'll give him hell for that later." Armie relaxed enough to manage a grin. "Used to be, Cannon would have closed out the place with me. Now, with Yvette, he's always in a hurry to get her alone. The wedding can't happen fast enough for those two."

"A few weeks after his next fight," Denver said. If it

was up to Yvette, they would have already been married because she didn't care about the fancy wedding.

But Cannon considered the guys family and knew they'd want to celebrate with him, so they'd set up the wedding in a way that wouldn't conflict with anyone's competition schedule, most especially Cannon's. "Looking forward to being best man?"

Armie snorted. "You all expect me to balk at the sight of a tux, but what the hell, man, you'll be wearing the same monkeysuit."

Watching Armie to gauge his reaction, Denver said, "Mostly I expect you to balk at the idea of being in the wedding with Merissa."

Looking past Denver, Armie narrowed his eyes. "Who's that dude hitting on Cherry?"

Twisting around, he forgot all about harassing his friend—which had probably been Armie's intent. But damn, he hadn't lied. Denver watched Cherry laughingly refuse an insistent guy bent on gaining her cooperation. The slow, thrumming music would have meant a different type of dance and Denver let out a breath when she didn't give in.

Seeing her body to body with another man, this time someone he didn't know, would have made him nuts.

Stack sat to one side of her, also watching the idiot who refused to take no for an answer.

To her other side, Miles started to frown.

Suddenly Cherry pushed back her chair and an ugly tension sank into Denver's chest—until she grabbed up her purse and made a hasty getaway toward the restrooms.

When the idiot started to follow, Miles blocked his

way while Stack spoke close to his ear. Whatever he said made loverboy frown and search the bar.

It wasn't until his gaze clashed with Denver's that he gave up and stalked away—in the opposite direction that Cherry had gone.

Smiles quirking, Stack and Miles both saluted Denver, then went back to their table and the other women there.

He was wondering what Stack had said when Armie shoved him, and Denver almost dropped off his seat. Righting himself, he muttered, "What the fuck?" and shoved Armie back. But since Armie wasn't daydreaming as Denver had been, he barely budged.

Snickering, Armie shook his head. "Damn man, get it together or go after her."

"No need. Stack got rid of him."

"Yeah," Armie said, his tone mocking. "Stack handled it."

Sarcasm? "What's that supposed to mean?"

"We both know Stack just threatened that poor bozo with *you*."

"Me?"

"Yeah, *Predator*, you." After emphasizing Denver's fight name, Armie sipped at his third drink. "You have a nasty death stare and you know it. That chump probably felt your evil intent all the way down to his balls."

"You are so—" Just then, Denver spotted Havoc scanning the crowd before a group of fans stopped him. "Think he's looking for you?"

Armie slunk lower in his seat. "No."

"You are so hopeless."

"Know what's hopeless? This denial you have where Cherry Peyton is concerned. Give it up already."

Denver glared at him. Why the hell did everyone want to butt into his private business? "Why don't you at least talk to the SBC? Maybe—"

"Why don't you talk to Cherry?" He tossed back his shot and asked for another. "Better yet, don't talk. Take her straight to bed and work off some tension."

Armie fought hard, played hard, but usually didn't drink hard. Denver eyed him. "This isn't about Cherry and me."

"It's about you trying to avoid talking about you and Cherry." He grabbed a handful of peanuts while waiting for the next drink.

Disgusted, Denver said, "Are you going to turn around everything I say?"

"Know what I'd like to turn around?" Armie nodded at someone. "That."

When Denver looked up he saw a stacked redhead coming their way. Lips pursed, eyes big, expression coy.

Definitely on the make.

"She looks ripe to ride doggy style, doncha think?"

At times Armie's brazen outspokenness bordered on obnoxious. Often, actually. But in this instance, with that girl's hips, Denver totally got his meaning and even had to grin in agreement.

Seeing their humor, the lady narrowed her coal-lined eyes.

Thank God it was Armie she'd zeroed in on. "You know her?" Denver asked.

"Nope. But give me a minute."

The redhead stopped in front of Armie and touched a finger to his chest. "You're Armie Jacobson."

"Guilty."

"So are the rumors true?"

"Sure."

Denver stifled a laugh; Armie hadn't even asked her what rumors she meant. But when it came to Armie, just about anything was possible.

Bracing her hands on his thighs, she leaned in more, making sure to put her cleavage on display. "I watched you fight."

"Yeah?"

"You're a beast." With a little shiver, she added, "I think that's sexy."

Armie smiled.

Denver lifted an eyebrow. He felt like a damn voyeur, but he wasn't about to budge. This was too entertaining.

"So…" Pretending modesty, she ducked her face while still watching him. "Was it…naughty of me to confront you like this?"

Armie stared her in the eyes while murmuring, "Real naughty. And you know what I do with naughty girls?"

"You…you punish them?"

Denver almost choked, yet Armie didn't miss a beat.

"That's right." Armie's smile had the woman ready to swoon, especially when he added, "Even if they're really, really good."

On an indrawn breath she straightened, all but vibrating with excitement.

"You got a room anywhere close, honey?"

Breathless, face flushed and one hand splayed over her upper chest, she whispered, "Right across the street."

Stern, his stare intimidating, Armie told her, "Then

we should probably get to it." He finished off his shot and put the glass on the bar.

To Denver he said, "Settle my bill, will ya?" and with a stinging swat to the gal's derriere, he started her toward the exit.

Shaking his head, Denver turned back to the bar—and almost bumped into Cherry Peyton. The time of the night and so much dancing had left her bouncy blond hair a little messy, her makeup a little smudged, her skin flushed and dewy.

A soft V-necked shirt clung to her breasts and tight jeans hugged her ass.

She looked so damn hot, his dick twitched and his guts tightened.

Breathless, eyes wide, she asked, "Was Armie serious?"

Just to tease her, Denver asked, "About what?" when he knew damn good and well what she meant. He also knew he shouldn't be engaging her more than necessary—except, well, his convictions had already started to fade.

After glancing around to ensure they had privacy, she whispered, "Spanking?"

Damn, but she always smelled so good. "I doubt it." Settling back some so he wouldn't keep breathing her in, he shrugged. "Armie's into sex however he can get it. But I don't think he particularly gravitates to the whole discipline scene."

Scandalized, she said, "He's awfully blatant about it."

True, but her interest in Armie annoyed him. Her interest in *all* guys was the number one reason he'd always tried so hard to avoid her.

Because he flat-out didn't share.

Cherry Peyton might be the most appealing woman he'd ever met—sexy, sweet, funny—but she was a world-class flirt.

That fact bugged him just enough that he asked, "Why?" He leaned to the side a little to see her heart-shaped ass. "You like the idea of getting your back-side warmed?"

Instead of embarrassing her, the question made her smile bright enough to stir him.

He almost got hard before she said, "No, so don't go getting any ideas."

Too damn late for that. He'd had ideas from the moment he'd laid eyes on her.

One hand on the stool next to him, she asked, "Mind if I join you?"

Yeah, he did. It would have been easier for him if she kept her distance. So far she hadn't done that. She teased and toyed with him constantly—along with every other guy in the vicinity. Tonight had seemed different and he'd thought maybe she'd finally given up—but now that she was done dancing with everyone else...

Struggling with himself, Denver hesitated too long, causing her to retrench.

"Unless you'd rather I didn't?" Watching him with big dark eyes that now looked wounded, she let out a breath. "You're probably hoping to hook up, right? Stack and Miles already did, so I didn't want to get in their way."

So she'd only approached him to give them space?

When he still said nothing, Cherry took a step back. "Guess I shouldn't get in your way, either."

Yeah, until he'd gotten preoccupied with watching her, that had been the plan. A one-night stand with a nameless woman he'd never have to see again. Relieve some stress. Get his head together. Then walk away.

Man, had shit gone awry on that plan.

He'd known all along that Cherry had driven down for the fights; she was as supportive of Armie as everyone else in their group. At the venue, with every seat filled, he'd barely seen her. Here at the club, he couldn't keep his gaze off her.

And again, he'd hesitated too long.

Twisting her mouth, she nodded. "Got it." She tucked her hair behind her ear with trembling fingers. "Sorry I intruded. It won't happen again." Her cheeks were hot, her eyes glassy as she turned away.

"Hey." Before she'd taken a full step, Denver gestured at the seat. "Suit yourself."

Given the length of time it had taken him to issue the invite, she should have been insulted. He half expected her to tell him to go to hell.

Instead, after considering him for several heartbeats, she slid that shapely ass up next to him.

He wanted her enough that small talk wasn't easy. He had to concentrate to say, "You want something to drink?"

The shake of her head sent all those soft curls tumbling over her shoulders. "I better not." Without looking at him, she wrinkled her nose. "Three wine coolers is my limit."

Was she toasted? If so, he couldn't very well leave her on her own, right? He glanced back and sure enough, as she'd said, Stack had one lady on his lap while Miles made out with another.

Worse, the guy who'd hit on her was across the floor keeping her in his sights. Denver mean-mugged him until he averted his gaze.

"You're staying in the hotel across the street, too?"

The question brought Denver's attention back to her. With an elbow on the bar and her chin in her hand, she looked tired.

The damn music was so loud he felt the beat in his chest.

Or maybe sitting so close to Cherry caused the heavy thumping of his heartbeat.

Why did she ask about the hotel? Looking at her lips, he said, "Yeah."

"So am I."

Damn, he didn't need to know that.

She blew a curl away from her face. "I'm glad I decided not to drive back tonight." Releasing a deep breath, she closed her eyes. "I'm beat."

Driving home to Warfield, Ohio would have meant two hours in the car, and it was already one in the morning. The after-party was in full swing even though Armie, who would have been the man of the hour, had already booked with a babe.

Denver didn't know if it was the kinky redhead or the threat of interest from the SBC that had driven Armie off so quickly.

Seeing Cherry rub her temples, he asked, "Headache?"

"It's so loud in here."

A hint that they should go? Having her this close tempted him… "Maybe you're hungry. Want me to get you—"

"No." She shook her head in denial. "I don't even

want to think about food." Curving an arm around her middle, she said, "I'm starting to feel a little green."

Frowning, Denver stroked back her soft hair and put his palm to her forehead. Damn it. "You're hot."

At first she froze, while the rise and fall of her breasts gave away her deeper breathing.

Because of a simple touch? *How was he supposed to resist that?* Slowly, he withdrew.

And she relaxed. "Thanks. I think you're hot, too." She smiled at her jest. "Too much dancing, I guess. It's so noisy and warm and…I should probably turn in."

Denver watched her slide back off that barstool without commenting, without an offer to walk her over, without…anything.

She hesitated, giving him plenty of opportunity, and he saw the moment she gave up—probably on more than tonight.

Maybe for good.

It'd be for the best, but damn, the idea bothered him.

After a soft sigh, she said, "Good night, Denver."

He felt like a fickle prick. Worse, he felt like a coward. "Cherry." Reaching out, he caught her wrist.

She turned, her gaze searching his.

"Hang on."

Her short, humorless laugh cut him. "Why?"

Without meaning to, he rubbed his thumb over her knuckles. Her hand was so small, delicate and soft.

There were a lot of rowdy guys hanging around, adrenaline pumping from the fights, either from watching or partaking, their discretion weakened by alcohol.

That excuse served as good as any.

"I'll walk you over."

"You really don't need to do that. It's just across the street." She stared up at him. "Unless you *want* to."

Yeah, he wanted that—and so much more. They both knew it. The only question now was whether or not they'd each follow through.

"Give me one sec." He settled up his and Armie's tab, all the while telling himself all the reasons why he should be on his best behavior. *Walk her over, see her into her room, then go to your own.*

But yeah, even he knew that was bullshit.

When he turned, she put a hand to his chest.

He felt that touch *everywhere*.

"I don't mean to be pushy, but…I'm tired of playing guessing games."

Is that what she thought? "No games."

Exasperation brought her brows together. "I need to know, Denver. Are you dropping me off at my door…" Her gaze searched his. "Or sticking around for a while?"

Did she mean for sex? Or just to visit?

He couldn't tell, was afraid to assume, but he'd vote for sex. Maybe once he had her he could end his obsession.

Curling his hand over hers, he lifted her knuckles to his mouth. If she wanted to leave it up to him, he had no problem making the final decision. He wanted her too much to keep fighting it. "Sticking around."

She inhaled…and smiled. "Seriously?"

Such unguarded pleasure. "You like that idea?"

"I'm not the one who's been unclear on things."

Knowing he'd been far from decisive, Denver took that one on the chin.

"Didn't you ride down with Stack and Miles?"

Trying to ignore how warm her hand felt in his, he said, "Yeah, why?"

Her small pink tongue came out to dampen her bottom lip, forcing him to swallow back a groan. "Well, they might leave early."

Aware of his blood pumping hotly, his muscles tensing, he waited.

"I could offer you a ride."

Lord help him. He didn't need her saying suggestive things when his brain was already centered on getting her naked. His resolve had already weakened, but with such an open invitation, he lost the fight completely.

As if she'd read his thoughts, her eyes widened—and she laughed. "That sounded bad, didn't it?"

"No." Sounded really good to him.

Slanting him a look, her smile still in place, she clarified, "I could give you a ride home—in the morning, I mean."

It wasn't natural, how she teased and smiled and no matter how badly he behaved, kept her good humor. He hoped she wasn't drunk. "Sounds like a plan." Because now that he'd given in, he knew it would take the entire night to get his fill.

Holding her hand, he went in the same direction Armie had gone earlier.

Along the way, he paused by Stack and Miles long enough to say, "Don't wait for me in the morning."

Leaning away from the lady in his lap, Stack glanced at each of them, then at their entwined hands before breaking into a slow smile that made words unnecessary.

Miles reached around his own lady-friend to offer Denver a high five.

Ignoring his raised hand, Denver gave him the bird and walked away.

Laughter erupted behind them.

With a hand over her face, Cherry muttered, "Well, that was embarrassing."

"You expected anything else?"

She dropped her hand and showed him a rueful smile. "With those two? No, not really."

That she knew them both so well ramped up his jealousy, but he refused to react to it. From the moment the guys knew he was interested, Cherry had gone off-limits to them. Not for a second did he think they'd overstep, not unless he called the all clear.

And he wasn't about to do that.

Slipping his arm over her shoulders, he drew her into his side and damn, it felt right having her close. She surprised him by resting her head against his shoulder for a second. When he glanced down at her, he saw she looked happy.

More than anything else, seeing that particular look on her face sent a heated rush of lust through his bloodstream, and convinced him he'd made the right decision—for both of them.

They passed Gage Ringer with his new bride Harper, both regulars at the gym, Gage as a fighter and Harper as a helper. They were so engrossed in each other that they didn't notice Denver or Cherry.

Anticipation growing sharper, Denver led her through the throng, steering her around small clusters and heavier crowds. The loud, pulsing music and clamor of laughter and conversation made it difficult to talk until they finally reached the entrance.

As he drew her out the doors and into the quieter

night, Cherry tipped up her face and drank in the humid evening air. "Ohhh, this is so much better."

A storm gathered in the distance, sending brief flashes of lightning across the horizon. He could smell the rain in the air, and he felt his own mounting tension.

While a frisky breeze played with her hair, Cherry ducked against him comfortably, as if they'd been cozy forever.

She couldn't know how it affected him, feeling her sweet body so close, inhaling the hot scent of her skin mixed with the dampness of the night.

He couldn't help but touch her cheek, smoothing back her hair. She turned into his hand, smiling.

Would she look like that, all relaxed and satisfied, after she came?

Her lashes lifted and she looked at him. "It feels good, doesn't it?"

Had she read his mind? He opened his hand, stroked his fingers through her silky hair. "What?"

"The quiet and the fresh air."

She felt good. But then he was so primed that everything she said and did felt like a come-on.

Thick clouds tumbled over the stars and moon, but street lamps illuminated the area. Sluggish traffic went by. People milled in and out of the bar and the hotel across the street.

Apparently in less of a hurry than him to reach her room, Cherry turned toward him to chat. "Yvette left with Cannon right after the fight ended."

Looping his arms around her waist, Denver nodded. "I talked with him." Cannon always came as Armie's corner man if his own fight schedule with the SBC didn't have him out of town. It was a treat for all the other fighters at the event, and a thrill for the locals. "He's as sappy as Gage."

Her smile twitched. "Guess it helps that the ladies really enjoy the fights."

Shadows played over her, emphasizing the swells of her breasts. With every move she made, that soft flesh drew his eye. He couldn't wait to get his hands on her.

And his mouth.

She didn't exactly flaunt her curves, but she was definitely aware of them and the effect they had. The V-necked T-shirt she wore tonight was casual, but the way it fit her rack kept distracting him. He could tell she wore a bra, but it had to be insubstantial.

He worked his jaw when he saw that the cooler air had tightened her nipples.

Or maybe it was his gaze that did that.

Aware of her watching him, Denver asked her, "What about you?" She attended all the local events and when possible, traveled with Merissa—her roommate, who was also Cannon's sister—to watch Cannon compete. She'd even gone with them to Japan.

As a day-care worker for preschool kids, Cherry had weekends free and could usually get Friday off by trading with another employee. But Denver knew some women liked the atmosphere, the excitement and interaction with fighters more than the actual sport.

"What about me?"

With the way he stared at her body, he could understand her confusion. Knowing he wouldn't last much longer, Denver got her walking again. "You enjoy MMA?"

"Mostly." As they crossed the lot, a trio of laughing men passed them. To make room, Cherry squeezed more closely against his side.

And damn, he liked how she fit. Her five-seven was a lot smaller than his six-two, but not too small.

"I don't understand all of it," she admitted, going back to their topic. "But it's exciting when someone I know wins."

The increasing wind slapped against them, carrying her hair up to his chin. Denver drank in the scent of her, wondering if she smelled that good—or better—all over.

"I could do without the blood," she admitted. "And once, I saw a guy's arm break." She winced as if she felt the pain herself.

Smiling, Denver paused with her just outside the hotel door to let another group exit. "I remember that fight. The idiot should have tapped. Injuries like that aren't common, but every now and then they happen."

"Have you ever been injured?"

He laughed. "Hell, yeah, but not bad. My worst injuries happened in training, not in competition."

"Like what?"

With a roll of his shoulder, he said, "Joint injuries mostly. A popped rib. Broken finger and broken toe. Torn rotator cuff. Concussion. Pulled hammy…"

"Good grief." Aghast, she said, "I had no idea."

"Comes with the territory. Like I said, nothing serious, and nothing too bad in an actual fight."

Still frowning with worry, she shoulder-bumped him. "Because you're good?"

"Sure." Modesty had no place in the life of a professional MMA fighter. "But I'm also trained, and that makes a big difference."

Hugging his arm, she said, "I'm really looking forward to seeing you fight."

Since he didn't know where things were going with her, he didn't want to plan that far ahead. Mostly he wanted to plan for the rest of the night. Period. "Headache better?"

Smiling, she said, "Mmm-hmmm."

She looked so sweet it was a challenge not to kiss her. If they were alone, he wouldn't bother resisting. But people hung around the hotel lobby and just outside its doors. Other fighters called out to him. A woman asked to get her picture with him. Denver let Cherry go long enough to oblige the fan.

When he rejoined her, she whispered, "You're so popular."

Only in certain crowds, and right now he could do without the recognition. "Come on." Taking her hand, he led her inside and went straight for the elevator. They had to squeeze in with other people...including the guy who'd hit on her earlier.

CHAPTER TWO

DENVER KEPT HIS mouth shut and his gaze vigilant. Cherry returned the man's smile with a polite nod, then looked away.

"Calling it a night?" he asked her, with a glance at Denver.

Denver stared back.

"Yes," she said around a yawn. "I'm exhausted."

Too dumb or too buoyed by liquid courage, the guy eyed Denver again. "You're a fighter, too?"

Too? Did that mean this bozo was trained? Perfect. Given how he'd panted after Cherry earlier, he'd love to meet him in a competition. "That's right. You?"

"Just this lame local shit."

He said nothing to that. Armie made one hell of a living off the "local shit."

Sticking out his hand, the man said, "Leese Phelps. You're a heavyweight with the SBC, right? Denver Lewis."

Without bothering to explain that he'd only recently been recruited to the SBC, Denver gave a brief handshake. "We've met?"

"No, but I follow the fights. I'm light heavyweight. Been thinking about moving up, though."

Probably to dodge Armie. "You fight in this venue?"

"Yeah. You gotta know someone to get in the SBC, right? So I'm stuck here. But I didn't fight tonight."

Put him and Armie in the cage together, and Denver knew Armie would annihilate him.

"The SBC lets you wear your hair that long?"

Denver cocked a brow. Yeah, his hair now hung to his shoulders. Long, but who cared? He didn't. "Doesn't bother anyone."

"Huh."

As the people behind Denver exited the elevator, he allowed himself to be pressed closer to Leese. He started to speak—and Cherry leaned into him.

"I like your hair," she said. Then she went a step further and reached up to tunnel her fingers through it. In a playful tone, she said, "It's *sexy*."

Denver frowned at her. Sexy was never his intent. He just didn't bother getting it cut. But sexy? There were still five people crammed in the elevator with them and he felt his ears getting hot.

Cherry looked at Leese. "When you're as successful at fighting as Denver is, I doubt anyone worries about the length of your hair."

Leese jutted his jaw enough to look obnoxious. "You've only had one fight with the SBC, right?"

Denver didn't get a chance to reply.

"And he *won*," Cherry said with emphasis. Just then, the elevator stopped at her floor and, clutching Denver's hand, she departed with a brisk, "Have a good evening."

The hallway was empty, so after the elevator doors closed, Denver drew her up short and backed her to a wall. "What was that about?"

"What?"

"I don't need you to defend me to that guy or any-one else."

"I just stated facts!"

"And that bit with my hair?"

"It *is* sexy." Again she trailed her fingers through it—and shivered—before getting serious. "But I wasn't really defending you."

"No?"

"You were giving poor Leese your patented death stare, and I figured you were about to level him, so…I wanted to defuse things."

He drew back in insult. "You think I'd start brawl-ing in a crowded elevator?"

"No. But you wouldn't have to. Your ability is light-years away from Leese's level and he knows it. He was already intimidated and acting like an ass. I didn't want you to say anything that would…"

"What?" Even more disgusted, Denver asked, "Hurt his feelings?"

Gaze softening, her attention went all over his body. "Seriously, Denver. Did you really want to argue right now?"

He searched her face. "No." *Hell no.* Especially not with her looking at him like that. He moved in again, one hand on the wall by her shoulder. "Thing is, I'm not sure you want what I want."

For the longest time, their gazes held while her breathing quickened and her cheeks warmed. Finally, in a whisper, she asked, "Do you want me?"

With one short nod, he pressed her to the wall, feel-ing her all along his length. "Have for a long time."

"You hid it well."

"Then I'm one hell of an actor." He brushed his

mouth over her forehead. "We have a lot of talking to do, but I'd as soon do it after."

"After?"

"After I've had you. Maybe several times."

She dipped her head down so that he stared at the crooked part in her fair hair. He brushed his nose against her, down to her temple, her ear.

Her hands clutched at him. "I got the feeling you didn't like me."

"I like you." It was how her flirting made him feel that he didn't like so much.

"We're finally going to have sex?"

Having her spell it out like that, as if he'd just given her a gift, added fuel to the fire. He closed his eyes, drew a breath. "That'd sure be my preference."

Pushing him back so she could see his face, she asked anxiously, "You won't change your mind?"

The laugh tried to escape, but he wanted her too much to take a chance on pissing her off. "Where's your room?"

"Close." On a sharply inhaled breath, she stepped him back a few paces and darted around him in a rush. "Come on."

At first he just watched her, the sway of that stellar ass, how her breasts moved, her obvious urgency, the way her hair teased over her shoulders. She stopped halfway down the hall and fumbled in her purse before pulling out a key card. She opened the door, jammed the key card back into her purse, and glanced at him.

Ah, hell. Definitely close. In a few long strides Denver reached her.

Seconds later they were in her room.

A second after that he was kissing her.

OH GOD, HE tasted good, even better than she'd imagined—which seemed incredible because she'd done a *lot* of explicit imagining. Big and bold, he slanted his head and nudged her lips open so he could lick in with his hot tongue.

Whoa, the man seriously knew how to curl her toes.

And so much hunger! If she didn't know better, she might think that he'd wanted her as much as she'd always wanted him. But that couldn't be true because *he* was the one who'd started avoiding her. No way had she misunderstood that.

She just didn't know why.

He was here with her now, though, and she wanted to do this right.

Gasping for air, Cherry said, "Wait." He lifted his head but stayed close, his hard body pressed to hers, thrilling her. She'd wanted him for so long that the reality of this happening, *finally*, almost made her frenzied to seal the deal. She could feel his warm breath, the flexing muscles in his chest and arms, and the intimidating rise of his erection.

But if she thought about *that* right now, she'd totally lose it. Better to concentrate to keep things on track.

Holding on to his biceps—*so sexy*—she licked her lips, swallowed, and managed to say, "The door?" It still stood open because the second she'd stepped into the room he'd kissed her.

Slow, methodical, he slid one hand up her nape and into her hair, clenching just enough to hold her securely, keeping her right there against him.

That possessive embrace sent another thrill racing through her, turning her breath short and shallow, her heartbeat fast and furious.

With the other hand he shoved the door closed and turned the lock, then went one further and flipped the security latch. That all seemed so final that her knees trembled.

His hand in her hair tugged, tipping her head back and away to give his open mouth access to her throat, tasting her skin, sucking and licking down to her shoulder, then concentrating where her frantic pulse raced.

She couldn't help but groan at the feel of his teeth, his hot tongue. "Denver..."

He kissed his way back up to her mouth.

So much heat suffused her, she felt light-headed. At the last second, she turned her head. "I need five minutes for a shower."

That clever hand in her hair brought her face back around. "Later." And then his mouth was on hers again, his tongue delving, consuming.

Making her forget herself.

She clutched at him, uncaring that she was a little worn from so much dancing, that she'd wanted this first time with him to be perfect.

His free hand went to her waist, kneading her before gliding up her ribs without quite touching her breast, back down past her hip to the curve of her backside. His big hand opened on her, cuddling, stroking her bottom, lifting her to her toes.

He was so big all over that she felt dwarfed next to him. He crowded her more, caging her against the wall as his hand teased back up her body.

When she made a soft sound of anticipation, he eased up, gently kissed the corner of her mouth, her jaw, then locked onto her gaze. Their breaths mingled as his fingers hooked in the V-neck of her shirt and stretchy lace bra, and tugged them both down until he'd freed one breast.

She felt the cooler air on her bared skin, her sensitive nipple. Low light filled the room from the bedside lamp she'd left on, but he didn't look at her there.

Still with a hand in her hair, staring into her eyes with an intent expression, he cupped her.

Her lips parted; his gaze went heavy.

"Fuck, you feel good."

Heart thundering, she closed her eyes as he drifted his thumb over her taut nipple.

"Look at me, Cherry."

Oh, that husky voice. She got her eyes open, and it was so startling, seeing him like this, being the recipient of that golden-brown, predatory stare.

"I like it when you breathe hard," he told her. "It does interesting things to you here."

Here being the breast that he continued to fondle so carefully.

"All this soft flesh." He finally looked down at her, made a rough sound and bent his head to draw her in.

Putting her head back against the wall, Cherry held her breath to smother a groan. From the moment she'd met him months ago, Denver had epitomized the elemental male.

As a heavyweight fighter, he was big and so incredibly strong, with amazing biceps, tight abs and thighs that made her breathless. All of the fighters at the rec center were big and brawny, but other than Gage, Denver was the biggest.

All of it honed strength.

He had confidence down to a fine art, but he never bullied. In fact, she'd witnessed his very big heart overflowing with kindness and generosity. She loved watching the men work with the at-risk neighborhood kids, but because of his size it always seemed more amazing to see Denver tussle with a child, coach a youth or instruct a high school kid.

He could break the average guy in two, but he tempered all that strength with gentle control. *Such a turn-on.*

With his sense of humor, he made her laugh as often as he made her sigh with lust. But when it came to those things that mattered to him, he had laser-beam focus.

Working with kids.

Supporting his friends.

Training for the sport he loved.

She so desperately wanted him to focus on her, too. But after what had felt like a great connection, their interest mutual, each of them flirting with the other, he'd suddenly cut her cold and she had no idea why.

If they weren't to have a relationship, she at least had to have this—the intimate knowledge of him, a memory to hold, a fantasy for the dark, lonely nights.

"Stay with me, honey." He took her mouth again, keeping her from giving a reply.

Stay with him? She was here, in the moment, 100 percent.

As he deepened the kiss more, he smoothed his hand down her back…and into her jeans and panties.

She went to her tiptoes in surprise.

He rumbled in appreciation at feeling her body go flush to his.

Finally freeing her hair, he lifted his mouth and melted her with his heated gaze. "You have the finest ass I have ever seen." As he spoke, he worked his fingers lower, cupping one whole cheek.

"Um…" Still up on her toes, she glanced toward the bed.

"Soon," he told her. "Once we're there, I'm done for, and I want this first time to last."

It could last forever if he'd let it. But of course she didn't say that. Just getting him to this point had taken a lot of work.

Lightning seared the dark night, illuminating the room for two seconds, followed by a crash of thunder that rattled the window. She felt all that turbulence deep inside, making her head swim and her knees shake.

Keeping her trapped in his sights, Denver brought his free hand around and opened the snap on her jeans.

Cherry held her breath as the material loosened. He eased down the zipper with excruciating slowness, then slipped both hands into her jeans to work them down her thighs.

Being mostly bare from the waist down was startling enough, but when he went to one knee, her heart almost popped out of her chest. She staggered slightly before his hands gripped her hips.

Looking up at her, he said with concern, "You okay?"

Denver Lewis was on his knees in front of her and her jeans were down.

Not wanting him to stop, she bobbed her head. "Yes. Fine." *In a frenzy of need. Taut with expectation. Incapable of more than one-word replies—but otherwise fine and dandy.*

Unconvinced, he continued to scrutinize her. "You're sure you're not drunk?"

"Swear." Yes, she felt a little dizzy and her head-ache lingered, but she knew exactly what she wanted.

Denver. This.

Now.

His hands never left her, but he settled back on his heels, a frown in place, and Cherry panicked.

"So help me, Denver, if you walk away now, I'll…"

"What?" Tipping his head, he looked her over. "What would you do?"

Lifting her chin, Cherry said, "I'll spread a rumor that you're a lousy lay."

His slow, crooked grin reassured her. "Can't have that now, can I?" Giving his attention back to her body, he touched his mouth to her skin, nuzzling her belly, nibbling over to her hipbone while his hands coasted up and down the backs of her thighs. "You are so soft, and damn girl, you smell good."

Again she wanted to melt, this time from sensation overload. His big hands continued to coast over her skin, lifting every so often to her tush to squeeze and cuddle. His lips were warm, his tongue teasing, and right through her skimpy panties he gave her a soft love bite.

Oh my God. Flattening her hands to the wall for support, Cherry stared down at him. She hadn't lied about his light brown hair; it really was beyond sexy. But then everything about Denver was downright scrumptious. "I'd love it if you took off your shirt."

He paused long enough to reach over his own shoulder, grab a fistful of material, and jerk the shirt up and over his head. He stood again, breathing a little more heavily, and murmured, "Your turn."

So many times she'd seen his gorgeous body in no

more than boxing shorts, but never before had she been given the opportunity to touch. She reached for him, but he caught her hands, kissed each palm, and lifted them high over her head.

"Keep them right there for me." And with that, he lifted the hem of her shirt, drawing it slowly up and over her face until he caught the material between her elbows one-handed—pinning her there, all stretched out.

Hardly fair! "Denver—"

"I've thought about stripping you a million times," he murmured. "Let me have my fun."

He'd been thinking about stripping her? Oh. Well then… "Okay."

"Good girl."

She frowned, but with his palm playing over her from shoulder to hip as if savoring her, she couldn't gather her thoughts enough to protest the ridiculous endearment.

Briefly, he came in for a hot eating kiss that left her shaking before levering back so he could open the front closure on her bra.

She heard the small catch of his breath as the cups parted, showing the inner swells of her breasts, but not quite revealing both nipples.

"So fucking stacked," he whispered roughly, lowering his head to nuzzle aside the material with his mouth.

Going perfectly still, her pulse buzzing and her vision narrowing to the crown of his overlong hair, she waited—and felt his hot breath, then the touch of his hotter tongue…

And he sucked her in.

The vibrating moan came out loud and high as she stiffened, her muscles all going taut in a rush of pleasure.

"Relax." He kissed his way to her other breast and drew that nipple into the damp heat of his mouth. At the same time she felt his fingertips lightly tracing over the crotch of her panties.

Frantic to touch him, Cherry struggled against the restraint of her shirt.

He released her, saying, "Take it easy," while helping to free her hands. The second she could, she leaned into him, her hands everywhere, all over him, relishing the light furring of hair on his chest, those sleek hard shoulders, the bulge of his rock-hard biceps. She trailed a hand down his abdomen, following that silky happy trail until it disappeared into his low-hanging jeans. Almost desperate, she suggested, "The bed…"

He caught her wandering hand. "I said no." With far too much ease, he turned her suddenly so that she faced the wall. Stepping in close to her back, he nestled his erection against her bottom. "Trust me, okay?"

She felt too warm, dazed with wanting. Nodding, she whispered, "Okay." But she honestly didn't know how much longer she could stand there. Her legs seemed almost incapable of holding her up and she had a rushing in her ears.

With a kiss to her temple, he slipped one foot between hers, nudging her legs wider apart. When she accommodated him, he murmured, "Good girl. Just like that."

Breathless, she said, "You are so sexist."

"Maybe. Sorry." His arms came around her, one

hand cupping a breast, the other wedging between her thighs. "I'm too turned on to worry about it."

He stroked and… Yeah. She didn't want him to worry about it, either.

Unless… "Wait."

His hands curled, holding her more firmly. And given where they were, wow. She just might faint.

"What now?" he breathed near her ear.

"You have protection?"

"A rubber." He nibbled on her earlobe, touched his tongue inside her ear. "More in my room if we get that far."

More if we… This time, her "Okay" ended on a squeak as he readjusted to put his hand inside her panties.

"Mmmm," he growled, his fingers already exploring lightly, opening her, playing with her. "You need me to take care of you first, don't you, girl?"

Be strong, Cherry told herself. Tell him you're a woman, not a girl. Tell him…

His finger worked into her.

"Yes," she moaned, arching back against him.

"That's good." He stroked into her, deliberately teasing. "You're nice and wet, but small, too. And since I'm not so small, I need to—"

"Armie told me," she admitted, her thoughts mostly centered on how it felt to be held to his hard frame, his strong arms around her, his fingers doing those amazingly erotic things to her.

Denver stilled. Quietly, his tone off, he said, "Armie told you what?"

"That you're big." She wiggled her bottom against him, both to acknowledge his size and to hopefully get him back to stroking her. She was equally excited and a little nervous.

From head to toes he went as cold and hard as granite, then in one quick move turned her to face him again.

Her shoulders touched the wall and Denver leaned into her. "Why the fuck were you discussing my dick with Armie?"

The whispered question sounded more lethal than a shout. Accompanied with that look in his eyes, she couldn't think.

"Umm…"

He waited with throbbing impatience, not budging, not asking again.

Man, she had a big mouth. "See…Yvette and I were talking." Mostly it was her, pretty much mooning over Denver. But he didn't look receptive to hearing that right now, so she did her best to summarize judiciously. "You know, about how nicely ripped fighters are? And Armie overheard us."

Denver's glittering gaze narrowed. But she wasn't afraid of him. Never that.

She just really wanted to get past this so they could get back to what they'd been doing before she so badly misspoke.

Clearing her throat, she offered, "You know how Armie is."

"I do," he agreed in an unsettling whisper. "How well do you know him?"

"Well enough that I was only a little embarrassed that he busted us. He accused us—"

"You and Yvette?"

She nodded, but admitted sheepishly, "Mostly me."

"Go on."

"He said we were being shallower than men just because we appreciate how sexy you guys are."

His jaw locked.

Very slowly, Cherry reached out until her hand cupped him through his jeans. Lips parting at the reality of his length and thickness, she wavered, for the first time wondering if maybe he was *too* big.

"You'll take me," he assured her, his voice low and rough. His eyelids went heavier, his mouth tighter, but he didn't move away.

When she stayed silent, overwhelmed, he encouraged her, saying, "Go on."

So she stroked him.

"No." His throat worked as he swallowed. "Get to the part where you and Armie discussed my junk."

"Oh." She would much rather explore him. "Armie overheard me talking about you and—"

He stopped her long enough to open his jeans, ease down the zipper, then carry her hand inside. Hot and sleek and big enough that her fingers didn't quite circle him.

Like a flash fire, heat rolled through her.

Denver gave a soft growl, covered her hand with his own, and guided her in a slow stroke. After three deep breaths, he asked, "What were you saying exactly?"

How could he chat right now? She certainly couldn't. "I don't remember."

"Cherry."

Wanting the discussion over with, she shook her head. "Something about liking your shoulders and your thighs."

He flattened his free hand on the wall next to her

temple and just stared at her while enjoying her touch. "Still listening."

"Right. So he, ah, suggested…" To get it over with before she fainted, Cherry blurted, "That you would happily give me a viewing, and that you were bigger than most."

"Those aren't the words he used."

"I can't think!"

He brushed his mouth against her temple. "Try."

How had she missed this bossy streak of Denver's? "He…he said you'd gladly give me a show and you were the best hung one in the bunch." The second the words were out, she felt his smile.

"Yeah. That sounds more like Armie."

"He was right." She lifted her other hand, now holding him in both. "Honest to God, Denver, I never imagined—"

His choked laugh was accompanied by a hug. "It's not all that."

"I…I need to sit down." She seriously did.

"Soon." With two fingers under her chin he lifted her face. "No more talking about my cock with other men."

For a second there, his wording dazed her, then she nodded. "Okay, sure." She hadn't meant to have that discussion with Armie anyway. "No problem."

Smile going crooked, he added, "You can brag to the other ladies all you want."

Jealousy spiked through her; he *wanted* the attention of the other women? "You—"

"Now, if we're done with interruptions…?" He pulled her hands away and went back to one knee, dragging her panties down at the same time. "Step out."

Sidetracked, she took in his position at her feet, his gaze level on her body, and nothing else existed. Another bright flash of lightning emphasized the stark intensity in his eyes as he took in her nudity.

No one had ever looked at her quite that thoroughly.

She no sooner had that thought than bad memories tried to intrude, memories of being scrutinized critically, against her will—

No. Ruthlessly, she quashed those thoughts.

She was with Denver—nothing bad in that. He was unlike any man she'd ever known, definitely better than most. When it came to ugly experiences, there was no comparison.

Keeping his focus on her body, he held her hand to steady her as she stepped free of the underwear. Brushing them aside with the rest of their discarded clothes, Denver said, "Jesus, Cherry, you have a smokin' body." He touched his fingertips down her belly to her sex. "I'm dying to taste you."

With no more warning than that, he cupped her backside, pulled her forward, and pressed his face to her.

Gasping, Cherry sank her fingers into his hair and held on.

Apparently done waiting, his hands—easily twice the size of her own—roamed over her body while he treated her to soft, devouring kisses that forced her to lock her knees and use the wall for support.

Putting his palms to the inside of each thigh, he urged her to widen her stance. Once he had her arranged to his liking, he stroked two fingers of one hand into her, and used two fingers of his other hand to part her.

Another throaty growl of appreciation, and he closed his mouth over her throbbing clitoris, suckling softly while rasping with his tongue.

Oh God, oh God, oh God... His hair felt cool brushing her thighs, his fingers working inside her, pressing, and he kept making those low sounds of hunger... and appreciation.

Thunder shook the floor beneath them. Wind lashed the rain against the window. The strobe effect of the lightning increased to an almost constant flash.

Locking her hands in his hair, she cried out as he drove her higher, as pleasure drew her tighter. Like a powder keg with a short fuse, she surprised herself by exploding so quickly. Denver supported her easily, and good thing because she went boneless, her tripping heart leaving her breathless and far too weak.

CHAPTER THREE

DENVER SCOOPED UP her lax body and carried her to the bed, putting her on her back and then taking a step away so he could look at her as he took off his shoes and socks, pushed down his jeans and removed his boxers. The storm raged on, matching his turbulent lust.

How she'd come, the sounds she'd made in her pleasure and the taste of her, left him primed. He'd always known they'd be scorching together; the easy way he'd just gotten her off proved it.

Now he wanted more. A lot more.

Eyes still closed, she half turned, drawing one knee up to help hide her sex while crossing her arms over her chest.

That pose just fired his blood more. She looked equal parts timid and boldly sexual.

She had the most amazing breasts, big and soft and real, trembling with her heavy, broken breaths. In her pale throat he could see her pulse still tripping.

"Let me see you." Gently, he clasped her wrists and moved her arms to her sides. "You don't ever need to hide from me."

Her nipples were softer now that she'd come, her hair more tangled. She wasn't as slim as most of the women who hung out at the rec center.

She was better.

Rounder in the right places and so damn sexy he knew it was going to be a struggle to hold back. Thinking that, he got the condom from his wallet, tossed his wallet on the nightstand and opened the rubber.

Cherry never moved.

Soaking up the sight of her, he smiled. "Girl, you didn't fall asleep, did you?"

She shook her head, sucked in air, and whispered, "No."

"Then how about you open those pretty eyes and look at me?"

She did, her gaze going straight to his dick. Eyes widening, she bit her lip and put a hand over her heart.

For some reason, that reaction almost made him laugh. "You're overreacting, honey." Coming down next to her, he promised gruffly, "I'm going to wear you out—and you're going to love it."

When he started to kiss her, she straight-armed him. "Can I ask you something first?"

Well, hell. He hadn't expected all this reserve from her. Most women were excited by the size of his package.

But from the get-go, he'd known Cherry wasn't like most women.

He smoothed back her hair, kissed her forehead. "Ask away." Not like he had anything else to do.

She looked from his eyes to his chest, his shoulders. Letting out a sigh, she gently pawed him, as if testing his strength. "You are so hard."

If she'd reach a little lower he could show her just how hard. "Comes with the territory."

"Being a fighter?"

He lifted a shoulder. "Nonstop training."

"Will you stay the night with me?"

After throwing that out there, she defiantly met his gaze—and bit her lip again.

"Yeah." He bent to her mouth to do a little biting of his own. When she groaned, he tangled his hand in her messy hair to keep her still. In so many ways he wanted to crush her to him and work off the raging lust until he could get her out of his system.

Then again, he hated the idea of *not* wanting her.

He kissed from her mouth to her downy cheek, her warm neck, her silky shoulder, and down to one plump nipple. "I'm not going anywhere unless you boot me out."

Her arms came around him. *"Never."* And now it was her kissing him and he felt scorched not just by her sexual need, but her unguarded caring.

She seemed to think he didn't like her, that he didn't want her, and still she left herself open. It made him feel ultraprotective—and even more possessive.

Her heated skin repeatedly drew his hands, his mouth. Over and over he breathed in her scent until it filled his lungs, his head and his heart. He'd never known a woman who smelled so good, her hair, her skin, the fragrant, moist heat between her thighs.

She'd tasted good, too, and thinking that, he worked his way down her body again.

"Denver," she moaned in protest. "No."

"Yes." Her belly sucked in as he licked her skin, and she squirmed when he teased over her hipbone.

Trying to draw him back up to her, she tunneled her fingers into his hair, but it didn't slow him down. She'd be more sensitive now, every touch and lick more acute, and they both knew it.

It left her trembling, and him determined.

As soon as he parted her soft thighs, she dropped to her back again, then arched up as he explored her with fingers and tongue.

"I can't," she moaned.

He took a lot of satisfaction in telling her, "You already are."

Refusing to be rushed, Denver took his time, and even after she came again, this time with high, weak, broken cries, he didn't move over her. He'd been wanting her long enough that savoring her was more his speed.

He got her right to the edge a third time, loving the way she quivered all over, her hoarse moans and dewy skin. With two fingers pressed deep in her, he moved up her body to kiss her parted lips. Damp hair clung to her temples and her lungs labored.

"God," she rasped, sliding one leg up and over his. "No more."

"I'm nowhere near done," he told her.

Her hand clenched in his hair, drawing him back so she could see his face. "Then please, at least stop playing."

"But playing with you is so much fun," he whispered, adding a third finger to ensure she was ready for him.

She gasped, and as her eyes closed she bowed her body, her head twisting on the pillow.

He kissed her hard as he moved over her, kneeing her thighs wider and slowly, very slowly, taking his fingers from her.

She tensed, but he murmured to her, calming her. "Shush. Just relax for me."

Breathless, she half laughed. "You're nuts."

"And you're ready."

"More than ready. It's just—" Her explanation ended on a sharp inhalation as he barely entered her.

Immediately she tensed up too much, forcing him to pause with his muscles locked, nowhere near buried the way he wanted to be. All that teasing left him with dwindling control.

Three deep breaths later, she whispered, "I'm okay."

He nibbled on her bottom lip. "I know." Now he needed her to believe it. He was hung, no two ways about it. But he'd never in his life hurt a woman and he sure as hell wouldn't start with Cherry.

On straightened arms, he watched her, eased out a little—and pressed in more.

She held on to his arms just above his elbows, her fingers gripping tight, her nails stinging as if she thought she could hold him back if she decided to.

"Tell me you want me." Again he withdrew, only to rock in farther.

"I do," she gasped. Her legs strained against him. "I have for a long time."

"Then stop fighting me."

"I'm not."

Wasn't easy, but he smiled. "You're tense from head to toes, girl. Take a deep breath."

She did, urgently, turning it into a pant.

"Am I hurting you?"

She shook her head. "It's just…I can *feel* you."

"Damn, I hope so."

Closing her eyes, she tipped her head back. "You know what I mean."

"Know what I feel?" He didn't wait for her to reply.

"I feel you squeezing my cock like you want it there."
Saying it only turned him on more, and he clenched
his jaw. "I feel you getting wetter. And hotter."

Another squeeze—this one of excitement, he was
sure.

He kissed her jaw. His voice rough as gravel, he
said, "You want more, don't you?" *Please say yes*. His
restraint was about to unravel.

She shifted against him, and moaned, *"Yesss..."*

Coming down to an elbow, he scooped one arm
under her hips for a better hold, and thrust in a little
harder, a little deeper.

Almost there.

As he filled her up and then some, her heels dug
into his thighs, maybe in protest, but he was lost. He
felt the giving of her body as she accepted him, knew
she squirmed to adjust, and it destroyed him.

He watched the movement of her breasts as he
rocked them both, saw her face as, amazingly, she
neared yet another release. Wanting that a lot, he kept
up a steady rhythm, each stroke harder, taking him
deeper, and when he knew she was ready to come he
encouraged her, doing his best to hang on, determined
to feel the grip of her body as she climaxed, this time
with him buried deep.

Legs wrapped around him and eyes squeezed tight,
she bowed her body hard. *"Denver."*

Fuck yeah. "That's it, baby. That's it." As soon as
he felt her winding down, he gave up the fight. Driving into her one last time, he held himself deep, groaning harshly as the pumping release drained away his
tension.

By small degrees, he sank down onto Cherry's soft, giving body.

He knew he should move off her, but he couldn't. Not yet.

She had both hands knotted in his hair.

From the inside out, he felt like smiling.

Her fingers loosening, she kissed his chest and went limp.

Lifting his head, he looked at her—and the smile turned into a grin. Ms. Cherry Peyton was dead to the world.

Carefully, Denver turned to the side of her and sprawled out, welcoming the cool air that washed over his damp, heated skin.

Lord have mercy, she was incredible, even hotter than he'd hoped for. His heartbeat still rocked him and getting enough air into his lungs wasn't easy, but he had to touch her.

He rested a palm on her silky upper thigh, amazed to find her skin still so warm.

She didn't stir.

Because lethargy pulled at him, too, he forced himself from the bed. Give him an hour and he'd be ready to go again, so he needed to run to his room to get his stuff, which included more condoms. As he stepped into his jeans commando, he glanced around her room, looking for the key card, but didn't see it anywhere. Not on the desk, the dresser, the nightstand. He eyed her purse on the desk chair, then her utterly relaxed body.

No reason to wake her, he decided, and he opened her purse, rummaging around a wallet, comb, cell phone, phone book and a few makeup items. No key card. He peeked in the wallet. She carried only forty bucks on her, a few credit cards and ID. Flipping open the small phone book, he finally found the key card jammed inside between the pages—and a listing of phone numbers for all the fighters.

Cannon, Armie, Stack, Miles…his number was there, too, though she'd never called him.

Had she called any of the other guys?

That damn jealousy nudged in, disturbing his peace of mind. Why the hell did she need contact info for men she wasn't dating? He knew for a fact none of them had been out with her. Their circle was a close one. He'd have heard. Hell, he'd have *seen*.

Feeling like a damned snoop, he dropped the phone book back in her purse.

If she'd had plans to play the field, he'd convince her otherwise. Together they were combustible; he'd keep her so satisfied she wouldn't even think of other men.

With that decision made, he gave another quick glance at her still sleeping form. The ways she affected him… He shook his head.

Forcing himself to head to the door, he slipped silently out of the room. Despite his current disgruntlement, he wanted her again. At times, he thought he might always want her.

Soon as possible, he'd spell out to her exactly what he needed: exclusivity—and no flirting with other men.

THE BANGING ON the door caused Cherry's heavy eyelids to lift. Her head hurt, her throat was scratchy, and she only wanted to go back to sleep.

But the knocking didn't stop.

When she sat up, the room seemed to swim around

her, causing her stomach to pitch. Whoa. She held on to the mattress a moment to get her bearings.

Shivers wracked her as she looked around the room in confusion—and realized she was naked.

Oh yeah. Denver.

Where had he gone? Her brows pinched, making her head pound harder as she tried to figure out how she'd gone from drowning in pleasure to waking alone and feeling so wretched.

More knocking sounded and, thinking that might be Denver, she tried to get herself together.

Wrapping the sheet around her body she made her way across the room, every step an effort. When she peered out the small security hole, she saw Armie instead of Denver.

With Denver gone, immediate worries settled in and she pulled open the door. "What's the matter?"

Until she spoke, she didn't realize how croaky her voice would sound. She tried clearing her throat, but that just made it worse.

Armie had his hand raised to knock again, his mouth open to speak—but the second he saw her, his gaze dropped to roam quickly over her sheet-shrouded body.

Brows lifting, his gaze finally met hers. "Damn, Cherry, way to stop my heart."

Feeling more miserable by the second, she slumped against the door frame to stay upright. "Where's Denver?"

"He's not with you?" He peered in around her with a frown. "Because honestly, doll, you look like he's been here."

Confused, she looked around the room, trying to sort it out. "He was, but I must have fallen asleep."

"Yeah?" Grinning, Armie sidled in uninvited. "So you two were together? That's what Stack told me."

Walking away, Cherry went to the bed and more or less collapsed to sit on the side. Staying upright took great concentration. Freezing, she hugged the sheet tighter and tried for a deep breath. But that hurt most of all.

"What's wrong?" Armie approached cautiously. "You're not going to keel over, are you?"

"No. I just don't feel well."

He put the back of his hand to her forehead, then whistled. Crouching down in front of her, he tried to see her averted face. "You're burning up."

Wrong. "I'm freezing."

"That'd be the fever." He reached around her for the blanket, and that's when Denver walked in carrying an overnight case. He drew up short at the sight of Cherry on the bed in a sheet, Armie touching her.

Even through bleary eyes, she read the suspicion in his gaze. Before he could speak, she did. "Where did you go?"

He dropped a duffel bag and crossed his arms. "I went to get my things."

So cold that she couldn't stop shaking, she wanted only to be alone. In her throaty voice, she said, "Will you two leave? I need to get dressed."

"Dressed to go where?"

"Back to bed?" She seriously wasn't up to anything else.

Denver's eyes narrowed. "I've already seen you."

"Lucky bastard," Armie murmured, and then with

a disapproving frown, "But I haven't seen her, so walk me out. I came to see you anyway."

Denver hesitated, studying her a moment, but finally he nodded. Thank God. A minute longer and she'd have crawled back under the covers just to hide.

As soon as the door closed, she dragged herself out of the bed and found a T-shirt and panties. Shivering almost uncontrollably, she went into the bathroom. One look in the mirror and hiding became a real possibility.

Such a mess. Wild hair, ruined makeup, red eyes and a pale face.

But she flat-out didn't have the energy to deal with it. Just getting her shirt and underwear on proved a trial. No way could she wash off her makeup or tidy her hair. By the time she staggered out of the bathroom, she felt weak as a baby. And that made her weepy.

This was supposed to be her big night with Denver—and here she'd gone and gotten sick.

"First," Armie said, the second the door closed, "get that shit out of your head."

Knowing exactly what he meant, Denver said, "Fine. Then tell me why you're here."

"Not to hit on her, and you know it."

For ten seconds longer, they had a stare-off.

And Denver realized he was being absurd.

Not only was Armie trustworthy, he didn't go for girls like Cherry. Hell, for the most part he avoided them.

Scrubbing his hands over his face, he dropped back against the wall. What he felt for Cherry blew his control. He had to get a grip, and fast, before he made an ass of himself.

Or rather, more of an ass. "Right. Sorry. I know she's not your type."

"Didn't say that."

New volatility demolished Denver's relaxed posture. With a half grin, Armie admitted, "If you hadn't stepped up, I'd have been all over it."

"Bullshit." Armie's preferences were well known—because he made them known. He was congenial with all women, but made it clear that he divided the fairer sex into three categories: women up for grabs because they were fast, nasty and rough around the edges, or in other words, perfect for his tastes; nice women, which he considered all fluff and uninteresting; and women related to anyone he knew, which put them off-limits—like Cannon's sister, Merissa.

Although Denver thought Armie might fight a losing battle with the last.

Through his teeth, Denver said, "I thought you didn't like *nice* girls."

With a shrug, Armie murmured, "Cherry is a different type of nice."

Didn't he know it. She was the perfect mix of sweet and sexy. Her brand of nice could give any guy a boner.

Determined to set Armie straight right now, Denver came forward in a single aggressive step—

And Armie laughed at him.

Far from amused, Denver warned him, "You're pushing your luck."

"And you're being entertaining." Armie shook his head, then said with mock pity, "I can be a prick, Denver, I know. But I wouldn't do that."

Shit. No, he wouldn't. Denver retreated with a deep

breath that didn't even come close to helping. "Yeah, I do know it. Sorry again."

"Tell it to her, not me."

"Already planning that particular chat with her."

Snorting, Armie said, "Good luck with that."

"Meaning what?"

"You're coming on too strong, man. But then, hey, who am I to say? Maybe she's into that caveman shit."

If Armie didn't stop being so deliberately provoking, he'd flatten him just for the fun of it.

With a clap on the shoulder, Armie said, "I can see you'll enjoy unleashing that big badass protective streak tonight, huh?"

Shaking his head, Denver scowled. "What the hell are you talking about?"

"That's why I'm here, actually." Going far too serious for Denver's peace of mind, Armie said, "I overheard some stuff and I figured you should know. When I didn't find you in your room, Stack said you'd be here."

"What stuff?" More than anything, he wanted to get back inside with Cherry. He'd lose his edge in her soft body and then maybe he could feel like himself again instead of suffering so many chaotic emotions.

"I went to my car, but Havoc, the sneaky bastard, was hanging around there, so instead I went back toward the bar—"

"You dodged Havoc? Jesus man, just talk to him already."

"And," Armie went on with emphasis, ignoring both the interruption and the derision, "off to the side of the bar, three guys were talking about Cherry."

Forgetting Havoc, Denver straightened. "What do you mean, they were talking about her?"

Armie rubbed the back of his neck. "See, that's the troubling part. It sounded all covert and underhanded, so I got closer."

"What did they say?"

"Something about having to see her, but knowing she wouldn't welcome them, so they'd have to catch her off guard then force the issue."

None of that made sense, but still it pissed him off. "You're sure they were talking about my Cherry?"

Armie grinned. "Already claimed her, huh?"

"Armie—"

"Yeah, I'm afraid so. See, when I heard the biggest one use her name, I interrupted. Not like Cherry is a real common name, ya know?"

Figured Armie would get involved. "What happened?"

"I asked if they were talking about Cherry Peyton. You should have seen their faces. They were busted and knew it. The youngest one got all shifty and asked if I knew her. I said yes, and he asked what room she was in."

When they traveled together, the group always shared room numbers for emergencies, but he knew Armie wouldn't give that info to an unknown. "I hope you told him to fuck off."

"Those exact words, actually."

Impatient, Denver glared at him. "Jesus man, it's like pulling teeth. Spit it out already, will you?"

Armie shrugged. "The biggest one—who, by the way, is bigger than you—tried to insist that I spill my guts. And by insist, I mean he went ugly real fast. Actually grabbed my shoulder and tried slamming me to the brick wall."

"Stupid."

"Yeah. But the dumbest part? The oldest one pulled a knife."

"Jesus," Denver breathed again. His brain scrambled, wondering what the men wanted with Cherry.

"Punches were thrown. I kneed the knife wielder in the balls. Decked the other one. Some other people got in on it and the oldest of the three called a halt. The cowards were going to limp off but I figured you'd want some answers, right?"

He didn't give Denver a chance to reply.

"So I...insisted."

"You insisted?"

"Yeah. I mean, Cherry's one of us, right? Like you said, she's your Cherry. And if they meant to hassle her—"

Jumping past all that, Denver asked, "What'd you find out?"

"They claim to be related to her." Armie heaved a sigh. "And given how they told it, I sort of believe them. I mean, they were snotty about it, like maybe defiant. I dunno. I'd have grilled them more, but Havoc nosed in and trapped me."

Damn. Lousy timing. "He interfered?"

"Not really." Now evasive, Armie glanced at the door. "You aren't going to rush in there and take care of her?"

Of all the... "That's none of your damn business."

Armie's smile cracked. "Yeah, see, I didn't mean in the sack. I meant because she's sick."

Denver gave him a blank stare.

"She has a fever, man." And then, "You didn't know?"

"No." Damn it, he'd thought she was too warm, but he'd still been wallowing in satisfaction and not thinking straight—or rather, he'd mostly been thinking about a repeat performance.

Fists low on his hips, Armie frowned at him. "Why the hell did you think I was feeling her head? Not exactly what I zero in on, you know."

Shoving the door open again, Denver stepped in to find Cherry back in the bed with the covers pulled all the way up to her ears. Even from across the length of the room, he could see her shivering.

His heart turned over as he strode to her. Sitting beside her on the bed, he smoothed back her hair. "Hey."

"I'm sorry," she said in a small raspy voice without opening her eyes. "I think I'm sick."

Heat poured off her. "Yeah, baby, you definitely are." He realized Armie had followed him in. Ignoring him, he asked, "Have you taken anything?"

"Don't have anything. I just want to sleep."

She'd said earlier that she had a headache, and she hadn't wanted to eat. She'd been unsteady on her feet— and he'd assumed she'd drank too much.

Armie shifted closer. "Want me to go grab some stuff before I head out?"

Head out? Denver turned to him. "You're not staying 'til morning?"

"Now that both Havoc and that crazy chick know where to find me, it's best if I just get on the road."

With a roll of his eyes, Denver said, "I thought you were taking the girl to her room."

"Did that, then left. But she followed me."

Cherry made a choked sound and Armie eyed her with interest. "Don't expire, honey. Turned out she mostly just wanted me to talk dirty to her."

She cracked open one eye. "Bet you're good at that."

Smiling, Armie said, "Yeah."

"Here's a news flash," Denver interjected, just to keep the two of them from teasing in front of him. "Havoc can find you at the rec center, too."

"Nah, he wouldn't bother coming to Ohio." Looking past Denver, Armie studied Cherry with concern. "Something for fever? Anything else?"

Again Denver stroked her hair away from her face, put his mouth to her forehead, and flinched. "The gift shop is closed."

"So I'll make a run to the store. Not a problem."

"You don't mind?" Denver didn't want to leave her.

Pushing herself up against the headboard, Cherry huddled a little tighter and, teeth chattering, said, "You can both go. I can take care of myself." That statement ended with a cough.

Which Denver had been expecting.

He needed to get her fever down. While walking Armie to the door, he rattled off a list of things for him to grab. When he reached for his wallet, Armie refused him.

"You paid for my drinks. We'll call it even."

"Thanks." Soon as he left, Denver went into the bathroom and dampened a washcloth. When he headed back, Cherry watched him with alarm.

"What are you going to do?"

"Smothering a fever won't help anything, babe. You need to lose the blanket."

"*No.*"

The demonic tone might have amused him at any other time. But not now. She looked miserable and it twisted his heart.

He sat beside her again. Putting the damp cloth on the nightstand, he took hold of her blanket.

"Denver, no," she whimpered.

"Trust me, okay?" Relentlessly he wrested the blanket from her, but let her keep the sheet—for now. "I'll make you more comfortable."

Around more coughing, she growled, *"You're not a damn doctor."*

"My father is."

That stalled her. "Seriously?"

"Yeah." He rarely shared his family history. No point to it. But if conversation helped her to relax, hell, he'd tell her fairy tales if she wanted to hear them. "He has his own practice."

While she licked very dry lips and thought about that, he stroked the cool cloth over her face and then her neck.

At first she sucked in a breath. A second later she leaned into his hand.

If, as he suspected, she had the bug that'd been going around, sex was off the table for at least a week. It'd take her that long to start feeling human again.

Her hair was smashed on one side, frazzled out on the other. And he'd never seen her makeup so wrecked. But he wanted to hold her close and care for her, and for however long it took for her to get well, he wanted to be with her. With or without her looking her usual irresistible self.

With or without sex.

Armie had great instincts and if he didn't trust the

guys claiming to be her family, then Denver didn't trust them, either. So at least for now he had a damn good reason to stick close—beyond the fact that for the first time in his life, a woman had him in over his head and he knew it.

CHAPTER FOUR

WHEN DENVER TUGGED her sheet away, too, and then urged her against his body, bone-deep chills had Cherry trying to burrow closer. "This is awful," she mumbled.

"Me holding you?"

Never that. His attention was the most wonderful thing to ever happen to her.

But the timing was the worst.

Almost too drained to reply, she whispered, "You seeing me like this." When he lifted up the back of her T-shirt, she braced herself. The first touch of that cloth felt like ice on her spine and she hissed in a breath that brought on a nasty coughing fit.

He stroked her, rocked her, made soft shushing sounds—those same husky sounds he'd made while holding her legs open and gently squeezing into her.

Remembering his size, the delicious sensation of being filled, Cherry ducked her face. "This sucks so badly."

"I'm glad I'm here with you." Holding her hair up with one hand, the cool cloth in the other, he stroked it from her nape all the way down her back to the top of her barely there underwear. "And I love your panties."

She groaned. "If I'd known I was going to be sick—"

"Don't say you wouldn't have worn them."

"I don't own any other kind." But by God, she'd have bought some briefs if she'd known it wouldn't do her any good to tempt him.

He went still, then hugged her carefully before easing her to her back on the bed. "Stay put. I'll be right back."

She reached for the sheet, but he stopped her, saying again, "Trust me."

Trusting him had nothing to do with the teeth-rattling shivers. "Hurry."

She watched through gritty eyes as he went into the bathroom to rinse out the cloth.

Trying to concentrate on something other than her discomfort, she rasped, "Tell me about your dad."

After a long pause, he said, "He's a terrific doctor. Well respected." He returned in less than half a minute and again sat beside her hip. He started on her legs, and sure enough, some of the awful chills let up so that she mostly felt lethargic and very achy all over.

She studied Denver's face. With his head bent down, his wavy hair hung forward, concealing his high cheekbones. This late in the day, he had a very appealing beard shadow on his jaw and chin. His nose was narrow with a slight crook from once being broken. Long lashes framed his amazing topaz eyes.

And his mouth, firm and sexy… "Does he look like you?"

"He's as tall as me," Denver remarked while working to cool her down. "Athletic, but never competed."

"Meaning he's not all buff like you."

Denver smiled. "Same features, but his coloring is different. Lighter than mine. He's fit."

As he leaned over her legs, she lifted a hand and

stroked her fingers through his shaggy hair. Jogging under the afternoon sun had added golden streaks to the light brown color. It was just long enough to be held in a rubber band when he fought. "Bet he wears his hair different."

"Military short." He lifted one leg and moved the cool cloth behind her knee. "He doesn't say much about my hair, but I know he doesn't like it. My stepmother does, though."

Cherry looked from his hair to his face and saw his lean jaw tighten. "Your stepmother?"

He tensed, then suddenly turned and lifted the front of her shirt all the way above her breasts. "Yeah." For just a moment he cupped his large hand over her left breast, his thumb teasing dangerously close to her nipple. "You are so damned pretty."

A sweet talker—who wanted to change the subject. "I look terrible."

He bent to her breast for a soft kiss, almost stopping her heart. "You just look sick, honey—but not here." He kissed her very briefly again, the press of his warm mouth gentle, and then he straightened. Gaze riveted, he touched the cloth over her upper chest, around each breast, down to her belly.

She squirmed, both from the coolness of the touch and from the absorbed way he looked at her body.

Tears burned her eyes and she sniffled. "I wish I wasn't sick, damn it."

One brow lifted. "I wish you weren't, either."

Melancholy weighed heavy on her, and she knew she had to ask. "Will this be it?"

With the cloth held still high on her inner thigh, his gaze locked on hers. "Come again?"

Scrambling away from his touch, she pushed her shirt down and pulled the sheet over her. Shoving her ratty hair back, she sniffled, feeling so dreadful it was almost unbearable. "It's taken me forever to get you here, and now—" That awesome accusation got interrupted with harsh coughing that hurt all the way through to her back.

Denver left the bed to fetch a juice from the in-room bar.

"Don't," she wheezed. "It'll cost a fortune."

Ignoring that order, he twisted the cap off the bottle and again sat beside her. "My treat." He tipped it to her mouth. "Come on, Cherry, drink."

Since he gave her little choice, she did, swallowing down half the container before stopping.

He stroked his thumb over her bottom lip. "Better?"

She nodded. It was, but the insistent way he had of making her feel helpless was both sweet and a little unsettling. "Denver…"

"To answer your question, no, this isn't it." He set the juice on the nightstand before giving her a direct look.

Complaints disappeared under his scrutiny. "It isn't?"

"Not by a long shot."

"Oh." A million questions came to her at once, but Denver spoke before she had decided where to start.

"Armie is picking up more juice. You need to stay hydrated. How's your belly?"

"Fine." She wasn't nauseous, thank God. "Well, unless I move too fast."

He cupped the back of her neck and looked into her eyes. "Head still hurt?"

"Some." Growing in intensity, but she really didn't

want to come off as whiny. It was bad enough that tears kept pricking her eyes.

"What else?" When she didn't immediately answer— *what woman wanted to spend her first night with the man of her dreams by complaining?*—he used both hands to hold her face, "You're right, I'm not a doctor. But I've learned a lot from Dad, and from the sport."

"The sport?"

"Sure. Fighters have to know their own bodies well enough to stay healthy. So quit stalling. Your head, your throat. I'm guessing your chest with that cough. What else?"

She didn't think he'd let it go, so she admitted the truth. "Pretty much everything."

"Body aches?"

She nodded. "And my eyes burn." Maybe that'd be a good excuse for the tears.

"That's probably from the fever. Soon as Armie gets back we'll get some meds in you." Once more his thumb teased over her bottom lip and he let out a pent-up breath. "I'm so damn sorry."

"You didn't make me sick."

"I also didn't pay close enough attention to realize you weren't feeling well."

She hadn't paid enough attention, either. At the time, with Denver touching and kissing her, she'd been focused only on feeling. "You thought I was drunk."

"I worried about it, yeah. I didn't want to take advantage of you."

Talking hurt her throat, but she still had to say it. "When I had to practically beg you?"

His eyes narrowed in thought. "You should have told me, you know."

"I didn't realize—" she started to say.

"Shh." He kissed her forehead, softening his rebuke. "Don't lie to me, Cherry. Ever."

How could he so easily make her feel guilty? She bit her lip. "Well…"

"There's no way you couldn't have known you were getting sick."

True enough—to a point. "I didn't feel well, but—" She coughed some more, then had to bite back a groan at the radiating discomfort.

Denver supported her, rubbing her back until she'd quieted again.

Holding on to him, she drew a careful breath. "I didn't know I'd be this bad," she wheezed. "Honest. I wouldn't have risked getting you sick."

"I'm not worried about that." He helped her resettle in the bed. "But why didn't you tell me?"

She started to again bite her lip, but when his gaze focused on her mouth, she stopped herself. In a hoarse whisper, she said, "It's embarrassing."

As if her embarrassment didn't factor into things, he shook his head. "I need you to always be honest with me, Cherry, no matter what."

It irked her, this persistence that she might not be truthful. "I'm not a liar."

"No. But there are layers of honesty." Firm, he tilted his head to stare into her eyes. "I have to have one hundred percent."

"Fine." Though she felt like death warmed over, she lifted her chin. "I was afraid if I told you, you'd use it as an excuse to walk away."

His piercing gaze softened at her admission. "Am I walking away?"

"No." And it confused her so much. "But I don't know why not."

He took her hand. "You think I'd walk out on you when you're so ill?"

She didn't want his pity. "If that's the only reason you're staying—"

"It's not."

"Oh." With her eyes gritty and her head throbbing, she could barely stay upright. She persisted anyway, drawing in a slow breath to keep from coughing. "Long as we're being honest, why did you ignore me?"

For the longest time he stared down at their clasped hands and she felt the tumult of his thoughts, his resistance and even a sort of muted resentment.

She got nervous, dreading what he might say. It had been tough to take his unspoken rejections on good days. Being wretchedly sick, this was not a good day. But if she cried in front of him, she'd just die.

Finally he lifted his head. The piercing focus of his attention unnerved her. "Mostly I avoided you because I wanted you too fucking much."

Wow. Never had she expected that. How did that even make sense?

"The way you smell," he murmured, dipping his nose to her temple and inhaling. "The way you look. How you laugh and the bounce of your hair, your tits, that amazing ass…"

She gulped. His tone was gritty, almost raw, and she couldn't think of a reply except to say, "Oh," again.

"Every time you'd get near me, hell, even in the same room, I could smell you."

"That's…unsettling."

"You smell good, girl. So fucking good." Keeping

her pinned in his gaze, uncaring about her mute surprise, he continued. "You know you're stacked. There's no way you could not know. But I've known plenty of built women."

She scowled, making her head protest with ramped up pain.

"But they aren't you. It's the combo, I think. Your bod, your attitude—which drove me nuts, by the way."

In a croak, she asked, "My attitude?"

"Party girl," he accused. "Tease."

Despite being ill, her shoulders stiffened. "I am *not*—"

"You tease every guy who gets near you."

Her gasp choked her, making it impossible to protest. *She did not tease.* How dare he—

"You do," he stated, "even if you don't mean to." Working his jaw, his gaze went over her body, his hands following suit until he clasped her hips. "You have no idea how it affected me."

If it got him to this point—in bed with her—then she'd accept the blame.

"I hate to admit it, but that's probably why I went overboard." His voice dropped. "Swear to God, girl, if you weren't sick I'd be inside you right now."

Her eyes widened on a startled breath, and of course that set off a spate of coughing again.

Denver pulled her against his hard chest, cradling her gently. "Easy now." She'd only barely gotten her air back when he added, "I'm betting I've wanted this longer than you have. So damn long, I was going nuts. Then to finally give in—"

Give in? What did that even mean?

"That's not an excuse for pushing you so hard, but

fact is, you do it for me. Around you, I stay so primed it's almost agonizing."

Ducking her face against him, Cherry said, "That's exactly how I felt, too. As to you pushing me…" She shivered, remembering. "I liked it."

She felt his smile when he kissed her temple. "I know you did. But you'll like it more when you're feeling like yourself." Almost as an afterthought, he added, "There's still a lot I want to do to you."

Oh Lord. Not with her, but *to* her? How was she supposed to breathe normally when he said things like that?

For Denver, it sounded like everything was sexual. It thrilled her to finally make some headway—but what she felt was so much more.

He rubbed his hand down her back toward her bottom—but stopped short. "Soon as you're well, we'll try this all again." His lips teased her ear, and he whispered, "When you can take it, I'll make you beg."

Wow. As unnerving as that sounded, she could hardly wait.

His fist under her chin tipped up her burning face. "Far as I'm concerned, there's no end date in sight." He searched her eyes, then focused on her mouth. "You okay with that?"

She'd been hung up on Denver Lewis from the day she'd laid eyes on him and every day since she'd fallen harder. If he asked her to marry him right now, she'd probably say yes.

Instead, he wanted unlimited sex, and the answer was still a resounding, "Yes."

"Good." He tucked her hair back, then leaned away to see her body. "You're shivering again."

With nervousness, excitement, and yes, fever. The way he'd cooled her down had helped, but not for long.

He pulled off his shirt—a treat no matter how sick she might be—and kicked off his shoes, then crawled into bed beside her and hugged her up to his warm chest. "Better?"

Heavenly. "Yes."

"Doze off if you want." Stretching out his long legs and then reaching for the remote, he got comfortable with the TV on low. "I'll wake you when Armie gets back."

Tired as she was, she didn't think she'd be able to sleep. Not with her head feeling like it might explode off her body and her throat getting scratchier by the second. "Could we chat some more?" By chat, she meant her resting against him while he shared details of his life.

"About what?"

So many things. "Tell me about your family."

"Already did. Dad's a doctor."

The way he summed that up, to the point of being curt, made her wonder. Did he have a bad relationship with his dad? "You mentioned a stepmother?"

"Yeah. Dad remarried years ago."

Curling up next to him, her cheek on his bare chest, his arm around her, felt more comforting than meds ever could. The heat of his body seemed to permeate her aching muscles, and his scent wrapped around her. When she rested a hand over his abdomen, the incredible muscles there tightened. "How old were you?"

"Nineteen." Covering her hand with his own, he moved his thumb over her knuckles. "You are so soft."

Changing the subject again? "You like your step-mother?"

Silence stretched out while Denver played with her fingers. She didn't rush him. If he chose not to answer, she'd let it go.

She knew all about family issues better kept private.

Then he said, "Dad loves her. I figure that's what's important."

She turned her face up to see him. "You don't get along with her?" Given Denver was so wonderful, she couldn't imagine anyone not loving him.

Again, he took his time thinking. Finally he pinched the bridge of his nose and muttered, "It's complicated." After a quick hug and a kiss on the top of her head, he promised, "We'll have plenty of time to talk when you're feeling better. It's late. You should sleep."

She didn't want to, but lethargy pulled at her. Soon as Denver tucked the sheet around her, she felt herself slipping away.

Sometime later, more sluggish than ever, she woke to whispering and realized Armie was back. While trying to orient herself, she heard a low, angry conversation on relatives.

If anything, she felt worse now, bad enough that she didn't even care what they talked about. Pulling the covers over her head, she groaned, "Thanks Armie. Now go away please."

He didn't leave, of course. In fact, she sensed when both men came to loom over her. The testosterone ramped up enough to strangle her.

Armie crouched down by her shrouded head. "How you feelin', doll?"

She curled a little tighter to ensure he wouldn't unwrap her. "Bad enough I don't want anyone to see me."

A big, warm hand settled on her shoulder—Armie.

She was still adjusting to the impact of that when another hand settled on her hip—Denver.

Good Lord.

Her heart almost stopped. *Were they trying to kill her with their combined machismo?*

One large, hunky guy focused on her was enough. The two combined left her shivering with awareness. Though she wanted only Denver, they were both studs and she wasn't used to anything even close to this. Beneath the concealing covers, she squeezed her eyes shut—and since she had no idea what to do, she played possum.

Until both men's hands sympathetically squeezed, rubbed...

Surprise wrought a groan that ended in a rasping cough.

"Move," she heard Denver say, and a second later he'd pulled the covers to her waist, leaving her hideous hair and smudged makeup exposed. At least they'd kept the lights low, giving her shadows to hide in.

Denver helped her to sit up while giving her a drink of cold juice.

She needed the drink—but he'd pulled the sheet so low that snatching it back up seemed her first priority. Once she'd preserved her modesty, she accepted the drink.

So very aware of Armie standing there, taking it all in, seeing her in such a mess, she wanted to wither. But the juice eased the pain of her throat so she ignored her awful embarrassment and drank it all.

When she'd finished, Denver smoothed down her hair. "Let's get you started on some meds."

She seriously hated being babied so much. Never, ever, had she been the center of so much attention. "I can do it. You should go home with Armie."

Grinning at her, Armie said, "Damn, Cherry, way to insult a guy."

Tone level but uncompromising, Denver said, "I'm not going anywhere." He opened two different pill bottles and some cough medicine.

"You don't need to be stuck here."

This time Armie shook his head and, deliberately provoking, said to Denver, "Women."

"We already settled this," Denver said as he handed the pills to Cherry. "Can you swallow them?"

"Yes." But man, it hurt getting them down. Soon as she finished, he held up the tiny medicine cup of cough liquid.

That went down easier and didn't even taste too awful. Pulling the covers tight around herself again, her vision a little muzzy, she asked, "What time is it?"

"It'll be dawn soon," Denver told her.

"I was gone an hour," Armie told her. "Sorry about that. The store wasn't quite as close as I'd figured."

"Thanks." She started to recline again.

Denver caught her shoulders. "I want to take your temperature."

"Can she hold the thermometer in her mouth?" Armie asked.

Denver grinned, but Cherry choked on a gasp then coughed hard enough that she dropped the sheet and covered her mouth.

And still she tried to curse Armie, assuring him that there was *no* way—

"He's teasing, girl. Calm down."

"Not funny," she managed to croak around broken breaths and a lot of glassy-eyed glaring.

Concern brought Armie's brows together. "Sorry. Didn't mean to cause all that."

She wiped her watering eyes and concentrated on carefully catching her breath.

Coming closer, Armie stepped around Denver and felt her head again. "You sure she doesn't have pneumonia?"

This was all too weird. No one would ever mistake Denver Lewis or Armie Jacobson for nurses. Big, muscular, macho guys should never tend the sick, especially not in freaking *pairs*.

Having them both try to pamper her at the same time was like an overdose of fantasy—only she'd never even dared fantasize anything that unreal.

How was she supposed to deal with it?

When Armie's warm palm remained on her forehead, Cherry leaned out of his reach. He looked surprised until he took in her expression, then he grinned and winked at her, all in all being far too familiar when she looked and felt as she did and clearly wasn't up to bantering with him.

Shaking the thermometer, Denver said, "Can't know for sure but I doubt it. You know something's been making the rounds." He turned, waited for Cherry to open, and slipped the thermometer under her tongue. "If her fever gets too high, I'll run her to the hospital to be safe."

How dare they make plans without her input? Around the thermometer she said, "No hospital."

"Not yet anyway," Denver agreed, tapping the bottom of her chin as a reminder to keep lips closed.

"Somehow," Armie remarked, "it doesn't seem as bad when it's a dude who's sick."

"I know."

"Sexist," she muttered, then slumped against the headboard.

While waiting the requisite time to get a temperature reading, they both watched her far too closely, making her almost squirm. She wore only a T-shirt and panties, in a bed, in a hotel room—and she had two megahunks focused on her.

The upside to this whole awful scenario would be telling her girlfriends, Yvette, Rissy, Harper and Vanity about it. She just knew they'd love the details and would embellish some for laughs.

They might even envy her...since they didn't actually have to suffer it.

Finally Denver deemed it time to take the thermometer from her mouth, and she collapsed back in the bed, pulling the sheet to her chin. He held it under the bedside lamp to read it, then with a frown told Armie, "A little over 101."

Well. No wonder she felt like crap.

"Damn." Armie checked the time. "I'd give it an hour and check again. If the meds haven't brought it down by then—"

"Yeah." Denver glanced at her, but said in an aside to Armie, "I'll take care of it."

Pigheaded men. She could damn well decide if she needed the hospital. Right now, though, all she wanted to do was hide, so she pulled the blankets over her head.

She heard Denver say low, "She's going to suffocate herself. You better go."

"You don't need anything else?"

"Got it covered."

"All right, then." Voices dropped more, moved farther away, and Armie said quietly, "You'll let me know if anything else happens?"

"Yeah. But I'll keep a close eye out, so don't sweat it."

A close eye out for *what*? Cherry lowered the sheet enough to see both men standing by the open door.

Armie half stepped out. "Think you'll be back at the rec center tomorrow?"

"Depends on how she feels in the morning." When Denver glanced back at her, she quickly closed her eyes, and he said to Armie, "I'll call in and let you know."

"I hate for her to go through that long drive home if she's not up to it."

If she'd had the strength, Cherry would have set Armie straight. She wasn't a frail little girl—but at the moment, she sure felt like one.

"I know," Denver agreed. "If it is the current bug, she should feel a little better tomorrow. Not as feverish anyway."

"But still wiped out." Armie hesitated before saying, "You had, what? A kids' class and then your turn at the self-defense for women?"

"Intermediates at five-thirty, then the women at seven-thirty."

Oh wow, Cherry thought. He wasn't getting any

sleep, and then he'd have all that way to drive, his own workout to do, then two classes… Guilt made her feel even lower. All the guys pitched in at the rec center. It was sort of a tradeoff for getting to use the place, being able to mix and mingle with the better established fighters that visited Cannon on occasion, but also because they were close friends with Cannon and enjoyed pitching in.

Armie said, "Why don't I just cover for you?"

"You're coming off a tourney," Denver reminded him.

"So?"

"You sure you're up for it?"

"Now you're just trying to piss me off."

Denver laughed. "All right, sure. Thanks."

More was said, but Cherry couldn't hear it all, and then the door lock clicked and she knew Denver was returning to her. Curious as to what he'd do, she opened her eyes and watched him.

"Medicine kicking in yet?"

She took stock of her body, realized she wasn't trembling as badly, and nodded. "I think so."

He smiled down at her. "You look drowsy."

She knew how she looked and she didn't want to talk about it. "Will you come back to bed?"

"Yeah. We both need some sleep."

Without a single care, he stripped off his clothes, even taking off his boxers.

Watching him, her eyes went wide, then wider still when he turned to fold everything on a chair. Figured he'd sleep naked, which added to her torment since she wasn't up to taking advantage of that hot bod. His muscled butt was a thing of beauty. And his wide, strong back and shoulders made her sigh.

Apparently he heard her wistful sigh because he glanced back at her. "No coughing. That's good."

She just might be too stunned by his nudity to cough.

Turning to face her, Denver said, "You don't mind?"

Seeing him in the raw? Heck no. She shook her head while letting her gaze track all over him.

"Give me five minutes and I'll join you." He picked up his overnight bag and disappeared into the bathroom. She heard running water and the sounds of him brushing his teeth.

That made her feel extra funky, and as soon as he finished she dragged herself out of the bed. Even knowing she walked like an ancient zombie, she couldn't move any faster.

Denver took her arm and helped her to the small john. He tipped up her chin. "If you need me, let me know."

"Thanks." She closed the door on him. It took the last of her reserves but she washed off her destroyed makeup, brushed her teeth, used the john, and knew she had no energy left for dealing with the impossible mess of her hair.

Denver was right there when she opened the door and he scooped her up and carried her to the bed. Once he had her tucked in, he turned out the lights and scooted in behind her, drawing her close. He slid one arm under her head, the other around her, under her T-shirt and over one breast. "Okay?"

His massive fists had knockout power, but right now

his open palm and long fingers were so gentle it left her awed. "Yes."

He kissed her shoulder. "Sleep. I'll wake you when you need to take more meds."

Relishing his nearness, she closed her eyes and faded away.

CHAPTER FIVE

DENVER HELD HER as she slept restlessly until bright sunshine shone through the curtains. An hour or so ago, he'd gotten up to cool her down again, to give her meds and get her to drink. He knew she needed time, rest and meds more than anything, and somehow he'd see that she got it.

He hadn't slept much, but then, she was so sick, and he felt so damn guilty, it was a wonder he could relax at all. Thanks to his colossal ego, and yeah, pent-up lust for her, he'd pushed her hard, making her come again and again. That hadn't helped her.

It definitely hadn't helped *him* any, because now that he knew the feel of her, the sounds she made in her pleasure, how she clenched all around him, he couldn't stop thinking about doing it all again.

He rubbed a hand over his face, then got himself together.

She was with him, thank God, not alone. When he considered his own stubbornness, how he'd almost let her go back to her room alone, it made him want to kick his own ass. Right now she needed someone.

He wanted that someone to be him.

Luckily he had time to spare, and though he hated to see her feeling so poorly and would have spared her if he could, he'd enjoy caring for her.

First thing was cancelling their checkout.

He slipped from the bed without disturbing her, then just stood there looking down at her.

During the night when her fever had broken, she'd turned to her back, one hand up above her head, the other resting over her middle.

The sheet and blanket were now down to her knees. Torture.

She had the sweetest, curviest little body he'd ever seen.

And those panties… They were mostly a strip of lace over the front, a thong in the back, and they made him hazy with churning lust.

Making himself turn away, Denver picked up his clothes and slipped into the bathroom to dress and shave. Shaving was a concession for her delicate skin. He rarely bothered anymore, except when meeting with clients through his work as an accountant. But since making the SBC, he'd cut way back on that—and on shaving. Now he only had a few longtime clients he continued to work with.

After brushing his teeth, he finger-combed his long hair and stepped out again.

Cherry hadn't stirred. Her badly mussed blond curls spilled out over the pillow. Sunlight cut across her face and even sick and without makeup, she looked beautiful, her skin creamy, her lips full and soft.

If he didn't have a fight rolling up, he wouldn't mind spending an entire week at the hotel with her.

Just the two of them.

Most of their time spent in bed. Or the shower. Hell, he'd enjoy bending her over the desk so he could appreciate that spectacular ass even more.

But he would never shirk his training, so a week was out.

They'd have most of today, but she wouldn't be up for any of the things he burned to do to her.

Looking away from temptation, he put his wallet in his pocket and picked up the room key card, then slipped out without making a sound.

At the front desk, he checked out of his own room and extended her stay, explaining that she was sick. There was a good chance that once awake, she'd feel up to the ride home later. But he didn't want her rushed.

With that done, he visited the hotel restaurant and grabbed an assortment of food for himself, drinks for her. Carrying his haul, he headed for the elevator...until he felt eyes on him. Pausing with a frown, he glanced over his shoulder.

From across the lobby two men tracked his every move. Being unshaven, rough and in sloppy clothes didn't conceal their bulky shoulders and probable strength.

Or their aura of danger.

Suspicion sharpened, while priorities left Denver divided.

He needed to get back to Cherry. But what if these two were part of the trio Armie had mentioned? They could be a threat to her.

Decision made, Denver turned and, never once breaking eye contact with the biggest guy, headed toward them.

Clearly that surprised them because the big guy lost the challenge in his gaze, straightening with new awareness. The smaller man—which didn't make him *small* by any stretch—said something to the other and... *Damn it*.

Denver watched them go through the rotating doors and disappear. His jaw ticked. Should he go after them? In his experience, men only ran if they had a reason.

So hell yes, he needed to go after them.

He saw a couple of female fight fans eyeing him and, ready to take advantage, gave them a smile. "Could I ask a favor?"

A slim brunette returned his smile. "Sure."

"Watch my food for a minute?"

"Oh...um..."

In a rush, he set everything on the top of her rolling suitcase. "Swear I'll only be a couple of minutes." He hoped.

A more petite blonde next to her bobbed her head. "Okay. Sure."

"Thanks." Jogging, he went out the same doors, looked left, turned right—and saw the two men duck around the side of the building.

He stalked forward and rounded the corner cautiously. Three hulking men now stood together, all openly belligerent. Idiots. Did they think being together somehow gave them an advantage?

And why would they need an advantage anyway? What were they up to?

If they were in any way related to Cherry, it didn't show. Though two of them wore hats, Denver could see they were dark-haired, muscular but with signs of dissipation, eyes reddened from drugs or alcohol, maybe both.

The third guy had a close-cropped Mohawk with the side of his head tattooed.

Taking his time, Denver looked over each of them, then raised a brow. "You ran from me."

One man spit tobacco that came entirely too damn close to Denver's foot. He waited without moving.

"Wasn't running."

"Looked like it to me." They had their backs to a long, narrow alleyway that opened to a cross street behind the hotel. If he had to chase them, he'd catch at least one, probably two, no problem. "Why were you staring at me?"

"Check your ego, man. I wasn't."

Smiling, Denver took another step forward, ready to provoke if that'd get him some straight answers. "That's a lie."

The big guy—who, as Armie had said, was taller than Denver's six-two—bunched up.

The one who had spit now laughed. "Chill, okay? We were jus' tryin' to figure out if you're with Cherry Peyton. We heard she's hangin' with a fighter, and last night a different fighter caused a scene—"

"Which one of you got it in the balls?"

None of them were amused. Denver knew one of them had pulled a knife. He almost wished the chickenshits would try that now.

Pulling off a trucker's cap, running a hand through his hair and then sticking the hat on his head again, the spitter glanced at the quietest of the three.

Taking that as his cue, the Mohawk wearer stepped forward. "That was Gene." He gestured at the spitter.

"Still got a knife on you?" he asked Gene.

It was Mohawk who answered. "Yeah, he does." The hand he offered showed tats on his knuckles, a few scars. "I'm Carver Nelson."

Denver ignored his extended hand.

"Gene always carries his knife. It doesn't mean anything." Pulling his hand back, Carver said, "These are my brothers. Mitty and Gene."

Mitty, the biggest, continued to glare. Gene, the knife carrier, spit yet again.

"That's a nasty-ass habit you have."

Gene bunched up.

"So," Carver said. "Are you with Cherry?"

"And if I am?"

"We're trying to find her, that's all."

No way could Denver reconcile the idea of Cherry with any of these men, but especially not the guy now talking to him. In the fight world, he saw every style there was; tattoos and crazy haircuts didn't faze him.

But he knew a thug when he saw one. Carver was that—and more.

"Why?"

Mitty said, "She's our little sis."

No fucking way. Knowing his disdain and disbelief showed, Denver again looked them over.

Cherry was bubbly, all smiles, sweet and stacked, soft and sexy.

These men looked like low-life goons. "Seems to me you'd have her number and know a better way to contact her than skulking around hotels."

The big guy fisted his hands. "Wasn't skulking."

"We got estranged a while back," Carver said, speaking over his brother. "Had a family disagreement and lost touch. That's all."

"But now we wanna reunite," Gene added with a tobacco-stained leer.

Hoping to get the truth, Denver fought to moderate his tone. "How did you know she'd be here, at the fights?"

Carver shrugged. "Knew she was a fight fan, knew she lived in these parts." He folded his arms over his chest, putting muscular arms on display. "Just figured."

He didn't want to, but to be fair, Denver made an offer. "Give me a number where she can reach you, and I'll make sure she gets it."

"No good," Gene told him. "She won't call."

More so than the others, Denver wanted to knock Gene on his ass, make him choke on his chew.

It seemed Carver attempted diplomacy, and Mitty was too stupid to do more than mutter incomplete sentences. He figured Carver for the leader, Mitty for the muscle when necessary.

But Gene had no problem inciting his rage. Denver would love to unleash it on him and a blade wouldn't make any difference at all.

Instead, knowing it'd bug the man, he directed his answer to Carver. "Then I guess you're out of luck, aren't you?"

After giving both of his brothers a quelling scowl, Carver stepped in front of them. "There's been a death in the family."

"Who?"

"Our pops."

If they were related, would Cherry be devastated? It wasn't something he could keep from her. "Sorry to hear it. I'll let her know." Anxious to get back to her, he said, "So you want to give me a number or not?"

"Yeah, sure." Carver patted his pockets with theatric flair. "Damn. Ain't got a pen or paper on me."

"I guess a business card is out?"

"Left mine at home," Carver joked.

"Go into the hotel and tell the front desk that you want to leave me a message. Ask them to hold it for Denver Lewis. I'll pick it up before checking out."

"Yeah? When is that exactly?"

Denver laughed, but he didn't feel even a smidge of humor. Carver tried to be slick and failed miserably. "I don't know yet, but you'd be smart not to be there when I do." He was just about to walk away when he felt the approach of someone behind him. He didn't take his attention off the brothers, but he did go more alert.

Until he heard, "Need a hand?"

Relaxing again, he turned to see Dean Connor, better known as Havoc, standing a few feet away, arms folded, expression amused.

"Thanks, but I've got it."

"I'll just wait, then."

Because he wanted to discuss Armie. Shit, shit, *shit*. Denver didn't have time for this. He wanted to get back to Cherry.

Damn Armie for being so stubborn.

No way would he disrespect Dean, so he said, "Suit yourself."

"Always do."

Facing the brothers again, Denver pointed at Carver. "Don't bother her. That's the only warning you'll get. Do we understand each other?"

In no way intimidated, Carver gave a slight nod. "Yeah, I think we do."

That Carver tried to say it like a warning didn't bother Denver at all. He walked toward Dean and the three yahoos went in the other direction. If they weren't as dumb as they looked, they'd keep walking.

"Friends of yours?" Dean asked when he joined him.

Shaking his head, Denver said, "They're nobody."

"Funny. That's the same thing Armie told me last night."

"Maybe because it's true."

"Or more likely, you consider it none of my business." When Denver would have backtracked, Dean held up a hand. "Whoever they are, I think you put the fear of God in them. Glad we already have you signed with the SBC."

"Like dealing with street punks would prove anything?"

Dean shrugged. "You handled yourself well and you kept your cool." And then, with an amused smile, "At least better than Armie did last night."

He'd met Dean a few times, but he wouldn't say they were friends. More like acquaintances. Being newer to the SBC, Denver always appreciated the time Dean, who was a legend, gave to him.

Except for now.

"Armie has plenty of control when he needs it." Because Armie didn't always show that control, Denver added, "Like when he fights."

"Agreed." Dean fell into step beside him. "You're in a hurry?"

"I don't mean to be rude—"

"No problem. I'll walk with you."

With no way around it, Denver said, "Sure."

They stepped through the hotel doors. "Actually, I wanted to talk about Armie."

Already shaking his head, Denver said, "Not my business."

"I get that. No pressure. Just pass along a message for me, will you?"

The two women were still there, anxiously watching for Denver. "Hang on." He went over to them, apologizing as he approached. "Sorry. That took longer than I thought it would."

The blonde beamed at him. "It's okay."

He picked up his bags of food and drinks. "Where're you both headed? The airport?"

The brunette nodded, but her gaze had moved beyond Denver to Dean and she looked ready to faint.

Pasting on his patented "fan smile," Dean stepped forward and offered his hand.

Things got smoothed over when Dean took a picture with the ladies and Denver paid for their cab.

With that resolved, Dean followed Denver to the elevator.

"Sorry about that," Denver told him. "What did you want me to tell Armie?"

"To quit running from me. Tell him I said to man up and give me an opportunity to talk to him."

Denver whistled. "That won't win him over."

"No, but it will force him out." He surprised Denver by stepping into the elevator with him.

"Was there something else?"

"Yeah, but I'll make it quick. I want to know how Cannon runs his rec center. It's unique, the combo of a top-notch training center, the opp to spar with and learn from him, while also helping the neighborhood. How's that work exactly? I'd ask Cannon, but he's too humble about it."

Now this was a topic Denver could sink his teeth into. He and Cannon had been friends forever, and he respected him more than any man he knew. "Cannon has it set up so that everyone takes turns pitching in, some once a week, some an hour every day. Now that Cannon's made it big, Armie carries the lion's share of the load. He sets the schedule and lines up the volunteers. Whenever Cannon is out of town, Armie runs things."

"He's an employee, or a partner?"

"Both, I guess." Denver had never really gotten into the details with Armie, but knowing Cannon, he assumed Armie was well compensated for all the time he contributed. "Armie has a high energy level and refuses to have idle time."

Grinning, Dean said, "I thought he spent all his free time with the ladies."

"He fits that in, believe me." There were times when it seemed Armie wouldn't sleep for days on end—and yet he never dragged.

Laughing, Dean pulled a card from his pocket. "Give Armie my message. And hey, next time you're in Harmony, let's grab dinner."

"Sure." Since Harmony wasn't that far, just a little south in Kentucky, he got down that way often. Denver pocketed the card. "I'd like that."

When the elevator stopped, Dean stayed inside, but held the door open after Denver had stepped out. "You know," Dean said, "I wouldn't have let that motley crew around my lady, either." After that parting shot he allowed the doors to close.

Huh. So Dean had understood more than he'd let on.

Denver had a lot to think about—later.

Right now, he only wanted to see Cherry.

To his surprise, when he opened the hotel room

door, he found the bed empty. As he slowly let the door shut, he heard the shower running. Heat expanded and his body grew taut as he set down his packages…and headed for the bathroom.

SHE'D STRUGGLED TO pin up her hair, to start the shower, to stand under the spray and wash from head to toe. Now slumped against the tiled wall, Cherry realized her mistake. Never in her entire life had she been so drained. Even staying upright seemed to take an incredible amount of energy—energy that had quickly faded away.

Home, *alone*, she wouldn't have bothered.

But it was bad enough to be so pathetically sick with Denver. She wouldn't be grungy, too. Besides, she honestly believed she'd feel better once she was clean.

Instead, she wasn't sure she could muster up the strength to turn off the taps, much less get dry, dressed and back in the bed.

She literally wanted to sink down to the tub and go back to sleep, even with the water raining down on her. If she knew for certain she wouldn't run out of warm water or drown herself, she might've done just that.

In fact, it was still a toss-up.

That thought had barely cleared her brain before the shower curtain opened and Denver stood there, his smoldering gaze going all over her. He appeared stern, and a little turned on.

A unique combo.

"Damn, girl, what do you think you're doing out of bed?"

A lump of misery caught in her throat. "I was… I

can't..." She braced a hand on the shower wall and said simply, "Big mistake."

He reached in and turned off the water. Grabbing up a big white towel, he wrapped it around her and, uncaring if he got wet, lifted her out against him. One-handed, he flipped down the toilet lid and lowered her to sit.

"Denver..."

"Hush. I'll take care of it." Going to one knee, he dried her calves, up her legs, over her belly.

She held herself as upright as possible, completely mortified, all too aware of where and how he touched her. For him it seemed so impersonal; for her it was as personal as it could get.

When his gaze met hers, he said, "Breathe, girl. Slow and easy."

The husky timbre of his voice made her want to melt. "I'm sorry. I thought—"

"You should have waited for me." More gently, he dried her breasts, and as the soft terry towel moved over her nipples, she swallowed hard. The cooler air after her shower made her shiver—and made her nipples draw tight.

"Almost done," he told her, and he sounded as strained as she felt. Finally giving up on her breasts, he briskly dried her shoulders and gently patted the towel to her face. "Up you go." He drew her to her feet and supported her against his body.

So warm. Closing her eyes, Cherry honestly thought she could doze off just like that, with him holding her so carefully.

After he dried her shoulders and the small of her back, he spent an inordinate amount of time on her bottom, looking over her shoulder until she said sleepily, "Denver."

He kissed her neck, wrapped the towel around her and scooped her up. She knew he was strong; anyone could look at him and see that. But he held her with such ease it still impressed her and made her feel like the quintessential "little lady."

As he strode to the bed, he said, "I'm glad you didn't try washing your hair."

Resting her cheek against his hard shoulder, one hand over his heartbeat, she admitted, "I couldn't."

He paused by the bed with her still comfortably in his arms. "Are you feeling any better at all?" His mouth brushed her temple. "You don't feel as feverish."

Around a yawn, she whispered, "That's why I thought I could shower." But halfway through she'd known it was a very bad idea.

"I'm sorry I took so long." He tilted her back a little to look at her. "Do you have anything to wear?"

With the way he held her, the towel barely kept her concealed. Then she noticed Denver glancing at the dresser mirror beyond and when she looked… *Oh God*. She squirmed to get free.

He only tightened his hold. "Settle down."

"Stop looking at me!"

He gave one more long perusal at the mirror. "Sorry, but that's not going to happen."

The image in the mirror showed her legs tucked up over his arm, the loose towel hanging well beneath her backside, and a whole lot of nakedness in between. He could literally see from back of the thighs to the middle of her back.

Her heart hurt in her chest and red-hot humiliation scalded her. "Denver…"

He hugged her—and turned so that her behind was no longer aimed at the mirror, but still didn't put her down. "You have no reason to be embarrassed. I like looking at you."

"Not like that!"

"Especially like that." He nuzzled against her. "I want to see every part of you."

Tucking her burning face against his throat, she groaned, "This is so awful."

"You're beautiful," he said, low and rough near her ear.

That was not a beautiful shot, but she didn't have the will to debate it with him right now. "My shirt…" She glanced at the same shirt she'd removed before getting in the shower. It was now badly rumpled, but anything would be better than staying so vulnerable.

Denver continued to study her face. "One day soon, you'll show me everything I want to see."

Ready to die of embarrassment and half afraid he was right, she said nothing.

He took in her expression, then turned his head to eye her discarded shirt on the dresser. "I brought a few extras if you want one of mine instead." His smile went crooked. "Much as I enjoy seeing you, it'll probably be better for my sanity if you don't stay naked."

"I wouldn't!"

He grunted. "Left on your own, we both know you wouldn't have had the grit to worry about it."

True enough. "Somehow," she muttered, "I'd have figured it out."

"Maybe." After lowering her to the bed, he pulled

away the towel and his attention moved over her in minute detail again. "Now you don't have to." He kissed her forehead, her shoulder, and the top of one breast before going to his bag and removing a black SBC T-shirt.

Hating her own weakness, Cherry managed to sit back up before he got to her, but she let him drop the shirt over her head and even tug her arms through the short sleeves.

Wearing an indulgent, very male smile, he said, "Poor baby. You're really shot, aren't you?" He pulled the sheet over her lap and propped the bed pillows behind her.

"I'm sorry—"

"Stop apologizing." He pulled the band from her hair and ran his fingers through it to smooth it out. "I told you there's something going around. I've seen a few fighters go down for the count."

And she wasn't a big, muscled, extremely fit fighter. "Really?"

"Yeah, really. You just need to take it easy a few days." He cupped her face in his hands. "Think you can stay awake long enough to take some medicine and get down some fluids?"

"Yes." Honestly, now that she was back in the bed, she knew she *did* feel better for being clean. "What time do we have to check out?"

He opened an orange juice and handed her pills to take, then liquid cough medicine, before answering. "I extended your stay another day."

Something must have shown on her face, because he said, "Don't worry about it. I've got it covered."

Cherry shook her head. It was enough that he'd

taken on caring for her. She did not want him financially taxed, too. "I'll pay you back."

"No, you won't." Ignoring her indignation, he said, "I'm staying here, too, so don't sweat it. Now stay put while I go get some ice. I'll be right back."

"Wait a min—"

He bent and kissed her forehead. "You're not up for arguing with me, girl, so just relax, okay?" Another kiss and then he strode to the door.

The shower had cleared the fog of lethargy enough for reality to intrude. The timing was a problem in more ways than the obvious.

The second Denver returned with the ice bucket filled, she said, "I have to work tomorrow."

"Around kids?" His brows climbed high. "That's not happening."

"I'm feeling better." Better, but still on the dark side of rotten. And since she worked in a day care, she probably shouldn't be around little kids. Still...

"Hate to tell you, honey, but you're going to need at least two more days. Maybe three." He looked her over. "Or more."

Unacceptable, but knowing he might be right got her head to pounding.

The ice clinked in a glass as Denver dropped it in, then poured juice over it. "You want a straw?"

Her shoulders slumped. "No."

He handed it to her and went to the small table to open up some bags. "I grabbed food for myself, but I wasn't sure—"

She held up a hand. "No. No food for me."

"I figured." His expression softened. "Will it bother you for me to eat?"

"No, just…don't talk about it."

Smiling, he shook his head and pulled out a seat. "If it makes you nauseous, tell me."

Turning to her side, she snuggled down in the bed. Keeping her eyes open wasn't easy, but she'd been enough of a pill already. "What will you do today?"

He opened several containers. "What do you mean?"

"You usually work out? Or jog?"

"Both, but I can miss a day."

She watched him dig into what looked like cottage cheese. She closed her eyes. "Denver?"

"Hmm?"

"Would you do me a huge favor?" When she opened her eyes, she saw that he'd turned toward her and was waiting. "Please, will you go make use of the gym? Or at least jog?"

"You planning another shower?"

His teasing made her smile tiredly. "No." She yawned, sank a little deeper into the bed. "I'm going to doze and I'll feel better knowing I didn't completely ruin your day."

He pushed his chair back and came to sit on the side of the bed. "I like being here with you."

"Not like this."

"Even like this."

Could that be true? And if so, did that mean he actually cared for her? They had so much to work out, but first… "Please?"

Hesitation showed through his frown. "You promise to stay in bed?"

Since she didn't think she could move anyway, she nodded.

"All right. I'll finish eating then take off for an hour

or so." He bent to put his forehead to hers. "Be good while I'm gone."

Soon as she got well, Cherry decided, she'd set him straight on his bossiness. But until then…yeah, sleep seemed like a very good idea.

CHAPTER SIX

DENVER HAD TO ADMIT, the jog did him good. He'd still been tense from his clash with Cherry's supposed family. He hadn't gone too far from the hotel and he'd stayed alert while pushing himself, but he hadn't seen them anywhere when he left or when he returned. With a little luck, they'd taken his advice and split.

Most of the fight crowd had finally cleared out by the time he returned so he made it to their floor without getting stopped even once. Wearing a sweaty T-shirt and running shorts, his phone and the key card in a special carrier strapped with Velcro around his wrist, he headed to the door.

The sudden splitting noise of a fire alarm obliterated the calm he'd just achieved by the long run. Jogging the last few steps to the door, he jerked it open and found Cherry sitting up, groggy and confused.

"What happened?"

"Fire alarm." In rapid order he went about shoving his things into his overnight bag, then started on her stuff, grabbing up discarded clothes, shoes, makeup she'd left in the bathroom...

"What are you doing?"

"We have to clear out," he said while finding her a pair of jeans and her underwear, "and I figure we may as well head home."

"Oh." Little by little the sleepy daze cleared from her eyes.

Odds were the cough medicine had wiped her out as much as illness.

She started to leave the bed so he went to help her.

"I need the restroom."

"Okay, but we have to hurry." A voice came over an intercom of sorts in the room, directing guests to follow the guidelines on the backs of their entry doors. He led her to the bathroom, put the jeans and panties on the vanity, and stepped back. "Where's your phone?"

"Nightstand," she said, and shoved the door closed.

He saw she'd missed a call on her cell and on the room phone. Everything about this situation felt wrong, from the roughnecks claiming a relationship with her, to the sudden fire alarm and evacuation.

Damn it, he would not take chances with her.

He listened to the voice mail on the room phone first.

"Listen up, Cherry. You need to get in touch. I mean it. No more fucking around."

Angry tension invaded every muscle in Denver's body. When the caller, who he thought might be Carver, left a number, Denver held the phone between his shoulder and jaw and scrawled it down on a notepad. He tucked the paper into his wallet.

"Tonight, Cherry. You've caused enough trouble. Don't make me chase you down." And with that, the call ended.

He needed to know what the hell was going on. Now, before anything else happened. To be on the safe side, he glanced at her cell and saw that the missed call was from her roommate, Rissy. There was also a text that said only, Rissy was here. Typical MO for Merissa Colter. Under other circumstances, Denver might've smiled.

Right now he was as far from a smile as a man could get.

When he dropped the cell phone and charger into Cherry's purse, he saw her car keys. He fished them out and stuffed them into his front pocket. He'd just finished gathering up the meds and putting them in her purse when the bathroom door opened.

Cherry more or less crept out, now in the jeans, pale with fatigue, exhaustion showing in every line of her body.

He grabbed up the bags and put an arm around her. "Come on, honey, we need to go." He didn't think there was a real fire, but he wouldn't take any chances.

"My shoes."

"Damn. Sorry, but I already packed them. I'll find them for you in the car." He got her out the door and then had to veer her away from the elevator. "Not with a fire alarm going off."

"Oh, right."

He took in her red eyes, her defeated posture, and shook his head as he transferred the bags and her purse into one fist. "Sorry."

"Wha—" The word ended on a gasp when he dipped, caught her around the hips, and hoisted her up and over his shoulder. "Denver!"

"We're on the sixth floor, girl. You can barely go six steps."

To his surprise, she didn't fight him. She just clutched at his shirt and said, "Don't drop me!"

"Never."

He tried not to jostle her as he went down several flights of stairs. On the second floor, they ran into other people so he lowered her back to her feet to keep from embarrassing her, but put an arm around her waist to help support her. Near her ear, he asked, "Okay?"

With the strain obvious on her face, she nodded. When they finally reached the lobby, guests congested the front entrance, so Denver detoured with her down a short hall and out a side door.

The storms had moved out even before his jog, leaving the air fresh and clean. A blinding sun shone in a cloudless blue sky.

"Come on. You're parked this way, right?"

"Yes." She stumbled, coughed, and righted herself.

Worry stopped him. "Need me to carry you again?"

She shook her head, firm. "No."

"That'd be pride talking."

Mouth pinched, she trudged on.

Rocks and weeds littered the walkway. "Watch your step then." They were almost to the car when he spotted her supposed "brothers" in front of the bar across the street—in close conversation with Leese Phelps, the same idiot who'd hit on her yesterday.

The reservations were adding up.

And so were the men.

They all kept their eyes trained on the front of the hotel, probably hoping to hijack Cherry when she emerged. *But why?*

Had they pulled the fire alarm? It seemed possible and damn it, he didn't like it, any of it.

An approaching fire engine, sirens and lights blazing, thankfully drew their attention and kept them from searching beyond the front of the hotel.

Cherry had her head down so she didn't see them. Denver hustled her along a little more quickly and got her into the front seat before dumping the bags in the back.

"My purse."

"I'll get it in a minute." He freed the keys from his pocket while circling the car, and got behind the wheel. "Buckle up, honey." He was just pulling out when the men looked up and saw him. Leese shaded his eyes, just watching them go. The others straightened, cursed, and started off, presumably for their own transportation.

His sweaty T-shirt stuck to his back. He'd rather be wearing jeans than running shorts.

He would have loved a shower.

But he blocked those discomforts as he drove straight for the expressway, repeatedly checking the rearview mirror for anyone following. Cherry slumped in the corner of her seat, her eyes closed, shivering.

Working his jaw, Denver wondered when would be the best time to question her. His instinct was to coddle her, to make her as comfortable as possible.

But somehow she was embroiled in a whole bunch of brewing trouble. Even if the guys *were* her brothers, he recognized them as bad news. And that ominous phone message...

When he saw the second exit he took it, drove down to a small convenience store and pulled around back.

He didn't think anyone had tailed them, not that it mattered much.

With Leese's help, if Carver and the others wanted to track her down, it'd only be a matter of time before they showed up at her front door.

Even to Denver, his reaction to that was telling. Brothers or not, he didn't like the guys and he didn't want them anywhere near Cherry. How he'd keep them away, he wasn't sure yet. Maybe, he decided, it'd be best if he just stuck close so he'd be with her when they finally showed up.

When he put the car in Park, she stirred. Soft, sick, trusting.

His.

No, he couldn't think like that. Not yet. Contrary to the belief that athletes were all brawn and no brains, he wasn't an idiot. He learned from his experiences, especially the experiences that altered life.

There were facets to Cherry that he might never be able to accept. But while he figured that out, he'd damn well see her safe.

"Why are we stopped?"

Her voice sounded raspy and rough, her eyes looked sleep-heavy. Being near her and not touching her proved impossible. Knowing his expression to be grave, he stroked her thigh through her jeans. "I wanted to get you better settled. It's a long drive."

"I'm okay." Straightening, she unhooked her seatbelt and looked around before turning a quizzical gaze on him. "I just realized we didn't officially check out."

"The hotel has our info. I'll call once we're home." He put the back of his hand to her forehead. Warm. Too warm. Snagging her purse from the backseat, he opened it between them and dug around for the medicine.

Cherry looked at him, then at his hands in her purse. "Sure," she said, her gravelly tone dry, "help yourself."

He moved aside the phone book. "Have anything to hide?"

"No. It's just—" A big yawn took her by surprise. "Sorry."

"It's just what?"

"I don't know." She chewed her lower lip. "Personal?"

He handed her two aspirin, then reached back again for a bottle of water. "And having sex with me wasn't?"

"It's different and you know it." She swallowed the pills without complaint, then eyed the store.

Denver took her hand. "These are odd circumstances, right? I don't want you to think I'm just snooping through your stuff. But with you pretty much out of it, and—"

"The fire alarm at the hotel." She leaned toward him and put her forehead on his shoulder. "The way we had to leave there."

"Babe." He levered her back. "I'm sweaty."

"Because you didn't have a chance to change." She nestled up against him again. "You're so warm."

If she didn't mind, he wouldn't worry about it, either. He brushed his fingers through her hair. Usually she had soft curls, but now her hair was straighter, tangled. He tucked it behind her ears. "I was already in your purse once before."

Stiffening, she tipped her head back to share her displeasure.

This close, her brown eyes looked bigger and softer. And damn, he wanted her bad, maybe even more now that he'd had her than before getting a taste.

Smiling, he touched her mouth, amused by the mulish set to her lips. "I had to find your key card." He let his hand drop to her narrow shoulder. "Wanna tell me about that phone book?"

Her brows puckered. "I usually keep numbers stored in my phone, but if my phone dies—"

"Sure. But why are you carrying numbers for Armie, Stack or Miles in the first place?"

Very slowly she eased away from him, her breaths slow and shallow. The lack of makeup added to her wounded expression, and her cough-strained voice finished it off. "What are you accusing me of?"

"I'm just asking." *Because you're mine.* Damn it.

Her eyes searched his. "No, I think it's more than that."

Right. It was the near-savage need to stake a claim. Knowing he couldn't say anything that over-the-top, he said instead, "I think you and I need to come to an understanding."

"What kind of understanding?"

"Several actually, but let's start with exclusivity."

Uncertain, she slicked her tongue over her bottom lip. "So…you won't be seeing anyone but me?"

Hell, since meeting her no other woman had appealed anyway. "And vice versa."

Her chin lifted. "For how long?"

She'd come around in one hell of a mood. His jaw ticked, but he wasn't about to say how much it mattered to him. "As long as it lasts."

Looking like that answer bothered her, she deflated, closing her arms around herself and putting her head back on the seat. "Cannon insisted I have the numbers. I live with Rissy and you know how he is." She lifted a hand, flapped the air. "Two women, all alone. He wants me able to reach him—or one of you—if anything happens."

Yeah, that made sense. And now, seeing her so closed off, he felt like a damned bully. He tugged on a lock of her hair. "If there ever is reason to make that call, call me first."

She flashed him a weary smile. "Funny, but Cannon insisted the same thing."

Denver held silent. Cannon had rights that he didn't have—yet.

Saving him from coming up with a reply, Cherry put a hand to her stomach. "You know, I think I'm actually a little hungry."

A good sign. "Perfect timing, since we're at a quickie mart."

She looked down at her bare feet, touched her mussed hair. "I'll need my sandals."

"I can run in for you."

Relief showed, though she tried to hide it. "You wouldn't mind?"

How could he *not* kiss her? Drawing her close, he touched his mouth to the bridge of her nose. It wasn't enough. Not even close. Soon as she was well, he planned to taste her again. All over. "Glad to do it. What would you like?"

"Maybe…pretzels? And a cola?"

It'd be better if he let her eat before grilling her more. He should have talked with her about her damned relatives instead of the phone book anyway. "You got a call from Merissa while you were sleeping. Why don't you text her back while I'm in the store. And Cherry? Stay in the car with the doors locked, okay?"

Busy digging out her phone, she said, "I don't suppose you'd let me pay—"

"No." He caught her chin and turned her face toward his. "I'm serious, girl. Promise me you'll stay in the car, doors locked."

Confusion tweaked her brows, but she nodded. "All right."

"I'll only be a minute." He took the keys with him, pressed the automatic door locks, and closed the door behind him.

There were only a few teenagers in the lot, an older man walking with a cane and a mother with two kids. Still, he rushed through buying her things and was back out to the car in under three minutes.

With the phone to her ear, Cherry smiled and nodded, but when she saw him, she hastily ended the call.

As he got in, he asked, "Merissa?"

"Mmm-hmm."

Something in the way she acted, avoiding his gaze, her cheeks flushed, got his attention. "You told her you were sick?"

"Yup."

"Cherry." When she looked up, he cocked his head. "What else did you talk about?"

A darker rush of color stained her cheeks, but it wasn't from fever this time. "She, um, wanted details."

"About?" Able to guess and entertained by it, Denver opened her cola and handed it to her. "Us?"

In a rush she said, "Everyone knows I've been hung up on you forever."

Hung up on him, so not just looking for some fun? Nice. And if true, it gave him plenty to think about.

She gulped, and her voice faded. "I probably shouldn't have said that."

"You don't want me to know you care about me?"

Making a rude sound, she asked, "How could you *not* know? I've been so obvious."

True, but he hadn't realized anyone else was paying that much attention—especially with the easy way she teased with *every* man who got near her. "Others picked up on it?"

Nodding, she shifted nervously. "Rissy said I should stop chasing you so hard. She said I made it too easy for you."

"Rissy was wrong." His feelings for her had never been easy. *Had Merissa warned her off flirting with other men, as well? Or had he been singled out?*

Confused, she chewed her lower lip. "She and Vanity both told me I should accept a few other dates."

Jesus, he hated the games some women played. "Other guys asked you out?"

"Well…" She looked at him like he was nuts. "Yeah."

Of course they had. He knew how badly he'd wanted her, so it stood to reason other men reacted to her the same way.

Her smile flickered and she teased him, saying, "You know, Denver, I don't always look like this."

No, she usually looked hot as hell. "First, you don't look bad, so stop saying that. Actually, if you were up to it, I'd be all over you right now."

She blinked in surprise. "You would?"

He let his attention drift over her face, her throat, her body. "You look soft and mellow and extremely fuckable."

"Oh."

"Second, these other guys sniffing around—you refused them?"

"After meeting you, why would I want anyone else?" The second she said it, her eyes widened and she fell back in her seat with a dramatic groan. Given her thin, raspy voice, that groan held a lot of effect. "I probably shouldn't have said that to you, either."

By the second his mood improved. "You can say whatever you want to me."

Her disbelieving laugh turned to a cough.

Denver waited until she'd caught her breath again. "Merissa and Vanity are wrong, okay? Just be honest with me, always, and things will work out better."

She didn't look convinced, but she agreed with a nod anyway.

"So, what'd you tell Rissy about us?"

Her gaze skittered away and she cleared her throat.

"Come on, Cherry." Despite himself, he felt his mouth quirking. "What details did you share?"

Lacing her fingers together and again looking at her feet, she muttered, "Only that you're amazing."

Nice. But not for a second did he think that covered it all. "And?"

She lifted her shoulders, looked out the window. "That you're—" she toyed with her hair, took time for a big swig of cola, and finally muttered low "—even bigger than we'd imagined."

"What's that?" Pretending he hadn't heard her, Denver hitched a brow.

Wincing, she faced him again and said in a rush, "You said I could brag to my girlfriends, and Rissy is my best friend. She knew I wanted you forever and that you'd been dodging me and—"

"Slow down before you get yourself coughing again."

"—she'd heard the same things I'd heard."

Unbelievable. "About the size of my cock?"

Again her eyes flared and she inhaled so sharply that she coughed, then had to swill more cola before she could answer. "We're close, Denver," she explained, still wheezing. "We talk all the time."

More amused than bothered, he thought it would have been terrific to be a fly on the wall during those conversations.

"Being with you was so awesome—well, except for the part where I got sick—"

"Gossiping women." Shaking his head, feeling indulgent, Denver said, "I guess you both heard it from Armie?"

"Welllll… After I heard it from Armie, I sort of told Harper and Rissy."

Harper, too? Too funny. "You *sort of* told them?" Damn, he'd never really pictured a bunch of women—especially women he knew as friends—sitting around and discussing his package.

She carefully drank in a breath, then went on the offensive. "You can't tell me men don't gossip about women."

Shrugging, he said, "Sometimes."

She squared her shoulders, which made his attention drop to her impressive rack.

"Guys talk about boobs *all* the time," she accused.

"Maybe not as often as you think." *But yeah, often enough to make her accusation accurate.* Reaching out, he cupped her left breast. She was braless, her breast heavy and firm. By habit alone, he moved his thumb over her nipple. "As nice a set as you have, you can believe I won't be sharing details with any of the guys at the rec center."

She stared at him, guilty and flushed, and he felt bad for continually doing this to her, touching her in ways that excited her—and him—when he knew they couldn't do anything about it.

He withdrew his hand even as his curiosity ramped up. "What else did you tell her?"

Struggling to compose herself, she braced one hand on the door, the other on the seat beside her hip. "You want to hear it all?"

"Hell yes." Though God knew there were other far more important things they should be working out while she felt up to it. "You can summarize for me."

Bracing herself, she stated, "I told her how incredible you are. You know. In bed." And then, with feeling, "Because, Denver, you really, *really* are."

Sensation washed over him as he recalled how it had felt to be inside her, feeling her squeeze him tight as she rocked out a hard release. The way she affected him, visually, emotionally, with her body and her words and those damn sweet smiles, was almost alarming. "I think maybe we were just incredible together."

"And see, you're humble, too." She gave him another of those boner-inspiring sweet smiles. "I also told her how hot you look naked, how indescribable you smell—"

"Yeah?" Bragging was better than if she'd been disappointed and complaining to her friends.

"—and how badly I wanted to do it all again and

again, and instead you're stuck taking care of me."
She grabbed another pretzel. "Rissy was appropriately
bummed for me that I'd get sick now."

All in all, Denver figured he could take that type
of gossip.

"I'm where I want to be, so don't think I'm stuck,
okay?"

Unconvinced, she hunched her shoulders. "You're
a trooper, I'll give you that. But no way can you be
enjoying this."

Her being ill, no. But caring for her? He sure as hell
didn't want anyone else doing it.

"Granted, it's not how I thought I'd be spending
my time with you." He made a point of looking at her
body—specifically her lap. "I'd rather have you naked
on your back again."

She went wide-eyed, her gaze locked on his face,
slowly eating a pretzel without blinking.

He thought about her breasts, her narrow waist, and
that gorgeous ass; the sounds she made while coming;
how physical exertion had intensified the scent of her
heated skin.

Thinking it fired his blood, because *damn*, she had
a gorgeous body.

Shifting, he murmured, "The things I want to do
to you…"

She stopped chewing.

He had to get it together. She wasn't up for sex, so
there was no point in continually teasing them both.
Plus, he had ground rules to set up. When she was
well, that needed to be his priority—before he got involved any deeper.

Scrubbing a hand over his face, he said, "But shit happens and we'll both deal with it."

"You sound…"

"Turned on? I'll probably stay that way until I can have you again."

She swallowed hard. "I was going to say annoyed."

"No." He cupped his hand around her nape. "It's just now that I've seen you and tasted you, I know what I'm missing and it's making me nuts." True, she looked more with it, as if the nap and fresh air had done her good. But even though her skin wasn't as hot as it had been only hours ago, she was still too warm.

Nowhere near ready for everything he wanted.

Trying to lighten the mood, he said, "If you want to make it up to me later, I won't complain."

Putting the pretzels aside, she whispered, "I do. *So much*."

Even sick, she sounded almost as turned on as him. "Good."

"I already feel a little better." She laid one small hand on his chest, stroking him and inflaming him. "I think I'll be okay pretty soon."

"Hope so." But he figured it'd be at least two more days. "We'll both be patient and it'll just add to the anticipation."

Her fingers trailed up to his neck, then his jaw. "You're being so nice about all this."

Horny men tended to be real magnanimous. But with Cherry, it was more than that. A lot more.

He leaned across the seat to kiss her forehead, and decided he should get them back on the road before he forgot his better intentions. "Stay put. I'm going to change out of this shirt, find your sandals, and then we can get back on the road."

Now that they had a few minutes, he dug out another of his shirts for her to use if she started shivering again, and made sure everything else she might need was in easy reach.

She twisted around to ogle him as he changed his shirt, then kept watching him as he got back behind the wheel and drove them out of the lot. He could almost read her thoughts and that kept him on the ragged edge.

Knowing he needed a distraction, he waited until she'd eaten half the pretzels and drank most of her cola before he got her talking again. "Tell me about your family."

She froze up, purposely not looking at him. "There's nothing to tell."

"Mom, dad?" He glanced her way. "Siblings?"

"Mom and Dad are gone." She curled up in the corner of her seat.

Away from him.

Seeing her stare out at the passing roadway at nothing in particular told him more than she probably realized.

"Brothers? Sisters?"

As she closed the pretzel bag, apparently done eating, she said, "You didn't get anything to eat?"

He refused to take the hint. Gentling his tone, Denver hoped to coax her into sharing. "By gone, you mean your folks passed away?"

She nodded, and said nothing more.

Feeling his way, he asked, "Will you tell me how?" The silence grew, and so did her tension.

Denver reached for her hand. "If there's a reason you don't want to talk about it—"

"They were murdered." As she blurted that, she squeezed his fingers—still averting her gaze.

"Murdered?" Never in a million years had he expected that. His thoughts scrambled and the protectiveness he already felt for her expanded. "How? When?"

In the barest of whispers, she said, "It's not a good story, Denver."

"I'd still like to know." He *needed* to know.

Her eyes dark with shame, she hesitated. "I've never told anyone about it. Not even Rissy."

That, too, made him want to shield her from the world. "I don't want there to be secrets between us." Yet he knew there were things he didn't want to share, not with her, not with anyone. Knowing himself to be a hypocrite, he lifted her hand to his mouth and kissed her fingers. "You can trust me."

"It's just…it embarrasses me."

"Why?"

"It says a lot about my childhood, and because it's so awful."

"Then I'm doubly impressed with how sweet and caring you are." He continued to hold her hand, to rub his thumb over her knuckles, to wait.

Finally she said, "Dad dealt drugs and Mom helped him."

Drug dealers? He thought of Carver, Mitty and Gene, and new possibilities made his heart pump harder—with suspicion, and with determination.

To shield her.

To insulate her.

Even when younger, he'd never used recreational

drugs. He'd always been an athlete, a fitness buff. What he knew of drugs he'd learned from the news, never from firsthand experience or exposure. "A deal gone bad?"

"Something like that." She finished off her cola, then rested back in the seat. "This sucks, but I'm ready for another nap."

Despite how worn she looked, he needed to press her. When they got home, he'd have no excuse for moving in on her, yet until he understood everything, especially the level of threat, he didn't want her alone.

"I'm sorry, honey. I know you're tired." She should be in bed right now, not going through the inquisition. But he pushed her anyway. "Tell me what happened with your folks, then you can nap more if you want."

"I don't know where to start."

"When did they die?"

"When I was fourteen. A little over ten years ago."

If she'd lost both her parents, where had she lived? Who'd raised her? "They were killed together?"

She breathed deeper, distressed at sharing. "Someone knew they were delivering drugs and they got sidelined on the way to the drop. No one knows for sure what happened, but there was a lot of speculation."

So the murderers were never found? He supposed a lot of drug crimes went unsolved. "No arrests? No witnesses?"

She shook her head. "The theory is that Dad fought them and got hurt. Mom was driving the truck. He must have been in the truck bed, because there were bullet holes and his blood and…"

Denver waited as she composed herself.

"At some point, he fell out and they…" She looked at him, then away. "They ran over him."

Jesus.

"The truck was found half a mile away so Mom had probably kept going until they ran her off the road. Her body was several yards from it. No one knows if she was dragged out or tried to run." Cherry freed her hand to close her arms around herself, retreating both physically and emotionally. "She'd been shot three times. Once in each knee, and then in the head."

Emotions bombarded Denver, anger and sympathy the most prevalent. Thinking of what she'd gone through nearly broke his heart. "You're right. That does sound pretty awful."

She curled tighter into the corner, her eyes getting heavy.

And so damned sad.

She let out a slow breath. "Mostly, it just sounds like my life." She turned her face away. "I hope you don't mind, but I'm fading out again."

Denver cupped a hand over her knee. "Go ahead, baby. I'll wake you when we get home."

In a mere whisper of sound, she sighed, "Thanks." Using the extra shirt he'd given her, she cushioned her cheek against the door and within minutes dozed fitfully.

He had a million questions, most of all how a girl with such a terrible background could always be the life of the party.

But he'd literally *felt* her discomfort, her sorrow over the past, and it devastated him. He appreciated the reprieve, because he needed to regroup as much as she probably did.

Who knew that a woman being sick and vulnerable, sharing a tragic past, would grab his heart quicker than amazing sex?

CHAPTER SEVEN

STILL BLEARY-EYED, Cherry stood beside the car in the driveway of the house she shared with Merissa Colter. The midday sun baked down on her head, sending waves of heat up from the pavement, adding to the discomfort of her fever. Lethargy pulled at her, but she resolutely stayed on her feet.

In the home's open doorway, Merissa, known as Rissy to her friends and family, waited for them.

As Denver gathered up all their bags, she wanted to help, but of course he'd already refused her. The man was too damn macho for his own good. Then again, she knew just getting herself inside would tax her enough.

Best to get things going. As she stepped away, Denver followed.

Before they'd gotten even halfway up the walkway, both Cannon and Armie came to the door, too.

Stalling, Cherry mumbled, "Oh great."

Denver glanced down at her. "Problem?"

"Why do they have to be here?" She tried to step behind Denver, but he turned with her, keeping her in his sights.

"Cannon and Armie? What does it matter?"

"I look like death on a bad hair day."

Smiling, he bent and kissed the bridge of her nose. "I think you look cute."

Right. "No makeup, hair destroyed, clothes frumpy—"

All too seriously, he said, "Eyes big and dark, cheeks all pink." His gaze dropped to her chest and he frowned. "But I probably should have found your bra for you to put on."

"Denver." Given the gravelly roughness of her voice, her censure sounded like a growl. She crossed her arms around herself and glared at him. "Now I'm going to feel self-conscious about *that*, too!"

He searched her face. "Other than that, how do you feel?"

His continued concern and understanding humbled her. "Tired, even though I've slept endlessly."

"Come on." He stepped behind her and nudged her forward. She felt both Armie and Cannon looking her over as she went up the walkway. Or more like she dragged herself. She would have loved to pick up the pace, put some spring in her step.

Instead, it seemed putting one foot in front of the other took all her concentration.

Everyone stepped back to let them enter.

"Damn, Cherry," Armie said with sympathy. He put the back of his hand to her forehead. "Feeling worse?"

"Better, actually."

Cannon's hand went to her forehead next. "Sorry, but no one's going to believe that with your red eyes and nose."

Freaking great. She stepped out of reach and clutched the railing of the stairs leading down to her part of the house.

Cannon asked Denver, "She has that bug that's been going around?"

"I think so."

Was Cherry the only one to notice how Rissy stared at Denver's lap? Giving her friend a pointed look, she cleared her throat—loudly.

Which drew Armie's notice to Rissy, and then his scowl.

Grinning, Denver said, "Hey, Merissa. What's up?"

Her face went so hot, she looked more feverish than Cherry. "Want me to put on some tea or soup?"

Denver deferred to Cherry.

She shook her head. "Thanks, but I'm fine." Going down one step, then another, she said, "I'm…just going to go…" *Hide.* "Yeah." Giving up on lame explanations, she held on to the railing and fled.

If you could call creeping at a snail's pace fleeing.

Behind her, Denver said, "Hang around a minute, okay? I wanted to talk to you."

Cannon said, "No problem."

And then Denver was right beside her, holding her elbow on the other side, patiently helping her down the stairs and into her bedroom. She'd always considered her living space on the lower level of the house to be generous. She had her own bathroom, small kitchenette that included a stacked washer/dryer unit, a small sitting area and a large bedroom. But now, with Denver's presence, the walls closed in until it felt like they'd crowded into a closet.

Denver, being six-two, muscled head to toe, honed by confidence, took up a lot more space—physically and mentally—than most would. But truthfully, she'd never had a man in this bedroom.

Heck, she'd no sooner met Rissy and moved in than she'd met Denver and quickly fallen for him. After that, no other guy had appealed to her.

"This feels weird."

He'd left his own bag up by the front door, but carried hers in and set it by the closet. "How so?"

"You being in here with me."

Giving her a heated look, he pushed the door shut. It closed with a click.

Oh wow. She didn't mean to, but when her knees went weak she dropped to sit on the side of the bed. Keeping his gaze locked on hers, Denver closed the small distance between them, took her shoulders and pressed her flat, coming down to his elbow beside her. He slipped one big rough hand in under her shirt to rest on her bare midriff, then bent and nuzzled her throat.

"You…you're going to get sick too if you don't stop that."

"I never get sick," he told her, and nibbled his way around to her collarbone before raising his head.

"Well, still…" The touch of his warm, damp mouth lulled her. She so badly wanted to take advantage of all this awesome attention. Knowing she didn't have it in her left her even more maudlin. "Honestly, Denver, the spirit is willing, but the body is just kaput."

One corner of his mouth lifted. "Relax, girl." He stroked his hand up and over her breast. "I just want to touch you. That's all."

But the way he touched her was enough to fry what few wits she had left. "Yeah, but—"

"Shh." As he sat up, he lifted the shirt to expose her. Cupping one breast in his hand, he cuddled her.

It was a sexual touch—but then again, it wasn't. Sexual, because it was her breast. However, he didn't ply her nipple, didn't try to excite her.

If he'd held her elbow like that, no problem.

But whether he meant to turn her on or not, she was so acutely aware of him and where he had his hand, she almost couldn't bear it.

Under his breath, more to himself than her, he murmured, "Damn, you are put together fine." As if they'd been together forever, he kissed the top of each breast, pulled her shirt back down and stood. "Do you need anything?"

You, definitely. She shook her head. "No, thank you." Anxiety crept in. Would he leave her now? And if so, when would she see him again?

"You can take your meds in an hour or so." He dug them out of her bag and put them on her nightstand. "Even if you're feeling better, be sure to take the cough medicine."

"Okay, thanks." Trying to figure out what to say and do, she lay there like a washed-out mop.

"I'm going to make you more comfortable, then I need to head home for a bit."

Make her more comfortable how? And how long was a bit? Surely he didn't plan to return yet again today, not after all that driving and— Her thoughts scattered when his big hands went to the waistband of her jeans. Whoa!

Warm fingers curled under the material and inadvertently brushed her stomach. He opened the snap, slowly slid down the zipper, and by small degrees tugged the snug-fitting jeans past her hips, her thighs, her knees, and off her feet.

Yes, he'd seen her naked already, but this was different in so many ways! Her hands knotted in the coverlet and she bit her lip.

Drawing in a deep breath, Denver surveyed her

body. Even though she knew how wretched she looked, she saw his appreciation, and so much more.

He definitely still wanted her.

Nervous chatter erupted. "You've already done so much for me—"

"You need a little help right now." His attention lifted, locked on her eyes, and no matter how she tried she couldn't look away. "When you're well, I plan to see to you properly."

The roughness in his tone teased her nerve endings like a warning, causing her heart to skip a beat, then lurch into double time. She tried a laugh that came off nervous and squeaky.

His intent expression didn't change.

And that, too, rattled her. "I… What does that mean?"

Resting a hand on her belly, he narrowed his eyes. "It's a lot to take in, I know, because I've been living with it since meeting you."

"Living with…?"

Silently, he considered things, almost stewing before flashing his predator's gaze to her face. "The overwhelming need to fuck you senseless, to make you come again and again until the only man you can see is me."

Wow. He said that so calmly, all while watching her to gauge her reaction.

The words sounded both sexual and forceful. A hot combo—at least when coming from Denver.

Any other man and she'd—

"I want to see you sweat," he added, interrupting her thoughts. "Hear you panting, maybe screaming."

Screaming?

He visibly struggled with himself. "I need to hear you saying my name."

Something dark and vulnerable shadowed his expression. "Denver?" she whispered in question.

The slightest of smiles curled his mouth. "Not like that, girl. I want you to want me so much you're crazy with it. I want to hear it. I want to fucking *feel* it. And I will." The fingertips of his right hand teased the inside of her thigh, and then fell away. "When you're well."

The seconds ticked by while Cherry struggled to get her thoughts ordered. Everything Denver had done to her she'd loved. A lot. But what he mentioned now, well, she just didn't know. "That sounds…a little intimidating."

With a casual shrug, he cupped his hand over her sex and looked into her eyes. "You're going to love it, I promise."

Somehow everything had gotten badly off track, leaving her tongue-tied when she hadn't been for years.

His attention went to her breasts, then her panties. "You can consider our first time just a taste, okay?"

Wow. Okay, that might finish her off right there. To add to it, he shifted her around in the bed, tucked her under the covers, and kissed her forehead. So gentle and attentive. He was the strongest man she knew, and the sexiest.

Until now, she hadn't realized he was also the sweetest.

"Before I let you sleep, I need to know something."

"Okay." True, she felt like crud, but she wasn't as weak as he thought. Not anymore anyway.

"How close were you to that dude from the elevator? Leese something?"

"Phelps?"

He gave an impatient shake of his head. "Yeah. Whatever. How well do you know him?"

Never could she believe Denver was jealous. So why did he ask? He had to know that no other man measured up to him.

"Stop trying to analyze things, Cherry. It's important, so just tell me."

"I don't like your tone."

He tipped his head back, frustration showing. When he looked at her again, she saw the heat in his eyes but he sounded calm enough when he said, "I'd appreciate it if you could tell me about your relationship with Phelps."

Much better. "He flirted a few times. We talked. But that's it."

"Does he have your number?"

She shook her head.

"You never told him where you live?"

"Not my house address or anything."

"Shit." He stood and took a few steps away. Keeping his back to her, he asked, "So he knows you live in Ohio? In Warfield?"

"Yes." She didn't understand this strange mood of his. "Casual conversation, Denver. That's all it was."

"Maybe. But I don't trust him." He turned back to her with new resolve showing in every line of his big, hard body. "Tell me about your family."

The shift in conversation threw her, making her wary. "I already did."

As if that reply displeased him, his eyes narrowed. "You told me about your parents."

"Right." It made her want to squirm, the probing way he watched her. "There isn't anything more—"

"What about your brothers?"

A scalding wave of heat rushed over her and for one blinding second, she felt light-headed.

Denver wasn't asking. He mentioned her brothers as if he...

He *knew*, and damn him, he dared to look at her as if she might be holding back? "You bastard."

His brows went up.

The shout she'd intended came out as a hurt, pathetic whisper.

That wouldn't do.

Throwing back the coverlet, she swung her feet over the side of the bed—and would have dropped if Denver hadn't moved close to grab her shoulders. "Settle down."

"Go to hell." Remorse gave her strength to struggle, but not enough.

Not nearly enough.

He pressed her flat to the bed, sprawling out over her. When she shoved against his shoulders, he trapped her hands and pinned them down at her sides.

Looming over her, his eyes bright with concern, his hair dropping forward, almost touching her cheeks, he held her immobile. "Tell me what's wrong."

That calm tone infuriated her. "You know them!" Oh God, it hurt. Worse than anything she'd ever imagined.

Had she really been such a fool? *Again?*

"Of them, at least." He raised her hands above her head so he could hold them in one of his. With the other, he tenderly tucked her hair behind her ears. "I didn't like what I saw, and liked even less talking with them. But I have to say, you've thrown me for a loop." Obvious restraint held him in check as he bent to lightly kiss her open mouth. "Tell me why they upset you so much."

Panic ebbed beneath the sincerity of his words, leaving behind only a dull throb. She had a million questions, but first...*she had to know*. "Is that why you finally slept with me?"

He stared down at her with blank confusion. "What are you talking about?"

"Did they put you up to it?"

For what felt like forever, he contemplated her accusation. Concern drew his brows together, made his gaze more intrusive. "We had sex because we'd both gotten to the boiling point."

"You didn't want to!"

"I always wanted to, but I resisted." He moved against her, settling in and getting comfortable. "You and I still have differences to work out, but that has nothing to do with the trio of idiots."

Was that really how he saw them? They were idiots. They were also cruel and manipulative and a very real threat. Always.

Beginning to feel a little foolish, Cherry did a quick comparison between Denver and the trio. No, she couldn't see them as Denver's friends. She definitely couldn't see them as cohorts.

Closing her eyes did nothing to salve her shame. "Will you let me go?"

"No."

Her eyes popped open again.

"Not now," he said. "Not tomorrow. Not for the foreseeable future. Anything else you need to know before you explain?"

Her mouth opened, but she had to think what to say. "I meant will you let me up—"

"The answer is still no."

Resentment left her bristling.

"Sorry, girl, but I like you right where you are. Now talk to me."

"Fine." It seemed he only called her "girl" when sexually charged. "I don't have any brothers or sisters."

Doubt and suspicion tightened his mouth. "Cherry—"

"I *don't*!" If he accused her of lying, she'd— Cough.

Damn. Her raised voice brought it on, and once she started coughing, she couldn't seem to catch her breath.

Denver moved quickly to her side, then helped her to sit up. He stayed beside her, one hand bracing the middle of her back. "Slow, shallow breaths."

When the fit subsided a little, he stood and walked out of her room but returned seconds later with a glass of water. Again he sat by her, causing the bed to dip so that she tilted into him. With his arm around her, keeping her close, he handed her the glass.

She sipped.

"The nasty cough is going to hang around a few days, so try not to screech at me anymore."

Her glare, she hoped, was more effective than a screech.

But given his smile, maybe not.

He relieved her of the glass, looped both arms around her, and said, "I only met Carver, Gene and Mitty today."

Just hearing their names made her skin crawl. She would have launched herself away from Denver, but apparently he'd been prepared for that because she didn't manage to get a single inch of space between them.

Denver drew her against him. "I hope it's true, that they're not related to you. But could you tell me why they claimed to be, and why you freaked out over it?"

"I didn't—"

"Total freakout, girl. Don't deny it, okay?"

Hedging, she asked, "Why were you talking to them?"

"You first."

If she weren't so weak, she'd elbow him, hard, right in the middle. "They're part of the foster family that took me in after my folks were killed."

His stroking hands paused, but only for a moment, then they resumed. "Huh. I hadn't figured on that. Actually, I hadn't thought far enough ahead to wonder who had raised you."

"It wasn't them," she assured him with more sarcastic bite than she intended. No, instead of becoming family support they'd been another hardship—the worst one that she'd had to endure. "I was already fourteen and I raised myself."

"So…" Denver tipped her back to see her. "I take it you don't like them?"

Dislike didn't even come close to conveying how she felt about them. She loathed, despised, detested them.

And she feared them. Horribly.

Saying all that would leave her emotionally raw, so she settled on a less volatile truth. "I'll be happy if I never see them again."

"Tell me why."

Cherry shook her head. Even sick, she refused to be

a complete pushover. "It's your turn. Why and when did you meet them?"

"They were hanging around the hotel we just left."

Alarm squeezed her throat and she almost lost her breath again.

Standing, Denver stared down at her, visibly pondering her reaction. "Armie overheard them ask about you. When he questioned them, it didn't go well. He tussled with them, and then he told me."

Oh God. "They tussled?" Shock kept her voice a whisper of sound. *They were looking for her.* Had Armie inadvertently put himself on their radar? No, no, no.

Seeing the alarm she couldn't hide, Denver crossed his arms. "Don't worry about Armie. He's fine."

"But—"

"The next morning, I saw some disreputable-looking dudes watching me in the hotel, figured it was them and decided to ask a few questions."

Good Lord, was he nuts? "Why in the world would you do that?"

Denver held up a hand. "You aren't up for a long convo, honey, so forget it. The bare bones are that they claimed to be your brothers and wanted me to lead them to you. I already told you that I didn't like the looks of them, but I also figured siblings would have your number, right? Unless you were avoiding them for a reason." He shrugged. "So I said no."

And yet he was here to tell her about it. There must be a reason they hadn't attacked him.

She knew they still could.

"How did they know we were...friends?"

"I'm guessing Phelps. They were probably asking around until they found someone who knew you."

Leese Phelps. She worried for him, but other, bigger worries took precedence.

"They'd already seen me in the hotel," Denver said. "It didn't take a genius to know you were there, too."

She rubbed her temples, trying to wrap her mind around it.

"They left you a message on the hotel room phone. You must have slept through their call."

Her head snapped up and she stared at him. "Do you know what they said?"

"That you needed to get in touch." His eyes narrowed. "To be exact, the caller said you shouldn't fuck around."

Closing her arms around herself, Cherry resisted the urge to rock in restless anxiety. She didn't want to be in touch. One demand always led to another and another until… "When?"

"By tonight."

In other words: now.

Denver stood there looking at her, so she had to say something that didn't give away every awful emotion she felt. She sat up a little straighter and looked him in the eyes. "I'll take care of it."

Maybe seeing too much despite her attempt at bravado, Denver shook his head. "I'd rather you didn't."

It'd be so easy to let him guide her—but he didn't know them, didn't understand the situation and what could happen if she ignored a summons now that they'd actually found her. She'd thought they'd given up on her, had prayed it was so. Instead, they'd tracked her down.

Never had she felt so lost.

"We'll work it out, okay?"

Cherry blinked away the fog. *We*, as in the two of them? God, no. He'd taken care of her, driven her home, been downright amazing. But this was different.

No way would she further involve him with her twisted, redneck foster brothers. *Brothers.* She laughed at the absurdity of the concept, then slapped a hand over her mouth when apprehension brought Denver closer. No, they were no relation to her, not in any way at all.

Thank the heavens.

Somehow, she'd deal with them. "It's my problem."

Denver studied her. "You must be feeling a little better."

Just because she didn't agree with everything he said? "I am."

"There's more." He propped a shoulder against the wall. "I hope it won't hurt you, but I think you need to know."

What else could there be? She waited, braced for the worst.

"They said their pops had passed away."

Breath left her and her shoulders slumped—this time with relief. No, she hadn't wished anyone dead. She'd only wished to be free of them. But she wouldn't mourn, either. "Thank you for telling me."

Tone thick with irony, he replied, "You're welcome."

Why did they want to see her? Not because they thought she cared. They knew better. So then what?

"Will you promise me something?"

Not trusting that silky tone, she eyed Denver warily. "I don't know. What?"

"Promise me you won't contact them." Pushing away from the wall, he stalked closer. "Promise me you'll take your meds, rest up and get well. Then we can talk about it."

"It's not your problem."

He frowned. "I don't want you to shut me out."

That's what he thought? "I'm not." She wouldn't.

"Then promise me."

He asked for the impossible. "I'd rather get it out of the way. I need—" *It and them out of my life* "—to give my condolences." The lie hurt, but what else could she do? She couldn't tell him the truth, so a lie was her only option.

He sighed his disappointment, making her feel even worse. "All right, honey, have it your way."

Seeing him turn for the door stopped her heart. "Denver, wait—"

"I'll tell Merissa I'm staying over."

"Don't— *What?*"

Crossing his arms over his chest, he gave her the full force of his daunting stare. "They were talking with Phelps at the hotel, so they might already be figuring out where you live. Not like Warfield is a sprawling city."

Oh God. She hadn't considered that.

"And if you call, they'll have your number, too. You won't tell me why they scare you—"

Her gaze shot back to his. "I didn't say they scared me."

Sympathy smoothed out his frown, filled his voice with compassion. "But they do."

Yes, they did. Very much. It made her skin crawl to even think of them. But to know they'd mentioned her, that they were close, possibly looking for her...

Rather than lie again, she looked away. "I don't want to impose on you more than I already have."

"I need to run home and take care of a few things, rearrange my schedule, and set up—"

"Okay, *fine*! I won't call."

Her acerbic tone didn't put him off. "Growling like that is only going to get you coughing again."

She flung a pillow at him, and damn it, it taxed her and fell short of hitting him.

Denver looked at the pillow by his feet, then at her. "I need to teach you how to fight, *and* how to be a good sport when you lose."

She wouldn't lose. She couldn't. This was too important.

It startled her when his finger touched under her chin and raised her face. "Promise me."

"I already did," she grumbled.

"Yeah, but now I get the feeling you're scheming."

Maybe because she was. "I won't call them tonight."

Exasperation had him stepping back. "Damn it, Cherry, don't play word games, either. I want you to wait to call until we've had time enough to talk it out."

"It won't matter."

"What won't?"

She shouldn't have said that. Shaking her head, she said, "I'll wait. But not too long."

"Thank you." He checked the time, came forward to give her one last kiss on her forehead, and headed out.

She didn't mean to, but she asked, "When will I see you again?"

Pausing in the open doorway, he thought about it. "I don't want to take a chance on calling and waking you up, so how about you call me in the morning? We'll figure it out from there."

"Okay, but—"

"Sleep. Rest." He stepped out and started to pull the door shut, but at the last second, he smiled at her. "And think about everything I'm going to do to you once you're back in fighting form."

When the door closed, she curled up tight on the bed. Holy smokes, if Denver kept making those dark, sultry promises about things he planned to do, she just might have to hurry along her recuperation.

That is, if her foster brothers didn't ruin her life first—as they probably planned to do.

CHAPTER EIGHT

On his way upstairs, Denver passed Merissa coming down. "She's resting," he said, hoping Merissa wouldn't want to have a gabfest, as the ladies so often did.

Merissa struggled to keep her attention on his face. Twice she failed as her gaze dipped down his body to zero in on his crotch.

Shaking his head, Denver stopped and crossed his arms. "Sorry, but it's not performing tricks right now."

"Wha…?" Surprise gave way to exasperation and she punched his shoulder, mumbling, "Shut up."

"Then quit eyeballing me."

Her mouth twitched. "Sorry, just curious." After flipping back her long dark hair, she went on down the stairs. "But I'll get the nitty-gritty from Cherry."

He watched her tap on the bedroom door, slip in, and seconds later both women roared with laughter. Cherry's cough immediately followed.

Women. Smiling, Denver bounded up the rest of the steps and followed the voices down the hall and to the kitchen. He found Armie and Cannon sitting at the table drinking coffee and eating cupcakes. Cannon lounged back in his seat, at ease in the family home he'd gifted to his sister after much success in the SBC.

Armie, however, still looked wound too tight— meaning Merissa must have been with them before leaving the room to visit with Cherry. Every time Armie was around her, he struggled like a sweet-toothed fighter in a candy store trying to make weight for an important match.

Did Cannon see it? Everyone else did—except maybe Merissa herself.

Not that Cannon's little sis was obtuse. As a bank manager, she put in a respectable amount of hours growing her career. While Cannon might have gifted her with their family home after they lost their mother, she kept her own budget and lived within her means. And she understood more about the fight world than many competitors Denver knew.

But when she chose to, she completely ignored the finer points of being a professional athlete—like her refusal to take into account their specific healthy diets. Merissa Colter was a junk-food junkie who loved to bake, and did so often.

Being the generous sort who liked to share, she usually left a plate of her irresistible desserts sitting around as temptation.

Knowing he'd indulge, Denver glanced at Armie as he headed to the coffeepot. "Havoc wants you to give him a call."

"I'm not—"

"He said to quit running from him." Denver poured a cup, black. "He wants you to man up and talk with him."

Predictably, Armie went coldly defensive. "What the—"

"I agreed about the running part, of course. Told him you were probably home sniveling, hiding under the covers, whimpering and shit like that."

As Armie came halfway out of his seat, Cannon laughed at his outraged expression and grabbed his shoulder. "Don't start brawling in my sister's house. She won't like it."

At the reminder of Merissa, Armie looked more ill at ease than a badass ever should. He also retreated. Ribbing Armie was easy and Denver didn't have to feel guilty about it; everyone knew Armie cowered from no man.

Now women, or more specifically one woman… Yeah, Denver wouldn't go there.

Pulling out a chair, he sprawled into his own seat and gave a "whatever" shrug for Armie's decision. "I passed along the message. My responsibility has ended."

"Thanks for nothing."

Done with that futile effort, he looked at Armie, then over to Cannon. "I have a problem."

"Honey-blond hair?" Armie guessed. "Big boobs?"

He took a cupcake off the table. "I told Cherry we wouldn't be discussing her body, so shut up."

Cannon cocked a brow. "How exactly did that conversation come up?"

"Because asshole here—" he pointed the cupcake at Armie to make sure they all understood who he meant "—discussed the size of my junk with all and sundry, apparently."

Armie grinned. "Nah, dude, just the ladies."

Cannon choked on a laugh.

"I was giving you a boost," Armie claimed. "I figured once Cherry knew what you're packing, she'd come after you, sort of force the issue since you won't tell her how you feel."

"I told her."

"Yeah, right." Armie settled comfortably in the seat, tilting the chair on its back legs. "Told her you were going ape-shit lusting after her and that you wanted to bang her senseless?"

"Pretty much."

The chair dropped forward again. "Seriously?"

"Yeah."

Cannon shook his head with sympathy. "And then she got sick?"

"Luckily," Denver said as he peeled the paper off his cupcake, "that happened after."

"After you two hooked up?"

Denver glanced across the table at Armie. "You didn't tell him?"

"Do I look like a gossipy old lady?"

Grinning, Cannon pointed out the irony of his objections. "Man, you talked about his dick with the ladies."

"Okay, yeah. *That.* But no, I didn't say anything about your personal business."

"My dick isn't personal?"

Grinning, Armie said, "Not anymore."

Getting even for that crack, Denver took a big bite of the cupcake and groaned in bliss. He looked at Armie and said, "Man, Merissa is such a good cook, and supercute to boot, it's a wonder guys aren't lined up begging to marry her."

Shoulders bunching up and neck going red, Armie flattened his mouth and kept quiet.

"Got her own house," Denver added, just to goad him, "a great job, a famous brother…"

"Don't even go there." Cannon gave a mock shudder. "I'm not ready for that yet."

"She's what? Twenty-two?"

"Damn near a kid," Cannon said. "If she ever gets serious about anyone, then I'll deal with it." He crossed his arms on the table. "So what's the problem?"

Again Denver glanced at Armie. "Cherry's supposed brothers? They're from a foster family. Given her reaction when I brought them up, they're guys she'd really like to avoid."

To catch Cannon up to speed, Denver shared what had happened at the hotel first, then told them both more about Cherry's background.

"Jesus," Cannon said. "I had no idea."

"She's never even hinted," Armie agreed. "Hell of a background, poor kid."

She wasn't a kid, far from it, but Denver let that go. "I doubt she'd like it shared, so—"

"Not a word," Cannon agreed.

"Except for the guys," Armie added. "I'm heading to the rec center next, but figured you might want a ride."

"I do, thanks. And yeah, the guys need to know."

"Gage and Miles are there now," Armie told him. "We can clue them in tonight."

"Stack will be in tomorrow morning," Cannon said. "I'll let him know then."

So they were all getting together tonight, minus Stack. No surprise there, since it happened often enough. Camaraderie wasn't always the only incentive for hanging out.

Long ago after his dad died, Cannon had taken to prowling the neighborhood, keeping watch over those who couldn't protect themselves—the elderly shop owners and retirees, the school kids, the single moms.

In many ways, Warfield was much better than it used to be, no longer threatened by extortion or gangs.

In other ways, especially when it came to drug dealers, it was worse. The bastards skulked about, hiding in the shadows, drawing in the kids who didn't have much else to look forward to.

The rec center helped a lot, gave at-risk kids an opportunity to focus in a different direction. Far as Denver knew, none of the guys resented the extra time they put in there. Together, they kept their own small part of the neighborhood friendly for all.

Discontent chewed on Denver's peace of mind. "I know everyone has some loony relative they don't want to see, and there's a black sheep in every family."

Armie raised his hand.

Ignoring him, especially since Armie was one of the most honorable guys he knew, Denver said, "I don't mean to make a big deal out of nothing, but I have a bad feeling about this."

Armie flexed his shoulders. "I disliked the pricks soon as I saw them, and that one bozo did pull a knife on me, so I'm happy to go with your instincts."

"Appreciate it." Denver finished off his cupcake in one big bite. He washed it down with the last of his coffee. "When I get more from Cherry, I'll update you." He turned to Cannon. "Until then, you should know that I'm going to stick around as much as I can."

Not that long ago, Cannon had objected to Denver's pursuit of Cherry. Denver followed his reasoning: Cherry was roommates with Merissa and the idea of anyone making a booty call to his sister's house didn't sit right with him. What Cannon thought about it no longer mattered, though.

He wouldn't leave Cherry alone, sick and vulnerable.

"Not a bad idea," Cannon said, surprising him. "Anyone can see you're invested beyond a quick lay."

True. There wasn't anything at all he wanted to be "quick" with Cherry. "I'll be here whenever I'm free. It's just that—"

"Free time is scarce these days, I know." Cannon clapped him on the shoulder. "Try not to sweat it too much. Rissy has a good security system but I'll explain things to her, too. She's smart, so she'll be careful. And I'll be in town for a stretch, so someone will always be around."

Watching Cannon, Denver said, "Both girls have a list of phone numbers." He understood it now, but it still bugged him.

"Rissy has always agreed to carry them, but I made sure Cherry did the same." Cannon obviously thought nothing of it. "In a lot of ways, Rissy accepts all of you as family."

Armie seemed to choke a little on that.

"She and I both trust you. All of you. I know even when I'm not around, she has backup. That's important. Not that I expect trouble, but you never know."

All of the rationalizations helped—and yet they didn't. A sense of danger kept Denver on edge.

It was too personal for him to tell the others, but he knew by Cherry's initial reaction that she'd thought him somehow allied with those creeps. She'd pegged him as using her in some way—but how?

Knowing there was nothing else he could do right now, Denver put his coffee cup in the dishwasher and left with Armie. He knew he'd feel better if he could trust Cherry, but on a gut level he was sure the girl had secrets. How long would she hold out on him?

What if she *never* opened up?

It was his biggest gripe, the main reason he'd tried to steer clear of her.

He was damn near obsessed—how had Armie put it? Ape-shit with wanting her—and she wouldn't commit 100 percent.

Somehow he'd have to work through that, wear her down, and win her over. He wanted Cherry.

But only if he could have every part of her, including her deepest, darkest secrets.

LEESE ACCEPTED THE shot glass and tossed back the contents. It sent a fiery burn down his throat that pooled in his gut. He screwed his eyes shut, clamped his teeth together and let his breath out in a hiss.

Carver laughed. "A man who knows how to drink. Hell yeah."

Then he threw back his own shot of whiskey.

As the liquor flowed through Leese's blood, the world tilted, went fuzzy, then righted itself again. He knew he'd already drunk too much. But Carver, Mitty and Gene were so admiring, like his own personal fan club, he wasn't ready to call it a night.

They sat on the open hatch to Mitty's truck bed beneath a night sky fat with black clouds that concealed even a hint of the moon. A light glowed and he turned his head to see Gene lighting up. A red sheen covered his face as he inhaled—and then the sickeningly sweet smell hit Leese.

"Want a hit?" Gene offered, holding the joint out to him.

"No thanks." He propped himself against the truck.

Mitty laughed. "The little fighter is afraid to take a toke?"

"Afraid? No." He wasn't afraid of jack-shit. "Just not my thing."

Gene passed it to Carver, who closed his eyes as he sucked it in and held it.

Smoke hung in the thick, humid air, turning Leese's stomach. It had to be late. Or early. Whatever. He looked around at the nearly deserted streets. The last thing he needed was for a cop to show up. "I should get going."

As he exhaled Carver asked, "Why the sudden rush?"

Tension knotted up his neck; Leese clutched his stomach to keep it from pitching. Damn. He'd gotten drunk plenty of times in his life, but it never made him feel like this. He took a step away from the truck, and almost fell to his knees.

Laughing again, the sound warbling like a strobe light, Mitty caught him and held him upright.

"Pathetic," he heard Gene mutter.

Then Carver's breath was on his jaw. "Hey, buddy. You okay?"

Too close, crowding against him. He tried to push away, but got pushed back. As if from a distance, he again heard the laughter. He couldn't seem to draw his thoughts together enough to figure out why the earth kept moving or why his tongue felt so thick. He reached out, and his hand connected awkwardly with the truck, busting his knuckles. It hurt.

"Take it easy, friend."

Carver again.

A hand steered him and he found himself hefted into the truck bed, then reclining. He opened his eyes and stared up at the sky. So black. So endless. "I need to get home," he thought, then realized he'd spoken aloud.

"Yeah, sure," Carver said. "We'll take you. Where is home?"

His brows squeezed down. He didn't want to tell them but he couldn't figure out why.

When he felt a hand in his jeans, he panicked. Real, sick, twisting panic. He reared up, lashing out until he heard a curse.

Mitty shoved him back so hard that his head collided with the rusted truck bed. "Asshole."

Blinding pain exploded through his skull.

Carver said, "Relax, dude. Just getting your wallet so we can figure out where to take you."

Shit. Going lax, Leese closed his eyes and drew a slow breath that still didn't give him enough oxygen.

"Got it." Carver spoke low to someone, truck doors opened and closed, the world moved—this time for real.

He realized Carver was still beside him when he nudged him with his boot. "You with me, buddy?"

Leese groaned as the truck hit a bump. "Yeah."

"You need to stay awake."

Distrust was a live thing inside him, screaming a warning that he couldn't quite heed. "Yeah."

"There you go. So let's talk."

He wasn't sure if he could. But Carver was insistent, and the wind blowing over Leese, the sounds of traffic around him, revived him enough to clear some of the ever-growing cobwebs.

The boot hit him again, this time in his biceps. "Stay

with me, damn it. You won't like it if I have to keep getting your attention."

Leese concentrated, but that just made his brain pulse.

"Where does she live?"

"Who?"

"Cherry." And he sneered, "My sweet *baby sister.*"

Oh no, he didn't want them going after Cherry—not that he knew where she lived anyway. Cherry had been friendly, willing to share a fast dance and a few smiles, but nothing more.

Leese got several more kicks before he recalled that Cannon Colter and Denver Lewis were her friends, and Cherry was seeing Lewis. That meant they were probably from Warfield, Ohio. Yeah, Warfield. That sounded right.

"Good, that's good," Carver said. "What else can you tell me?"

So he'd spoken aloud once more?

This time the boot heel caught him in the ribs, then the hip. "Yes, you're talking, you idiot. Now answer my question."

Instinctively Leese rolled away, but that just left his spine exposed, his kidneys. *Fuck.* Between the jostling of the old rat-trap truck and the sporadic kicks to his body, he couldn't get his bearings.

He needed to fight back, but his arms didn't respond right to his brain's commands, too sluggish to do more than fan the air. Getting his legs under him was a no-go, too. He crawled up to his knees, and took a kick to the nuts that had him collapsing hard on his face.

While pain dug into his consciousness, he tried to

understand. He was good in the cage. Why the hell couldn't he fight now?

"Because you stupidly drank what I gave you, you trusting, pathetic ass." *Thump.* "Now stop wasting my time. You said something about a gym. Where is it?" *Thump.* "Who runs it?" *Thump.*

Curling in on himself, Leese accepted his own weakness. If he could, he'd go down fighting.

But he *couldn't* fight.

Still, he tried to keep silent, to deny them the answers they wanted, but whatever they'd given him left him babbling. Carver kept prodding him, and with each reply his apprehension grew. It didn't take this long to make it to his apartment, damn it. Or did it?

Finally they stopped and he awkwardly, with Carver's help, sat up.

"This is it. Time for you to go." Mitty hauled him out with a complaint. "Jesus, he's a heavy fucker."

Leese tried to get his feet under him, but something was wrong with his legs. Mitty half carried, half dragged him to the front of his apartment building, banging his shins up each concrete step to the landing. He got callously dumped against a wall, arranged more upright than supine, with his shoulders wedged into a corner beside the door and the railing.

Someone said, "Good enough. If he wants the rest of the way in, let him crawl."

A rough palm slapped his face to regain his attention. "It's been fun, man. Thanks for all the info."

Info? Oh God, they'd been asking something about Cherry—

A meaty fist slammed into his jaw, and a welcome blackness closed in.

When Denver knocked very early the next morning, Cherry answered the door. She'd called half an hour ago to say she was up, feeling much better and on the mend. He'd just finished showering after his jog, so he threw on jeans and headed over, anxious to see her.

Taking her in head to toes, he believed she felt better. Lingering shadows remained beneath her dark eyes, but she stood stronger, steadier. Still no makeup, but with her looks she didn't need it. She must have washed her hair; the scent of hyacinth filled his head when he bent to put a kiss on the side of her neck. He breathed her in and didn't want to stop. Thoughts of stripping her clothes away so he could again touch that sweet, curvy little body tested his better intentions.

That wouldn't suit his agenda, so he shored up his resistance and took a step back. "How'd you sleep?"

Her gaze skittered away from his. "Okay."

Another fib. Had she gotten any rest at all? "No more coughing?"

She wrinkled her nose. "Only a little."

"Still taking the medicine?"

"It makes me sleepy."

Meaning no. "Sleep is the best thing for you."

Rolling her eyes over his excess concern, she moved back. "Come on in."

When he said, "I can't stay long," he saw a subtle tension release from her posture. Had she dreaded his visit, assuming he'd press her for explanations?

She was right, he would.

Holding out a bag, Denver offered an olive branch. "I brought you breakfast."

"You didn't need to do that."

He absently tugged at his ear. Things were definitely different today. Less intimate.

He'd have to see what he could do about that. Yes, he'd get some answers. But he'd like her to be willing to talk, or at least not so resistant.

The way Cherry held herself now, the careful way she watched him, he could tell she wanted to act as if nothing had happened, as if she didn't have three psycho punks hunting her down for some reason.

Would she try to derail him by claiming herself well, by rushing him out the door? Did she *want* to call Carver now? Or was it that she felt she had to?

He looked around at what he could see of the empty house. "Where's Merissa?"

"Gone to work about ten minutes ago."

He checked his watch. It was barely seven thirty. "Already?"

"She said she had an early meeting at the bank. I should have gone to work, too. I'm well enough today—"

"One more day off won't hurt." He well knew the level of energy it took to deal with young boys. With preschoolers? He didn't want to find out. Taking her elbow, he said, "Couch or kitchen?"

"That probably depends on what you brought me."

"A muffin and juice."

"Kitchen, then, I guess." As they headed that way, she peeked into the bag and the scent of warm blueberries escaped. "Mmm, that smells so good."

He pulled out a chair for her. "Got your appetite back?"

"With a vengeance." She didn't sit. "Can I get you anything?"

"I already ate." He'd have to be at the rec center within the hour. Workouts and keeping up with his remaining accountant duties severely strapped his time. But thanks to his success in MMA, stellar endorsements and good investments, he'd been able to pare back on the job enough to dedicate more effort to growing his fight career.

So far, so good—but still time-consuming.

Getting involved hot and heavy now with Cherry put a slight kink in the works, but it was a nice kink, one he'd definitely enjoy working through.

She sat, opened the juice for a sip, then bit into the muffin with a look of rapture.

Denver smiled. "Good?"

"Heavenly."

Pulling a chair out, he turned it around and straddled the seat. He waited until she had her mouth full. "How long did you live with the foster family?"

A vague dread froze her in place. For a few seconds, she even stopped chewing. Time ticked by. She swallowed, picked up a napkin, patted her mouth, set the muffin aside. Took another drink.

Stalled.

"Cherry," he whispered.

"Four years."

That's all she said, making him frown. "How old were you when you went there?"

"Fourteen."

So she'd been on her own ever since? "You're twenty-four now, right?"

"Yes."

Six years on her own. "Where'd you go when you first left them?"

Her eyes flickered away again. "I moved here, to Ohio."

Getting answers from Cherry was like pulling hen's teeth. "From where?"

"Kentucky."

Eighteen and alone, no job, in a new state… He wanted to know everything between when she'd left and now, but at the rate they were going that could take a while. So instead he got back on track. "When you lived with them, was it just the three boys? No other kids?"

"Yes."

Done with the curt one-word replies, Denver tilted his head. "Why do you despise them so much?"

She stared him in the eyes. "You met them. They're terrible people."

"Now."

"They were terrible then, too!" She snatched up her muffin and took another big bite.

This time Denver let her eat. The muffin was fresh, healthy, and she needed food as much as she needed sleep. Though she was recovering quicker than he'd expected, a slight rasp still sounded in her voice and her skin remained a little pale. But she no longer looked feverish or ready to keel over. Progress.

By tomorrow she should be just about there—just about well enough for him to taste her again, to feel her soft skin all over. To sink into her warmth—

"Am I holding you up?" she asked.

"No."

"You're just sitting there and staring at me like you're waiting for something."

He smiled. "I was thinking about tomorrow, hoping you'll be ready for me."

The empty muffin paper crumpled in her hand when she braced it at the edge of the table and leaned forward. "I'm ready now."

So anxious. It was a very nice thing to be wanted by Cherry Peyton. "Not just yet." She furrowed her brows, ready to debate it with him, so he threw out his biggest question. "Why'd you freak, girl?"

Her eyes widened.

Denver pushed back his chair. "When I admitted I'd met them, you lost it."

She pressed back in her seat as he circled the table. "You only call me 'girl' when you're thinking about sex."

He confirmed it. "I'm thinking about sex." But he didn't relent. "Why'd you freak out?" And just in case she was considering it, "Don't lie."

"Stop accusing me of that!"

"Then stop fudging the truth." He took her shoulders and eased her from the chair. So soft and female. Without meaning to, he caressed her. "You thought I had some kind of association with your brothers."

"*Not* my brothers."

"I'm glad of that." He kissed her soft mouth, but kept it brief. "What did you think?"

The way she tasted her lips with her tongue made him a little nuts. "Kiss me again?"

"All right." There were few things he'd enjoy more—other than getting his answers. "After you tell me."

Shoving away from him, she wrapped her arms

around herself. "Maybe I wouldn't have to fudge things if you didn't keep trying to take over."

Is that what he was doing? "I thought we were involved."

She whipped back around, her eyes big. "We are."

"But you expect me not to care? You think I shouldn't bother to understand?" He crossed his arms over his chest and stared down at her. "That's the kind of man you think I am?"

Using both hands, she tucked her hair behind her ears. "I think you're wonderful."

Keeping his stern expression wasn't easy, not when he wanted to pick her up and hold her and tell her to stop worrying. But he honestly believed the best way to ease her worry was to get to the truth. Once he knew it all, he could help her come up with solutions.

Breath left her in a defeated sigh. "It's not an easy story to tell."

"You can tell me anything."

With a negative shake of her head, she paced away. "It makes me sound stupid and gullible."

All that? "I would never think those things about you." To reassure her, he stepped up close and put his hands on her shoulders again, this time standing behind her. "How about you tell me and together we figure out what to do?"

He heard her swallow, felt her blond curls tease his chin when she finally nodded.

Hugging her, Denver wrapped her close and waited.

"They liked to set me up. A lot."

That didn't make any sense to him. "Set you up how?"

She put her face in her hands. The silence stretched

out, but he didn't rush her. He could sense her collecting her thoughts, searching for the words.

And working up the guts to tell him.

He kissed her temple and just held her, giving her the time she apparently needed.

Her hands came down and rested on his forearms, which were crossed under her breasts. "They would get guys to pretend they liked me. Sometimes to ask me to school dances or stuff like that. The guys…a couple of times they were their friends. Other times they were just dupes like me. Boys forced to do…mean things."

It was the "mean" part that stirred his anger, and the fact she sounded so embarrassed told Denver it was still raw for her.

Yet what she said didn't really explain anything. They pretended to like her? How could that have been so bad that she'd never stopped hurting over it?

He brought her around to face him, but let her huddle close. "Can you give me an example?"

As if she needed to ground herself, her small hands fisted in his shirt. "The first time it happened was when I was a freshman. A senior asked me to prom and I was…ecstatic. Life with the Nelsons was as far from fun as a girl could get."

"How so?"

She waved a hand. "Small, dirty, ramshackle house. Tons of drunken fights. Foul language and fouler attitudes. For me, getting away from there, being with the other kids at prom, being *normal*, would have been like a Disney vacation."

Everything she said just brought up more questions. Denver thought he could probably dedicate an entire

day to interrogating her and still not know everything
he wanted and needed to know.

"I spent two weeks cutting grass for Gene and Mitty,
and they gave me a percentage of the money they would
have made."

"If you cut the grass, why didn't you get all the
money?"

Leveling a look on him, she said, "It was Gene and
Mitty."

Right. "What does cutting grass have to do with—"

"I used what I made to buy a dress and shoes at the
thrift shop."

Did she have any clue how she broke his heart? "I
bet you looked sexy even then."

That must've been the wrong thing to say because
she jerked away and put several feet between them.

"It was all a sham. I was there that night, stupidly
giddy, dressed up and waiting. And then still waiting."
With demons chasing her, she paced the room, always
keeping her face averted. "Finally he showed up—in
jeans and a T-shirt. I didn't understand…until they all
cracked up, laughing hysterically. It was a joke." She
shook her head, and said with emphasis, "I was a joke."

Oh God. He wanted to kill them. All three of them,
Denver decided.

"That game became their favorite sport." She'd
walked to a corner of the kitchen, her hands braced on
the countertop. "Prom was the worst, but it happened
four more times, each time more convincing than the
last. And I guess I was just so…so stupidly desperate
for something *real*, I was easy to convince. But I finally got smarter and I gave up on the idea of dances,
or going to the football games or…anything like that."

"I'm so damn sorry."

She accepted that with a nod, her expression distant with her thoughts. "The last time it happened," she whispered, "was in the summer when all the neighborhood kids were getting together to head to the lake."

A hollowness filled her voice. Worse than the cough, because although her expression was carefully void of emotion, in her voice he heard the edge of hurt...and maybe a hint of tears. If she cried, Denver didn't think he could bear it.

"This nice, shy boy talked me into going along and swimming with them. He said all the right things, telling me not to let Carver or the others know, like we had a special secret between us."

She looked so delicate standing there, her eyes haunted—but her shoulders were straight and proud.

"I didn't own a suit, so I wore a T-shirt and shorts." Her voice lowered and her eyes narrowed with a touch of anger. "He kissed me in the lake. He...touched me."

"You liked him?"

She laughed without humor. "I think I would have liked any guy that wasn't one of the brothers."

Any guy who'd been nice. "I can understand that."

She twisted her mouth with rueful contempt. "I was so pathetically desperate..." The words trailed off and she straightened again. "He was kissing me, both of us mostly submerged in the water, and then Carver applauded on the shore and I looked up and *everyone* was standing there, some of them confused, some full of pity. Others, Carver and Gene's friends, laughed until they couldn't stand up straight. The boy who'd been kissing me like he actually liked me just waded out and I was left there in the lake."

Alone.

Denver took two big steps that put him directly in front of her, caging her in.

She held up a hand, maybe to deny the need for comfort. Maybe to block him from getting too close. He stepped into it until her palm flattened on his chest. He put his hand over hers and his forehead to the top of her bowed head.

And he struggled. With himself, with what he wanted from her.

How he wanted to find the miserable fucks and tear them apart.

"After that," she whispered, "I just refused to speak to boys, and I didn't make friends with girls. Because I stopped participating, Carver was forced to give up that particular game."

That game—but had he found other games to play? Denver wanted to know everything, especially whether or not the brothers had ever physically hurt her. But she'd spent enough time reciting bad memories.

A deep breath lifted her breasts against his ribcage. She shifted, slowly raised her face and looked at him. "It wasn't until that day at the lake that I realized why Carver did the things he did."

Hands shaking from several emotions, but mostly debilitating fury and a staggering tenderness, Denver cupped her head. "Why?"

"He said he didn't want to share."

"With you?"

She shook her head. "He didn't want to share…me."

CHAPTER NINE

AN AWFUL EXPRESSION fell over Denver's face. She'd seen him fight, but she'd never been up close when he went into battle mode—as he did now. He looked ruthless. The hardness in his golden hunter's gaze, the flexing of steel muscles, might have unsettled someone else.

Before this moment, she'd touched him because it gave her comfort. Now she touched him to offer it, smoothing a hand over the tension in his chest, up to those bulging biceps and hard-set shoulders. "Carver said it was seeing me in the wet T-shirt that did it. His way of blaming me. But later, when I thought about it, I knew he'd been thinking along those lines for a while."

Eyes narrowed and jaw tight, Denver growled, "He touched you?"

He'd done so much worse than that. She squeezed her eyes shut, trying to block it out. "He never raped me." *Not for lack of trying.* Her words sounded like gravel, and she hoped Denver attributed it to lingering sickness instead of deep-rooted fear and revulsion.

"That's not what I asked you."

She shrugged as if it didn't matter, when it mattered far too much. "He liked to manhandle me. They all three found one reason or another to yank me around, shove me. They threatened plenty, but they never outright hit me."

He breathed harder and his eye flinched. "That sounds pretty awful for a young girl."

Too awful to bear—especially when she knew it was leading up to worse. "After that day at the lake, everything changed. It's like they were no longer rough just to be mean. It was more about..."

Denver waited, and under her palm she felt the strong thumping of his heart.

"About getting their hands on me."

Though anger came through in the tightening of his muscles, his tone emerged as calm and controlled as ever. "Did you tell anyone?"

This particular calm, she realized, had a definite chill to it. "Being a ward of the state meant we got occasional checkups. Janet and Gary kept the boys in check." *For the most part.* Going on tiptoes, she brushed her lips over his collarbone. "And they kept me in check."

His big hands wrapped around her upper arms. "Meaning they didn't let you talk?"

Concentrating on Denver's appeal made talking about the past easier. "They told me what would happen if I did."

Tone deadly, he whispered, "Tell me."

There'd be no point. "You can already imagine."

Disgust knotted his jaw. "Janet and Gary are the parents?"

"Janet is their stepmother. Gary was their dad." At times it felt like Denver looked into her, like he already knew her every secret. It could have been intimidating but instead his concentrated attention felt like a balm. "You said he's dead now."

"That's what they told me." He pulled her closer

until her body pressed into his and she either had to rest her cheek against him, or tip her head back to maintain eye contact.

She chose to cuddle closer.

"Gary knew what they did to you?"

This was the difficult part, what scared her the most and sometimes still gave her nightmares. "He caught them trying to get into my bedroom." She hated thinking about it, definitely didn't want to talk about it, but she needed Denver to understand so he'd let it go. "They did that a lot, *accidentally* busting in on me in the shower, in my bedroom." None of the locks in the house were secure. It took little ingenuity to open any door and she'd forever been fearful. "More often than not, I took a two-minute shower when none of them were around."

Whenever Carver drank, she found a place to hide—even if it meant staying out all night.

And that experience had its own terrors…

Denver muttered a low, foul curse. "What did Gary do about it?"

Hoping he wouldn't notice, she squeezed in as close to him as she could get. "They tussled. That happened a lot, too. He'd belt one of them, they'd shove back. Same with Janet."

"They hit their stepmother?"

"They had massive brawls." And she'd known if Janet accepted the violence without leaving them all, she herself wouldn't be exempt. "The fights were endless. That night it happened against my door with a lot of shouting. Carver…accused his dad of looking at me, too." She appreciated it when Denver's arms tightened. "Their voices dropped and, I don't know, I felt like I had to hear what they were saying. I crept to the door to listen."

She could still remember the exact words Gary had muttered to his twisted sons.

"You heard what he said."

The words would forever be trapped in her brain. Nodding, she repeated, *"She'll be eighteen soon, so lock that shit down until then."*

Denver stared in stunned disbelief.

"Carver argued with him." As she'd later learned, he didn't want to wait—and wouldn't. Carver wasn't known for denying himself once he'd set his sights on something.

The fight between father and son had been brutal, which maybe explained why Carver both hated her and wanted her.

An evil combination.

"Hey." Denver smoothed back her hair, tipped up her face. "You're here now, with me. No one is going to hurt you."

"I know. I wouldn't let him. Like I told you, I'm not a scared kid anymore."

Brushing his thumb over her chin, he murmured, "Such a hardass."

"No. But I'm not a wimp, either." At least, she hoped not. Certain things, things she would not talk about right now, still had the ability to freeze her in terror.

"Carver's father should have protected you."

She shrugged with acceptance. "I guess because the state wouldn't pay for me after I turned of age, Gary considered me fair game."

Denver's hands tightened on her in a gentle but unbreakable hold. "I'm glad the bastard is dead."

She shared that sentiment. "I left a few days after that." But it hadn't been soon enough.

She wouldn't go into how she'd managed to get away, the cruel nightmare that made it clear she either had to leave, or pay the consequences.

She said only, "I didn't stick around to finish high school."

"Knowing you had a very limited grace period left, it's smart that you didn't."

All the mean tricks and torment had been bad enough, but what Carver had planned out... Feeling defiant, she raised her chin. "I was nineteen before I got my GED." But by God, she'd gotten it. "I later got my associate's degree through an online college."

Denver rubbed her back, kissed her forehead, and then abruptly set her away from him. "You thought I knew them, that I'd go along with that warped shit?" The words were gentle, but his burning gaze scoured her face. "You actually thought that? About *me*?"

She shook her head in denial, but they both knew she had. "Not until you mentioned them and then it was just like a...a knee-jerk reaction or something." She'd worked hard to put the Nelson family out of sight and out of mind. "I hadn't even thought of them in so long, but when you said their names it came flooding back in on me." Meaning it as an apology, she said, "It leveled me, Denver, thinking you would do that." Because he was important to her when no one else had been.

It fascinated her, the way Denver popped his neck, then his knuckles. An enraged sort of energy pulsed off him in waves.

"Understand something, girl." He pinned her with his gaze. "I would never hurt you."

He looked hurt, so with apology she whispered, "I know."

Thank heavens he was headed for the rec center and a prolonged workout. Not that Denver maimed innocent people. He had awesome control and from what she could tell, a real leash on his temper. But he still looked like he needed to blow off some steam.

"We're clear?"

"Yes."

"And you trust me?"

She'd been waiting for that trap. "As much as you trust me."

His demeanor darkened even more. "I trust you."

Baloney. "Great. Then let me handle this."

"After what you just told me?" His expression went from clear annoyance to accusing her of being nuts. "Fuck no."

"It's my business," she reminded him.

He gathered her close. "And you're my business."

That was…okay, sweet. But he didn't understand just how psycho the brothers were—and she'd prefer to keep it that way. "If I call him, he might not show up here." But he probably would, because whatever Carver wanted, she couldn't give it to him.

"Come on, girl, we both know if he can find you, he will."

"You're not turned on right now, so why did you call me—"

"Who says I'm not?" He pressed his mouth to hers in a quick smooch, then slid a hand down her back to her bottom. Against her lips, he murmured, "I'm pissed, yes. And it's still undecided if I'm going to take them apart or not."

"Denver—"

"But no matter what, when I see you I want you. Hell, I think about you and I want you. You plastered against me? Finally opening up to me a little? Yeah, I'm turned on. Never doubt it."

She sighed. "I'm the same with you."

Groaning, he hugged her off her feet. "Thank you for telling me."

"It wasn't news. You already knew how much I cared for you."

"No…" He looked struck, then resigned as he shook his head. "Not that—and quit talking about it or I'll blow off the rest of the day when I shouldn't." He sucked in a chest-expanding breath. "I meant about the foster family. The Nelsons. Their asshole sons. I know it wasn't easy to tell me everything."

Telling him *everything* would be impossible. Whoever said sharing problems made them easier to bear didn't understand her problems.

"Know what I think we should do?"

Every time he said "we," her heart leaped, and then her stomach cramped. She'd never really known love before. It was as foreign to her as wealth or security. But with Denver, she was so ate up with him, she loved him more than she'd ever thought possible. No way did she want him anywhere near Carver.

But how could she both keep him, and keep him away? No words would emerge, so she mustered a questioning look.

"I'll call him."

"No." No, a million times *no*.

"I'll set him straight."

The laugh nearly burst out. Carver was so crooked,

so bent, no one, not even Denver, could set him straight. If Denver tried, he'd end up on Carver's radar—more than he already was.

His brows tweaked down, and he half smiled. "You're worried for *me*? Seriously?"

Oh crud. He sounded disbelieving and irked. How did he do that? How did he read her thoughts even before she'd sorted them out?

Her mouth felt dry. "I know you can take care of yourself." Denver was an amazing man and an incredible athlete.

But he wasn't superhuman.

And he wasn't the scum of the earth, willing to stoop as low as it took to get his way.

His advancement to the SBC was still new enough, his career so fast-growing, that she didn't want her troubles to interfere in any way.

Carver was that type of man, the kind who brought destruction. He didn't fight fair. Not face-to-face, man to man, as Denver was used to. No, he'd fight dirty in ways Denver would never expect—and couldn't prevent. She knew well the cruel and abnormal way Carver's brain worked. He justified the most unjustifiable forms of brutality. He made up reasons for unreasonable acts of violence.

He did it all without a conscience.

And took pleasure from it.

She couldn't tell Denver everything she knew about Carver and his brothers, because that would only encourage him to want to defend and protect her. But she had to try to talk him out of digging in. "You don't understand how Carver is."

"I met him, spoke with him. I understand plenty.

And, honey, hate to break it to you, but he already sees me as an obstacle, guaranteed."

She was very afraid he might be right.

"Talking with him again isn't going to make that more of a fact. But it might reinforce for him that you aren't alone. Maybe," he said, then more firmly when she tried to interject, "*just maybe* it'll deter him."

Out of ideas, she said, "I don't want you to." That sounded petulant, but damn it, how could she convince him without spilling her guts about things better kept private? "I just need to find out what he wants." Because Carver had to want something. She couldn't imagine what, but—

"And if he wants you?"

For a split second, her heart stalled, then started again in a rush. "Why would he after all this time? No, it has to be something else." Though sure, once Carver found her she didn't doubt he'd revert to his same grabby, obnoxious self. "I'm not a kid now. He can't bully me anymore."

Denver didn't buy it—but then she didn't, either.

"You'll give me his number, okay?"

What a mess. She could really use a sounding board, but she didn't want her friends to know about her awful upbringing. It was painful and very private. It killed her that Denver now knew.

The many worries lay heavy on her shoulders, wearing her down. "I just wanted to be with you, that's all. And everything is screwed up. First I'm sick and now the idiots want to see me again—"

"But I'm going to take good care of you, remember?" He gently held her face. "You're not alone, girl, so stop acting like you are."

Right now, maybe being alone would be better. Except that she loved Denver and the thought of losing this time with him…

Exasperated, he tipped her face up and gave her another, slightly longer kiss that sent a pool of warmth through her belly and obliterated clear thought. "You'll stay in today?"

She wanted to say no, to tell him she had a life to get back to. But she'd already called off work, her friends were all at their jobs and her body declared it time for another nap.

"Yes." Before getting sick, she'd had a ton of energy. Staying in would have been unthinkable. Now, even with a megasexy guy kissing her senseless, she had to fight off a yawn.

"It's going to be okay. You'll see." His attention went from her face to her body. Briefly, he cupped both her breasts, made a low sound in his throat, and stepped away. "I'll be back over tonight, okay? Not sure when yet, but it won't be real late. If anything comes up, call me."

He expected her to think after how he'd just touched her?

"Cherry?"

She got her head to bob a few times. "All right." She'd take her nap and maybe afterward she'd be refreshed enough for a solution to come to her. Doubtful, but she'd give it a try.

Together they walked to the door.

"Lock up behind me."

"I will." Even before Carver resurfaced, she and Rissy kept the doors locked.

"Cherry?" He paused in the open doorway. "I can't

imagine any male of any age not wanting you. Odds are every guy who played you for Carver did so with regrets. Know that, okay?" He pulled her in for one last, blistering taste of her mouth, then jogged down the walkway to his car.

After closing and locking the door, Cherry leaned back against it. As bad as things were right now, she realized she was smiling—because of Denver.

Now, if she could just figure out what Carver wanted, if she could deal with him and his perverse demands without drawing anyone else in as a victim, she could get back to the fantasy of finally having Denver Lewis's attention.

A SLASH OF sunlight warmed his face and caused him to flinch when he cracked his eyes open. He closed them again, went to stretch—and stilled with agonizing aches and pains.

What the hell?

A whisper drifted past his ear: "So he ain't dead?"

Pausing, Leese peeked his eyes open again. The sunlight blinded him, but he heard traffic and more whispers. Weird. Had he left a window open last night?

"Mister, do you need a hospital?"

That voice came entirely too close. He got one eye open and found a very dark face with wide, even darker eyes, close to his, blocking the morning sun. Startled, he sat up—and groaned. Jesus, it felt like a herd of buffalo had stampeded over him.

With another, more cautious peek, he saw that the dark face belonged to his neighbor's ten-year-old kid. Beyond her stood another girl wearing mismatched clothes, with red pigtails and freckles everywhere.

Disoriented, Leese looked around and realized he was on the steps to his apartment building. He had drool on his chin. A very bruised chin, judging by how it hurt to move his jaw.

"Can he talk?" the redhead asked.

"I'm okay, Mayla."

Even as she nodded to her friend, Mayla didn't move away. "Why'd you sleep outside?"

How could he tell a ten-year-old girl that he'd gotten stinking drunk and apparently… No, wait. That wasn't right. Memories tried to nudge in, but that sent his stomach roiling.

"He's gonna puke!" the redhead yelled with horrified excitement.

"No." At least, if she'd stop screeching he might not. "Shh…" Remembering something he'd heard Mayla's mother say, he told her, "Inside voice."

"But we're outside."

Yeah, there was that. Grabbing the iron railing at the side of the stairs, he dragged himself—slowly—up to his feet. "You know what time it is?"

She shrugged. "Play time."

He dug in his pocket for his phone, saw it was nearly nine, and swallowed back a curse. Another search of his pocket produced his keys, but no wallet. Son of a bitch.

He'd gotten played, big-time. How many people had seen him passed out? His neck burned thinking about it. "Does your mom know I was here?" Hard to imagine or she'd never have let the girls out to play.

"No. Want me to go tell her?"

He couldn't ask a kid to lie to her mother. Mayla's mom was the good sort, babysitting other kids, taking in laundry—including his own—and playing manager of the beat-up apartment building in order to stay at home with her daughter. She made ends meet, but Leese knew it wasn't always easy.

Ignoring the question since he didn't have an answer, he glanced around the neighborhood. In this neck of the woods, drunks sleeping on doorsteps weren't a totally uncommon thing.

That he'd fallen into that category shamed him.

The little redhead, who up 'til now had warily kept her distance, drew closer. She scrunched up her blue eyes and her nose, making her freckles more pronounced. "You're bleedin'."

He touched where she pointed and found dried blood near his ear. "I must've fallen." Glad for an excuse to escape their innocent curiosity—and doubly thrilled to still have his keys—he turned for the door. "I'll go get cleaned up right now." He half stumbled, realized his legs were shaky, and gripped the entry-door handle. Fuck him for living on the third floor.

At the last second, he turned back to the kids. "You stay right in front here, where your mama can see you."

All wide-eyed and watchful, Mayla nodded. "Mama says there could be bad people around."

"That's right." And last night he'd become one of them.

DENVER WALKED INTO Rowdy's bar, hoping to meet with the guys before he headed over to see Cherry. He figured if they put their collective brains together, they could come up with a way to draw out Carver and his brothers without upsetting Cherry in the bargain. She'd been as clear as she could be that she wanted to handle things on her own.

It was going to bother her enough that he wouldn't let her. If he cut her out completely, as he wanted to, she'd be majorly pissed. He didn't want that.

He wanted to get her under him again.

And he wanted to claim her in some way. Longer term than just here and now. The thought of any other man getting near her heated his blood with possessive rage. Again he popped his neck, but the tension had crawled in with a vengeance and sunk its claws deep, and short of a good fuck or a real fight, he didn't know how to shake it off.

He was making his way through the bar when he drew up short.

There, sitting at the bar and chatting up Vanity Baker, was none other than Leese Phelps. Was he here for Cherry? Working with Carver? The impulse to drag the bastard outside and get some answers the old-fashioned way got his feet moving forward.

Rowdy intercepted him. "Is there a reason you're looking bent on murder?"

As the owner of the bar and a certified hardass, Rowdy never missed a thing—especially not trouble. Because Cannon used to work with him, and many of the fighters considered the bar a favorite neighborhood hangout, they all knew him well.

And vice versa.

If he thought it necessary, Rowdy would go toe to toe with a heavyweight champion. Thing was, everyone respected him too much for that to ever be necessary.

With a nod of his head, Denver indicated Phelps. "What's he doing here?"

"Hitting on Vanity from what I can tell. That bothers you?"

"That he's here?" Looking beyond Rowdy, Denver stared daggers into Phelps's back. "Yes."

"Not because of Vanity?"

"What?" That sidetracked his attention. "No. Her life is her own."

"I ask," Rowdy said, still blocking his way, "because Stack has been bristling since he got here, too."

Denver searched the crowd and sure enough, Stack sat at a table with a couple of women, but his gaze continually went to Phelps. "He knows the douche." Maybe he had his own reason for wanting to take him apart.

He'd damn well have to get in line.

"Knows him how?"

Impatient, not that Rowdy gave a shit, Denver rolled a shoulder. "He was around at the after-party when Armie fought." Unsure of how much to tell him, Denver added, "He hit on Cherry a little too hard until Stack warned him off." *By using Denver as a threat.* But hey, whatever worked.

"Well, Vanity doesn't seem to mind his chitchat." Rowdy moved into Denver's line of vision to ensure he had his attention. "If there's going to be trouble, take it elsewhere."

Holding up his hands, Denver indicated compliance. "Got it."

"Thank you."

Denver didn't move. "You really think I'd—"

"Stir up trouble? No. But I've seen that look before, worn it a few times myself."

Denver snorted. Rowdy used to wear it more often

than not. Since marrying, though, he'd mellowed. A little.

"You're itching for a fight or a fuck."

Damn, hadn't he just thought the same thing? "The first won't happen in here, you have my word."

Rowdy must've believed him because his frown eased and his mouth went into an amused smile. "And the second?"

"Since the right lady isn't around, that's not happening, either."

"Ah." The smile turned into a grin. "Hopefully later, then." Rowdy went about his business, collecting empties off tables, but Denver knew he'd see every little thing that went down.

Instead of heading to the bar, Denver headed for Stack.

When he reached the table, he hooked a chair with his foot, pulled it out and sat, then braced his forearms on the small round tabletop. With speculative smiles and suggestive body scans, the women welcomed him.

Stack barely acknowledged him. He was too preoccupied with his own thoughts. Dark thoughts, given the expression on his face.

Watching his friend drink from a longneck, Denver said, "Got a favor to ask."

One of the women practically sat in Stack's lap, her hand on his chest, his free arm around her. Absently, as if he did it out of habit, Stack stroked her narrow hip, then down so that his hand encountered her thigh beneath the hem of a denim miniskirt. "Sure, what is it?"

Model-thin chicks never did it for Denver. Apparently Stack felt differently.

"Need you to lend me a hand with something." *Or more like someone.*

Still playing with the chick one-handed, Stack finished off his beer and set the empty aside. "Let's hear it."

Giving an apologetic glance to the ladies, Denver said, "Sorry, but it's best explained in private."

Nodding, Stack turned and planted a long wet one on the girl, gave her hip a pat and levered her away from him. "If you'll excuse me?"

She crossed her arms and struck a pissed-off pose.

The other chick sent a hopeful glance at Denver, but he held up his hands. "Sorry. I'm taken."

"Yeah?" Ignoring his angry lady, Stack grinned. "Cherry?"

Denver nodded.

It took some convincing, but Stack finally got the two pouting ladies to depart.

Never, not once, had Cherry been that tenacious. Whenever Denver had been less than inviting, which sadly had been most of the time, she'd accepted it and moved on.

Had to admit to himself, he respected that about her.

He was also damned grateful that she'd been persistent enough to try that one last time.

"So." Stack slouched back in the hard chair, the bottle held loosely against his abs. "What's up? And it better be important given you just chased off my entertainment for the night."

"Both of them?"

He shook his head. "That'd be one more piece of trouble than I wanted. I leave that headache to Armie."

He glanced at his watch. "Miles is supposed to join me in an hour. The second was hanging around for him."

"Gotcha. Well, do this for me and then you can call them back."

"All right." He sipped at his beer. "Let's hear what it is."

"I need you to hit on Vanity."

CHAPTER TEN

UNSURE IF HE'D heard that right or, if he had, whether Denver's suggestion was serious, Stack took his gaze from his friend to the killer lady at the bar.

Damn, but her ass looked sweet on that bar stool. Megasweet.

Maybe too sweet.

He'd never seen a woman so drop-dead gorgeous from head to toe, and God knew he'd known plenty of sexy women. To make it even more confusing, Vanity Baker was nice. And funny.

And while she had to know she was hot, she didn't seem to care that much about it.

"So I have your attention?" Denver asked with a low laugh.

"Yeah." Still looking at Vanity, he said to Denver, "I'm listening."

"You remember the creep she's talking to?"

"Dude from Kentucky." Stack scratched his jaw. "Leese Phelps. He was pestering Cherry before I pointed out that you were keeping watch. That seemed to discourage him."

As if the reminder bothered him, Denver worked his jaw. "I need to have a word with him."

Ho, what was this? "I know for a fact Leese struck out, the poor schmuck." That made Denver frown—

which had Stack laughing. "Why are you thinking about dismembering him, given that Cherry wasn't interested, much less involved?"

"The others already know, and Cannon was going to tell you tomorrow, but since you're here…"

"Damn, man. Now you've got me curious."

The story Denver shared took care of any humor Stack felt at his predicament. Cherry was a sweet girl. Funny, lively and completely hung up on Denver. Since Denver hadn't seemed to reciprocate, had instead chosen to wallow in misery, it had been a little sad to watch. That was the major reason he and Miles had tried so hard to cheer her up, while also doing their part to needle Denver.

Stack slanted his gaze back to Leese. "Funny that he'd show up here after all that going down."

"If you think that's funny, you must have a twisted sense of humor."

"Nah, Leese is okay. You'll see." Cutting off Denver's curse, Stack said, "Did you notice he's beat all to hell and back? I saw him walk in, and let me tell you, he's moving like a man who went five rounds in the cage and lost them all."

Brows shooting up, Denver twisted in his seat to view Leese with new awareness.

From the back left angle they had, only a few war wounds showed: a big, purple bruise above his ear, with less colorful shading under his eye and across his nose.

"Hell of a coincidence, right?"

"Huh." Denver didn't show any sympathy. If anything he looked a little more volatile.

"So I'm to interrupt and lead Vanity away." Stack said that as if there was no question of her following, but for once in his life, he wasn't sure of his success. "Then you're going to…what? Add more bruises to Leese's black-and-blue camouflage, or just talk?"

"That'll depend on him, now, won't it? But Rowdy already read me the riot act about anything going down in here."

"As if." Denver wasn't a barroom brawler. It wasn't his MO. Then again, he'd never been this strung out on a chick before. The fact that it had taken him and Cherry so long to work out whatever it was keeping them apart only made Denver tetchier when discussing her.

"If necessary, I'll *lead* him outside."

Lead, as in drag, given the way Denver said it.

If that happened, Stack would follow, because Denver would only end up feeling bad for pulverizing a lesser fighter. That, too, was his MO. He had the greatest sense of fair play Stack had ever run across.

Pushing back his chair, aware of profound anticipation zinging through his bloodstream, Stack affected the cockiness necessary to convince his friend and said, "Give me two minutes."

Vanity Baker had only recently moved to the area and joined their group. Hailing from California, she had the surfer-girl look with crazy long, pale blond hair, a light tan, sexy toned legs that went on forever and curves that'd showcase any bikini. The day she'd walked into the rec center every guy had immediately gotten snagged by her big blue eyes and easy smile. In a nanosecond, they'd all had carnal ideas on their brains. But because she was Yvette's best friend, and Yvette was engaged to Cannon, no one went after her hot and heavy.

As they all surely wanted to do.

Then again, maybe Vanity intimidated the others. Wasn't every day a guy saw a classy, confident, happy, spellbindingly gorgeous woman—who was still single.

Stack slid onto the stool beside her, gaining her notice. Probably thinking a stranger had joined her, she cast a quick glance his way, then realized it was him and turned back for a longer, more familiar look.

Big blue eyes started by locking with his before, with a slow smile, she dipped them down and over his dark T-shirt, his worn jeans, all the way down to his cowboy boots and back up again. Smiling as if amused, she lifted one slim brow. "Hello, Stack."

"Vanity."

Frowning, Leese leaned around her to see him. "Hey."

"Wassup, Leese?" He nodded at him. "Got run over, I see."

"Feels like," Leese grumbled.

"You were in a tourney?"

He shook his head. "No." Running his fingertips along a cut on his chin, he said, "Long story."

They stared at each other, Stack willing him to take a hike, Leese refusing to budge.

Vanity grinned. "Wow, don't I feel popular."

Her teasing made Stack want to kiss her until neither one of them could breathe, but he held it in check. Trying to look serious, he said to Leese, "Mind if I borrow her a minute?"

Wearing a black scowl, Leese spun on the stool to face him. "Matter of fact—"

Vanity made a loud "ahem" sound before speaking to Stack. "That's up to me, not him, and no, I don't mind." She turned back to Leese. "Thank you for the drink."

Stack resisted the urge to whistle in sympathy. Talk about a dismissal…

Glowering, Leese lowered himself carefully off the stool, his limbs unbending and awkward, testament to some nasty body shots that must still hurt.

He took one step away, glanced beyond Stack to where Denver stood staring a hole in him, and huffed out a breath. "Now I see. Okay, then." He managed to straighten. "It's why I'm here, so I might as well get this over with."

Hobbling in a broke-ass gait, he headed toward Denver.

That'd gone easier than Stack had expected.

After taking it all in, Vanity angled her body around to face his. "So you were the sacrificial lamb, huh?"

"Actually, I'm known as the wolf, not the lamb."

"Your fight name, yes? Something about the way you stalk your opponents like prey in the cage."

"That's ri–"

"And in the bedroom you make the ladies howl."

His mouth snapped shut. First time he'd heard that one. And damn, she looked serious—like she believed it.

He tugged at his ear. "Who told you that?"

"About the cage? Yvette and Rissy."

He shook his head. "No, the part about the ladies." *About them howling.* It was almost laughable.

Idly, Vanity traced one tapered finger over the polished bar top. "Apparently it's common conversation for the ladies' room." Her lashes swept up and she met his gaze. "I've heard it twice now."

"Here?"

By small degrees her mouth slipped into a smile. "Well, it wasn't at Rissy's or Yvette's."

He pulled back over that appalling thought. "Yeah, I haven't ever—"

"Been intimate with them? I know." She put her elbow on the edge of the bar and propped up her chin with a palm. "So let me see if I get this right. You were sent here to draw away my attention so those two, Denver and Leese, could get some private chat time in?"

"I volunteered," Stack lied. Her drink was empty so he made the offer. "Can I get you another?"

She turned her head, sending that long fair hair cascading down to her thigh. "I can entertain myself, you know. No reason for you to give up your earlier pursuits."

Still thinking about her hair, about how he'd like to wrap it around his hands and hold her steady for some hard sex play, he murmured absently, "How's that?"

"The two hopefuls fawning over you earlier?" Feigning sympathy, she asked, "Did Denver's storm-cloud impression chase off your prospects?"

"They were done deals, not prospects. But that's over." She'd noticed him with the other women? Wondering what that meant, if anything, Stack gave her a once-over. "What about you? Meeting someone tonight?"

Pretending a forlorn sigh, she pouted. "No. I'm all alone."

On her, the pout tempted far more so than on the two ladies he'd sent from his table. With her sky-blue eyes, straight, narrow nose, smooth cheekbones and that full, soft mouth… Yeah, she could make him lose his thoughts. "Same here."

"Now we both know that's not true."

"Is since I sent them off." Even better than her face was her body—all sweet, supple, curvy perfection. He needed to get his head on straight, and fast. "So how about we keep each other company?"

She seemed to think about it for far too long, making his left eye twitch. Not since high school had he been rejected, mostly because he knew how to hedge his bets. If it hadn't been for Denver, he might not have ever approached her like this—

"I would love the company." Lifting her glass, she said, "And another drink."

Score. Stack ordered them each a drink, considered asking her to move to a table with him, but decided it'd probably be safer to stay at the bar.

He'd just tipped up a fresh beer when she said, "Do you have a date for the wedding?"

He choked, damn it. Grabbing for a napkin and trying to ignore the way she rubbed-pat-rubbed between his shoulder blades, he concentrated on getting his breath back. Not easy when her hand stroked down, then paused at the small of his back.

Even after he caught his wind, she stayed too close, her hand still touching him, the warmth of it sinking right through his T-shirt.

If he thought much about her small, soft hand on him, he'd get a boner for sure.

He cleared his throat. "Sorry. Went down the wrong pipe."

"I was talking about Cannon and Yvette's wedding."

She tipped her head. "Not asking for your hand in marriage."

Jesus. Much more of that and he'd be strangled again. "I never take a date to a wedding." Best to clear that up right now.

"Because women get ideas?"

The back of his neck prickled. "Yeah. Something like that." He cast a look at Denver, but he and Leese had their heads together, both of them looking far too serious.

No help there.

He hated to ask, because he just knew it'd be a trap, but he heard himself say, "What about you? Got a string of guys waiting for the word?"

"Like you, I hesitate to go with anyone." Finally she retreated, leaning out of his space to sip at her drink.

But with her body aimed toward his—for the sake of conversation, maybe—and her legs so long, her knees bumped the outside of his thigh.

Since when did an innocent touch like that become so hot?

Since the knees belonged to Vanity Baker.

Thank God she wore jeans. He'd seen her in itty-bitty skirts and shorts and it never failed to inspire lust.

"Stack?"

"Hmm?"

The smile flickered into place again. That, too, was a turn-on, how her lips always twitched and one side went up first, then the other, as if she fought every grin.

"You're here to keep me engaged in conversation, but you're not holding up your end of the bargain."

"Right. Sorry." What the hell had they been discussing? Oh, yeah, Cannon's upcoming wedding. "You hate to take dates to weddings, too? How come?"

She lifted her glass as if in a toast. "I lose my better judgment when I drink too much."

He eyed her half-empty glass. *Do tell.*

"So it's risky to have a guy in the line of fire. But I'm the maid of honor and I'm going to look pathetic to be there solo."

Oh hell. He felt the noose closing.

Very softly, she said, "You did run off Leese."

No fucking way! "You were going to ask *him*?"

Again she sipped. "Actually, I think once I mentioned the wedding he would have asked me."

Knowing what he did now, Stack couldn't stop obsessing on how much she might have imbibed already. "And you'd have accepted?" She deserved better than a new fighter with a shit attitude.

So what was he? A better-grade fighter with a shit attitude?

When she sipped again, self-preservation sank in. Stack took the glass from her and set it out of reach.

Her eyes flared. "You didn't just do that."

"Did." He braced an arm on the bar and leaned into her. "Stay away from Leese."

This time when she tilted her head, her hair drifted over his wrist. "Giving me an order?"

"Call it a concerned suggestion."

"I'll think about it," she said, and her gaze was on his mouth, making it harder for him to breathe. Just… making it harder all around.

He needed to put some space, emotional and mental if not physical, between them pronto. "Mostly I don't take dates to weddings because it's a good place to score."

"Really?" Looking intrigued instead of insulted, she said, "Tell me."

"What?"

Her eyebrows wiggled. "Details. You pick up women at weddings…one at a time?"

Shit. "One at a time."

"Okay, you pick them up and take them to your place? Isn't that dicey? I mean, not that they might molest you." Her soft, husky laugh did crazy things to him. "That's the point, right? But how do you get rid of them afterward?"

Another glance at Denver showed no end in sight. He and Leese were now seated at a table. Double damn. Vanity waited, her gaze searching his, occasionally dropping over his body, so he had to answer. "I don't bring chicks to my place."

"Chicks," she said with a smile that mocked him. "So where do you take these *chicks*?"

And now she was making fun of him. He leaned in, annoyed enough to be blatant. "In a closet or the men's room usually."

"Eww. Really?" She reached past him, her breasts brushing his biceps, and retrieved her glass. "I mean, a closet…*maybe*. But the bathroom? Foul."

"The walls are usually clean enough."

"So." She swirled the ice. "I take it these are quickies, yes? I mean, surely there can't be much foreplay in a public bathroom. It's a disappointing image, I guess because I had this vision in my… Never mind."

Oh, hell no. "What?"

She looked him over. "All that wolf and howling

gossip." She lifted a bare shoulder that made her breasts move softly. "Guess I never envisioned you as a minute man."

Stack locked his teeth. "I'm not."

"You just said you are."

"That is," he growled, overly enunciating, "I only am when it's the right way to be."

"Always choosing the best path? I see. So there are times when some speedy action in a bathroom is the proper course?"

He leaned closer still, his gaze holding hers. "When the woman is so hot for it she's begging, yeah, a few minutes is long enough to get her off."

Someone bumped his arm and he turned to see both Denver and Leese standing there. Denver looked startled, Leese disgusted.

Well, hell.

Vanity said, "Hello, boys. All done with your chit-chat?"

Denver's gaze bounced back and forth between them before settling on Stack. "I hate to interrupt, but—"

"Yeah, give me a minute."

"He's the minute man, you know," Vanity said sotto voce.

"That's enough from you."

She tried to look innocent, but another twitching smile ruined it.

Stack turned his frown on Leese. He wasn't about to budge until that dude was long gone.

Denver said, "I'll grab us a table."

"If his lady friends come over," Vanity called after him, "tell them he'll be right there."

Bemused, Denver looked back and forth between them again. "Sure."

And he took off, the coward.

Leese stuck around, and it annoyed Stack enough that he said, *"What?"*

"He's surly," Vanity explained with a gentle pat to Leese's forearm. "Something about quickies in a closet."

Not amused, Leese said, "I'll see you around?"

"I'm sure you will." And then softer, with concern, "Are you okay to drive?"

That caused old Leese to straighten. "Yeah, I'm fine. Thanks." And he walked out stiff-legged while trying to hide his discomfort. Pride, Stack knew, could be a bitch.

"That poor man," Vanity said.

Though Stack almost thought the same thing, he didn't like hearing it from her. He also knew it was the very last thing Leese—or any fighter—would want her thinking. "Jesus." He stood. "You want a date for the wedding?"

"Well, I did," she clarified. And before he could say more, she added, "I already assumed you didn't want any one woman getting clingy. I also don't want any man getting clingy." She wrinkled her nose. "I'm well-to-do. Don't know if you knew that."

As in wealthy?

"Anyhow," she went on as if she hadn't just said something so startling. "It gives guys ideas."

Stack laughed. Seriously? How much money could a midtwenties California surfer-chick have? "I don't know anything about your finances—"

"I could live comfortably without ever again working." Her bare shoulder lifted again. "But sometimes I get bored."

That was a mouthful. He knew she worked part-time for Yvette at the resale shop, so he'd just assumed...

Shaking that off, Stack said, "Doesn't matter if you're a millionaire. Listen, any guy that gets ideas about you, gets them from this." He waved a hand, indicating her face, down to her painted toenails and back up to that sinfully long, pale hair.

"But you've never had ideas?"

He laughed. "I'm breathing, right?"

Her eyes smiled even if her mouth didn't. "So will you be my date to the wedding?" She held out a hand to strike a deal. "No strings attached."

Still stung over how she'd harassed him, Stack hesitated. "I don't know. It'll mean I have to give up getting laid—"

"Not necessarily."

Wait, fast rewind. Trying to look merely curious, he said, "What's that?"

"I mean, I won't do anything in the bathroom." She wrinkled her nose in distaste. "And honestly, a closet isn't sounding all that appealing, either. I prefer a bed. And nakedness." Her attention dipped over him. "Overhead lighting wouldn't hurt."

His brain refused to function so he just stood there staring at her—visualizing every damn thing she'd just said, which included her naked in a bed under lots of light so he wouldn't miss a single sizzling thing.

She kept talking, that slim hand extended, waiting for his agreement. "But I'm open to using my place—bed and light provided."

The visual turned hot and vivid.

"That way you won't have to worry about getting rid of me afterward. I promise to toss you out before you can even get nervous about it."

Too stunned to think clearly, Stack said, "I don't get nervous."

"And just think," she continued, "once you agree, then if any other men, like Leese for instance, ask me, I can say I already have a date."

Blackmail. Very effective blackmail. "It's months away."

She nodded. "You're free and clear in the meantime to carry on however you please. We can tell people we're friend dates, if you want. Like I said, no strings attached."

With his temples—and his dick—throbbing, he ran a hand through his hair.

Finally dropping her hand, she went on tiptoe to smooth the hair he'd just rumpled. "Relax, Stack. You have yourself all mussed and I really didn't mean to rattle you so badly."

His back teeth locked. "I don't get rattled and I don't get nervous." She made him sound like a schoolboy.

"I take it your lack of an answer *is* the answer?" She gave him an indulgent smile and patted his arm. "Don't worry. I understand. But I need to go see if I can catch up with Leese, maybe make him the same offer—"

Stack caught her elbow, and even that sent sensation from his palm straight to his already alert gonads. "Not rattled," he clarified again. "But yeah, you surprised me."

"Good thing we weren't in the cage, huh?"

He smirked. "I've yet to have another fighter make the same offer you just did." A deep breath helped him to feel his legs again. "So yeah, not a bad deal." Fuck him, that sounded lame.

"Sex with me is *not a bad deal*? Why, Stack, I'm completely charmed."

He rubbed a hand over his eyes. "That's not what I meant."

"Such a relief."

"Sex with you—" He mentally cast around, but couldn't come up with the right words.

She stepped closer. "Yes?"

Not kissing her was tough, but hey, *he* was tough so he could handle it. Maybe. "How the hell am I supposed to think about anything else between now and the wedding?"

Her slow smile this time was genuine and sweet. "Aw, now I *am* charmed. Thank you."

"So we have a deal?"

"Ironclad." She patted his chest, lingered as she had on his back, then scooped up her purse in a rush. "I'll see you around."

That's it? See you around? "You're okay to drive?"

"Since the first drink was cola, and you only let me drink half of the second, yes, I'm fine." She waggled her fingers at him in farewell and left with that shapely ass drawing attention from every red-blooded male in the joint.

But she wanted *him* to take her to the wedding.

She'd offered *him* sex.

He'd either just made the best deal of his life, or tied his own noose.

DENVER DIDN'T GET to the house until damn near nine o'clock. After sharing with Stack this new turn of events, he needed to see Cherry. To his surprise, he found her and Yvette sitting on the front porch talking to two of his fighter buddies, Miles and Brand, beneath a yellow porch light. As he opened his door and got out, he heard Cherry's laugh. It carried on the night, curled inside him. Turned him on.

Nudged his possessiveness.

Which was dumb because any idiot could see they were just sitting around chatting. Being that they were part of the group, backup whenever Cannon needed it, he assumed Miles and Brand were there to keep a watchful eye out. Better the porch than cozy on the couch.

He trusted them, all of them.

Heading up the walkway, his small overnight case in hand, he saw Brand lean in and say something low to Cherry. While watching Denver she listened to Brand, and her smile made his jeans feel too tight. When she burst out laughing again, it did insane things to him, even when a spate of coughing followed the laugh.

Brand patted her on her back. Miles fanned her face.

She'd regained her breath before he reached her, leaving him free to catch the back of her neck and take her mouth in a kiss that no one would misunderstand.

When he finally lifted away, she said, "Denver," in a breathy, surprised reprimand.

Brand, sitting closest to her, said, "If he pisses on you, don't be surprised."

"Marking his territory," Miles agreed.

Rissy laughed. "You guys are so gross."

Both men stood, stretched.

How long had they been there? Denver reached a

hand down to Cherry and pulled her to her feet and into his side. "Still coughing?"

"Not much." She slanted her attention at the guys. "Only when *some* people keep making me laugh."

With two fingers under her chin, Denver brought her gaze back to him. "How do you feel?"

"Fine."

"You sure?"

"Denver," she whispered again, embarrassed. "Stop fussing."

"I don't *fuss*."

Too late. Given their grins, the guys heard her and now he knew they'd be ribbing him for a month. He took the seat Miles vacated and, setting the overnight case aside, pulled Cherry into his lap.

Rissy gathered up half-empty glasses of iced tea and put them on a tray. "I need to head in, too. Tomorrow is another superearly day."

"You work too much," Miles told her.

She smiled, shrugged. "Not like I have much else to do."

As she started in, all three guys shared a look. Damn.

Miles jumped forward to open the front door for her. "Thanks for the food."

"I'm glad you liked it."

Brand asked, "You aren't dating what's-his-name anymore?"

"That ended a while ago."

"He's still calling," Cherry said. "He wants her back."

Rissy rolled her eyes. "Not happening. Right now I'm just concentrating on a promotion at work. Fingers crossed." She went on into the house, then said through the doorway, "Good night."

After a round of good-nights from everyone, Denver teased his fingers up and down Cherry's bare arm. She wore polka-dot flannel pajama pants and a cute matching T-shirt. A high ponytail held her blond curls away from her face and her bare feet, toenails painted pink, poked out from the hem of the overlong pants.

He wanted her, in too many ways to count.

"I feel like a voyeur," Miles said. "Rein it in until I'm out of here."

"We're not doing anything!" Cherry protested.

Denver just smiled. No doubt both Brand and Miles knew the direction of his thoughts. Guy instinct.

Brand dug keys from his jeans. "We're heading out, too." He gave them each a devilish grin. "You kids be good now, you hear."

As they walked away, Cherry tried to stand but Denver held tight. "What were you laughing about?"

"It's terrible." She turned her face into his neck, but he could feel her smile.

"Tell me." He kissed her jaw, along to her ear. Breathing softly, he touched with his tongue, teasing the lobe, then inside the whorls.

She shifted and he felt her shiver.

"I want to know," he whispered.

A balmy evening breeze drifted over them, heightening his senses. It seemed the more he wanted to protect her, the more he just plain wanted her.

She ducked her face again. "The guys were discussing close calls."

"In the cage?"

She nodded, then looked at him. "Miles said you got…hit in an unfair place."

The grin tugged at his mouth. "No way is that how Miles put it."

"No."

"Say it." Teasing her, his tone a dare, he whispered, "Say it."

Trying not to smile, she slicked her tongue over her lips. "He said you got nutted."

"Yeah." When she smiled, she looked even prettier— if such a thing were possible. "I remember that fight well." A car door closed quietly, then another. An engine started. He turned his head to watch Brand's SUV pull away from the curb. They'd parked a few houses up, maybe to keep any creeps from knowing they were around.

Since they all ended up on the front porch, it didn't much matter in the end. But he appreciated their forethought.

"When you get racked, at first it doesn't hurt," Denver explained. "It takes a few seconds for it to sink in, but you know it's coming, and then you just go sick and weak."

"Miles said the ref didn't see it."

"Not until he watched the replay, and then he was full of wincing apologies." Remembering made him grin. "Bastard kneed me so hard he cracked my cup."

"On purpose?"

Her outrage almost made him laugh. "No, he was going for an inside leg kick. It happens and sometimes even the best ref misses things."

"Tell me how you won."

"If you know I won, then Miles and Brand already told you."

Resting her cheek against his shoulder, she slipped her hand under the neckline of his shirt to stroke his heated skin. "I want to hear you tell it."

Since it ended well, he didn't mind. Shortly they'd have much more serious things to go over. Maybe that's why she wanted to hear it, too.

"When the pain sank in, I dropped my guard. He caught me with a wild haymaker, then followed up with a jab that got me right on the chin. I went down and I swear, I thought that might've been it."

"I'm glad I wasn't there," she said, squeezing him tight.

Usually a woman fussing would grate on his nerves. Not so with Cherry. He liked the shielding way she hugged him.

While rubbing her back, he inhaled her scent. "Every fighter gets caught now and then. Stick around long enough and you will see it."

She sat up to meet his gaze. "I am sticking around."

"Yeah, you are." He gave her a quick kiss.

Appeased, she settled against him again. "So then what happened?"

"He landed on me, going for some ground and pound. Instincts kicked in and I defended by rote, gutted it out, and finally my head cleared. When he thought he'd finished me, he got sloppy and I caught him with an arm bar. He tapped out."

"Miles said the audience went nuts."

"Yeah." One by one, stars burst into the sky. It was a quiet night, only the distant whine of a siren and the occasional bark of a dog disturbing the peace. Such an illusion. They both knew trouble waited right around the corner.

"That's the night the SBC called?"

He nodded. "Signed my first contract with them."

"And soon now you'll be on the main card."

Something in the way she said that set off alarm bells in his head. "A couple of months from now."

"That is such an amazing thing."

It was, but he'd worked so long and hard that it had felt inevitable more than anything else. He curved a hand around her nape, kissing her forehead, the bridge of her nose, nudging her face up until he got to her mouth. "You're amazing." He tried to kiss her hotly enough to show her he meant it.

But she pulled away. "I need to talk to you."

Groaning, he dropped back against the porch steps, arms and legs thrown out, eyes closed. "Somehow, I knew this was coming."

CHAPTER ELEVEN

CHERRY'S SMALL HAND smacked his chest. "You do not read my mind!"

"No, but I understand you." Still with his head back, his eyes closed, he blew out a breath. Damn, he really just wanted to take her to bed and hold her all night—then in the morning, assuming she'd be recovered enough, he'd finally have her again. "Let's hear it."

Scrambling off his lap, Cherry sat beside his shoulder. "You can't dictate to me."

"Never tried to."

Her knee gave a rude shove to his shoulder. "Baloney. You—"

"Cut to the chase, honey, because I have things to tell you, too." And the sooner they got to it, the sooner he could get her inside, in bed, and against him.

Drawing her knees up and closing her arms around herself, she said, "Fine. I want to have sex with you. I want to be with you."

He cracked one eye open. "If only we could stop right there."

"But," she said, not stopping, "there are some things I have to take care of on my own, and you're just going to have to accept that."

"We're talking about your foster brothers?"

She rolled her eyes. "Yes. I know you want to help."

"Help?" She made it sound like he wanted to carry groceries for an old lady.

Appealing to him, she added softly, "And I love how protective you are, I really do."

He clenched his molars. Was that all she loved? "Protective, huh?"

"It's part of who you are."

Did she think he got this involved with every woman he'd slept with? Soon he'd have to explain a few things to her.

Once he figured them out himself.

She forged on. "The thing is, I've thought about this all day."

He should have been with her. Never before had he resented his various training, but today his thoughts had stayed centered on her even as he went through his routines. He'd sweated his ass off doing cardio, then strength building. He'd sparred, working hits and kicks, different combos, and then concentrated on his ground game.

And through it all, a part of his mind had been centered on seeing Cherry.

"If you interfere, it will only make things worse."

If he interfered? What a joke, since already she'd interfered with his life in a big way. Heaving a frustrated sigh, he stared up at the moon. "A lot happened tonight."

Jerking around, expression stricken, she stared at him. "What?"

"I think Stack and Vanity are...I dunno. In an arrangement."

The fear faded from her widened eyes and she repeated, "Stack and Vanity?"

"Yeah, surprised me, too," he said, though he knew that wasn't what she'd meant. His change of topic threw her off, and maybe that was a good thing. It'd give him a moment to regroup. Plus, surprising her just might make her less guarded—then he could really make some headway in the trust department. "Stack is such a player and from what I've seen, Vanity hasn't dated at all since moving here."

"You're all players." Diverted, she said, "I kept thinking you'd ask Vanity out."

"No." Even when he'd been resisting Cherry, he hadn't wanted to do anything that might hurt her. As she'd already pointed out, he knew how she felt about him—physically at least.

Knowing he could have her had kept him awake many nights.

Getting together with Vanity without Cherry knowing would have been difficult since they all hung together. It hadn't seemed worth the trouble, and beyond that, it wouldn't have been honorable.

"She's beautiful."

"That she is." But he'd already met Cherry by then, so no one else had appealed to him. He glanced her way. "So are you."

Cherry didn't respond to that, choosing instead to keep speculating on Vanity's social calendar. "It's odd that she doesn't get asked out. I think guys are intimidated by her. Nothing else makes sense."

"I hadn't even considered that." Maybe he'd clue Stack in, give him an excuse to jump the gun a little since the wedding was still a way off.

"She's nice."

Did he hear jealousy? He looked over at her. The

porch light behind them made a halo of her fair hair. "Stack's going to take her to the wedding."

Cherry relaxed enough to smile. "Do you realize we all talk about it as if it's the only wedding to ever happen? It's not Cannon and Yvette's wedding. It's *the* wedding. Like for royalty or something."

It amused him, too. "Yeah."

She leaned into him. "I assume we'll go together?"

He caught her wrist, pulled her hand over to his mouth and kissed her knuckles, then her palm. "Already looking forward to it." Knowing she wouldn't expect it, he kept hold of her hand as he told her, "Leese Phelps is in town."

He felt the flinch of fear as her fingers tightened on his. "What?"

"Found him in Rowdy's bar." Hoping his casual attitude would calm her, he remained lounged back, relaxed. "He knows I go to the rec center, but it was closed by the time he got to town. It was just happenstance that we ran into each other at the bar."

"Wait." She pulled away from him and shifted so he could better see her frown. "What were you doing at Rowdy's?"

Cute, how she looked so suspicious. If she knew how much he wanted her, how badly he'd wanted her all day, she wouldn't give it another thought. "I wasn't there looking for a hookup, so don't get riled."

Typical for women, his reassurance only riled her more.

With her so disgruntled, he sat up, too. He propped his elbows on his knees and let his hands hang between. "I finished up my workouts and training and wanted to talk to Stack before I came back here."

She chewed that over. "And Leese was there?"

"Worked over pretty good." Watching for her reaction, he told her what he knew. "Carver and the others took him drinking, drugged him, beat a few answers out of him and then dropped him unconscious at his doorstep."

Anger shadowed her expression. "He's okay?"

Denver saw no surprise, leading him to believe she expected no less from the brothers. "Mostly he's sorry. Asked me to tell you he never meant to hurt you."

In a faint voice, her thoughts already elsewhere, she whispered, "No, I'm sure he didn't." She drew in a single deep breath, as if bracing herself for the inevitable.

He wanted her to know he'd keep her safe, and to do that, she had to level with him completely. "They drugged him, Cherry. Drugged him, questioned him about *you*, beat him up and discarded him."

"Yes." She tried to hide it, but she was shaken, and somehow shamed.

So she expected no better from them? She knew their violent tendencies extended well beyond punking out a young girl? And yet she wanted him to step aside and let her handle it alone?

Like hell.

For her benefit, so she'd know Leese's remorse, Denver shared the conversation. "He said that once he realized how dangerous they could be, he wouldn't have talked if he hadn't been drugged, even with a beating. And I believe him."

He hadn't much liked Leese when he first met him. But after talking with him more, seeing his remorse, his shame, he better understood him.

Leese wasn't succeeding in MMA as much as he'd

like. He covered with more cocky confidence than actual talent and heart. Good training could change that, but not every fighter could afford it. Inviting him to the rec center might help remedy his situation.

Denver felt indebted to him for coming forward and sharing what he could about Cherry's foster brothers. He'd stepped up, and he wanted to do what he could to make amends.Denver had to respect that.

"Soon as he woke up this morning, he came to find me, to let me know."

"He should have come to me."

Denver carefully tempered the surge of anger; she didn't completely trust him yet, but he'd work on that. "Finding me was easier."

Leese had stared at him with blackened eyes and a swollen nose. *"Thing is,"* he'd said, *"if I can find you, they can find her."*

Denver wasn't going to let anything happen to her. Now he just needed to convince Cherry.

Standing, he took her hand and pulled her to her feet. After chasing him down and finally getting him, she now wanted to retreat, to cut him out. He wouldn't let her. "Come on. I'm beat and you could use another good night's sleep."

Her uncertain gaze lifted to his. "You're leaving?"

He retrieved his case, tugged her through the door, closed and locked it, then shook his head. "Tonight, I'm staying."

CHERRY SAT AT the foot of her bed, listening as Denver brushed his teeth. He'd waited for her to go first, and while she'd been in there he'd folded down her bed.

What a novel thing to have not just any guy, but *this*

guy, staying the night with her. It didn't escape her notice that Denver hadn't exactly asked, either, had instead just informed her.

He was protective, autocratic, capable, bossy, sexy, insistent and sweet, and she loved him. So, so much.

She should protest his pushiness, but tonight…she just couldn't.

She'd never brought another man to this place, much less to sleep over. Since meeting Denver, there hadn't been any other men for her.

Did he stay because he suddenly cared for her, or because he worried for her safety?

He seemed plenty into her right now, but she couldn't forget that everything had changed at lightning speed.

Not just her relationship with Denver, but…her entire life.

Shivering, she accepted that eventually Carver and his brothers would find her. They'd already hurt Leese and they wouldn't mind hurting others until they got what they wanted.

If only she knew what that was.

Despite Denver's protests, she probably should have called Carver—but would it have made a difference? Even though she'd gone along with Denver's insistence that she wait, in the end they'd get to her anyway. More than anyone else ever could, she understood the lengths Carver would go to once he'd set his mind to something. Petty, mean and vindictive; one way or another Carver always came out on top.

If Denver knew the whole truth, what would he do?

"Ready?"

The sudden intrusion of his deep voice made her jump. Embarrassed, she put a hand to her heart while turning toward him, a nervous laugh bubbling up—until she saw him. Then she went mute.

Denver stood there wearing only dark snug boxers.

He'd probably showered at the rec center, but now his hair was wet at the temples, showing he'd splashed his face. As usual, he hadn't bothered to shave. The scruffy stubble, longer hair and those amber eyes somehow made him even more handsome. With his gaze direct, he waited to see how she'd handle his aggressive intrusion into her life.

Ha! She had his attention, and one way or another she wanted to enjoy as much of him as possible before it all fell apart.

The extended visit from Miles and Brand had surprised her; they dropped by occasionally, but usually didn't hang out, not without Cannon there also. But Rissy, who had known them all much longer, took it in stride, so she assumed it was no big deal. While there, they'd regaled her with stories of Denver's ability. She'd already learned what she could about his fighting career, but the guys were always a fount of eclectic information.

Denver's style was that of a champion wrestler. Not only did he easily take opponents down—*hard*—but he had such good balance that other fighters couldn't take him down. He blocked every shot with ease and usually turned the tables, with his opponent caught in a submission.

Commentators called him unmovable like a mountain, impenetrable like a steel vault. His winning streak made him the talk of the MMA world, and a lot of people anticipated his next fight.

What she hadn't known was that he'd lose more

weight as he neared the next competition, or that his body would get leaner, more shredded, stronger and faster. She couldn't see how. He was already such a specimen, perfected in incredible ways.

Body relaxed, limbs loose, he tipped his head. "What are you thinking?"

So many things. "How breathtaking you are."

He snorted and started across the floor. Wavy brown hair skimmed his broad shoulders, a few shades lighter than the hair on his powerful chest, muscular forearms and strong calves. She especially loved the treasure trail leading from his navel into the waistband of his boxers.

While she visually devoured him, he set his folded clothes and a small travel case on a chair, put his cell phone on the nightstand and walked over to stand in front of her.

Wow. That left her eye-level with his lap. He was semierect now, and even that was impressive. Badly wanting to touch him, to stroke him through the soft cotton, she curled her fingers into the bedspread folded down at the end of her bed.

She tried to blink but didn't quite get there. "Are you hoping to distract me with sex?" It'd be a really awesome distraction, but she needed to assert herself first. She had to make him understand that she could deal with Carver. Ugly as it would be, she wanted Denver out of it.

With one finger under her chin, he got her attention northward. "I usually sleep in the nude."

If he wanted an objection, he'd be disappointed. Already warm, turbulent need expanded inside her—

typical whenever she got near Denver. "I'm okay with that."

The side of his mouth lifted. "I figured it'd be better just to strip down to my underwear." He toyed with her ponytail. "I'd love it if you did, too."

Standing, she tugged her shirt off over her head and tossed it. She reached for the loose drawstring waistband of her pajama pants and Denver caught her wrists.

"Just to sleep, girl." He eyed her taut nipples, and she saw he, too, breathed more deeply. "Tonight I only want to hold you."

That had to be a joke.

Pulling her wrists free, she ran her hands up his chest and around his neck. His hands dropped to his sides.

"I don't want to wait." Brushing her nose against his soft chest hair, she kissed his sternum, up to his shoulder, then nuzzled against his warm throat. He smelled like sunshine and warm skin and musky male. "I *can't* wait."

"Cherry." Clasping her waist, he kept his tone far too calm and insistent. "You're just getting over that bug. You need rest."

She straight-armed him. "Listen up, Denver. You don't just get to play with me."

Eyes heavy, sensual, he slid his hands down and around to her behind to draw her closer. Bending, he teased soft kisses over her temple to her ear. "You like it when I play."

Damn it, she did, but… "Not if you're only going to frustrate me."

Propping his chin to the top of her head, he hugged her. "It'll be better if we wait, I promise."

What if she waited and lost the opportunity? There was no guarantee that Carver's bizarre torment wouldn't eventually drive Denver away. She wanted to make memories with him, to soak up as much time with him as she could while the ugliness remained unconfirmed.

"Cherry." With one hand, he eased the band from her hair, then worked her curls loose with his fingers. "I have a full day tomorrow that starts early with conditioning." Those clever fingers continued on down her spine until he palmed her backside.

She rushed to say, "And I'm going into work tomorrow, too." Tonight might be their best chance to be together until the following weekend.

That is, if Carver didn't show up and nix the entire relationship.

Denver continued to tease his fingertips over her rear. The man did seem to have a fixation with her body.

He dipped lower, delved deeper, explored her. "What time do you get off?"

How could he talk while doing that? "Any minute now, if you'd just move those fingers where I need them most."

He grinned down at her. "Cherry," he chastised playfully.

She must be a masochist, because his denials only made her want him more. "Not until three."

"I'll be at the rec center then." Watching her closely, he shifted and slid one hot hand into her pants, now doing all that tantalizing touching without any material to blunt the heat of his warm, rough hand.

And then he talked some more.

"Want to come there?"

Barely biting back a groan, she said, "I'd rather come here. Right now."

He squeezed her cheek. "Gage will be there, so odds are Harper will be, too. You can hang out until I finish, then we can go to my place where there's more privacy."

She'd never been to Denver's house and the idea appealed to her. "You don't think this is private?"

He shook his head. "Fighters come and go here more than at the rec center." He leaned down, his forehead to hers. "I need at least a few hours alone with you."

"If you don't want to have sex now, then why are you doing all this?"

"Seriously, girl?" He angled his head to study her while his fingers did some especially tantalizing exploring, making her breath catch. "You think I can be this close to you and not touch you?"

He said that with a straight face as if he expected her to agree! Swatting at him, her temper frayed, she stepped out of reach. "If you aren't going to do anything about it, then you can damn well keep your hands to yourself!"

Satisfaction glittered in his mesmerizing eyes. "I'll try." Raising both hands, palms out, he offered compliance.

And damn it, she already missed his touch. "Are you sure I can't convince you—"

"We both need some rest and I'm not into quickies. Not with you."

Clearly, it was for her that he wanted to wait, no matter what excuses he gave. And that bit about visiting him at the rec center—he wanted her where he could keep an eye on her to know she was safe.

He didn't yet understand that having her there would only endanger everyone else.

But she'd pushed him enough tonight. She wouldn't beg for sex. She put her chin in the air. "Fine—but I'm agreeing under duress."

"Noted, and I promise to make it up to you later. So." Tentatively, as if he expected her to smack him again, he reached for the waistband of her sleep pants. "Mind if we lose these?"

She didn't see the point, but only shrugged.

With a half smile, he said, "Thank you." Pushing them past her hips, he let them drop in a puddle around her ankles. Holding her shoulders, he looked at her body with fixed absorption, as if this was the first time. After a deep breath that he let out slowly, he took her arm and led her to the bed.

Still peeved, Cherry crawled over to make room for him, turned her back and tugged the sheet up to her chin. He got in behind her, stretched out one long arm and killed the lamp.

Dark silence filled every inch of the room.

Never before had she thought about the quiet, but now it smothered her. Maybe because she'd let things end on a tense note. But how to fix it?

The bed dipped when Denver turned and slid an arm under her pillow, wrapped another around her waist, and drew her into the strong cradle of his big body. "Okay?"

Now that he couldn't see her, she closed her eyes to relish the moment. "Yes." Better than okay.

Heat, scented by his skin, enveloped her. After a few minutes, drowsiness set in. Maybe he was right. Maybe she did need to sleep. Too much had happened, with an ominous dread leaving her splintered. She yawned wide enough to hurt her jaws.

"Do you mind if I touch you?"

Her groan, long and dramatic, made him chuckle. She honestly didn't know how much more teasing she could take.

"Like this." Giving her time to object, he scooted her closer, fitting his strong legs to the backs of hers, tucking her so close that problems faded away.

If she could sleep like this, safe in Denver's arms, it wouldn't be too bad.

Time drifted by, but she didn't doze off.

"You're not sleeping," he murmured.

"Not yet." She curved her fingers over his forearm. "I'm keeping you awake?"

"No. I was just thinking. When did you paint your toenails?"

Surprise got her eyes opened wide. "You noticed?"

"That you changed the color?" Husky and low, he said, "I notice every damn thing about you, girl. You should know that by now."

"Oh." Well, that was nice because she noticed every single thing about him, too. "I got antsy midday and didn't have anything to do."

"Except worry?"

"And paint my toenails."

He squeezed her in a quick, gentle hug. "I wish I could have been here with you."

Somehow, she knew that talking with him like this in the quiet dark was deceptive. It felt like nothing bad could happen, like the future held only promise.

A false illusion.

"No." She turned her head enough to kiss his bulg-

ing biceps. "I don't want to interfere with your routine."
More than I already have.

"You won't." He nipped her earlobe. "I can multitask." A warm kiss behind her ear had her brain wandering to sex again, until he added, "It's going to take
some juggling, fitting everything in—and no, I'm not
talking about the size of my pipe."

She closed her mouth, but laughed.

"Brat." Another kiss, this one on the side of her
neck. "Weekends are mostly free," he continued. "But
the weekdays start early and run late."

In case he made assumptions, she offered tentatively, "I'm nine to five, so I'm happy to adapt to your
schedule."

"We'll work it out."

He fell silent after that, giving her thoughts room
to roam. "Denver?"

"Hmm?"

"Why didn't any of you ask to date Vanity?"

She felt his grin against her shoulder. "Most of us
don't do a lot of steady dating. You know that. The
other guys are like me. None of us has the time."

True. They all kept grueling schedules, at least when
prepping for a fight. Their social hookups seemed to
happen in spontaneous ways and almost always on a
weekend. "So forget dating. None of you tried to sleep
with her, either." Or had they? Maybe Denver had and
she just didn't know, and why would she? Until a short
time ago, he hadn't shown interest in her, either.

He shifted, moving one leg over hers. "She's Yvette's
best friend. She'll be maid of honor at the wedding."

When Cherry tried to turn and face him, he held
her secure. "So?"

"So she's too close for comfort if things go sour. That takes her out of bounds for casual sex."

Possibilities churned in her brain, keeping her so unsettled she knew she wouldn't be able to sleep. Toying with the soft hair on his forearm, she asked, "Did you want to go after her, though?"

"No."

Disconcerted that he said nothing more, she nudged him. "Are you sure?"

"Positive."

Not quite satisfied with his one-word replies, she decided to go to the crux of her restlessness. "Did you consider me too close for comfort, too?"

"Not really, no."

"Then why did you leave me hanging when I made it so obvious I wanted to be with you? Why did you always ignore me?"

He growled, "Don't fool yourself, girl. I could never ignore you, no matter how hard I tried." He lightly bit her shoulder, then smoothed the spot with his hot tongue. "Anytime you were around, I knew it. I *felt* it. Clear down to my bones."

"Then why make us both wait?" *Why make me so miserable?*

He held himself still; she could hear them both breathing, the tick of the clock.

The beating of her own heart.

"At first," he whispered, "I hesitated because of the closeness. You live here with Merissa, and Cannon gets all big brotherly about any of us getting ideas." Leisurely, his hand cuddled her breast. "He tried to warn me off until he realized I wanted more than one night."

That was news to her. "Cannon told you not to date

me?" If he was the reason for the long delay, Cherry just might smack him.

Denver gave a gruff laugh. "I don't think it was dating he had a problem with. When he and I *discussed* it, there was one point where Yvette thought we would come to blows and it scared her."

No way. Yvette had never told her!

"I don't take orders well, Cannon's too damn watchful over his sister—and his sister's roommate—but we settled it peaceably enough."

"You *still* didn't ask me out."

"No, I didn't."

Fed up, Cherry demanded, *"Why?"*

His long hesitation made her wish she could take the question back. Would he tell her something awful? Like she hadn't appealed to him or her personality was annoying?

"Truthfully, honey, you scared me."

She scoffed. Far as she could tell, nothing scared Denver. Even when walking into the cage to fight, massive crowds screaming and hot lights shining down on him, he looked rock steady, like it was just another day. "That's a little hard to swallow."

"Don't know why. From the day we met, you've been under my skin."

That didn't sound all that complimentary. More like an aggravation—or an itch. "What does that mean?"

"I liked you too much, and wanted you more than that. I've known plenty of chicks that just wanted to sleep with a fighter. I thought you were different, but then you flitted from guy to guy, and it made me nuts. *Too* nuts."

Now wait a minute! This time he couldn't hold her back as she half turned while sitting up. "I did not!"

With what sounded like a groan of annoyance, he moved away. Her eyes had adjusted enough that she could see the shadows of his large form as he settled onto his back and folded his arms behind his head. "Girl, you flirt with every man in sight."

Her mouth fell open. "I've been after *you* since I met you!"

"Me, and every other dude in the room." While she tried to absorb that insult, he added, his voice firm, "But that's over now."

After that accusation, he wanted to dictate to her? She couldn't see well enough to judge his expression and, by God, she wanted to see him while he spouted so much nonsense. Reaching over him—which made him groan as her breasts grazed his abdomen—she flipped on the light and then sat back on her heels.

She'd totally displaced the sheet and, oh wow, Denver could so easily throw her off with his big gorgeous body. Never had her bed looked better than with him stretched out on it.

"You going to give me hell or strip me with those pretty eyes?"

"Both," she snapped right back. He'd pushed his way into her private room, so he could damn well deal with her physical fascination. "Understand, Denver. Talk is one thing. Maybe I joke around a little—"

"You *flirt*, Cherry. A lot."

Her brows came together. Stubborn, annoying man. "And you don't? Every female fan you meet is the recipient of your flirting. But do I complain?"

"That's business," he said as if it didn't matter.

"Ha! Don't tell me you never slept with a groupie, because I've heard the stories."

He wisely kept silent.

"But I haven't been with anyone else, heck, I haven't even *kissed* anyone else, since meeting you!"

Going still, he asked, "No?"

"No." Her hand went to his abs, drawn extra taut with the way he reclined, and her fingers idly dipped over each and every solid ridge of muscle. She managed to stop short of going after the erection now straining his boxers, but it wasn't easy.

Cutting a glare to his face, she asked, "Insulting me makes you hot?"

"Never insulted you. I just spoke the truth." He caught her wrist and carried her hand up to his chest. "But angry girls near my jewels make me nervous, so how about we get this over with?"

She snatched her hand away and crossed her arms tight beneath her breasts. "You hurt me, Denver."

"I would never."

"You already have! Too many times for me to count." Maybe it was time for a little truth. She made herself look at him. "If it had been any man other than you, I'd have given up long ago."

"I'm glad you didn't."

Fidgeting under his direct stare, she admitted, "I do like to talk, I can't change that."

"There's nothing wrong with talking."

"Carver and his brothers always made it impossible. I couldn't smile at anyone, or even say hello, so you know I couldn't flirt. I guess… I maybe sometimes go overboard. But only because I *can* now."

"That makes sense," he agreed. "They never should have been allowed to stifle you like that."

Relieved that he understood, she touched him again. "If I seemed too familiar with the other guys, it was because you'd rejected me and I didn't want you to know how bad I felt. I have my pride, too, you know."

A turbulent mix of emotions sharpened the color of his hunter's gaze. "So because I didn't jump fast enough, you wanted to make me jealous?"

"No!" Indignation swelled until she almost vibrated with it. "You always think the worst of me."

That made his eyes darken, narrow. "Cherry—"

"I never expected you to jump. But you were so disinterested it humiliated me. You gave me no reason to think you'd even care who I talked to." She steadied herself with a deep breath. "But you can believe me, never, not once, have I wanted anyone else since meeting you. They know that."

"They?"

"Stack, Miles, Brand…any guy I come into contact with."

"Leese didn't know it."

"Leese was just…a few dances, some laughs." It scared her, sharing so much of herself while Denver remained remote. But it was important for him to know. He wanted honesty, and so she'd give him what she could. "Cover."

Rubbing the bridge of his nose as if pained, he said, "I don't know what that means, honey."

"It means I used the poor guy because I didn't want anyone, including you, to know that I wanted to go home and cry."

They stared at each other, both breathing hard.

Denver's expression faded from annoyance to something else, something more acute than mere apology even though he whispered, "I'm sorry."

"You should be."

Coming up on one elbow, he fixed his attention on her breasts. "Damn, you're hot when you're pissed."

She thought her head might explode.

"Or maybe it's knowing you were never really into anyone else that's making me so horny." And with that, he snagged her waist and pulled her down to sprawl over him.

"Wha—"

His mouth met hers, warm and firm. She reared back, "You—"

"Want you." He took her mouth again, moving until her lips opened and his wicked tongue could lick in, then do even more wicked things that made her unable to think straight.

The leap from anger to lust left her heartbeat galloping. She didn't know if she should give in or toss him out.

"I'm sorry, baby." His hands went to her backside and rocked her against his powerful erection. "So damned sorry."

"Mmmm…" Okay, so lust won out. Cherry sank against him, knotted her hands in his hair and held on.

CHAPTER TWELVE

As SOON AS she stopped resisting, Denver cupped one hand around her head, the other over her ass, and turned her under him, fitting his body to hers but keeping most of his weight off her. He kissed her again, deeper and hotter, wanting to consume her.

He'd hurt her. Damn, that tore him up.

But more devastating than that was her insistence that she'd never really been into any of the other guys... he couldn't bend his brain around it. He had so much resentment built around *nothing*.

Knowing she'd been as obsessed as him from the day they met started a slow burn that quickly grew hotter until all he could think about was getting inside her.

He'd wasted so much time steering clear of her, protecting himself because he thought she'd be like his stepmother... *No.* He didn't want Pamela intruding into his thoughts. Not now, not with Cherry kissing him like she needed him more than her next breath.

The reality of how he'd hurt her made him determined to show her how much she mattered to him.

It also filled him with a savage need to keep her safe. She was his, period. He would never hurt her again—and he damn sure wouldn't let anyone else hurt her, either.

All the reasons he'd given her for waiting—her illness, their early days—were still there. They just didn't matter enough for him to resist her.

Leaving her mouth, he kissed her slim throat and her narrow shoulder on a path to her lush breasts. God love the girl, she had a great rack, full and firm with nipples already drawn tight.

When he played a thumb over one sensitive tip, she arched up, encouraging him. He put an arm behind her to keep her like that, offered up to him. "I should let you sleep," he growled before closing his teeth around that small, taut tip.

Her gasping sound of pleasure vibrated in the air between them, sweet and anxious. Gently, Denver tugged.

Catching fistfuls of his hair, Cherry kept him close and bent one knee up alongside his hip. The adjustment left his boner nestled against her hot sex with only their underwear as barriers.

His heart thundered against his ribs. He grew even harder, hurting with this sudden, crushing need to consume her.

Carefully, he nipped at her other nipple, then tugged on it, too, until she cried out. *"Denver."*

He sucked her deep, stroking with his tongue and rocking against her while using care to untangle her fingers, one by one, from his hair.

To keep her from rushing him, he pressed her hands up alongside her head. "Patience."

Lips parted, gaze smoky, she nodded. "I'll try."

Grateful that she'd turned on the light, he rose up the length of his arms to see her, to soak up the sight of her in nothing more than itty-bitty panties, her breasts flushed and her hair tangled.

So much temptation. He wanted to be sliding deep right now. He wanted to kiss every inch of her.

And oddly enough, he wanted to just hold her.

She shifted her feet for leverage, then writhed against him. "I need you, Denver."

Her enthusiasm scorched him. "So hot." *And all his.* "Let me grab a rubber." He was already so far gone that if he didn't take care of it now, he might not get around to it. That would leave them open to one consequence neither of them needed.

Giving him a heated look, she whispered, "Hurry."

Lust darkened her face, left her brown eyes smoky. Her nipples were tight points, her belly hollowed out, and she couldn't keep still, shifting in ways that looked sexy as hell. "You really are in a bad way, aren't you, girl."

"I'm in bed with you, Denver." Stark emotion sounded in every word. "You always make me this way."

Sitting up, he snagged his jeans off the chair and fished in a pocket for his wallet to retrieve his lone condom. As he fumbled with that—literally fumbled, with shaking hands and heavy breathing—Cherry came up behind him, moving against him. He felt her nipples on his back, then she reached beyond him and dropped her panties to the floor.

Damn.

Her hot little tongue came out to lick his ear. "Soon," she whispered, "we're going to have time enough for me to explore every inch of your big body."

He closed his eyes and fought for control, but he knew it'd be a very close thing. "Damn right." He could barely keep himself in check. "But tonight isn't it."

Naked, the condom in place, he turned and kissed her. Together they dropped back to the mattress, his hands on her everywhere, her hands just as busy.

He needed her ready. *Now.*

With openmouthed kisses, he made his way down her throat to her breasts where he spent a few minutes suckling her again. He loved the ragged catch in her breathing, her lusty sighs and soft, high gasps.

Wanting to eat her up, he took a gentle love bite of her midriff, her flat belly, the tender inside of her thigh.

"Denver."

"Shhh." He opened her, looked at her, breathed her in—and tasted her. Her hips rose against the stroke of his tongue, letting him know how much she liked that. No problem, because he loved it. The taste of her, the feel of her sleek, swollen flesh, her scent and the provoking sounds she made deep in her throat.

He ate her gently, forcing himself to be patient until he knew she was close. He levered up to see her, pleased that she had her head back, her bottom lip caught in her teeth, her hands held tight in the sheets.

Needing her, now, he pressed two fingers deep, then groaned. "You're wet, girl. But so tight." Moving over her, he opened her legs and positioned his straining boner against her. He was met by silky wetness and heat and it nearly destroyed his determination. "I'm going to work in slow and easy. Just relax for me."

Instead she hooked one leg around his hips while running her hands over his chest and shoulders. "Now, Denver."

As he rocked in she winced, causing him to slow even more. "Relax," he told her again.

Her eyes opened, big and dark and dazed with need. She looked at him with love, leveling him.

"Cherry…"

"I need you. All of you." She braced herself, and whispered, *"Now."*

"Fuck." He tried to hold off, tried to temper the raw explosion of emotions, but she broke him. Gathering her closer, holding her tight, he gave one hard thrust that sank him deep.

On a cry, her sharp little teeth closed on his shoulder and her sex squeezed him even tighter. The bite turned into a hot, wet kiss; the cry into a hungry purr.

She squirmed as she adjusted to him, each small movement urging him on.

The things she made him feel, disturbing in their intensity, encouraged him to ride her hard while also cherishing her.

He settled for a deep but steady rhythm and she kept pace, her pleasure building, her low cries growing sharper, higher. He kissed her even as he felt her tightening, her fingertips digging into his back, her body lifting—she freed her mouth as she came, keening sharply, and that turned him on, too, enough that he immediately joined her.

Little by little the blinding pleasure receded, taking with it all his tension. He rested over her on his forearms, careful not to give her all his weight.

Softly, sweetly, Cherry kissed his shoulder.

"Now," she whispered, "wasn't that better than sleeping?"

His laugh turned into a groan as he moved to the side of her.

Laying his hand on her thigh, he tried to come to

grips with his feelings for her. He had a lot on his plate, including the big fight coming up. He needed to refocus on that, and he would. But he'd also make time for this, for being with her, being there for her, enjoying the way she ramped up his lust only to numb him with mind-blowing pleasure.

Turning into him, Cherry glided her hand over his biceps and let out a satisfied breath. "I hope Merissa didn't hear us."

Oh shit. His breath stalled, his eyes widening.

He'd totally forgotten that they weren't alone. Looking at the ceiling, he wondered how soundproof the house might be.

He turned his head to look at Cherry, and crushing emotion struck him again. Damn, she was so beautiful, and right now she looked like a satisfied, well-laid woman.

Curiosity got the better of him and he asked, "Have you ever heard Merissa having sex?"

Eyes closed, Cherry smiled in that womanly, secretive way. "No. Not ever. Rissy doesn't really bring guys here." Her lashes lifted. "I think she's in love with Armie."

"Yeah."

Her brows lifted. "You knew?"

"I think about everyone does except him."

She let that go and instead concentrated on his torso, her fingers drifting through his chest hair, following that down to his abs. "You're going to destroy that guy when you fight."

"You think so?" He knew he would, but he wondered at Cherry's level of understanding of the sport.

Giving him an impish smile and wrinkling her nose,

she said, "He waxes everything. His chest, his legs. Even his underarms."

Denver grinned. "And that somehow means I can beat him?"

"Yes. While you're working out, staying so fit and strong, he's off grooming. He's a wuss. You'll annihilate him."

"You're nuts." He dipped his head to kiss her nose. "Guys get rid of the hair so it doesn't snag or pull when they're grappling."

"You don't." Crawling up and over him, she shifted her ministrations to his overlong hair, loosely tangling her small hands in it. "God, you are such a hunk."

Settling both hands over her ass, he smiled. "It was a really long day away from you, Cherry girl."

Her expression changed, going serious, even grim. "Denver." She moved to the side of him to sit—leaving the sheet rumpled beneath her. "I have to call him."

They both knew who she meant. "Yeah." He'd been thinking about it, and he wanted it behind them. "I know it's bothering you. Best to get it out of the way."

Hopeful, she asked, "You understand?"

He nodded. "As long as you understand that I won't let him hurt you."

Her smile looked so sad it bothered him. "It's not your responsibility—"

"Hush with that, okay? If you want to be with me, then you need to know who I am. And, girl, I'm not a guy who'd let you be scared or worried. Not ever."

She wanted to argue the point, he could tell, the same way he knew she was holding back when she said, "I'll call him tomorrow."

"I want to be there with you when you do." If the

bastard threatened her in any way, he wanted to know about it. And damn it, he couldn't trust Cherry to tell him. "Okay?"

Rather than agree, she evaded. "The longer I wait, the more annoyed he's going to be."

"Am I supposed to give a shit if he's annoyed?"

"You should." She chewed her bottom lip in indecision, but then must have come to a conclusion. "He's dangerous, Denver."

"So am I."

As if to pacify him, she touched his arm. "I know, but not in the same way."

For whatever reason, Carver and his brothers had a stranglehold on her. He'd have to tread lightly, because no way would he hurt her—not ever again.

Stomping down his irritation, he removed her hand. "Give me a second, okay?" He left the bed and went into her small bathroom to get rid of the condom, giving himself a moment to get his thoughts together.

When he returned, he found Cherry sitting there exactly as he'd left her, unconcerned with her nudity.

It was a wonder he could think at all, seeing her like this, knowing she was his for the taking.

He got into bed with her, sitting with his back against the headboard. "Let's call him now."

Her face went blank. "Now?"

"Yeah." He had a feeling if he didn't press the issue right now, while he was with her, she'd take care of it as soon as he was gone.

"You said you understood."

"I do. Now you need to understand that I want to share problems. And he's a problem."

Her eyes narrowed. "Share problems?"

Why did that bother her so much? She professed to care about him. She'd chased him 'til she got him. Now she could deal with the reality of it.

Feeling magnanimous, he explained, "That's the way relationships work."

"Oh, really?" She rose to her knees. "So you'll discuss with me how what's his name—" Snapping her fingers, she said, "You know."

"Who?"

"The guy you're fighting next."

"Packer?" What the fuck?

"Right. Packer. Are we going to work out *together* how to keep him from fighting dirty?"

Denver scratched the top of his head, unsure where she was going with this. "I don't know what—"

She almost pounced on him. "The guys told me he's a dirty fighter. That he keeps his open hand out so he can poke his opponents in the eyes."

Snorting, Denver explained patiently, "It's happened a few times. Doesn't mean he—"

"Yes, it does!" She leaned into him, all ready to make a point of some sort. "Miles said Packer can't win against you unless he cheats. He said the last three guys who fought him ended up hurt. Brand told me that the ref gives a warning, then maybe takes away a measly point, but—"

Denver laughed, he couldn't help it. She looked damned cute in her umbrage.

Apparently humor was the wrong way to go. His laugh set her off, but he tumbled her before anger could drive her from the bed. Wrestling with her was fun, especially since she didn't actually try to hurt him.

He watched her boobs as she struggled against him, kneed her legs open to settle over her, then smiled.

"Get off," she insisted.

Keeping her pinned down, drawn to the mulish set of her mouth, he kissed her.

She shoved against him. "No!"

"Yes." He kissed her again, then kept on kissing her until she went soft beneath him. "You always taste so damn good," he murmured as he worked his way along her jaw, her throat, her shoulder. "You have the sweetest, softest skin." He released her wrists so he could cup her breasts. "All over."

She slid her fingers across his shoulders. "You're like hard, warm steel."

"My shoulders?" he teased.

"Mmm," she teased right back. "And other places."

It amazed him how quickly Cherry could lose her pique and get interested, sexually, again. Amazed and pleased him. A lot.

Gathering her close, Denver sat up with her on his lap. "Problems."

Groaning, she went limp in his arms in a dramatic fall.

He laughed, cuddling her closer to give her a smacking kiss on her mouth. "First, you told me no and I ignored it."

"Yes, you did."

"We were tussling," he explained. "I need you to know that if you're ever serious, I wouldn't—"

"Denver." She teasingly bit his bottom lip. "I already know you would never cross the line. You respect women too much for that."

Damn. It humbled him, her faith and her understanding. "True. Thank you for knowing it." But she needed to know the full truth. "With you, it's more than that. I care about you."

Her eyes warmed, and her smile went sweet and silly. In a whisper, she said, "I care a lot about you, too."

Did she love him? No, he didn't want to ask. They had too much to deal with already. "Now, second." Boasting only a little, he explained, "Packer isn't going to get a chance to poke me in the eye."

"But Miles said—"

He'd share his ire with Miles later. "I've watched Packer's fights, I know how he thinks and how he moves, I have a plan, and yes, I'll take him apart— without an eye poke. So don't worry about it. But," he said over her protest, "if I do have a problem, I'll discuss it with you. I promise."

She clearly hadn't expected that. "Even with fighting?"

"Sure. I don't expect you to totally grasp all the nuances of the sport, but it's always nice to talk things out anyway."

Looking absurdly pleased, she said, "I could be a sounding board."

"You're too sexy to ever be called that," he growled against her neck. "But I enjoy talking with you. You're a good listener."

"I'm also smart."

"Yes, you are.And that brings us back to Carver."

Not liking the way he'd circled that around, she frowned. "I don't want you in the middle of this."

Calm, he reminded himself. Stay calm. "What does that mean, exactly?"

"Carver might...shoot off his mouth. Make threats. Say...ugly, idiot things."

"Things he'll mean."

Her frown didn't ease. "Please don't let him provoke you."

"I like to think I have more control than that."

Her huff blasted him. "You're going to insist on listening in?"

"Not insist, no." Though he wouldn't mind laying on the guilt, not if it got him what he wanted. "But if you trust me, why can't I listen? Especially when you know it'll make me feel better."

After a lengthy, strained silence, he decided no answer was her answer. He picked up his cell. "Want me to do the honors?"

Looking more troubled than a woman ever should, she shook her head and held out a hand. He gave her the phone.

"Put it on speaker," he told her.

"Fine."

He knew her disgruntlement came from fear—for herself, and for him. Hoping to soften her temper, he said, "Thank you."

She sat there just looking at the phone until Denver finally asked, "Do you know the number?"

"No."

For some reason that made him feel better. Maybe because it meant Carver had truly been removed from her life.

He reached for his wallet and withdrew the slip of paper. "I wrote it down at the hotel when he left the message."

She took it from him, smoothed it out over her thigh.

"Will you just listen? Not interrupt, not speak, not... let Carver know you're here?"

It was the oddest thing ever, having a woman worry for him. All his life he'd been bigger than most, strong, confident. People sometimes came to him with their concerns, but he couldn't recall anyone fretting for him since his mother's death. "If that's what you want, then I'll be so quiet he'll never know I'm here."

Extreme relief stole the tension from her spine. "It is."

"Then I'll be silent." *For now.* "But Cherry, if he shows up here, if he even thinks about touching you—"

"Let's hope he doesn't." Before Denver could expound on dire threats, she touched in the numbers.

Her face stark with anxiety, she held the phone in both hands and waited for Carver to answer.

Hoping to soothe her, Denver tucked her hair back, then stroked his hand along her narrow back. Another novel experience, having a naked woman on his lap, making a call to a deranged punk while he promised to stay out of it.

On the fourth ring, Carver said, "Yeah?"

For the longest time, Cherry didn't speak.

Denver watched her, waiting, wanting to understand the awful hold Carver had her.

"It's me," she said at last.

A static charge came through the silence, building in intensity until Carver sneered, "Well, well, Cherry darlin'." Thick with malice, his laugh taunted her. "'Bout fucking time."

Cherry said nothing to that.

"What took you so long? Your boyfriend occupying your time?"

She didn't look at Denver when she whispered, "No." She inhaled, straightened her shoulders. "I don't want to talk to you, Carver. Whatever it is—"

"Did loverboy tell you Pops died?"

"Yes. You have my condolences."

Mocking, he asked, "But you aren't sorry to see him go?"

Before his eyes, Denver saw her getting her sass back. He wanted to hug her, applaud her and somehow emotionally protect her.

"You know I'm not."

"You little bitch," Carver jeered. "He took you in, he fed you, he—"

"The state fed me." She narrowed her eyes. "Now what do you want?"

Denver smiled at the bite in her tone, encouraging her and doing his utmost to keep his presence unknown. It wasn't easy. He wanted to spare her—but he also wanted her to understand that he'd respect her wishes. Always.

"You can start with a fucking apology for not calling me back sooner!"

"Hold your breath while you wait for that."

He laughed. "Getting ballsy, huh? Guess I'll have to see what I can do about that."

Cherry's posture showed both anxiety and anger, but her tone remained credibly strong. "I'm hanging up now."

"If you do, I will make you so fucking sorry."

No mistaking that threat, and Denver shifted, his muscles automatically bunching in preparation for violence.

Touching his forearm, Cherry silently willed him

people around. But she said you'd know. She said to get you back here."

This time her laugh reeked of sarcasm. "That's not happening."

"Oh, it's happening, Cherry darlin'. Resign yourself."

She shook her head in denial. "No."

"One way or another," Carver warned.

"Carver—"

"Think of it as a homecoming."

"That place was never my home!"

The panicked pitch to her words had Denver sitting up more, getting closer to help her remember that she wasn't alone.

Carver snickered. "What're you so afraid of, Cherry darlin'?" He spoke in a malicious, singsong voice. "You know you'd enjoy playing in the woods again, this time without Janet around to ruin the fun."

She dropped the phone to the bed and leaned away from it. "Don't you *dare*—"

Tone hard again, he said, "You know I dare a lot, don't you, little sister?"

Furious, she yelled, "Stop calling me that!"

Denver didn't like the way things had suddenly turned, with Cherry losing her control. Ignoring the cell phone, he reached for her, but she dodged him.

Breathing hard, she told Carver, "I am *not* your sister."

A beat of silence built the tension, then Carver whispered, "Nice of you to remind me."

That made her blanch—and Denver understood why. Despite her resistance, he drew her closer, reminding her that he wouldn't let anyone touch her, definitely not Carver.

Relenting, she leaned into him as she said to Carver, "You disgust me."

"Stop being such a spoiled bitch. If you get your ass back home where you belong, I promise to play real nice."

"Not in a million years."

"It's late. Sleep on it and I know you'll come to the right decision. I'll expect a call tomorrow. No longer than that." He paused. "Oh, and Cherry darlin'? Dream of me." The call died.

She sat there, still staring at the phone.

After moving the cell to the nightstand, Denver rubbed her nape. "Hey."

Very slowly, Cherry looked up at him. She drew in a slow breath, blew it out and tried to relax her shoulders. "I'm sorry you had to hear that."

"I wanted to be here, remember?" He pressed a warm kiss to her forehead. "You want to explain any of that?"

Wary, she shook her head. "I wish I could. But I have no idea what Janet meant. I was never involved in their business. Never."

"He said she ruined the fun."

Uncomfortable with the reminder, Cherry waved it off. "She sometimes defended me against the others."

"But not enough?"

She looked away. "Janet was sometimes…kinder— but she considered me an outsider, same as they did." Her dark eyes met his. "I have no idea how I could help them find anything."

"Do you think the same people who murdered your

parents could also be responsible for killing Carver's dad and putting Janet in the hospital?"

"I don't know." Sliding her gaze away from his, she toyed with the edge of the sheet. "It seems possible."

There was that lack of trust again. What did she think he would do after he found out the whole truth?

Or was she more worried about what Carver would do if she told anyone?

He should insist on more answers, but she looked to be at her limit. "It's late. How about we get some sleep and tomorrow we can talk about it more. Maybe something will come to you."

The reprieve had her melting against him in soft, sweet relief. "That sounds good." She yawned theatrically. "I really am beat now."

She really was elusive, but he let it go. He wanted to know it all, everything that concerned her, now and in the past. One way or another he'd uncover all her secrets—whether she wanted him to or not.

Denver didn't miss the irony of that, since, despite his assurances, he had no plans to unload his burdens on her. His family issues were private, unsettling, and as far as he was concerned, not up for discussion.

"Come here." He stretched back out in the bed with Cherry tucked safely against his side, then reached out an arm to turn out the light. They both needed a good night's sleep.

After a quick kiss, she let out a sigh, shifted to get more comfortable, and fell silent. Despite all the unanswered questions and vague threats, it was nice holding her like this, ending his day with her gentle scent in the air, her warm body curled to his.

Unfortunately, an hour later, Denver's thoughts continued to churn. He'd listened to Cherry fade into sleep and now enjoyed the feel of her gentle breath over his chest, the soft sounds she made in slumber.

Soft...until she seemed to hold her breath.

Attuned to her, he went still and alert. The arm she had around his abdomen flinched.

Raising his head, seeing her through the shadows, Denver whispered, "Cherry?"

She made another small sound—this one of distress.

Turning to face her, he clasped her shoulder. "Cherry."

Her eyes popped open and she stared up at him, breathing shakily. "Denver?"

Who else? "Yeah. You okay?"

She nodded, swallowed hard. "Yes."

"Bad dream?"

Even in the darkness, he saw the confusion in her eyes before she claimed, "I was dreaming...of you."

CHAPTER THIRTEEN

CHERRY WRAPPED HER arms around Denver's neck and hugged him tight to calm her trembling. Though now wide awake, emotionally she remained trapped in that damn strange dream—that had taken such a treacherous turn. She could still feel the cold, rocky ground cutting into her knees, smell the thick, dew-wet vegetation of the woods, hear the rustling of leaves high in the trees—and the drone of insects.

Over and over, the laughter of a cruel audience seemed to echo in her head.

She lifted a shoulder against her face to wipe her eyes and realized she wasn't sweaty from the hot summer day. No grime clogged her pores. Her hair felt soft and clean.

It had been so real—*because she'd once lived it.*

Except for the ending.

"Tell me," Denver said quietly.

No. Her heart raced as she remembered her cowardice, her pathetic struggles and useless tears.

The laughter over her spineless fear. The clicking of the bugs that drew nearer, the vision of multiple legs and antennae and sometimes even eyes.

And then the sound of a gunshot fractured the night.

In reality, she hadn't been able to move.

But in her dream, she'd turned to flee—and run headlong into Denver. His arms had closed around her and everything else had faded away.

Denver ran a hand up and down her back. "Tell me what you really dreamed about."

Danger and fear with Denver somehow mixed up in the middle of it. In the dream, he'd wanted her.

She wanted him now.

Kissing his shoulder, she tasted his sleek, hot skin over firm muscle. That was so nice that she nibbled her way up to his throat, raspy with beard shadow, then to his strong jaw. "I need you."

He pried her arms loose and rose over her. "Cherry—"

"It was just a nightmare, but in it you showed up."

"And saved you?"

No. She wouldn't let him play macho protector. *She would protect herself.* What she needed most from him he could damn well give her right now.

Sliding a leg up and over his hip, she insisted, "You're here, in my bed." Dragging her fingernails lightly over his chest, testing his muscles, she insisted, "Kiss me. Please."

The merest hesitation had her holding her breath, then he bent his head and brushed his mouth over hers with such tenderness, her heart wanted to break.

"Not like that," she begged, pulling him back, licking over his bottom lip before nipping him with her teeth. "Kiss me like you want me."

Husky, concerned, he whispered, "I always want you, girl."

So then why did he sound so somber? She lifted

against him, and sure enough, he had an erection. To convince him, she said, "I have condoms in my night-stand."

That got her a tight squeeze, and a tighter, "Why?"

Silly Denver. It would take her a while to get used to the idea of him being jealous.

Lifting her legs around him, she locked her ankles at the small of his back. "In case I ever talked you into coming over." Stroking her hands down his broad back to his muscled tush, she squeezed him. "And I have—so give it up."

His resistance wavered, she felt it in the way he breathed, how he settled more fully atop her.

Taking advantage of that, Cherry trailed her finger-tips up his back to his wide shoulders. "You are such a stud. Please Denver, stop denying me."

Almost as a nonargument, he murmured, "You need sleep."

Sleep dredged up ugly memories that were better left buried. "I need *you*." She tangled her fingers in the silky hair at his nape and pressed her pelvis up against him, then hummed with satisfaction. "Feels like you need me, as well."

He turned so that she rested atop him. "I don't know," he teased. "Maybe you should convince me."

"Oh, I love a challenge." Almost as much as she loved him and the understanding way he allowed her the diversion without asking too many questions.

Staying perched on Denver's hard abdomen, she reached for the nightstand drawer and withdrew the box of rubbers. After she opened one with her teeth, she smiled at him. "Consider it done."

THE SLAPPING OF his running shoes on dew-wet pavement lulled Denver, but then he was working on less than three hours' sleep. He hadn't planned to do that. A good night's rest was as important as the proper diet to his regimen. But when Cherry set her mind to seducing him... Yeah, zero resistance.

He'd wanted her far too long to say no when she insisted yes.

When he'd left at 5:00 a.m., she'd been dead out with a few more hours to sleep. Other than a soft kiss to her forehead and a long perusal of her naked body nestled on the bed, he hadn't disturbed her.

The note he'd put on her dresser would suffice as his morning goodbye. Already he missed her, which was absurd. Usually when he jogged he got in a zone where the rest of the world ceased to exist.

Not this time.

Yawning wouldn't cut it, so he concentrated on the rhythm of his jog and tried to ignore his exhaustion. He needed to get the cardio in before an early meeting with a client, then conditioning at the rec center, then sparring with Cannon and lastly a class with high school boys.

The damp morning air smelled like rain as he breathed deeply, loping past houses and toward the park. He was halfway through his run when Cannon joined him. Judging by the sweat, Cannon had been at it almost as long as Denver.

When he came alongside him, Denver said, "Hey."

"Morning." Cannon adjusted his stride, picking up the pace to match Denver. "Need you to come by the rec center a little earlier today."

Damn. "What time?" Maybe he could change the meeting with his client.

Cannon dropped his head forward with a laugh. "You don't want to know why?"

"Figured something came up." Cannon had been so good to all of them, no one asked "why" when he made a request—whatever the request might be. Denver loved him like a brother, valued him as a friend, and like most in the town, considered him a local hero.

"Yeah." Cannon rubbed a shoulder over his face to remove a bead of sweat. "Sponsors."

"Sponsors?"

"New clothing company." They jogged around an elderly couple making their way to a bench. "Athletic wear."

Talking and jogging was never easy, but especially not without sleep. "What's that got to do with me?"

"It's you they want."

Sponsors weren't new to him; every fighter established in the sport had at least one sponsorship, if not many. "So why not call me?"

"Because they want me, too. And Stack."

Denver slowed. "I'm not following."

Grinning, Cannon said, "They want to sponsor the rec center and any fighters there. You and me specifically since we're already with the SBC, but on a lesser scale they also want to help support the place, and they want the guys wearing their shirts. Said they'd donate some youth shirts, too."

Thinking of the ragtag kids that came to the rec center, Denver smiled. Most of them got excited over a piece of candy. "The boys will love it, especially if their shirts match ours."

"Yeah. I thought it sounded like a sweet deal, particularly with the influx of cash they're donating. We'll be able to upgrade some old equipment and add in some new. My manager jumped the gun and worked out the details, but I told him I'd have to clear it with you and the others first." He glanced at Denver with a conspiratorial smirk. "With all the shirt designs similar, Armie is going to see it as a uniform."

Picturing it, Denver laughed. "Yeah, probably. Maybe he can chop off the sleeves or something."

"Maybe." They rounded a bend and by tacit agreement, slowed to a walk. As he opened his water bottle, Cannon asked, "What's happening with Cherry? Anything?"

Amazing sex around the clock. He shook his head, not about to share details on that. "She called that douche foster brother of hers." And then had bad dreams that she'd combatted by wringing him out with pleasure.

Lifting his shirt to wipe sweat off his face, Cannon asked, "How'd that go?"

"I'd like to kill him, that's how."

While they walked, Denver told Cannon everything he'd heard while listening in on the call.

"So what do they want her to find?"

Shaking his head, he admitted, "Cherry says she has no idea."

"You don't buy it?"

Thinking of the day ahead, he said, "She's holding back, but I don't know what or how much." Not her body. Not her affection for him. But…something. "I'll get it cleared up with her later. Last night, she was just too stressed to talk about it." And she didn't trust him with the truth.

"There's a cure for that, you know."

"Yup." He grinned. "She was still asleep when I left."

"Your place or hers?"

"Hers."

Cannon went quiet, which made Denver tense.

As he'd just told Cherry, Cannon made it clear how he felt about any of the guys going for a casual hookup with his sister's roommate. But Cherry was more than that to him. More than a mere hookup. More than anything casual.

How much more, he didn't know yet. They hadn't really had time to figure it out.

But Denver knew what he wanted involved far more than a quick lay. Hell, he'd already had a sexual marathon with her, and it only whet his appetite.

He planned to spend every night with Cherry, so it'd be best for him to work this out with Cannon right now. "If you're still against me staying the night—"

"No, I'm not." Two women strolled past, blatantly eying them. Not that long ago, they'd both have appreciated the female attention.

Not so much now.

Cannon pretended not to see them and Denver just nodded.

After they were out of earshot, Cannon continued. "If it was Yvette, I'd have found a way to stay over, too. Actually, I'm relieved my sister and Cherry aren't alone at the house."

"I'm glad you get it, because Cherry doesn't."

"She doesn't want you there?"

"She does." For *sex*. And just when did he start complaining about that? "Thing is, she's *worried* about me. Like she thinks Carver might hurt me or something."

Cannon's commiserating grin came slowly. "Ouch."

"Yeah." Kids kicked a ball in their direction. Denver loped a few steps past Cannon, caught it, and tossed it back to the boys. "The thing is, she expects me to lose my cool."

"Sorry, but it happens." His thoughts traveling back to a bad memory, Cannon murmured, "When that fucker tried to grab Yvette…"

Denver stayed quiet, knowing it was still tough for Cannon to think about everything his fiancée had gone through. Yvette was awfully sweet, mostly quiet and very contained. She hadn't had an easy time of it, but with Cannon she was a very happy lady.

"I like to think of myself as controlled, too," Cannon said. "But that day I totally lost it."

Unsure what to say, Denver kept quiet. Under the same circumstances…well, he just didn't know. So maybe Cherry had reason to fret after all.

They'd just about circled around to where Cannon had started before he spoke again. "What are you going to do?"

A shrug didn't really convey the frustration smothering him. "Try to get her to open up. Level with me." *Love me.*

No, screw that thought. He wanted her to stop keeping secrets from him more than anything else. Before he'd think about getting too emotionally involved, he had to be able to trust her.

Almost as if Cannon had read his thoughts, he asked, "And until then?"

"I'll watch over her, keep her safe." As any good man would do. But he'd also keep trying to figure her out.

"What if she gives you reason to think her old foster brothers are a serious problem?"

"I won't let them be a problem, not for her." Never again. He had a feeling they'd already caused Cherry enough grief to last a lifetime.

As he followed Cannon to his car, Denver checked his watch. Talking about Cherry made him want to see her. He could probably squeeze in a quick visit, but for reasons he didn't want to examine too closely, he decided against it.

"Need a ride?"

Denver shook his head. "I'll finish up my jog, but thanks."

Cannon nodded. "You'll let me know if there's anything I can do to help with Cherry, right? You'll keep all of us updated?"

"Count on it." Denver knew the value of help from a well-trained, disciplined, capable fighter—even if Cherry didn't.

AFTER SHOWERING AND fixing her hair and makeup, Cherry dressed in a long, summery, floral skirt and pink tank top with sandals. To finish off the look, she slipped in hoop earrings and headed for the kitchen upstairs. She had her own small kitchenette in her living area, but overall she and Merissa shared the storage space in the main kitchen.

Merissa was just rinsing out her coffee cup, but the second she spotted Cherry, she abandoned the task to rush her. "Oh my God, you hussy!"

Freezing in her tracks, Cherry tried to look innocent. "What do you mean?"

"You molested that lucky man through half the night." Merissa beamed at her. "Woke me up twice and I am *soooo* jealous."

In wholehearted support, she offered Cherry a high-five.

Given that Merissa stood just shy of six feet, and Cherry was several inches shorter, she had to stand on tiptoe to smack her palm.

"You really heard us?"

"My brother probably heard you—and he's on the other side of town!" Not appearing bothered by the inconvenience, Merissa pulled her into a tight hug. "I'm so happy for you." Shoving Cherry back the length of her arms, Merissa gushed, "So spill the beans. Denver is a certified hunk, yes? I mean, not just what he's packing, but how he's dishing it out. Tell me everything so I can live vicariously."

Dodging her, Cherry went to the coffeepot and poured some liquid energy. Last night...well, she hadn't gotten much sleep, but she sure wouldn't complain. Poor Denver, though, had crawled out of bed before sunup. "I feel guilty."

"For waking me?" A chair scraped across the floor and Merissa said, "I have five minutes. Tell me everything."

"Not for waking you, no." Cherry turned to see Merissa settled in her seat, her elbows on the table, her chin in her hands, her attention rapt. "Though I *am* sorry about that."

"Don't be." Using her foot under the table, she pushed out another chair. "Sit. Spill." Bobbing her eyebrows, she added, "Tell me all the nasty things you have to feel guilty about."

Laughing, Cherry added sugar and creamer to her coffee, then took the offered seat. "I knew Denver had to get up superearly this morning and I still… Well…"

Eyes going round, Merissa supplied, "Gave him superhot sex?"

The sigh came out softly. "Oh, Rissy, it really was hot. Like supernova hot."

"*Pfft.* Then ten to one he's *not* complaining."

"No, he wouldn't." She bit her lip, but it couldn't hold back her very satisfied smile. "He's the most wonderful guy ever. And in bed he's…" She couldn't find an adjective good enough.

"No words, huh? Wow. Now I really am jealous."

Given the smile Merissa wore, she didn't harbor any hard feelings. "I'll try to dial it down from now on."

"Don't you dare!" Merissa winked. "I'll turn on the sound machine when I sleep. Someone in this house ought to be making profound whoopee, and it sure isn't me."

Since breaking things off with Steve, Rissy seemed to have given up dating, but she didn't appear all that sad about it. Mostly she'd just thrown herself into her work.

Cherry knew she was truly blessed for having such a terrific friend in her life. "Can I tell you something?"

"Something juicy?" Anxious, Merissa leaned in. "Heck yeah. Lay it on me."

Merissa's continued upbeat encouragement almost made her laugh again. "No, it's nothing like that." Desperate to clear her thoughts, Cherry gulped down half the cup of coffee, crossed her arms on the table, and admitted, "I want Denver to want to be with me."

One of Merissa's brows went up. "So…are you saying you kept him here under duress? Kinky. Were ropes and chains involved?"

"Sometimes you're worse than Armie!"

Feigning affront, she drew back. "You take that back."

"Sorry."

"Okay then." Merissa got serious, even taking one of Cherry's hands. "So tell me what you meant about Denver. Why do you think he's here?"

Knowing Merissa needed to head out the door, and that she only had a few more minutes herself, Cherry decided it was best to just say it. "Because he wants to keep me safe."

A very slow eye blink, followed by a dry, "Yeah," and a patronizing hand pat made up Merissa's reply. "That's what all that moaning and groaning was about last night."

"That was sex," Cherry stated. "And we both know guys are easy." Only Denver hadn't been. Not even close.

He'd been so difficult that there were times she'd almost given up. But she flat-out cared about him too much to do that.

Merissa searched her face. "You're serious?"

Dreading explanations, especially since neither of them had time for it, Cherry said, "It's my stupid foster brothers."

To her surprise, Merissa nodded. "Yeah, Cannon told me."

Oh God. Shame sent a wave of heat burning through her. Did the whole world know the ugliness of her past?

"Don't sweat it, okay?" Merissa squeezed her hand again, this time in commiseration. "The only people who know are your friends, and friends don't judge."

Friends, plural. "Who?"

"Me, Yvette, the guys—"

"Guys?" she squeaked. It was bad enough that her girlfriends knew.

Shrugging, Merissa said, "Yeah, you know, Stack, Armie, Miles, Brand, Gage—"

Horrified, she moaned, *"Nooo."*

"Hey, stop that." Her wail made Merissa frown. "We care about you, Cherry. You're one of us, part of this big, insane, goofy family and that means your problems are our problems."

She didn't want them to suffer her problems, damn it! "You and Cannon are the only two related."

"So? Blood ties mean next to nothing. I know without a single doubt that if I needed help I could count on any of the guys, Armie included, even though he acts like he doesn't like me for some reason." She tipped her head, encouraging Cherry with a smile. "You're the sister I never had. If you don't feel the same, tough. I'm keeping you anyway."

How had she gotten so lucky? Emotional overload had her softly confessing, "The best decision I ever made was moving to Warfield, Ohio."

"And rooming with me?"

"That was the best of the good decisions." Deciding a little honesty was in order, she said, "And I'm thrilled to have you for my sister. Thank you."

For a moment, both of them just enjoyed the candid

friendship. Then Merissa sighed. "So you think Denver is playing big, bad protector?"

"I know he is."

"Then surely you know why, right?" Without waiting for Cherry's opinion, Merissa stood from the table and pulled her purse strap over her shoulder. "Because he cares."

Afraid to believe that, just in case it proved wrong, Cherry asked, "How can you tell?"

"I've known Denver longer than you. Trust me on this, okay?"

She and Denver sounded the same. But not everything was about trust. Some things, she knew, were about survival. Independence. Responsibility.

And caring enough not to draw others into the mess of your life.

Pausing next to her chair, Merissa put her hand on Cherry's shoulder. "We're both supposed to be on guard until things are resolved. I had to cross my heart and swear to report any and every sound that might spook me."

Cherry could almost picture Cannon giving that lecture. "Your brother is pretty terrific."

"Yeah, he is." Bending down, Merissa gave her a hug. "I've gotta run. Try not to fret too much, not about that loony foster family or Denver's feelings. I have a hunch everything is going to work out just right."

Wishing she could share that belief, Cherry finished her coffee and grabbed up her own purse. When she stepped outside, she realized storms were moving in again. Instead of being greeted with a blue sky, fluffy white clouds and sunshine, she got hit with angry, humid winds that immediately curled her hair. Off in the distance, a flash of lightning lined the gray horizon.

"Great. Just freaking great." Rushing to her car in hopes of getting to the day care before the skies opened up, she hopped in, put the key in the ignition, and... nothing. Not even a pretense of starting. "No, no, *no*."

Trying again—and again—got her the same results. She dropped her head to the steering wheel, thought about calling Denver, and immediately scrapped that idea.

Instead she yanked out her phone and, with a deep breath, typed in the number for the only person she thought might not be busy.

FUNNY, CHERRY THOUGHT, but not in a ha-ha way. After discussing Vanity last night, basically doing her best to find out if Denver had ever lusted after her, Vanity was now her rescuer.

It was still early, and she had a feeling she might have woken her, but damn it, Vanity looked as gorgeous as ever. The humidity didn't frizz her hair as it did Cherry's. No, Vanity's long, pale blond hair, which easily reached to the small of her back, only had a sexy wave to it.

Even without makeup, her skin looked flawless. Vanity had just the right amount of tan to make her blue eyes stand out.

If she wasn't so nice, it'd be easy to dislike her for her perfect looks alone.

But she was nice, so nice that she'd gotten out of bed to chauffeur Cherry to work. Having her own little pity party, Cherry slumped in her seat.

Glancing her way, Vanity asked, "What will you do about your car?"

"I don't know. I have no idea what's wrong with it." Hopefully nothing too expensive, because missing work had already seriously cut into her paycheck. Expensive car repairs would devastate her meager bank account. "It's old and loaded with miles so it could be anything. But I'm praying for just a dead battery."

While she'd waited for Vanity, the sky had darkened even more, leaving everything cast in gray shadows. The wind bent branches and sent debris scuttling across the roadway. The storms would be heavy today.

"I know nothing about cars," Vanity admitted.

"Me, either." But she'd think of something. Somehow she always did. "Your car is really nice." For the twentieth time, Cherry ran her hand over the buttersoft leather seat.

"I know, right?" Vanity smiled. "Nice things don't have to cost a fortune."

Cherry gaped at her. The car, a brand-new, loaded Mustang convertible, probably cost more than she made in a year. She knew nothing about Vanity's finances, except that she always dressed in pricey but comfortable clothes, worked only when she wanted to and seldom seemed to give money a thought. She never flaunted her wealth, but she was as casual about expenses as she was her clothes and hair.

"I bet one of the guys could help."

By "guys," Vanity meant any of their group at the rec center. Did Vanity and Rissy both consider the fighters at their disposal? It seemed so.

Cherry quickly shook her head. "I don't want to bother them."

"I doubt they'd consider it a bother." Vanity flashed a knowing smile her way. "Men love to feel useful."

"Maybe." She'd have to take Vanity's word for that. "But it's my problem, not theirs." Even if Vanity had been told about her foster family, she didn't know everything else that was going on. She couldn't see that this would just be one more mess on top of the rest, making Cherry feel like a walking disaster. "I'll figure it out."

Rolling her eyes, Vanity hit a button on her steering wheel. "You don't have to."

Not until a ringing sounded in the car did Cherry realize she had hands-free calling. Taken by surprise, she gasped, "What are you doing?"

Just then Armie answered, saying, "Hey, Vee. What's the haps?"

Momentarily sidetracked, Cherry mouthed, "Vee?"

"For Vanity," Vanity explained, holding up the peace sign one-handed. "That's Armie being Armie."

"Who're you with?" asked Armie.

"Cherry." And before she could stop her, Vanity spilled her guts. "See, her car wouldn't start this morning so I'm driving her to work. It's her first day back after being sick so she couldn't miss or go in late. But who knows what's wrong with the car? Could be something simple like a dead battery, which she's hoping for because, really, who can afford major car repairs? But I'm thinking if she takes it to a garage, they'll try to rip her off and she'll be paying for repairs whether she needs them or not. Plus she'll need a ride home from work, too, only she didn't want to bother anyone."

Cherry stared in appalled admiration of the verbal

maneuvering. Vanity had run that all together without a breath and left no room to interrupt.

Armie laughed. "Can she hear me?"

"Yes," Vanity said with a fast, satisfied smile. "She's sitting next to me stewing right now."

"Cherry Pie," Armie murmured, "why would you not call me?"

She did a double take. "Cherry Pie?"

"That's what Denver used to call you when he openly lusted. Now that you two have a thing, he'd probably want to squash me for saying it. But I like it. It sounds both familiar and a little bit nasty."

Wow. Armie had done his own verbal maneuvering there, leaving her mute. *Denver used to call her that absurd name?*

"So," Armie said with a smile in his voice, "what weak-ass excuse do you have for not calling me?"

"You're busy," she squeaked, horrified at the use of the nickname and for being put on the spot.

"No, Denver's busy. But I just finished fighting so I'm free and clear for a bit."

Such a gigantic fib! "You work at the rec center all the time!"

"Yeah, well, I'm looking for an excuse not to be there this afternoon, so I'll come by the school and get you, and then check on your car. What time do you get off?"

When she stalled, trying to think of an alternative, Vanity nudged her with her elbow.

Blast. With a long sigh, she said, "Today's my short day, so I'll be off at three."

"Perfect timing. Thanks for giving me a reason to duck out of the gym. See you soon."

Grinning, Vanity disconnected the call. "There, you see? He appreciates it."

"My luck sucks lately."

Ignoring that, Vanity said, "If my car broke down, I'd call Stack in a heartbeat. Or no, wait, maybe I'd call someone else so that it wouldn't be too obvious."

Eyes widening, her own concerns disappearing under intrigue, Cherry slowly turned her head to face Vanity. "Too obvious about what?"

"How hot he is, how sexy he is and how much I'd love to get horizontal with him. Well, the horizontal part he already knows." She winked. "He's agreed to take me to the wedding, and I agreed we'd have sex."

Whoa. "So…" Assuming she had to have misunderstood something, Cherry tried to sort it out. "You agreed to an…exchange?"

Laughing, Vanity pulled up in front of the day care. "Sex for a date—isn't that the usual exchange? No, I'm kidding. I know it's not. At least not always."

"I am so confused."

"Because I'm deliberately confusing you. Sorry. I'm just…giddy, I guess." Leaning in toward Cherry, voice hushed with excitement, Vanity said, "I'm going to have sex with Stack! Isn't that amazing?"

"Vanity, seriously." Cherry gave her a critical once-over. "Have you looked in a mirror lately? You could have sex with anyone you wanted."

"I'll take that as a compliment. Thank you."

Of all the— "Of course it was a compliment. You're drop-dead gorgeous!"

"But no, I can't," Vanity said, disregarding her clarification. "Denver and Cannon are both entirely off limits, right?"

She frowned. "What?"

"For sex."

Snapping her back straight, Cherry said, "Most definitely!"

"And I'm pretty sure Armie is, as well."

"I—" Venturing into dangerous territory, Cherry cleared her throat. "You're saying you want to have sex with Cannon, Armie and—" *no, no, no* "—Denver?"

"No, just proving a point." She flapped her hand. "I'm all about Stack."

Head swimming, Cherry stared at her. "You're hung up on Stack?"

One brow went up. "Is there a reason you sound so incredulous?"

"*No.* Of course not. Stack is terrific. You're terrific. I just… You've never mentioned him before." At a loss, she lifted her shoulders. "Or dated, or far as I know, even talked to him that much."

Vanity looked at her nails. "I think he's yummy."

"He is." Not as hot as Denver by any stretch, but Stack was certainly as fit as the other fighters, and with his dark blond hair and smoky blue eyes, he drew a lot of attention. "I'm glad things are working out."

"It's just sex," Vanity said, but her lips played with a smile. "Well, and a date to the wedding. Win-win."

Cherry had to laugh. "Stack's a lucky guy."

"And I won't let him forget it." When the first raindrops splashed on the windshield, Vanity said, "Go, before you get soaked."

Cherry hurriedly opened her door and as she stepped out, she said, "Thank you so much for the ride."

"It was all my pleasure! Let me know how it goes with the car."

With a final wave, she dashed inside. For the next few hours, she stayed too busy to worry about ex-foster brothers, hunky fighters or car troubles. Half the kids were afraid of the lightning, and the rowdier unafraid half couldn't get outside to run off their energy. Midway through the day, the electricity went out. Luckily, things finally cleared up some and the lights came back on, making storytime easier. By the time Armie was due to arrive, the rain had even stopped.

Now if only the rest of her luck would improve.

CHAPTER FOURTEEN

DENVER AND ARMIE went through some conditioning exercises together. The high school boys always bitched about jumping rope, like they thought it wasn't macho enough or something.

Armie snorted. At the moment, with sweat soaking his spine and the waistband of his shorts, he'd love to see one of the cocky boys keep up.

"Double jumps," he told Denver, and they both adjusted, pushing themselves through two sets of twenty until Armie called a halt.

Denver tossed the rope aside and threw a few kicks at the heavy bag, then a series of punches.

Grinning, Armie watched him. "You're going to make Packer wish this fight never happened."

"That's the plan."

"Go take a break. No reason to overtrain."

"Look who's talking."

Doffing an imaginary hat, Armie said, "You know it takes a lot to get my heartbeat up."

"Because you're insane." With that parting shot, Denver went to the other side of the gym where he'd left his gear.

Armie headed to a bench to fetch his own water bottle and towel. He only had a few minutes before he had to take off, and he still needed to tell Denver that he was picking up Cherry. Didn't want to look sneaky or anything.

But then, Denver knew he usually dodged sponsors, even sponsors not solely focused on him.

He'd just finished dragging the towel over his drenched hair and hot face when the chime on the door sounded and Havoc walked in.

Seeing him did what other conditioning couldn't: Armie's heartbeat went haywire.

Cannon walked up to the man, shaking his hand and greeting him like a long-lost pal.

Neither of them looked his way.

What the fuck were they up to?

He had to shower before going after Cherry, but no way would he walk off now, not after that jibe of "running." It'd look bad and—screw it.

Tossing the towel aside, Armie took a step.

"Planning a frontal attack, huh?"

He spun around on Denver. "Did you know about this?"

"About one of Cannon's friends dropping in? No. He doesn't run his social calendar by me."

"Screw you, that's not what I meant."

"Armie."

Shit. Holding his breath for a count of two and clearing all expression from his face, Armie turned to Dean "Havoc" Connor. And said nothing. Hell, he didn't know what to say.

Havoc held out a hand, so Armie took it.

"Glad I could finally catch you."

His eye twitched.

Havoc—damn him—laughed. "Bad choice of words?"

"Did you want something?"

"Yeah. Let's start with a lack of hostility."

To give them privacy, Denver slapped Armie's shoulder and headed off to talk with Cannon. Traitorous bastard.

"I'm not hostile," Armie said, sounding well beyond that namby-pamby word.

"Good. Could I have fifteen minutes?"

"Shit." He ran a hand over his face. "Here's the thing. I need to shower and head out."

Havoc stood there, judging him, measuring him.

"It's the truth." Going for a casual vibe, he shrugged. "I'm helping a lady in distress."

"Then pick another time."

How about never? "I can be back here in a few hours." He may as well get it over with.

Havoc checked the time, then nodded. "I'll take you to dinner."

A muscle in his jaw ticked. Hands on his hips, he frowned. "Thought you said it'd only take fifteen minutes?"

"If we did this now." Havoc never blinked. "But you're talking dinnertime, so we'll eat." Cocking a brow, he said, "Unless you have a problem with that?"

A flat-out challenge. That deserved another heartfelt—but silent—*fuck*. Pasting on his most disingenuous smile, Armie nodded. "Dinner it is." And now he only had about two minutes to get out the door or he'd be late getting to Cherry. He still hadn't told Denver about her car, but Havoc headed over to Denver, so he'd just have to clue him in later.

Hustling, Armie headed for the locker room and the fastest shower of his life.

"I'M TAKING YOUR class for you," Stack said.

Having just finished a shower after sparring with Cannon, Denver sat on a wooden bench, taking a moment to rest. He'd thought he was alone, but there stood Stack fresh from his own shower, wearing only a towel around his hips. "Why's that?"

"Because you look like shit." Speculative, Stack said, "Don't suppose Cherry kept you up all night?"

"Actually, yeah." Rubbing the tired muscles in the back of his neck, Denver flexed and popped his head to the side.

In the middle of finger-combing his wet hair, Stack paused, intrigued. "Seriously?"

"Yeah." He stretched, so tired he didn't even care that Stack was probably imagining all sorts of things he shouldn't, like Cherry in excess-sex mode. "But I can handle the class."

"You sure? I don't mind."

Rather than admit he'd feel like a wuss if he let a woman throw him off stride, Denver asked, "No big date tonight?"

"Later," Stack said as he pulled a clean T-shirt out of a locker. "I have time." He stepped into jeans.

It was Denver's turn to speculate. "I thought you and Vanity were getting together."

"Not until the wedding." Taking his own seat on the bench, Stack pulled on socks and athletic shoes and pretended not to see Denver scrutinizing him. "You can quit that shit any time now."

Grinning, Denver said, "You weren't going to ex-pound?"

"On the date tonight? No. Just a friendly hookup."

"Will Vanity be pissed?"

"She said not." Stack rolled a shoulder, looking a little pissed himself. "She more or less told me to go about my business until the wedding."

To make sure he understood, Denver asked, "Go about your business with other women?"

Suddenly, Stack turned to blast him with his frustration. "That's fucked up, right? I mean, she comes on to me, only to set a date—*for sex*—that's *weeks* away, but doesn't care what I do until then. Have you ever heard of a woman making that arrangement?"

"Ah…no." But it made him wonder if Vanity had suggested it specifically to make Stack nuts. If so, she was succeeding.

"Know what I think?" Stack stood to slam his locker. "I think she's off doing God-knows-what with other guys and that's why she made the deal in the first place."

"That matters to you?"

He stalled. Dropped his head. Muttered, *"Fuck,"* in a really mean way. Then he shook it off to glare at Denver. "I don't know."

Doing his best not to laugh, Denver stood, too. "Some unsolicited advice—if it does matter to you, then don't wait for the wedding." As a man who'd waited, he knew the regrets that could bring.

What if Cherry hadn't pressed the issue when they were out of town for Armie's fight? What if he hadn't finally broken?

She'd have been in that hotel room by herself, sick without anyone to help her.

And she'd be dealing with Carver and his dick brothers all on her own.

The idea tormented him. Especially when he thought about how different she might be now if he'd gotten together with her a lot sooner. Maybe she'd be more open already.

Maybe she'd have already given up her secrets.

"I don't know," Stack muttered in disgust. "She was pretty clear."

"About wanting to wait? Maybe she just used the wedding as an icebreaker. You know it's impossible to figure out women. Your best bet is to ask her outright."

With a rude snort, Stack dropped back against the locker. "Like you did with Cherry?"

"Freely admit it, I fucked up."

"Yeah, says the man who spent the night getting laid."

The laugh came before he could stop it, then he immediately pointed at Stack and said, "Shut up."

Still grinning, Stack held up his hands in understanding. Jokes about a casual hookup were no big deal, but with Cherry it was more than that. "If you don't want me to do the class, then I'm heading out for some relief sooner rather than later."

"Will you at least think about talking to Vanity?"

He ran a hand over his face. "I'll think about her all right, even when I shouldn't be if you know what I mean, but talking won't be in the equation."

Denver gave an exaggerated wince. "Just don't admit to your lady friend that you're picturing another woman."

"Yeah, I'm distracted, not stupid." He grabbed up his gym bag. "That's the kind of loose talk that could put an end to friends with benefits."

Denver headed back out to the main area with Stack. His class would start in just a few minutes.

The high school boys were already in place, warming up, goofing around with the heavy bag, all in all being healthy, athletic guys. Denver was headed toward them when, one by one, he saw them look toward the door.

His neck prickling with unease, Denver turned—and found Pamela Barnett Lewis standing there.

The quintessential evil stepmother.

Claws of hostility soured his mood. Disdain overshadowed exhaustion.

He did not need this shit today.

Of course she made a smiling beeline for him, looking around as she strode elegantly across the floor.

At twenty-nine, she was only four years older than him—making her twenty-three years younger than his dad.

Straight red hair, the color enhanced by a pricey salon, hung loose to skim just below her shoulder blades. The curve-hugging dress and high-heeled sandals showcased her body.

Behind him a whisper sounded and Denver realized that not only the high school seniors were ogling her. When Pamela walked in, she deliberately drew attention, so now most every male in the place was appreciating her curves and poise.

Right before she reached him, he called out to Stack, who'd paused at the reception desk on his way out to talk briefly with Gage's wife, Harper.

Stack looked at him, then at Pamela. Curiosity lifted his brows high as he said one last thing to Harper and headed over.

"Hello, Denver."

For the moment, Denver ignored her. "Sorry, Stack, but I might need you for a few minutes after all."

"Sure." He started away, but of course Pamela didn't let him.

"Hello." She held out her manicured hand. "I'm Pamela Barnett Lewis, Denver's stepmother."

She stressed the relationship, waiting for Stack to show his shock, to tell her she was too young, anything, as long as it was a big reaction.

But still Stack didn't take the bait. He accepted her hand in a brief greeting, said, "Ma'am," with enough respect for a grandmother, and excused himself to get the boys going.

Damn, he had terrific friends.

Puzzled, Pamela gave a reasonable facsimile of a frown without actually puckering her perfect brow. "Denver—"

"This way," he said, unwilling to have any discussion with her, for any reason, out in the open. Not bothering to see if she'd follow or not, he headed for the breakroom.

The click of her heels right behind him made him feel stalked. When he finally got into the room with relative privacy he released a pent-up breath.

Pulling out a chair, he seated himself and waited for her to do the same.

She tsked. "You still haven't learned any manners."

Censure from her was laughable.

But sitting was a bad move on his part because

instead of taking a seat, she propped her hip on the table—right next to him.

Letting his revulsion show, Denver pushed back his chair and stood.

Her long sigh sounded both seductively breathy and reproachful. "I see you're still holding a grudge, too."

"There's no grudge."

Lined green eyes taunted him. "Your father chose me over you and you're understandably bitter."

One step brought him nose to nose with her. Low, his anger somehow fresh and still raw, Denver said, "Who he fucks is his business. But when you try to fuck *me*, it becomes my business, too."

"I was young."

"You were a lot of things. Let's not go through the list."

Her voice rose with her snapping temper. "Can't you be civil for even five minutes?"

Apparently not. Taking a step back, he crossed his arms. "What do you want, Pamela?"

With an effort, she pulled herself together, needlessly toying with her hair and smoothing the short skirt of her dress. If he didn't know better, he'd almost believe her act of distress.

"Your father's birthday is coming up and I expect you home for his party."

Denver barely heard the words since Pamela said them while ogling his body. His eyes narrowed.

She caught herself and actually flushed. "I'm sorry. It's just…it appears you've gotten even bigger."

His jaw locked.

She gasped. "I don't mean… I wasn't…" Stammering didn't suit her. She righted herself and said with formality, "Clearly you've been taking good care of yourself."

His mood growing more frigid by the moment, Denver considered walking out on her. But she was so tenacious she might follow, and then he'd be back out in public with her again. "I'll try giving Dad a call, but we both know he doesn't want to talk to me."

"No, a call isn't enough." She took a stance. "I'm having an intimate family party and that means *you*, dear son, need to be there."

Soon as she saw Armie pull up, Cherry raced out to meet him. Holding her purse close to her side, avoiding the deeper puddles, she bopped along the sidewalk like a woman on a mission. The light sprinkling rain, she decided, wouldn't be so bad as long as she didn't linger.

Unfortunately, halfway to Armie, the skies opened up and a deluge of freezing rain, carried on a high wind, drenched her to the skin.

Armie threw open the door. "Damn, Cherry, why didn't you wait for me?"

As she jumped in, he handed her several napkins that she used to dry her face and throat, then she immediately wrapped her arms around herself to try to fight off the shivers. "What would you have done? Gotten drenched, too?"

"I have an umbrella and a windbreaker."

"Oh." Yeah, her umbrella was in her car. So dumb. "I'm getting your seats soaked."

"They'll dry." Reaching into the backseat, he dug out the nylon windbreaker and handed it to her, then slowly pulled forward with the line of cars picking up kids.

"Bless you." The jacket didn't do much to help, but it was better than nothing. After she had it on, she buckled her seatbelt.

"Want me to turn up the heat?"

"No, that's okay." He was in no more than a T-shirt and looked comfortable. No reason to roast him. "Once I get to the rec center someone will have a T-shirt I can change into." Maybe even Denver, although his shirts were enormous on her, better suited for a nightshirt than to wear in public.

"I thought I was taking you home."

"Denver wanted me to meet him there." It was along the way, closer than her house. "Do you mind?"

"I was going back anyway. But what about your car?"

"You can't look at it in this rain."

"Why not?" He grinned at her. "I know I'm sweet, but I won't melt."

"No, absolutely not."

"You don't think I'm sweet?"

Rolling her eyes, she said, "Yes, you're very, very sweet. And I appreciate the offer, I really do. But my car is on the street, not in the garage, and I can't let you fiddle with it in this storm."

His fingers drummed the steering wheel. "Okay, then how about tomorrow?" He cut off her reply to add, "That is, if Denver doesn't see to it himself."

"Maybe." If possible, she'd get it figured out on her own without burdening either of them. "I hope this storm lets up soon."

"Don't hold your breath." Rain lashed the windshield, making the wipers almost useless, and wind buffeted the car, howling around them. He glanced at her, then fought another grin. "You might want to make use of the mirror before we get there. You're looking a little...smudged."

She pulled down the visor—and screeched. "Good heavens. I'm glad you told me."

"It's not that bad," he said, while fighting a laugh.

"Yeah, for a clown!" Luckily she had makeup in her purse, and with Armie driving so slowly by necessity, she was able to do a few repairs. It wasn't enough—she still looked a wreck—but it was better.

One of these days Denver would again get to see her at her best—independent, strong and put together.

Sadly, today was not that day.

AFTER MENTALLY WRESTLING his temper under control, Denver prepared his arguments, looking for sound reasons to refuse Pamela other than the obvious ones. He didn't want her to know that he still harbored animosity.

He didn't want her to know he felt anything at all for her—good or bad.

It was enough that he had to live with the damage she'd done to him. Because of her, his relationship with his father had been forever changed. He loved his dad. In most ways, he respected him.

But when it came to his second marriage, Denver had nothing but contempt.

"I don't like it when you're quiet this long," Pamela said. "It usually means you're thinking horrible things about me."

"Wrong. I don't think about you at all." He turned and walked to the open door, giving her his back. "I was just wondering what Dad will think of your invite. He might not thank you for asking me back."

Her hand touched his shoulder, making him stiffen in revulsion.

"He misses you, Denver. You should know that."

Yeah, that's why he called so often. How long had it been? Going on five years now. Long years.

He shook his head—and shrugged off her hand. "Paws to yourself, Pamela."

"It was a commiserating gesture."

Laughing, Denver turned to look at her. She wore the perfect expression of remorse mixed with hope. He marveled at it, saying softly, "If I didn't already know what a lying...*witch* you are, I would almost be convinced."

"Witch," she repeated, her facial muscles drawing tight despite her effort to hide emotion. "I appreciate the censorship on that one."

"We both know the truth, no reason to belabor the point."

Tensed to strike him, Pamela barely held herself in check.

He almost hoped she'd do it. Then he could tell her to fuck off and be done with it.

Instead she drew a deep breath, shook back her hair, and stabbed him with her rock-steady gaze. "I can guarantee you that he wants you there."

"Just like you guaranteed me no one would ever know if we fucked?" He straightened. "The way you guaranteed me that my dad would never get hurt?" Growing anger took him one step forward. "The way you guaranteed him of your innocence?"

Her chin quivered. "You're scaring me, Denver."

"Lady, a fucking typhoon wouldn't scare you."

She ducked around him and into the open hallway leading back to the gym.

Smirking, Denver took a step out, wanting her to run, hoping she'd run all the way back out of his life.

Voice shaking, she whispered, "People change, damn you."

"You?" he asked with caustic humor.

She gave a sharp nod.

Bullshit. "Does that mean you've told my dad the truth?"

Tears glistened in her eyes. "I love him."

Not for a second did he buy into the weepy desperation. "You aren't capable of love."

Pretending he hadn't spoken, she insisted, "I love him and I want my marriage to work."

"You want the perks of what he gives you."

She actually stomped one foot in temper. "You could repair your relationship without this ever having to come up again!"

"Dream on." There were times when he still heard the cold fury in his father's voice during that awful time. Disgust. Disappointment. Blame. He'd made one mistake, and it had irrevocably changed his life. "Dad is never going to forgive what *you* made him believe."

Trying a new tact, she pleaded, "Denver," and in a rush, stepped up to him again, this time daring to put her hands on him.

Rage all but blinded him. He clasped her wrists, meaning to toss her hands away from him—and just then Cherry and Armie dashed in through the front doors, followed by a loud clap of thunder.

They fell against each other laughing, a puddle forming around their feet.

After saying something to her, Armie struggled with an umbrella that had gone inside out.

Grinning, Cherry pushed hair from her face and removed a sodden windbreaker.

Denver's eyes flared.

A long skirt was glued to her hips and thighs, and her pink shirt stuck to her breasts like a second skin, showing the darker bra beneath. Thanks to the bra, nothing actually showed through, but given her rack and how everyone looked at her, that didn't matter.

Irritation—at the situation with Carver, the way Cherry cut him out, Pamela's appearance and now this—all coalesced into a red-hot fury.

"Denver?"

Dismissing Pamela and her small plea, he set her aside and strode purposefully toward the door.

"Denver, wait!"

He barely heard Pamela with the rush of his heartbeat sounding in his ears.

With all eyes on Cherry, no one else noticed his approach. He watched as Armie tried to stuff her back into the windbreaker.

As she laughingly smacked his arm.

As drips of rainwater fell from her hair to slowly track over her boobs and into her cleavage.

Two steps from them, he growled, "What the fuck is this?"

Stunned, Cherry pulled up short, her smile disappearing in the face of his obvious anger.

Stepping in front of Cherry—shielding her from

him?—Armie held up both hands. "She's oblivious, dude. Take a breath."

"You brought her *here*?" His gaze transferred to Cherry, and he easily pushed Armie to the side. "Looking like *that*?"

Hurt, Cherry pokered up just as she had while talking to Carver. Keeping her voice low in a laughable bid for privacy, she whispered, "You *told* me to come here!"

Uncaring that the entire rec center watched, he leaned into her, jaw muscles knotted and his irritability spiking. "Jesus, Cherry, you look *naked.*"

"What are you talking about?" Hastily she peeked down at herself, plucking at the sodden material of her skirt.

He narrowed his gaze on her jutting nipples.

That drew her attention there and she gasped, slapping her arms around herself.

Reaching to his back, Denver grabbed a fistful of his shirt and in one jerk stripped it off over his head.

Cherry snatched it from him before he could offer it, holding it in front of her chest.

"Put it on," Denver told her.

She went from embarrassment to a flash fire of anger. "Are you *ordering* me?" she asked, incredulous over the possibility.

For a single second Denver thought she might throw the shirt back in his face. He braced himself—

And Armie stepped up next to her, snarling to Denver, "Ass." Then to Cherry, "Jealousy makes guys nuts, honey. Ignore him."

Going combustible all over again, Denver knotted

up from the soles of his feet to the top of his ears. "You—"

"Dating groupies again?"

Ah, hell. He'd forgotten all about Pamela.

Both Armie and Cherry leaned to look behind him, Armie with male interest, Cherry going red in the face, the shirt clutched tight in front of her body.

Fed up, Denver faced his stepmother. "Later, Pamela."

Ignoring him, she smiled at Armie. "Introduce me."

Armie cocked his head to the side, giving her a thorough once-over.

On the ragged edge, polite manners well out of reach, Denver growled, "I'm busy."

Of course, that didn't stop Pamela. She stretched out a hand. "I'm Pamela, Denver's stepmother."

Cherry's mouth dropped.

Armie adjusted from interested to cold but polite civility, saying, "Nice to meet you, ma'am." After the briefest possible handshake, he said to Denver, "I'll be in back. We need to talk."

Glowing with mortification, Cherry tried to drum up a smile. "Hello. Nice to meet you. Clearly I got caught in the rain and I didn't realize—"

To cut off her groveling, Denver slung an arm around her. "Pamela was just leaving."

Like the cunning bitch he knew her to be, Pamela showed her teeth in a "got you" grin and spoke only to Cherry. "So nice to meet you…Cherry, is it?"

"Yes."

"Such an unconventional name." *Not* said as a compliment. "You and Denver are dating?"

She licked her lips. "We're…"

When Cherry looked at him with so much uncertainty, he wanted to rip through the concrete walls. "Not your business, Pamela."

"Denver!" Cherry tried to free herself, but he didn't let her. It sucked, but he needed her at the moment. To apologize for that, he kissed her forehead.

Stymied, Cherry stared up at him, then at Pamela.

Pamela watched with shrewd speculation. "Never mind him, Cherry. I understand Denver and his... ways."

What was that supposed to mean?

Cherry must've wondered the same thing because she quit resisting him and instead leaned into him. "What ways would that be, Ms. Lewis?"

"Call me Pamela, please."

"All right."

Wow. Denver stared down at Cherry in awe. She was always so sweet, occasionally defensive, but never curt. Now, though, her tone held as much cold bite as Pamela's.

"Despite Denver's surliness, it's clear the two of you are...involved? So I'll just include you in my invitation. You see, my husband's birthday is coming up and I know Denver's dad would not only love to see him again, but he'd enjoy meeting you, as well."

"I see." Cherry put her shoulders back, her little nose in the air. "Has Denver accepted the invitation?"

Pamela's smile slipped. "Not precisely."

"Then I certainly can't accept." She snuggled closer under his arm. "But he and I will talk about it, and if necessary, he can get in touch with you."

Making her mouth smile seemed to strain her, but

Pamela managed it. "Thank you." She peered out the window at the blowing rain. "Nasty weather."

"As I said, it caught me," Cherry explained, and now she stepped away from Denver. "I was halfway across the parking lot when the downpour started and of course I'd forgotten my umbrella."

Critical, Pamela said, "But you did have that handsome young man to assist you."

Crossing his arms, Denver waited to see how Cherry would handle Pamela's veiled accusation.

She surprised him by smiling, the first mean smile he'd ever seen from her. "Yes, he's a very good friend of Denver's and so he gave me a lift. Now if you'll excuse me, I need to go change."

"You keep clothes at a gym?"

"No, but one of Denver's *good friends* will loan me something." She looked at Pamela with a mix of loathing and pity. "It was nice meeting you." Her gaze flashed over to Denver, but only for a split second before she again focused on Pamela. "Quite…educational."

Denver watched as she exited the confrontation, drenched, makeup destroyed, holding his shirt in front of her. She didn't look back, and she kept her shoulders squared, her chin lifted.

He realized he was grinning.

"Very odd, Denver."

"Yeah. She's something." He gave Pamela a mock salute. "Later."

"Wait."

His long sigh made his impatience plain.

"Will you attend?"

"Like Cherry told you, we'll talk about it." And suddenly he meant it.

Just last night he'd made her a promise to share everything with her, get her thoughts on problems.

Pamela was a problem. The estrangement from his dad was a problem.

His jealousy was the biggest problem.

Starting right now, he'd keep his promise—and hope she'd forgive him.

CHAPTER FIFTEEN

NOW WEARING DENVER'S SHIRT, Cherry poked her nose into the locker room. It fascinated her, this all-male domain. The rec center got some female members, but not many, not on the scale of the fighters, so while they had a small changing room that included two toilets and sinks with some hooks on the wall, they didn't have this elaborate setup, an expanse of lockers, benches, open showers…

Did men have no modesty at all? If it weren't for the wall of lockers, she'd be able to see all the showers. *Into* the showers. Anyone who might be *naked* in the shower.

She heard water running, and sucked in a breath. It almost made her cough, but she fended it off in favor of another deep breath.

The room smelled good. Like clean male sweat, aftershave and soap.

The water shut off and she decided it might be prudent to announce herself.

Sounding like a strangled frog, she called out, "Yoo-hoo?"

A static moment of silence preceded a softly muttered curse, then she heard the sound of big feet padding across a wet concrete floor.

Using a towel to dry his naked chest, another towel

around his hips, Armie poked his head around the corner. His eyes widened at the sight of her standing there just inside the doorway. "Cherry?"

"Hi."

Dumbfounded, he looked around her, beyond her, saw she'd come on her own, and gave a slight frown. "This is the locker room, hon."

"I know." She nodded down at herself and rushed to explain. "I need something dry and it's not like there are clothes in the breakroom." Feeling wicked, she asked, "Anyone else down here?"

"Just me."

As he walked toward her, one hairy, muscled thigh playing peekaboo with that loosely wrapped towel, she quickly backed up a step.

Expression mocking, he reached past her for a locker, drawing out jeans, a T-shirt and Captain America underwear.

She stared at the bright briefs, inadvertently imagined him in them, and snorted a laugh even as her face went hot.

Lifting a brow, he asked, "Plan to stick around while I dress, or you want to give me a little privacy?"

From behind her, Denver said, "She'll give you privacy."

Cherry went rigid. She locked eyes with Armie, taking strength from his amusement, and finally turned to Denver. "Excuse me," she said, as haughtily as she could, and she stepped out of the room. But since she still needed a change, she only went to the other side of the door and leaned back on the cool, painted concrete block wall.

For a few seconds, no one said anything. Then a locker closed and that seemed to break the silence.

"Listen," she heard Denver say. "That shit earlier—"

"You," Armie said, "better start apologizing to her."

"I figured I'd start with you."

Yes, Cherry thought, he did owe Armie an apology.

Apparently Armie disagreed. "Not necessary. Desperate men do stupid things. And you, my friend, are desperate."

"What are you talking about?"

Armie snorted. "One look at you and anyone can see you're a man fighting a losing battle."

What battle? Cherry wondered.

"Yeah," Denver said as if making a grand confession. Then, *"Fuck."*

"Sucks, I guess," Armie commiserated. "But I hear tell it's easier once you give in."

"Somehow, with Cherry, I don't think it's going to be easy no matter what I do."

Cherry was so put out by Denver's forlorn tone that she pivoted from the wall and right back into the locker room.

Where Armie stood naked.

She squawked.

He jumped and quickly covered his goods with big hands.

Denver jumped in front of her and just as quickly covered her eyes with his hand. *"What the hell, Cherry?"*

She sputtered. Didn't matter what Denver or Armie covered—the image was emblazoned on her brain. "I thought he'd gotten dressed!"

Suddenly Armie cracked up. His roar of laughter bounced off the walls of the locker room.

Cherry just stood there, Denver's palm covering the top half of her face.

"It's not funny," she groused.

"Maybe a *little* funny," Denver told her. "How much did you see?"

Her shoulders slumped. "Everything in the front."

Armie got it together long enough to ask, "Did you want me to turn around and give you another peek?"

Cherry bit her lip.

Denver stiffened. "Damn it, girl—"

"No!" She cleared her throat, blindly reaching out to find his chest and pat it. "No, I don't. Truly."

"See, there, Denver. Truly she's not interested."

"You're not helping, Armie!" Cherry wanted to smack him. "I'll be embarrassed for the rest of my life, thanks to you."

"No," Denver told her. "You won't—because you're going to forget what you saw."

Once Armie stopped laughing, he said to Denver, "I see what you mean about it not being easy."

"Shut up, Armie!" she and Denver both said almost in unison.

Putting an arm around her, Denver ushered her out of the room, saying over his shoulder to Armie, "Get dressed."

"Spoilsport," Armie called after them.

Outside the room she was finally able to face Denver—and got a good look at his scowl. *How dare he?*

She shored up her umbrage, ready to give him a sizzling piece of her mind—and people crowded into the hallway behind her.

Cannon, Gage, Harper—and Leese.

Good Lord! She flashed a look up at Denver, but he didn't appear surprised by Leese's presence. Confusion left her blank.

Cannon glanced at each of them. "What's all the commotion?"

Armie stepped out, now in jeans and a mostly ragged gray T-shirt that said: *I like girls for their hearts. Their big, bouncy, jiggly hearts.* Another T-shirt hung loosely in his hand. "Cherry got an eyeful, that's all. Isn't that right, Cherry?"

New heat suffused her face. "If you didn't go prancing around naked—"

"Don't start rumors, hon. I do not prance."

Harper laughed. "He's shameless, Cherry. Don't let him make you blush or he'll forever be teasing you."

"Harper doesn't blush," Armie said. "She punches instead."

Gage kept Harper at his side when she started to step away, then said to Armie, "Nice shirt."

Leese even grinned over that.

Unable to take the suspense or the teasing a minute more, Cherry said, "Hi, Leese. What's going on?"

Denver hugged her. "I invited him."

"You did?" That was news to her. She knew they'd talked, but not that they'd…gotten friendly? Or just less hostile?

"Come on. We're blocking the hallway." He got her several feet before she stopped. "I'll explain it all to you in the break room."

She didn't budge. Cannon and Leese went around

them and disappeared into the locker room. Gage bent down to give Harper a soft but passionate kiss, then said, "Be right back," before following them.

Watching him go, Harper let out a long sigh.

Armie nudged Denver. "Guess the honeymoon hasn't worn off, huh?"

Harper sighed again, then handed Cherry a pair of shorts. "I keep extra clothes here because I hang out so much." She eyed Cherry's chest concealed beneath Denver's enormous shirt. "Sadly for me, we have very different builds, so I'm pretty sure none of my shirts will fit you."

"Your husband will tell you that your build is fine," Armie said, then with a flourish, he handed over his extra T-shirt. "I have one for Cherry."

She shook it out, read the front, and threw it back at him.

Grinning with anticipation, Harper snatched it from him so she could read it aloud. "Less hugs, more head."

Denver took it from Harper and turned it inside out. "It'll fit better than one of mine."

Cherry sent him a mean look. "I'm not keen about wearing yours, either."

Taking that as her cue, Harper grabbed Armie's arm. "Let's go. You have a visitor waiting on you."

"Who?"

"Havoc."

"He's early!"

"So prance on up there and tell him so."

Armie pretended to smack her butt, but she bolted away. Once Harper was gone, Armie turned back. "You should know, Denver. Cherry's car died this morning.

Vanity gave her a lift to work and I picked her up." He leveled his brows. "She didn't want to bother you."

"Armie," Cherry protested.

Denver just let out a breath.

"I was going to take her home and check on her car, see what the problem might be, but with the downpour she didn't want me to, so we came here instead. Even with an umbrella, we got soaked to the skin."

Denver nodded.

But Armie wasn't done. "If I'd known you were going to be such a bully to her, I wouldn't have brought her here."

"Armie," Cherry said again, this time scolding him for using that tone. The last thing she wanted was a conflict between him and Denver.

"Thanks," Denver said, as if Armie hadn't just insulted him. "I appreciate it."

"No problem. But seriously man, get it together." He winked at Cherry and, with a somewhat lagging step, headed out front to meet up with Havoc.

As soon as they were alone, Denver tried to take Cherry's hand. "You can change in the office."

She held back. "I'm not sure I want to go anywhere with you."

Resigned, he stepped back from her. For what felt like forever, he searched her face before asking softly, "Will it help if I apologize?"

"I don't know." Crossing her arms under her breasts and cocking out a hip, she tried to disguise her hurt with annoyance. "Try it and see."

A small, sexy smile teased his mouth, but he looked at her with those beautiful golden-brown eyes and said with touching sincerity, "I'm sorry."

Damn it, her resolve crumbled. Dropping her arms, her throat swelling with a lump of emotion, she asked, "How could you do that to me?" She didn't give him a chance to answer. Not yet. "You humiliated me, Denver. And not just in front of people I know."

"Please don't be embarrassed. Like Armie said, it's on me and most everyone in the rec center will know where to place the blame." He touched her cheek. "If it's Pamela you're worried about—"

"She's your *stepmother*." Remembering the humor and disdain in the woman's expression as she'd looked her over, Cherry went hot again. "With your help I just made a terrible first impression."

His brows came together. "She's not a nice person. Don't worry about her."

"But I *am* nice, and the way you treated me…"

"I know." Tentatively, he gathered her against him, his big hands open on her back, his chin on the top of her head. "I really am sorry. It's been…a difficult day."

"Tell me about it."

"I'd like to."

Surprised, she pushed back to see his face. "Really?"

His hands cradled her face. "Stack is filling in for me, but I should really get back to it so he can take off. Would you mind hanging around? I won't be much longer, then we can spend the rest of the day together."

Did that mean he wouldn't be staying the night? She never quite knew with him. "You'll tell me about Pamela?" That alone would be worth swallowing her pride. She had a feeling the crux of Denver's possessiveness stemmed from that woman.

"Yeah, I will." He released her to put his hands in his

pockets, looking uncharacteristically unsure of himself. "And we can discuss the birthday party for my dad."

When Cherry heard Cannon, Leese and Gage returning, she nodded. "I'll stay." Going on tiptoe, she gave Denver a quick kiss and started to hurry away.

He caught her hand, drew her back for a longer, more satisfying kiss, then steered her in the opposite direction from where she'd been headed. "There's a room at the end of the hall where you can change. The door locks. And Cherry?"

She paused. "Yes?"

"I'll make it up to you."

For as long as she could, Pamela stood under the overhang of the rec center waiting for the rain to let up. Over and over she debated with herself; should she go back in and try reasoning with him further? Should she perhaps try to trap his little country bumpkin girlfriend to see if that avenue would provide an in?

That Denver had rejected her yet again left a cold ache in her stomach. What did he want? For her to crawl on her hands and knees?

One stupid mistake, and he'd never let her live it down. Lyle forgave her. Was Denver so much better than his father?

Or just more stubborn?

Okay, so Lyle didn't know the whole truth. If he did, he might feel differently. But she wanted to tell him. She wanted to confess. She was a better person now, if only Denver would let her prove it—to him, to Lyle.

To herself.

But before she could indulge a cleansing of her conscience, she needed father and son to reunite. If that didn't happen first, if she had to confess her sins to Lyle while father and son remained estranged, neither would forgive her.

In fact, Lyle might end up hating her as much as Denver did, and then she'd lose it all.

It hadn't helped that Denver looked even better now. He was so incredibly gorgeous, so massively built and powerful and self-possessed. The years of maturity, with his dedication to his sport, only made him more appealing.

No one could blame a woman for looking—except for Denver.

And probably Lyle.

Oh God, what to do?

She covered her face with her hands, but she was not a whiner, not a person to wallow in indecision. She'd give him a day, two at the most, to get back to her, and if he didn't, she'd go after him again.

Opening her umbrella, she dashed for her car—and ran headlong into a body. Her hand loosened on the umbrella, and wind stole it away.

Though she normally refrained from cursing, a shocked *"Damn"* slipped through her lips. She stumbled back two steps and became instantly soaked.

Hands grabbed her upper arms to steady her. Through the awful downpour she saw a smiling and appreciative male face.

Lifting a jacket over her head like a canopy, he shielded her while leaving himself exposed. "Sorry, honey, are you okay?"

Staying out of the rain necessitated a very close proximity to him. "What?" He smelled of smoke, had a rugged, dangerous look about him. The same confidence that Denver carried, but with an edge. "Who are you?"

"Friend of Denver's."

"A fighter?"

He grinned. "I've been known to scrap a time or two."

What did that mean? She wasn't sure if she trusted him. She *wanted* to. It'd be a step forward to make nice with one of Denver's friends. But—

"Saw you inside a bit ago. Couldn't believe you were leaving in this storm."

"Oh." Knowing he wasn't a total stranger helped her to relax. She peered about at the dark skies and sheets of rain. "It was time for me to go." Not that she ever should have come here in the first place. She'd hoped that introducing her association to Denver would gain her some leverage.

Instead his friends had politely cut her cold—all except this man.

As if they weren't standing out in horrendously nasty weather, he looked her over. "So you're with Denver, too, huh? Not surprised, really. The lucky SOB always did get the hottest girls. But you're a lot classier than Cherry Peyton, ya know?"

"Oh. Oh, no." She smiled, pleased by the observation and finally understanding why he remained friendly. Knowing she had to be fair, she explained, "I'm Denver's stepmother," and then she waited for his open rejection.

A low whistle and an even lower, *"No fucking way,"* should have offended her. Instead, after Denver's awful treatment and how his friends had shunned her, the reaction sent pleasure radiating through her.

"Yes. His father and I have been married six years now."

"He must have robbed the cradle with you. And I thought Denver was lucky."

Her smile brightened another few watts. "Why, thank you." Holding out a hand, she said, "Pamela Barnett Lewis."

Taking her hand, he frowned. "Denver should have walked you out." He inched closer. "Can't believe he didn't."

"He was in the middle of things," she said as if she knew that for a fact, when in reality, she had no idea what he did in the gym.

"Well, his oversight is my fortune, right?" Still holding her hand, he smiled at her, a bold smile that frightened her just a little. "Carver Nelson, at your service."

ARMIE LOOKED AROUND the restaurant and half wished he'd worn something different. It was upscale casual, not one of the fast-food places he preferred.

Then again, screw it. He didn't want to be here anyway. Besides, Cannon also wore a T-shirt. Sure, his was a nicer SBC T-shirt. But the other two...

And that was another point of contention, damn it. The other *two*.

He thought he'd be doing a quick burger with Havoc, and instead it was Havoc and Simon Evans both in a sit-down restaurant with starched tablecloths and fancy menus. That Cannon had been invited along... Yeah, he didn't yet know if that was a good or a bad thing.

Cannon had a way of pushing him, seeing the imagined "best" in him and wanting others to see it, too.

At the moment they all watched him.

Sitting back in the seat and sprawling out his legs, Armie quirked a brow. "I think I've forgotten my lines in this little drama. Someone give me my cue."

Simon laughed, then shook his shaved head and half the damn women in the place looked ready to swoon. Simon Evans, better known in the fight community as Sublime, always had that effect on females. Matrimony and a few added years hadn't changed anything. "You're a funny guy, Jacobson. Do they call you Quick because of your wit?"

"Not exactly," Cannon chimed in with a big grin. "But that's a long story."

No, actually it was a short story—one Armie had no intention of sharing.

Havoc said, "Let's order before we talk."

Simon gave a signal and a waitress rushed up to them. Less than half a minute later they all had drinks. Armie was the only one to order a beer, and worse, he'd ordered a loaded burger while the others had lean chicken and fish.

Havoc and Simon scrutinized him. He didn't know if it was over the food, which he wouldn't explain because, seriously, his record spoke for him. When he needed to be on weight, he was.

When he could cut loose and indulge, he did that, too.

"So," Simon said. "Explain *Quick*."

"Quick knockouts, quick submissions. Fast wins," Armie said before Cannon could tell the real story. "That's the basis of my fight name."

"Somehow," Simon mused, "I think there's more to it than that." Stalling Armie's protest, he continued. "But that's not why we're here."

Havoc sat back, his expression far too serious. "Tell me, Armie, what makes you tick?"

Ah, hell no. He didn't want to get into any psychobabble. "No idea what you mean."

"You just said it—quick, maybe even expedient wins."

"Low-level competition?"

"No," Simon said. "Many of the men you've handily beaten have gone on to join us."

"Every fight," Havoc added, "you go out dominant, you stay dominant, every move slick, ingrained."

While Cannon beamed like a freaking proud father, Simon chimed in again. "Never a glitch, you never falter."

What the fuck? He faltered. He just didn't let it show. Not in a fight.

Havoc drummed his fingers on the tabletop. "Something drives you and I want to know what it is."

Jesus, between Cannon soaking it all in, Havoc dissecting him and Simon remaining amused, he almost squirmed. Being in the hot seat sucked. Giving himself time to think, Armie took a long drink of his beer before asking, "Why the inquisition?"

"Because I want you in the SBC."

"*We* want you in the SBC," Simon corrected.

"And to do that we need to better understand you. I know guys who get off on the audience—they feed from it. I know guys with something to prove, either to themselves or someone else. I know guys who consider winning a badge of honor."

Cannon laughed.

Mouth quirked, Armie said, "Yeah, that's not me."

"Which part?" Simon asked.

"All of it." Didn't matter to him if the audience was friendly or hostile. He didn't have a damn thing to prove to anyone. As for honor… Yeah, as important as it was to him, it had zip to do with winning. For him, honor was more about how he fought than whether he won or lost.

Havoc pressed. "So what is it?"

An easy enough answer. "I like fighting, and I like winning."

"You could win bigger with the SBC."

Yeah, and that was the crux of his reservations. Bigger fights, bigger audience. Armie drew a breath to again, as politely as possible, refuse.

"Before you say no again—and you can quit shaking your head—I have an offer to make."

"I don't want to hear it."

"Tough. Sign on with the SBC, and we'll invest heavily in the rec center."

Oh, hell no! Alarm jolted him out of his slouched position—until Cannon leaned forward. "Not taking over, Armie. Never that. We'll always run it, you and me."

He relaxed…a little.

"But they want to take part."

Eyeing Cannon, he asked, "How?"

"Just…enhancing some things."

"We're talking scholarships for some of the at-risk kids. Transportation to and from the rec center, like maybe a small bus. Scheduled visits from some of the SBC stars that you can promote—"

"That's blackmail!" And really awesome shit. Damn.

"We don't mind a little blackmail every now and then."

Armie scowled. "We?"

"Simon and me for now, although Jude Jamison wants in on it, as well."

"Fuck me sideways," Armie whispered, his spine again hitting the back of the chair as he slumped. It was enough that he had both Simon and Havoc singling him out, but Jude Jamison, too?

Jude had started as an SBC champion, doing a lot to take the sport mainstream, then went on to become a world-famous movie star, only to return to his roots by buying out part of the SBC. If Simon and Havoc were big-time, Jude was…well, superstar status.

Armie knew Simon was smiling again, sensed Cannon watching him with satisfaction, and felt the pressure from Havoc's unwavering stare. *Dammit.*

"It's time," Cannon said softly.

Getting air into his lungs proved impossible. Pushing back his chair, Armie walked out.

Behind him, he heard Cannon say, "He'll be back. Just give him a minute."

That was Cannon for you, always assuming the best of him. As he stalked toward the exit he ignored the cute waitress trying to flirt, just as he ignored the sense of being hunted.

Going to the SBC would mean giving up the comfort of his anonymity. It would mean dredging up the past.

Eventually he'd have to fight the old accusations all over again.

And seriously, once had been enough.

Breathing deep, Armie pushed open the doors and stepped out into the early evening air. The rain had stopped, leaving the air fresh, but heavy and thick. The tires of passing cars hissed on the wet roadway. Overhead, gutters dripped. Birds, their feathers wet, sat all along the telephone lines, singing happily.

Armie walked to a bus bench glistening with little puddles. He braced his hands on the backrest, dropping his head forward in thought as he struggled against what he wanted and what he...feared.

That unbearable thought made him want to run. *He didn't fear anything.*

Such a gigantic lie. He didn't fear much.

He didn't *want* to suffer fear.

But he did. Fear, humiliation.

Helplessness.

The sudden buzzing of his cell phone made him jump. Cursing his own vulnerability, he dug it out of his pocket and answered without looking to see who called. "Yeah?"

"Did you know if you call the gym, whoever answers hands out your number, no questions asked?"

He got taken aback—completely sidelined from his own misery—by that recognizable voice.

Refreshing antagonism rushed through his bloodstream. "It works that way because that's how I want it to work." He cocked his head, popping the tension out of his neck and letting sarcasm sink in.

"You're responsible for that place?"

He wouldn't explain jack shit to the idiot. "What do you want?"

"To talk to Cherry."

He laughed. "No."

"Tell her to call me," the man said in low, lethal tones. "Tell her I will rain misery down on everyone she cares about if she doesn't."

"Tell you what," Armie said with snide joviality. "Go fuck yourself."

"You'll regret that."

"Yeah?" Glad to egg him on, to have a new focus other than his own haunted future, Armie smiled into the phone. "Let's get together and talk about it in person. What do you think?"

"Suits me."

Perfect. "Where do I find you?"

A laugh. "Don't worry about it. Now that I'm in Warfield, I promise…I'll find you."

The call ended.

It took two seconds for the implications of that to sink in, then Armie turned with a purpose and strode back into the restaurant.

When he reached the table, he saw the food set out—and everyone waiting on him. He'd dodged the possibilities long enough. Time to face reality.

Time to move forward.

Without sitting, he drew out forty bucks and tossed them on the table, then stuck his hand out to Havoc. "I'll take your offer."

Slowly, Havoc pushed back his chair, his mood wary. "We haven't discussed the contract yet."

"Cannon can deal with that for me." He shook Havoc's hand, then reached past him to do the same with Simon. "A pleasure to meet you both in person."

"Just that easy?" Simon didn't smile now.

"Something's come up."

"I see." Simon clasped Armie's hand. "You don't have any questions?"

"No time. Maybe later." He turned to Cannon. "I need a word with you."

Cannon had already stood, attuned to a problem. Armie decided he'd call Denver on his way to the rec center.

Nothing like facing someone else's troubles to put your own into perspective.

Together, they went as far as the front doors. In hushed tones, Armie explained about the call.

"You're sure it was him?" Cannon asked.

"Positive." And he had a bad premonition about things. "You haven't met the cretins, but Denver is right to be worried. I don't like them, any of them, and if they're actually here, in Warfield now—"

"I'll come with you," Cannon said.

"What, and leave things hanging with those two?" He hitched a thumb toward where both Havoc and Simon watched them from their table.

"They'll keep."

Meaning Cannon had his priorities, too, and as usual Armie was one of them. Facing a faulty future with a really great friend made it more bearable. "No, you stay. I've got it covered. We'll all keep an eye out. But maybe later you could—"

"Set up a network. Yeah, I'll do that. Tell Denver I'll give him a call tonight."

Long ago, Cannon had made connections to damn near everyone in the neighborhood, some older and retired, some young and at risk. He knew the good and the bad, and many in the middle who saw and heard things that others didn't. When necessary, he could glean information from the streets in a way the cops never could.

Nodding, Armie mused aloud, "Denver won't let Cherry out of his sight."

Cannon grinned. "I have a feeling he'd have kept her close regardless. Those two are constantly either antagonizing each other, or setting off sparks hot enough to start a fire."

Armie grinned. "Yeah, they're even more entertaining than Gage and Harper were." He rubbed his mouth, then glanced again at the two veteran fighters. "I didn't want to mention any of this in front of them. Don't want them thinking Denver is divided on things while he needs to be focused on his training."

"I'm guessing they've been around long enough to know fighters can multitask."

"Especially when a woman is involved?"

"The right woman, sure." Cannon crossed his arms. "You okay with how this rolled out?"

"What? Having my best friend sabotage me while colluding with the enemy? Sure. Why would I mind that?"

Censuring, Cannon said, "They're not the enemy."

Armie laughed. "Not anymore anyway." How did he feel about it? Guarded. Resigned. "You said it, it's time. Couldn't drag my feet forever."

"You're not facing anything alone. You know that, right?"

He did. For as long as he could remember, Cannon had been like a brother to him. Better than a brother, even. "It's fine—but right now, I want to get hold of Denver."

"I'll call him. You just get to the rec center in case

there's a setup." Cannon pulled keys from his pocket. "Take my car. I'll grab a ride with Simon and Havoc. And Armie? Be alert."

"Always." He hesitated. "Negotiate a good deal for me."

Cannon cracked a smile. "Plan to."

Once, years ago, Cannon had saved his ass. If he wanted Armie in the SBC, then that's where he'd go, and he'd face the consequences, whatever they might be, head-on. "Thank you."

"For?"

"Pushing me." *Everything.* "Not letting me be content."

"Hey, what good are friends if they don't shove you into uncomfortable situations?" After a brief, commiserating grip on Armie's shoulder, Cannon pulled out his cell and headed to a quiet corner of the entrance to call Denver.

He had a lot of shit on his plate, but Armie realized he was smiling as he headed out. Maybe things weren't so bad after all.

CHAPTER SIXTEEN

STACK MEANT TO leave as soon as Denver reclaimed the class.

Instead, when Vanity strolled in looking damp and appealingly windblown from the weather, he decided to hang around a little longer. He'd watched her shed a trendy raincoat and matching umbrella, then watched her make herself at home at the rec center.

Now he was late for his date—not that it was really much of a date. More like a mutual agreement to get laid, but still... Somehow the idea of heading out for "the sure thing" no longer appealed.

He got out his cell and went into the hall to make a call and cancel the plans. After explaining that he'd gotten held up and promising that he'd make it up to her soon, he realized he wasn't alone.

Without even knowing why, he felt guilty as he jerked around and found Vanity eavesdropping. She watched him without a single sign of remorse.

Keeping his gaze locked on hers, he said his good-byes and calmly tucked his phone, and his guilt, away.

Her blue eyes bright, she said, "Hi."

"Hi, yourself." Tonight she had her long hair in some sort of intricate braid that arrowed down her back as if pointing to that stellar ass. In stretchy running shorts and a matching tank, she couldn't hide a flaw—not that she had any.

His mouth went dry. This woman wanted to sleep with him.

But not until the wedding.

"I'm curious, Stack."

"Me, too." Like half hard with curiosity.

Her patented teasing smile played over her lips, making him nuts and showing a smidge of confusion. "What?"

He shook his head. "You first."

"I was just going to ask why you're still here if you had a date."

Oh. He cast about for an excuse, and settled on the obvious. "We had some drama, that's all. Denver's stepmother stopped in."

"Why is that drama?"

Shrugging, he said, "I haven't had a chance to find out, but trust me, it was not a friendly meeting." Rather than detail how badly Vanity had occupied his thoughts, he dug in on the topic of Denver and domestic issues. "Shocked me when I met her. She looks nothing like a stepmother."

"Oh? How should a stepmother look?"

"Like a mother? At least old enough to *be* a mother. This woman looked damn near Denver's age. And she was…" How should he put it? "Overdressed for the gym, that's for sure. Young and sexy, too. Long red hair, killer dress and body, bold attitude."

Her smile stayed in place. "You admired her. How… nice."

"Said I was shocked already, right?" He frowned. She had no reason—and no right—to act put out over his observations. "You don't think I'd hit on Denver's stepmother, do you? Because that'd seriously be out of line."

"So the fact that she's obviously married isn't what held you back? It was just her relationship to Denver?"

"No!" How did she always steer him down these awkward verbal paths? "Don't put words in my mouth."

Her smile widened. "Okay, sorry. You know what? I think I saw her, and yes, she's beautiful."

"She was gone before you got here."

"Well, there was a woman who fit that description hanging around outside."

Curious, Stack asked, "Doing what?"

"I don't know. Just talking with a guy. I noticed her because of her dress. Usually women who are dressed up don't linger in the rain."

Curiosity turned to misgivings. "What guy?"

"I don't know him. Dark hair and eyes. He held a jacket over her head while they huddled together under an overhang. Her hair—which was definitely red—kept blowing out with the wind."

Alarm bells had been dinging, but now they blared. "Come on." He grabbed Vanity's hand and dragged her over to Denver, who was wrapping up a class with the older boys.

Denver said to the group, "I want you to always press forward. Keep your opponent on his back foot. You don't want him to know what's coming, whether you'll be shooting in, throwing a punch or aiming a kick. As long as he's backpedaling, he's off balance. But that also leaves you open to walking into something…"

Waiting off on the sidelines, Stack folded his arms and nodded agreement with Denver's instruction.

Vanity nudged him with her shoulder. Speaking low, she said, "There are so many rules and moves and they all seem to be contingent on other factors. How in the world do you guys learn it all?"

"Muscle memory," Stack said, still watching the boys. "You do drills often enough, you practice moves, spar a lot, and it becomes automatic. Or at least it should."

"Does that mean the guy who loses didn't do enough practice?"

"Not necessarily." Girding himself, he turned to her—and damn, the sight of her looking up at him with interest hit like a wild haymaker. Did she know the effect her getup had on him?

Probably. Vanity Baker was not an obtuse girl.

Not all women looked good in clinging workout clothes. Vanity could be a walking ad for them.

"Some guys just have more heart and more innate ability. You have to be able to take the pain and keep your head, and you need to be able to adjust. If a move goes wrong, if the guy you're fighting is especially proficient at something, switching gears can help." His gaze dipped to her chest, but only for a second. She watched him so closely, she'd know if he started thinking lewd, awesome things. "And sometimes you just get caught. Happens to the best of them. You do one thing wrong, no matter how small, and it can change the entire fight."

"Wrong, like what?"

"A punch you don't dodge. A submission setup you miss. Hell, occasionally you can trip, or slip on sweat or blood. Break a hand or pop a joint." He shrugged. "Anything."

Nose wrinkled over that last comment, she asked, "Have you ever been caught?"

Big-time. The night she'd asked him to take her to the wedding would count. The second she'd mentioned having sex, all his better sense had flown the coop.

"Stack?"

He locked his jaw and tried to clear his mind of smoldering carnal images. Luckily Denver, who'd finished while they were talking, saved his ass by asking, "What's up?"

Redirecting his focus, he said, "I think your stepmama might've made nice with Cherry's wayward foster brothers."

Vanity said, *"What?"*

Before Stack could explain about the trinity of troublemaking brothers, Harper jogged over carrying the phone for Denver. "It's Cannon. He said he called your cell and when you didn't answer, he figured you were still in the middle of the class." She handed over the phone and then went back to the front desk where she often helped out.

Stack sensed plenty of things going awry. When Denver took the phone, he didn't excuse himself so Stack and Vanity were privy to the convo. From what Stack could tell given the one-sided dialogue, Armie had gotten a call from the brothers confirming they were in town.

Not good.

Soon as Denver ended the call, he said to Vanity, "Tell me what you saw."

She didn't ask any questions, didn't need clarification. She repeated to Denver almost exactly what she'd told Stack, but with more detail.

"Shit." Denver rubbed the back of his neck. "Carver claims he's here. He threatened Armie again, says he wants to see Cherry…"

"So it probably was him with your stepmama then, right?"

"Call her Pamela, okay? I don't claim any relationship."

Stack agreed, although given the hostility between her and Denver, he had no plans to call the woman anything at all. "If he was just outside, that means—"

"He's aware of the rec center." Denver's gaze went to Vanity and then back again. "And everyone coming or going from here."

Understanding just how risky that made things, Stack frowned at Vanity.

She lifted her brows in query.

"You'll take care of it?" Denver asked.

Meaning would he take care of Vanity? Stack inhaled. "Got it covered."

"Good. Cannon's going to set up a network to keep an eye on things, but it'll take at least a few hours, if not a day to get that in motion."

Nodding, he said, "Doesn't hurt to be extra careful." *Especially with the ladies.*

"I have to go find Cherry."

"She's in the restroom," Vanity offered. "Repairing her makeup and hair, I think."

Denver checked the clock and frowned. "Still?"

Vanity shrugged. "Not easy to do in a standard restroom without her usual…accessories."

He nodded acceptance of that, saying, "Thanks," as he strode away.

As soon as Denver was gone, Stack turned to her and asked, "Why are you here?"

"Sorry. I didn't think you would be."

How the hell was that an answer? With his hair nearly standing on end, he asked, "What's that supposed to mean, Vanity?" Was she dodging him now?

Hooking her arm through his, Vanity started them both across the floor. Given her skimpy outfit and his short-sleeved T-shirt, he felt skin on skin.

Their arms, he reminded himself, not that his brain or his dick seemed to care how innocuous the touch might be.

"That came out wrong," Vanity explained with a smile. "I just didn't want you to think I was chasing after you because we have an agreement for the future. I was surprised when I got here and saw you."

"Denver's stepmother..." He started to explain again.

"I understand. Sounds like it's been a hectic day." She hugged his arm just enough to make his muscles clench, especially when he felt the side of her breast against his biceps. "It was nice of you to stick around and lend a hand."

"Yeah," he said, not really hearing himself since Vanity led them to a quiet corner alone. This time of night, the place was clearing out. They'd close up soon and only a few of those in the inner circle might still hang around and use the equipment.

She paused by a heavyweight bag. "I came by to sign up for the self-defense classes and then figured I'd stick around and exercise."

Damn. He'd be taking a turn teaching the class to women.

Stepping around the heavyweight bag, she examined a rack of weights. "I used to go to the gym all the time back in California. Surfed a lot, too. But so far around here, I've been a complete slug. I don't want to get out of shape."

Propping a shoulder on the wall, Stack gave her body a lingering look. "Yeah, no worry on that."

"Stack." She trailed her fingertips over the equipment. "Have you thought about it much?"

"It?"

"Us. Having sex."

Jesus, the way she threw things out there kept him off-kilter. "Round the clock," he admitted. He thought about it to the point that hooking up with other women just seemed like a bother. *That*, he didn't admit. "You?"

"Yes." Staring at his mouth, she took a step closer. "I don't want us to jump the gun on that timeframe because it leaves the possibility that we might hit a conflict and then I'd be dateless for the wedding again."

His heart pounded hard—with lust. But he kept his tone expressionless. "Given what you're offering, you think I'd do that?"

Her gaze lifted to his. "If you did anything bad enough to irritate me, I might be the one backing out. Either way would still leave me trying to figure out my plus one."

Incredible. So she didn't want to fuck him yet because if she did, he might somehow piss her off to the point that she wouldn't want to be stuck with him at a wedding?

Keeping his narrowed gaze on her face, he said, "I think I'm insulted."

"Please don't be." The blue of her eyes turned smoky. "Especially not right now because…"

Charged chemistry drew him closer. "Because?"

"Well, while I don't think we should spoil the suspense, I really need at least a small taste."

His eyes widened. His dick said a hearty *hello*.

She inched closer, too. "Would that be okay, you think?"

"Define taste." Because seriously, just the word turned him on.

"A kiss," she breathed.

Okay, he could work with that. "Where?" he whispered.

She misunderstood and said, "Your mouth, for starters."

Much more of that and he'd be hard. "I meant where, as in here, at the rec center?" In front of everyone.

Not that anyone should be paying them any attention, but…

"If you don't mind." She licked her lips while looking at his. "Now that I've decided on it, I don't want to wait."

How surreal to be standing there with her in the gym, talking about a kiss, discussing sex that wouldn't yet happen, while being insulted—and still wanting that damn kiss so bad he needed it more than his next breath.

Not sure he could stop at one kiss, he said, "I'll be following you home." She tried to refute that, but Stack bent and took her mouth in a frustratingly brief touch. "I am," he insisted, while watching her lick her lips again.

Damn, but he wanted her soft pink tongue on him.

"You don't know the whole story," he explained gruffly, "but there's a threat so I need to see you get home safe and sound."

Rather than argue, she nodded. "I picked up on some of that, but didn't want to pry."

Amazing. No other woman he knew could have refrained from prying. "I'm sure you'll hear it all eventually." He didn't want to go into it now. "But do me a favor and be extra careful, okay?"

"Okay." She swallowed. "That kiss didn't count."

He loved the shaky way she said that. "No, it didn't."

"And I won't let you kiss me at home. It'd be too easy for me to get carried away."

He groaned. "You can't tell me things like that, Vanity."

Her smile teased before finally lifting into a grin. "A big, strong fighter like you can keep it under wraps."

"But you can't?"

Going serious, she sighed. "With you, I honestly don't know." She lifted both hands to his chest, stroked lightly and then leaned into him. Her head tipped back and her eyes grew heavy. "Now kiss me for real."

Hell yeah. Hooking one arm around her narrow waist and sliding his other hand around her nape, he drew her in tighter, aligning their bodies in a smoldering way. He took her mouth exactly as he'd been thinking about taking it since the day he'd first laid eyes on her.

And damn, it was even better than he'd imagined.

"You two charging tickets for this porno show?"

Groaning, Vanity pulled away and glared at Armie. "That was so mean. And here I thought you were my friend."

He teased her, saying, "C'mon, Vee. You know you don't want to be a spectacle."

Stack glanced around and realized Armie was right. Gage and Harper both grinned at them, two boys watched by the door, and Denver and Cherry were now glancing their way while also having what appeared to be a serious discussion.

Not that Stack cared who watched, but—

Sighing again, Vanity said, "I think it might've been worth it." After that bit of sweet talk, she hugged up to his arm again. "I'm ready to leave if you are."

"Seeing her home?" Armie asked without too much innuendo.

"He's my personal protection while I'm in transit. Isn't that sweet?"

"Downright syrupy," Armie agreed. When Denver called him over, he said, "Carry on, kids," before leaving them.

Stack hadn't said a single word. Caught in the vise-like grip of red-hot lust, he wasn't sure he could.

"After that kiss," Vanity confided, "it's going to be even harder to wait."

Screw that. The wedding was too far off; he'd never make it. But warning her now would steal his advantage, so he just smiled at her.

And for once she looked more confused than he felt.

STREET LAMPS HAD already kicked on by the time they left the rec center. The heavy storms left a bite in the evening air. Not a single star showed in the black sky.

If he'd known Carver and his fucked-up brothers would show up so soon, he would have parked closer to the rec center in the lot normally reserved for guests, instead of on the street farther away.

Keeping Cherry close to his side, Denver glanced back and saw Armie leaning in the doorway. If it was just Denver leaving, Armie wouldn't have bothered. Since he had Cherry with him, no one wanted to take a chance on an ambush that could leave her unprotected.

Even knowing Armie had his back, he checked out every shadow and movement along the busy street. The cool, damp breeze left goose bumps on Cherry's arms. She'd tidied up and even though she wore Armie's shirt inside out, she looked hot.

He figured she could wear a potato sack and he'd still want her because wanting her was about more than just her looks and her sex appeal.

Though she denied it, he could tell by her fast chatter she was nervous. She talked about everything from the rainstorm, to Leese at the rec center, to Vanity kissing Stack.

"I'm pretty sure he kissed her, not the other way around."

"That's not how it looked to me. Do you think Stack likes her?"

Denver shrugged. "Sure. Why wouldn't he?"

"Denver Lewis, you know that's not what I mean. Does he *like*-like her?"

Why did women always want to analyze things? "He's confused, far as I can tell." Wind shook overhead tree branches, and the wet leaves sprinkled them with rain droplets. Denver stepped her out from under the long branches. "Don't worry about your car. I'll take care of it."

She frowned at him. "I can—"

"No need." A truck drove slowly past, making Denver frown. Then he saw the driver smile and pull over to pick up a friend who stepped out of a building. "I'll take care of it."

Cherry grumbled, but didn't push him. "Are we going back to my place now?"

Absently, he shook his head. "We're going to my house tonight, remember? I need to soak my shoulder for a bit and all you have is a shower."

She did an about-face. "You hurt your shoulder?"

"It's fine." He'd overworked every muscle today in an effort to sweat off tension. It hadn't helped. "It's just sore, that's all."

"There's a bathtub upstairs."

"In Rissy's domain? Yeah, I can't see Cannon liking that idea."

She smacked at him. "It's not like she'd peek in on you." After only a short hesitation, she added, "I don't think."

He grinned, but remained watchful. "Maybe I should just show her the goods to take care of her curiosity." Across the street a group of people laughed as they walked along. Somewhere farther up a car door slammed.

Denver realized Cherry had stopped and he turned to find her standing stiffly, her arms crossed and her face tight.

The grin caught him by surprise. "Just a joke, girl. Don't get all huffy."

"It's not funny."

Reaching out, he caught her elbow and drew her forward and into his arms. There on the sidewalk, with the steady drone of dripping gutters around them, he kissed her. "We made that exclusivity bargain, remember?"

"It covers looking or showing?"

"Definitely." He didn't want anyone else even thinking of Cherry's body, much less seeing it.

Satisfied, she nodded. "Okay then."

He got her to his car and held the passenger door open for her.

As soon as she was seated, she said, "The bathroom door has a lock."

"Buckle up." He closed the door and walked around the hood to get behind the wheel. He started the car, but his thoughts were divided between danger and Cherry in the bath. "You soak in the tub a lot?"

"Often. Rissy doesn't mind."

"Damn." He could almost see her resting back, her blond hair pinned up while the water lapped at her big, soft breasts. He shifted in his seat. It seemed no matter how many times he had her, or what else might be going on—like a few lunatics offering up threats—she got him primed so easily.

"We could soak together," she suggested.

Yeah, he'd like that. But suspicion reared its ugly head.

He pulled away from the curb before asking, his tone as casual as he could make it, "Is there a reason you don't want to go to my place?"

"No. I'd actually like to see where you live."

"Then why all the hesitation?"

The seconds ticked by until they turned into a full minute.

"Cherry?"

She grumbled again, this time with more irritation. "I'm still annoyed with you."

"Really?" She'd hid it well. "How does that play into going to my place?"

"It doesn't. It's just…I wanted us to talk."

"We're talking." But yeah, he knew that wasn't what she meant.

"You," she said with emphasis, "have some explaining to do, but now we have to worry about stupid Carver, so I'm trying to put it aside for the moment."

So levelheaded. She had reason to be mad. She also had reason to prioritize. "Appreciate it."

Looking very pugnacious—and cute—she glared at him. "On the off chance that creep is hanging around, maybe following us, I don't want to lead him to your home. But I know admitting that to you is only going to fire you up more and I do *not* want to turn this into you being annoyed with me."

What the hell? How was that not supposed to annoy him? "So because you're still pissed, I can't react to you treating me like a wuss?"

"Yes!"

Huh. She didn't even deny the wuss part, meaning she must've still been plenty pissed regardless of how she'd covered it.

Going for the most expedient way to smooth things over, Denver offered his hand and was pleased when, after only a brief reluctance, she took it. "First, I've been keeping an eye out. No one is following us. But even if he did, my house is pretty secure."

For far too long, she mulled that over, then gave a nod. "Okay."

Gently, he squeezed her hand, knowing by that curt answer that he had a long way to go yet. "Second, but more important, I really am sorry about embarrassing you today."

Nothing.

"I've never been such a possessive jerk. Not blaming you, but damn, you leave me half-cocked."

She choked.

"Not just with lust, but...with everything. I trust Armie, I really do."

"Of course you do."

"Pretty sure of that, huh?"

"Of course." She twisted in the seat to face him. "When I was sick at the hotel, it didn't bother you when Armie loomed over me."

"He didn't—"

"He *loomed*, Denver." She fidgeted before adding, "And he touched me."

Denver frowned.

"No place important," she clarified before he could give himself an aneurism, "but still, it about stopped my heart having two big, gorgeous hunks—"

His body clenched with jealousy.

"—treating me with kid gloves."

Eyeing her amused expression, he accused, "Now you're just trying to piss me off."

And she laughed. Actually laughed—at *him*. "Misery loves company. But my point—"

"There's a point?" Because it seriously just felt like payback.

"—is that you trust Armie, so it must be me you don't trust."

That put the brakes on his annoyance. Damn, he had given that impression, which meant he'd have to give an explanation, too.

And that would involve baring part of his soul. *Shit.* "Denver?"

"I trust you. Completely." Since he didn't totally understand it himself, he had a hard time explaining his reaction to her. "It's not about that."

Tipping her head to study him, she said, "Armie is outrageous, no one could deny that." She held Denver's hand with both of hers. "But he's only friendly with the women he won't sleep with. You know that."

"Yeah, I do." Armie did a lot of superficial teasing with female friends. Only Yvette was different. She and Armie had connected on a more basic level, making them beyond mere friends, but nowhere near anything intimate.

"You're not suggesting I stop talking to him, are you?"

"God, no." He liked that she was so well accepted in their group. The other fighters recognized her as someone special, not just a casual hookup. That mattered.

Looking stern, she said, "Good. I adore you, Denver, but—"

She adored him?

"—I won't be bossed around, and I won't let you dictate to me."

Carver had likely done enough of that to last her a lifetime. "I wouldn't want to." He felt ridiculous saying it, but what the hell? "I adore you, too. Just as you are. I don't want you to change."

"Really?" Her smile nearly blinded him. "You adore me?"

Such a stupid word. To blunt it, he added a few he preferred. "Adore, enjoy, respect, lust after—"

She laughed.

After another squeeze, he released her hand to put both of his on the wheel, knowing he'd need them there while sharing a few truths. Just making the decision to tell her everything left him unsettled and raw with unfamiliar emotions.

He didn't want to drag it out, so he jumped right into the telling. "Not long after Pamela and my dad married, she came on to me."

Cherry stared at him slack-jawed. "How old were you?"

Tension sank in to his muscles, making his shoulder hurt like a sonofabitch, strangling him a little. "Twenty."

"A boy."

"No." He wouldn't let her sugarcoat things, especially when she hadn't yet heard the whole story. "I was a grown man. Dad knew it." He hated the memories. "So did Pamela."

"I imagine you were as impressive then as you are now."

He laughed without humor. Impressive? At the time he'd felt like a stud. Young, dumb, full of his own invincibility. "Dad was at the hospital for a long shift. I'd been out late the night before so I was still in bed." Jesus, he hated reliving it.

Cherry's small hand settled on his arm just above

LORI FOSTER 327

his elbow. She didn't say anything, but then, she didn't need to. He felt her silent support.

"She came into my bedroom. Naked."

"Wow." Her fingers slipped up under the sleeve of his T-shirt, touching the bare skin of his upper arm. "What did you do?"

Seeing it all in his head made him feel it again, too. "She was on me before I even realized what was going on. I woke up with her hand wrapped around my dick, her mouth on my neck." *Her naked body moving against me, her long hair sliding all over my chest.* "She said she'd heard from some of my dates how big I was and she had to find out for herself."

Totally deadpan, Cherry said, "Guess she needed it verified, huh?"

He scrubbed a hand over his face. Clenched and unclenched his teeth. "I had a boner," he admitted. "She carried on, saying a lot of stuff—"

"Denver, you *are* big."

"I know. But she took that for encouragement, carrying on like I'd gotten hard specifically for her."

"Awkward."

Was she teasing him? "Swear to God, Cherry, most guys wake up hard, especially at that age."

Her hand slid up to his shoulder. "How did she take it when you told her to get out?"

Unsure he'd heard right, Denver flashed a glance at her and saw she was dead serious. No doubts in her big brown eyes. No recriminations.

He heard himself say, "You sure I did?"

She said softly, "Yes."

Ah, fuck that felt great. Awesome enough that some of the suffocating pressure eased off of his chest, allowing him to take two big, cleansing breaths. "Thank you."

"I trust you, Denver. Completely." Her smile felt like a balm, but the words felt even better. "I'm sure at that age you were different, with a younger man's perspectives and priorities. But you would never sleep with your father's wife. That's just ridiculous."

"You can't know me that well." Could she?

"Maybe there are some things I still don't know. But you don't exactly hide the real you."

"The real me, huh?" By the second he felt better, as if he'd just shrugged off several years' worth of turmoil.

She nodded. "You can be really hardheaded. And God knows you're sexist. *Big-time* sexist." She scrunched her nose. "But in a nice way, like you want to take care of women."

"I—"

"And in bed you're a dominant force." She shivered. "Combined with how you look, and yes, your size, it's pretty hot."

She'd totally sidetracked him. "Cherry…"

"You're also pushy and way too autocratic, an alpha who always wants to run the show."

"Go ahead. Don't spare me."

"No, I won't. You can take the truth, and somehow I think you need to hear it."

Funny, but the string of insults really did make him feel better. If Cherry knew his faults, then maybe she also knew of the loyalty that would keep him from ever betraying someone he loved.

Even though his father hadn't known.

She wasn't done yet. "As much as you might deny it, you have a temper. I felt the sting of it today."

"We're back to that?" Shit. He hated that he'd made her feel so bad. "If I could redo it, I would. There's no good excuse, I know, but it was a totally fucked-up day, and with Pamela there and Armie with you and—"

She waved that off. "You're usually fair, proven by your willingness to apologize."

The praise was a little harder to take than the criticism. "Maybe I just want to get laid."

"There's that, I'm sure. You're the most over-sexed person I've ever known."

"No such thing." He couldn't get the smile off his face. "And if you weren't so sexy—"

"But," she interrupted, "it's also that you have a lot of honor. When you're wrong, you admit it." She took a deep breath. "So I know if you'd done anything with Pamela, you'd take half the blame. Instead, you seem to hate her."

He resented her more than anything, but didn't want to argue semantics.

Cherry's voice, her posture, her expression all softened. "So what happened?"

The complete and total faith humbled him. In that moment, he knew the truth. He more than adored Cherry Peyton, more than lusted for her.

He loved her.

CHAPTER SEVENTEEN

"DENVER?" HE WAS so quiet, so still, it worried Cherry. "You okay?"

Looking a little dazed, he nodded. "Yeah."

Did his voice sound funny? She leaned closer. "You're sure?"

"Positive."

Then why were his biceps bunched under her hand? Why did he keep swallowing? Hoping to soothe him, she rubbed his shoulder—and gave herself a thrill. She couldn't touch Denver without reacting.

Get your mind off sex, she ordered herself—a very tall order when it came to Denver. She licked her lips and made a magnanimous offer. "If you'd rather not talk about it right now, I can wait."

He checked the rearview mirror, the side mirror, then turned a corner. "It's okay. I was just thinking."

"About?"

His eyes narrowed. "How special you are."

"Oh." A little flustered, she sat back. "Really?"

"You don't know? Because girl, you are seriously a cut above the rest."

The flattery almost made her forget what they were talking about. But Denver hadn't forgotten.

"Pamela tried to kiss me on the mouth, but I dodged her. When I told her to stop, she said no one would ever know." He rubbed the bridge of his nose, the back of his neck. "When I reminded her that she was married to my father, she guaranteed me that Dad wouldn't find out, so how could he be hurt if we played just a little?"

"She missed the point that *you'd* know."

He drew in a shaky breath. "She figured I'd be all over it, like she was somehow irresistible or something."

"She misjudged you."

"I shoved her away, not to hurt her or anything, but I was so damned shocked I just reacted. She landed on the floor, buck naked, sprawled. Swear, I tried not to look. But she started scrambling, grabbing for me while I was just trying to get away. She made a lot of…promises." He glanced at her uncomfortably. "Things she'd do and stuff. Like she thought that would sway me."

There wasn't a single thing funny about what he described, but Cherry could almost see it as a comedy sketch. A young superhunk, a desperate woman offering herself. Nakedness. Rejection and confusion.

And to think *she'd* been embarrassed over how she'd looked when meeting Pamela for the first time. She wasn't one to judge, but God knew, Pamela wasn't in a position to be judging anyone, either.

Though she was curious about the kinky things Pamela offered, Cherry decided not to ask. Encouraging Denver, she said, "Go on."

"She trapped me by the damned door and at that point, with me being pretty blunt, she went from hoping to convince me to begging me not to say anything."

Oh no. Cherry's heart broke for him. She remembered conversations they'd had, how he hadn't wanted to talk about his family. "You told your father anyway?"

"Not at first. Dad was so damned happy with her, and other than sending me pleading looks Pamela acted like nothing had happened."

"But you couldn't?"

His jaw tightened. "I didn't want to talk to her. Hell, I couldn't even bear to look at her. Things got…tense. I tried to hide it, but I know Dad noticed."

Cherry watched him check the mirrors again, impressed that even while dredging up an ugly part of his past he remained vigilant. Such a remarkable man, even more so than she'd ever realized.

"Waiting to tell him what happened was a mistake." Disgusted, he said, "She told Dad that I hated her, that I'd been mean and disrespectful. She claimed I would do anything to get rid of her."

Disbelief widened her eyes. "He believed her?"

"He said he'd been watching me, that he could see the animosity every time I looked at her. I knew…" He squeezed the wheel, drank in a deep breath. "I knew it'd be useless but I tried telling him the truth anyway."

"Oh God, Denver, I'm so sorry."

"He kicked me out. Told me he wouldn't believe my lies. He said I should stay gone until I'd grown up enough to apologize to Pamela."

Cherry gasped, getting angry on his behalf. "Of course you can't do that!"

"No," he agreed. "We haven't spoken since and now Pamela wants me to just show up for a family party like the past isn't there between us."

Cherry wanted to make suggestions, but this was important—not just to Denver's feelings or for his re-

lationship with his dad, but maybe for his entire outlook on life.

Did he worry so much about her teasing with other
guys because of how Pamela had betrayed both him
and his father? She wasn't a therapist, but it seemed
pretty obvious to her.

Just as obvious was the fact that he needed to have
as much faith in her as she had in him.

"You need to accept her invitation."

His gaze cut her way, then returned to the road. "I
don't think—"

"You need to go, and you need to be nice."

His jaw worked. Probably trying to placate her, he
drew a breath, then asked mildly, "Why's that?"

"You need to prove that you've moved beyond it."
Though they both knew he *hadn't*, she felt that once
he confronted his father and Pamela again—this time
as a grown, confident man—he'd hopefully find some
closure. "You need to show that Pamela doesn't affect
you, that you've never wanted her that way. Not then
and not now."

"I don't care what Pamela thinks."

"You wouldn't be doing it for her. Not for your dad,
either. And definitely not for me."

His brows pinched down, but he listened.

"You need to prove it to you."

"Shit." He rubbed his mouth but he didn't disagree.
The seconds ticked by, and then a full minute before
he said, "You'll go with me?"

That was such an enormous sign of trust that her
heart seemed to leap in her chest. She tried to tamp
down the elation so he'd know she took it all very seriously. "Yes, if that's what you want."

He reached out for her hand, and when she put it in his, he gave her a squeeze. "It won't be pleasant."

"You might be surprised. But either way, I'd be happy to go with you."

He lifted her hand to his mouth and kissed her knuckles. "Thank you."

"You'll call her tonight to let her know to expect us?"

"Tomorrow is soon enough." He flashed a mean grin. "If I time it right, I can just talk with the house-keeper and she can give Pamela the message."

Cherry laughed. "Good plan." Sensing he could use a detour after the seriousness of their discussion, she said, "So then, you know what I'd like to do tonight?"

Without missing a beat, he said, "Head to bed where I can make you scream and groan and show you how sorry I am for insulting you earlier?"

It took a second for her to reply after he painted that particular, enticing picture. Trying for cavalier detachment, she quipped, "Really, Denver? That's the best you've got?"

"I'm horny as hell. How creative did you want me to be?"

Damn, she loved him. Someday maybe she'd get to tell him. "Know what? Yes, I want to do that."

He almost drove the car off the road. He slowed, straightened in his seat, and sent her a sizzling look of encouragement.

Not that she needed any. "Tonight in fact, even though I already forgave you. And then this Friday, I'd like us to just have a date."

Tense now that they'd discussed sex, he repeated, "A date?"

"Yeah, you know that unique concept where we actually go out together? And for a change I could look my best instead of like a train wreck." As an example she lifted the hem of Armie's too-big-for-her shirt, still inside out. "I deliberately put on a very cute outfit for you this morning, not that you can tell now. It seems ever since we got together, I've had one physical catastrophe after another. I want to look pretty for you."

"Damn, girl." He tugged at the leg of his jeans. "You're always pretty."

Aw, so sweet. "You know what I'm talking about."

Slowing the car, he turned and pulled into a driveway. "Sure. Girls like to doll up. I get that. But I'm serious. You need to know that never, not for a single second, not while you were sick and sure as shit not while you were soaking wet with clothes glued to your body, have I ever thought you didn't look amazing."

A bubble of happiness expanded inside her. "You are such a sweet talker."

"Lust inspires me."

"I agree to sex—which should be a given by now—and you go all poetic?"

"Actually, I've been halfway there ever since you handled Pamela so well at the gym. Strong, take-charge women are a big turn-on."

Quirking her mouth, she said, "That also describes Pamela."

"Not even close. She's weak and manipulative and needy. But you're…"

"What?"

His voice went soft and rough. "Strong, independent, loyal and sexy as hell because of it."

God, with the way he looked at her, she got entranced by his golden eyes.

Until he turned the car off and gestured. "My house."

"Oh." Given the turn of their conversation, she'd barely paid attention to him parking the car. Getting herself together, she peered through the windshield at a beautiful brick ranch. "Your house." Smiling, she tilted her head, taking it in, then opened her door and stepped out before he could do the gentlemanly thing and open it for her.

He joined her on the walkway to the front porch and took her hand. "What do you think?"

"It's wonderful."

That made him laugh. "It's just a house, not fancy or all that expensive."

"It's perfect for you." The house was simple in design but still looked welcoming, with just enough landscaping to feel homey, but not so much that it'd need a lot of upkeep. When she saw the rosebush, she stopped. "This is clearly a newly built house, so does that mean you planted the roses?"

He tugged at his ear. "Yeah, and the other bushes and stuff."

The garage opened on the side, but he hadn't driven into it, choosing to park in the driveway instead. Taking the cobbled walkway, they circled past the front of the double garage to the small porch.

Denver dug out a key, and as soon as they stepped inside he pushed numbers into a security keypad. "Come on, I'll take you on a quick tour then fix us something to eat."

Before he could whisk her off, she admired the

higher ceilings and the rich hardwood floors. An enormous rug rested beneath two couches, with a big lounge chair that faced a massive flat-screen television. "I see you have your priorities in line."

Laughing, he said, "Most of my priorities are in the basement."

"Workout stuff?"

"For when I don't spend as much time at the rec center as I should."

Far as she could tell, that never happened. It seemed to her that Denver practically lived in the gym.

They walked toward a big kitchen, but Denver steered her down a short hall to the left and pushed open a door. "Guest bathroom."

Cherry poked her head inside. "Nice," she said, though that single word didn't feel adequate. "I love the tile and the fixtures."

"Thanks. It opens into both of the smaller bedrooms on either side, but they're mostly empty." They went back to the living room and he gestured at the kitchen. "The dining room and breakfast nook are attached. Then over here is my room."

She stepped inside to tall windows, high ceilings, more hardwood floors and heavy masculine furniture. "Wow, your bed is huge."

"It's custom-made, an extra-wide king."

Extra-wide so he'd have plenty of room for sexual acrobatics? The sting of jealousy made her scowl. "You must've felt cramped on my full-size mattress."

Looping his arms around her, he nuzzled her neck and whispered, "Wrapped around you? Not a chance. I'd sleep on a twin as long as I was sleeping with you."

Wow, he'd really turned on the charm tonight. She

didn't quite know what to make of that. "That's a beautiful quilt."

Still holding her, he propped his chin atop her head. "My mother made it. It was for her and Dad's bed. When he remarried…"

"Pamela gave it to you?"

He released her and turned away. "She wanted to donate it along with everything else of Mom's, so I just took it—and a few other things." He moved to the dresser, opened the top drawer and got out a jewelry box. "I don't really know what to do with it," he said as he lifted the lid, showing some pricey pieces along with casual jewelry. "But it didn't seem right to just ditch it."

Cherry snuggled up next to him, admiring the tasteful designs. She touched one delicate silver chain that held an onyx teardrop pendant. "Beautiful."

He smiled. "That was Mom's favorite. She almost never took it off."

"Maybe someday you'll have a daughter and you could give it to her." Saying it made her think about it, picturing an adorable little girl with Denver's rich brown hair and intense golden eyes. One thought led to another and she also imagined a baby with her blond hair… Dangerous. Pushing away from the dresser, she pasted on a smile. "Wouldn't that be nice?"

He watched her closely, then carefully closed the jewelry box and put it back in the drawer. "Maybe." He laced his fingers with hers and led the way to the master bath.

As he pushed the door open wide, Cherry smiled at his Jacuzzi tub. "Big enough for two."

"Armie swears three could fit, but I'm the only one to ever use it."

"Really?" She had a hard time believing he hadn't *broken in* the tub already. "No bubbly bathtub sex?"

Smiling, he shook his head. "I only got the house a year ago and you're the first woman I've brought here."

"No way." Her heart tried to make that significant while her head said to slow it down and think it through.

"Way." He cupped her face, tipped it up, and kissed her. Against her parted lips, he whispered, "Maybe tonight we can try it out."

When she continued to stare up him, her expression dazed, he traced her mouth with one fingertip, gave a low rumbling growl, and gently turned her. "Come on, girl. Let's go to the kitchen and we can figure out dinner."

"Wait." He'd rushed her through the house so quickly, she barely had time to appreciate it all. "Where does that door go?"

"Just a closet." He opened it to show her a room as big as his bathroom but stacked with his clothes, a few random weights, sneakers and a laundry hamper.

Agog, she stared at all the available space. "This is an *amazing* closet."

He grinned. "Yeah, I figured a woman would like it."

Cherry stalled again. Had he bought the house with the thought of marriage in mind? Before they'd finally gotten together—*before she'd finally convinced him*—he'd seemed like the model bachelor, happy in his single life with no inclinations of settling down anytime soon.

Near her ear, Denver whispered, "Don't overthink it." With his arm around her, he urged her back out of the bedroom and into the kitchen where he pulled out a chair for her at the booth in the breakfast nook. "So what do you feel like eating?"

You.

"Girl," he groaned. "Don't look at me like that. I need to feed you, and much as I'd like to head straight to bed afterward, I really do need to soak my shoulder a bit."

Cherry popped right back out of the seat. "Sorry, I'm…" *In love.* "It's been a long day. How about you go take your bath and I'll fix dinner?"

He eyed her up and down. "You cook?"

Insulted, she crossed her arms under her breasts and cocked out a hip. "Do I look like I'm starving?"

Brows up, he said, "No."

So maybe he just found her so damned helpless he thought she couldn't do anything right.

"You look like a fuckable angel. Like a wet dream." He closed the space between them, brushed her cheek with the back of his knuckles. "If you can cook, too, I'm sunk."

Oh God, she hoped that was true because she'd gone under a long time ago. Shakily, she stated, "I'm adequate in the kitchen."

His hand went down her cheek to her jaw, then her collarbone. "Damn." With visible effort he stepped back from her. "Scrounge around, fix whatever you want, but nothing fancy. I'll be in the tub."

"Okay."

"And Cherry?"

"Hmm?"

"You should know that I'm sinking with a continual

hard-on—and a smile on my face." With that he turned and left the room.

And Cherry, feeling her knees go weak, dropped back into the seat. Was that Denver's way of telling her their relationship was more than just physical? For her it always had been.

For him...so darned hard to tell.

She needed several deep breaths before she felt capable of hunting through his kitchen cabinets. She discovered the man was entirely too organized.

Keeping his restricted diet in mind, she found skinless chicken fillets, brown rice and broccoli. He had it all on hand so she assumed he liked it, but to be sure she went to the bathroom and tapped on the door. "Denver?"

"Come on in."

She stepped into steam—and a carnal treat. Eyes flaring wide, she said, "Oh, umm..."

Keeping one shoulder submerged, Denver left exposed one thick shoulder and a long muscular arm, his lean waist, a paler hip and a strong hairy thigh. When she just stood there gawking, he said, "You've seen me before."

Yes, she had. But not like this. And seriously, every view proved inspirational. Right now, with the way his arm rested against his side, his biceps bulged.

Sexy personified, she thought.

She cleared her throat, watching the bubbling water move against his skin and slide over his muscles.

"At the rec center," he told her, "we have a hot tub that's deep enough for me to sit in and still soak my shoulder."

Guilt tripped over her. "We could have skipped tonight so you could—"

"No." His voice roughened, his gaze piercing. "I need you tonight."

Because of his stepmother and a past that had caused him a lot of pain. Wanting to be whatever he needed, she gave a small smile. "Then I'm glad I'm here."

"Me, too." He continued to watch her, waiting.

Oh. Right. She'd come in for a reason. "Chicken and brown rice okay?"

Visually stroking her body, he nodded. "Perfect."

Still hesitating, she asked, "Do you, ah, need anything?"

"Other than you? I'm good." He shifted, sending the water to slosh in the big tub and giving her a peek at the goods. Settling his head against the back of the tub, he said, "I feel like a hedonist. A hot soak, a hotter babe and dinner served. Doesn't get any better than that."

While she tried to think of something to say to that, his cell rang. They both looked at where he'd left it beside the sink.

"Want me to hand it to you?"

"Yeah, if you don't mind." Sitting up, he dried his hands on a towel hung over the edge of the tub.

Without really meaning to, Cherry saw Stack's name on the caller ID. "Here you go." She gave him the phone, then excused herself, pulling the door shut behind her.

He had her in his house and the last thing she wanted to do was make him regret it by eavesdropping.

Besides, she could already guess what the call was about. The big bad defenders probably wanted to coordinate their plans. She shook her head while tenderizing the chicken. It was a little annoying, and a whole lot endearing, how protective they all were.

Denver didn't emerge until half an hour later when the dinner was done. Wearing only loose shorts, his damp hair finger-combed back, he came in sniffing the air. "Smells good."

She glanced at him, all over him, while dishing up two plates. "Your shoulder feels better now?"

"It's fine." He came up behind her and kissed the side of her neck. "What can I do to help?"

"Everything is ready. Just take a seat and I'll serve you."

"I'll serve, you sit." He pulled out a chair for her and then scooted her in before fetching the plates. After sitting across from her, he picked up a fork and said, "Let's eat. Stack and Armie are stopping by in a few."

She had a bite halfway to her mouth but that announcement threw her. "Wait, what?" She'd had her heart all set on sex!

"Yeah, we have some plans to configure. Keep your motor running because it won't take too long. But they're both moochers and will steal part of my meal if I don't eat it fast enough."

"Oh." Her motor would definitely stay running. "Dig in, then." With her bottom lip caught in her teeth, she watched as he cut into the tender, seasoned chicken.

Two seconds after he got the first big bite into his mouth, his eyes closed and he gave a low growl of pleasure. "So good."

She beamed. "You like it?"

"Love it." In rapid order he tried the fragrant rice

HOLDING STRONG

and then the steamed broccoli, making his appreciation known. "Damn, girl, you do know how to cook."

"Told you."

He nodded at her plate. "Better get to eating. The guys aren't above stealing from you, either."

They ended up with a solid fifteen minutes before the doorbell rang. Plate empty, Denver stood, kissed her forehead, and went to answer.

He kept doing that, giving her small kisses in special places that felt intimate, but not necessarily sexual.

Again, her heart wanted to scream, *Significance,* while her brain cautioned, *Don't jump the gun.*

But being here with Denver in his house, talking to him while he bathed, cooking and sharing a meal…it all felt so homey, so domestic.

And yet Carver was out there somewhere, just waiting to wreck her world. That's why Denver's friends—now her friends, too, she reminded herself—were visiting.

She heard the multiple voices and realized Cannon had come along, as well.

Only half of her meal remained when they all shuffled into the kitchen. Sure enough, Armie made a beeline for her and snatched a bite of chicken right off her fork.

Stack eyed her plate. "Looks good. Who cooked?"

"I did." Smiling, Cherry pushed back her chair. "I'm done if you want—"

Before she could finish, they were both on it. Stack got his butt in her seat first, but Armie had her fork.

Cannon laughed at them. "Single men are so pathetic."

To her surprise, Denver grinned and said, "Yeah."

Flustered, it took Cherry a moment to react. "I'd be happy to cook something more—"

"Don't encourage them," Denver told her, drawing her into his side. "They're like wild animals. Feed them once and they'll always be underfoot."

"True story," Cannon said. "Ask Rissy. She'll tell you."

"That's your sister's fault." Denver grinned. "She ignores the diets and always cooks the sweet stuff."

Mouth full, Stack nodded. "Love her muffins."

Scowling ferociously, Armie smacked him in the head.

"Hey!"

Armie didn't back down. "That sounded bad and you know it."

"I wouldn't make a sex joke about Cannon's sister!"

"Yeah, well…" He frowned. "Never mind, then."

Denver and Cannon laughed. Stack just continued to eat, now leaning away from Armie, until the plate was empty.

After witnessing that exchange, Cherry realized just how difficult it might be for Merissa if no one could even joke without getting into trouble. Because she was Cannon's sister, the men all put her on a pedestal, and that pretty much made her untouchable.

Did Rissy know?

Did that have something to do with Armie always resisting her?

Interrupting her musings, Denver tipped up her chin and kissed her. "Why don't you go get your own bath and I'll put away the dishes?"

Every other guy in the room suddenly looked at her, making her feel like a spectacle. Pretending it didn't bother her, she teased, "Meaning the menfolk want to talk?"

"Meaning as soon as I can throw them out, I want to—"

"*Denver.*" Scandalized, she smashed a hand over his mouth. Heat throbbed in her face, especially when she realized all the guys were now smiling.

"You can quit smothering him, hon," Armie said. "It's not like we don't know exactly what he wants."

"*Exactly,*" Stack emphasized.

Only Cannon refrained from suggestive comments, but his grin said it all. "We'll make it quick, I promise."

Grabbing up her purse, Cherry nodded and left the kitchen with as much stiff dignity as she could. She felt them all watching her exit, so she did her utmost to keep her hips from swaying even the tiniest bit. Even after she'd turned the corner, everyone remained so silent that closing the bathroom door felt like an actual escape. Her heart finally slowed its mad gallop with her privacy ensured.

She didn't have a change of clothes but she found one of Denver's flannel shirts left in the bathroom for her to use as a robe. How considerate. She had work in the morning, and he had his usual full schedule. Did that mean Denver would take her home tonight? Or early in the morning?

With so many unanswered questions interfering with her contentment, she hoped Cannon was right, that they wouldn't be long. No way would she go back out there in the same wrecked clothes—or in nothing more than a flannel shirt.

In fact, once they were all gone, she wouldn't mind

just getting naked with Denver. She wanted to make love with him for the rest of her life.

But for tonight, at least, she'd make do with a few hours.

SOON AS THE bathroom door closed with a quiet click, everyone settled at the table.

Folding his arms on the tabletop, Stack asked, "You moving her in?"

Struggling with conflicting emotion, Denver shook his head and said, "I don't know." He wanted to, but was he ready for that?

Turning his chair to straddle the seat, Armie said, "He's an idiot." And then to Denver, "You're an idiot."

Cannon laughed. "I heard what happened at the gym."

"Gee, wonder how?" Denver gave a pointed look at Armie.

Shrugging, Armie said, "Why the hell are you dragging your feet anyway?"

That sentiment from Armie had Stack and Denver both staring at him with incredulity.

He lifted his arms, said, *"What?"* with a load of attitude, and then shoved back his chair to pace.

Cannon cocked a brow. "Am I missing something?"

"No." Armie quickly reseated himself. "But Denver is. How long do you expect a woman like Cherry to wait?"

Harking back to the conversation they'd had at the hotel, Denver said, "A woman like Cherry—who's a different kind of nice?"

"You remember that, huh?"

"Anyone can see you're hung up on her," Stack pointed out. "And vice versa."

Denver chewed it over, decided fuck it, and looked at each of his friends in turn. "It wouldn't bother any of you, the way she flirts? I mean, if you were involved?"

Armie frowned. "Get out of here."

"She's flirted with you," Denver said, and then to Stack, "You, too."

Stack laughed. "She jokes around, but I always knew it was you she wanted."

"Same here," Armie said.

"It's been pretty obvious," Cannon agreed. "The only one who might have misunderstood was you."

"And," Armie said, "it's past time for you to get it figured out."

Denver sat back in his seat. "I already did." Idly, he rearranged his half-empty glass of tea that Cherry had served with dinner. He looked at each of his friends. "She's something else, isn't she?"

A round of agreement made him smile. "Her fucking foster brothers are really starting to piss me off."

They all knew the petty thugs wouldn't just go away. That meant they had to ensure no one got hurt by them.

"I talked to Margo," Cannon said.

"Lieutenant Peterson?" One tough lady, Denver thought—although with her husband and baby daughter, she seemed much softer.

"What's the use in having cops for friends if you don't pick their brains every now and then," Armie explained.

Cannon nodded. "Right now there's not a lot they can do. But she said if they approach Cherry at all, give her a call. It wouldn't hurt to put restraining orders against the lot of them, but that'd require having them served with the orders."

"And we don't know where they're staying." Frustration mounted to the boiling point.

"You're in training," Stack said. "Want me to pick up Cherry after she gets off work?"

Denver shook his head. He had a feeling Cherry wouldn't appreciate everyone being involved in her business. He had his hands full getting her to let him in, much less everyone else. "I've got it covered."

"I can at least fill in for you at the rec center," Stack insisted.

"Thanks. If I need you, I'll let you know."

"I tried a return call on the number Carver used to call me," Armie said. "No go."

Denver hadn't expected it to be that easy. "Cherry has his number. I might give the bastard a call."

Silent surprise filled the room.

Armie sat forward. "If you have his number, what the hell are you waiting for?"

"She doesn't want me involved."

They all stared at him.

"Fucked-up, right?"

"Don't take it as an insult," Cannon advised. "Odds are she's embarrassed and trying to minimize things."

"That's part of it." Denver popped his neck, rolled his shoulders. He glanced back to ensure they were still alone. He could hear the shower running, turned back to his friends, and fessed up. "Seems Cherry and I work on some levels, but not on others."

"Bullshit," Cannon told him. "You make it work, that's all. No one said it'd be easy."

"But is she worth it?" Armie asked. And before

Denver could answer, he said emphatically, "You know she is."

"Yeah." More than worth it.

The silence held until Cannon shifted verbal gears. "If you're moving her in, let me know. I don't want Rissy at the house alone until all this is resolved."

For the next ten minutes they discussed plans. Cannon had already put the word out so anyone new to town asking about Cherry would quickly be reported. His network knew to get as much info as they could, which might include following the strangers. Because it was sometimes kids, late teens who, thanks to circumstances were tougher than many grown men, he also stressed caution.

"Cherry's convinced that they're dangerous." Denver hated thinking about what they might have put her through—things she hadn't yet told him, things she might *never* tell him. "No one take any chances, okay?"

They agreed, and Stack asked, "So what's going on with Leese? Why is he at the rec center?"

"I invited him." More comfortable with this subject, Denver finished off his tea. "He's not that bad."

"Never said he was."

"He's sweet on Vanity," Armie offered, and everyone knew he said it just to needle Stack.

Stack gave him one quelling glare but otherwise ignored him. "He hasn't had any real training, has never belonged to a camp."

"That's what I figured." Training with the best, Denver knew, made a huge difference. Each fighter learned from another. A few rose above the company they kept, but not often. "I checked out his record, watched him go through some drills. He's got respectable moves, especially considering he's taught himself."

Stack grinned. "I watched him do some cage work with Justice, specifically submissions."

Armie whistled. Justice was a big sonofabitch.

"He was getting tagged a lot until he caught Justice in a reverse triangle and skull-fucked the back of his head until the big man almost passed out. I tapped for him."

"He's too cocky," Denver said, laughing with the others. "But then so is Justice."

When the humor died down, Cannon said, "I like him. He's good with the kids."

"There is that." Armie looked at Stack. "Also good with the ladies, or so I hear."

Refusing to take the bait, Stack ignored him. "What if he's still involved with the foster brothers?"

Denver had already thought it all through. "I don't think he is, but we'll keep an eye on him." Even if he wasn't involved, Denver couldn't discount the possibility that the fucks would come after Leese again. "He was easy game for them once already. They'll take another shot at him."

Stack narrowed his eyes. "This time he won't be alone, or drugged."

"And he'll be better trained," Cannon said. "He's a quick study who needs some fine-tuning."

"And some humility," Stack added with an evil grin. "I call dibs on that one."

Armie laughed, opened his mouth—and Stack said to him, "Shut up."

The sudden quiet as the shower shut off had every guy going still.

Muscles drawn taut, a low burning lust flamed into an inferno inside Denver. Now that he knew he loved Cherry, he wanted her even more.

And more often.

In several various ways.

He shoved back his chair. "I know you're all scouring the neighborhood tonight, but—"

"But you're not," Armie finished for him. "Stay here with her. We've got it."

Cannon agreed. "It's covered."

"I was going to join you after." After he appeased the never-ending hunger. After he had her. Maybe twice. Then he'd get his head on straight and join them to do what needed to be done.

Stack laughed. "Cherry would wound you if she heard you say that."

"Seriously." Cannon clapped him on the shoulder, his expression firm. "Stay with her, get some rest, and we'll let you know if we find out anything."

On a regular basis they got together to walk the neighborhood, talking to business owners and the elderly...but they were right. He could skip a night.

"Then I guess I better get my car in the garage." Grabbing his keys, he followed them through the house and out the door, and he didn't even mind their ribbing.

He could take a few jokes.

And for now, he could take Cherry holding back.

What he couldn't take was losing her.

Somehow, he had to draw out the brothers and send them packing—once and for all.

CHAPTER EIGHTEEN

CHERRY WAS STILL drying her hair when the doorknob turned and Denver stepped in. He leaned against the doorframe, wearing that hot, intent look that never failed to fire her own awareness.

"Almost done," she promised as she finished smoothing her hair using his flat brush. She wanted to look as nice as she could after the calamity of the afternoon. Just being fresh and clean went a long way toward restoring her confidence. "Just so you know, I used your toothbrush."

"Help yourself to anything you need."

Oh, that husky timbre to his voice was so sexy. "Glad you feel that way." She set the brush down and turned to face him. "Because I used your lotion, too." Generic and unscented, but her skin was now soft and sleek.

"You're primping." He put a hand to his groin and drew in a breath. "It's not necessary, girl, you know that. It's impossible for me to want you more than I already do. But I can be patient."

"Such a champion." She caught the edges of the pale blue towel and drew it open wide, waited a heartbeat, then let it drop to the floor. "But I'm not as strong as you, and I can't wait."

Before she'd drawn her next breath he had her

scooped up in his arms and was striding for the bed-room. He came down on the mattress over her, kissing her long and deep while his hands cupped her breasts, kneading and cuddling.

He said nothing as he freed her mouth and kissed a path down her body, licking, biting gently…sucking.

Within only a few minutes she was lost. "Denver, *now.*"

Instead of prolonging the pleasure as he often liked to do, he launched himself away from her, dug in the bedside drawer for a condom, and was back over her seconds later, kneeing her thighs apart, settling his weight on her.

She braced herself, her breath held, her heart thundering. But he slowed, carefully holding her face, kissing her so tenderly while whispering, "Cherry…"

He entered her in one steady, relentless press, staying firm against her until her body softened and accepted every thick inch of him.

"There you go," he whispered huskily. "That's my girl."

She couldn't speak. By now she'd expected to be used to his size, but each and every time it thrilled her anew to be so completely filled, so totally possessed.

"Move with me," he urged her, sliding a hand under her bottom and guiding her into matching his rhythm. Faster. Deeper.

The pleasure tightened, sweeter and hotter.

Denver pressed his face into her neck and groaned, his muscles flexing, heat pouring off his body. That did it for her. She clutched at him, muffling her raw cries against his shoulder as she let herself go. Seconds later, he did the same.

It was nowhere near late, but as she felt Denver relaxing she trailed her fingertips up and down his broad back. "Know what I want to do?" she whispered.

He groaned again, but manfully worked his way up to his elbows. He looked at her, then kissed her, and kissed her again. "Tell me."

Knowing he hadn't had much rest lately, she hoped to persuade him to turn in early. "I want to sleep." The yawn snuck up on her, perfect timing to stress her point and hopefully convince him. "I'm zoned, and you could probably use a good night's rest, as well."

His beautiful eyes smiled at her. "God love you, girl, could you be more perfect?"

She opened her mouth, but he said, "It was a rhetorical question. Sleep would be good, so stay put while I get rid of the condom. I'll be right back."

As soon as he disappeared into the bathroom, she got up to smooth the quilt they'd displaced, then turned down the bed and crawled under the covers, still naked.

He strode back in, but paused to stare at her. "Damn, but you look good like that."

Cherry reached a hand to her hair. "Like what?"

"In my bed, in my house." He held her gaze. "With me."

It's where she'd always wanted to be.

He turned out the light and joined her, pulling her into his arms. "We need to see about arranging it more often."

It was dark, quiet, Denver's hold secure. She waited just a little too long before she got up the nerve to whisper, "Okay."

Denver was already asleep.

CHERRY STIRRED AWAKE to Denver making love to her—for the second time. The first had happened in the middle of the night. He'd roused her with a hand between her thighs, his mouth at her breast and before she had a chance to catch up she'd been coming.

Now as he kneed her thighs apart and pressed into her, she opened her eyes to predawn light filtering through the curtained windows.

At his easy entry, she realized she was ready for him and wasn't even a little bit amazed by that. *"Denver."*

He kissed her. "Say it again."

"What?"

"My name." He rode her gently, his breath hot against her throat. "Say it."

"Denver," she whispered on a moan, the word breaking as pleasure sharpened.

"God, I love hearing that little catch in your voice when I'm inside you." He closed his arms around her, sheltering her, cradling her close, bringing tears to her eyes as another release built and then shattered, making her cry out.

The next time she got her eyes open, sunlight brightened the room and Denver sat beside her on the bed, holding coffee.

He smiled when she looked at him in confusion. "Sorry, girl, but I think I loved you right into a stupor."

The mention of love threw her, then she turned her head and saw the time. Still early, thank goodness. "I need to get moving or I'll be late to work."

Denver helped her to sit up then handed her the coffee. "You want to get ready here or at your place?"

"Since I don't have any clothes here, I'll say home."

He grinned at her. "Clothes are good—at least when

you're with others. When it's only us, naked works for me."

She sipped the coffee and made appreciative sounds. "I thought you would jog this morning."

His smile went crooked. "Already did that while you recouped."

"Oh." Now she felt like a slug.

He tugged the sheet down to view her bare breasts, let out a slow breath, and stood. "It's going to take some getting used to, having you in my bed."

A complaint? She had her pride, too, so she lifted her chin. "If you'd rather I didn't stay over—"

His gaze shot to hers. "You're right where I want you to be." Then lower, more to himself than her, he added, "I'll just have to figure out how to rein it in."

The rest of the morning went the same way, with Denver touching her repeatedly, kissing her often, saying things that could be taken a dozen different ways. When he dropped her off at work it was almost a relief just to let her brain rest.

The weather was perfect and the kids got to play outside where they burned off some energy, which meant they were more settled when inside, too. It felt like she floated through the day, her happiness a live thing that made her heart beat faster and kept a smile on her face.

She knew Denver had arranged to pick her up from work and when it was finally time to call it a day, she had to resist rushing out to him.

But he didn't resist. He'd parked at the curb and stood outside his car, dark sunglasses hiding his eyes while he waited for her. The second he saw her she knew, because his teeth showed in a beautiful grin and he started striding toward her.

Oh, she could so easily get used to this.

When they reached each other, his grin settled into a smile. "I assume being we're surrounded by rugrats and their parents, I probably shouldn't grab you up and kiss you until you're talking to me in that hot, husky way, right?"

"Probably not," she said with disappointment.

"Then as soon as we're alone." He took her hand and led her to the car. Two miles down the road he pulled over, put the car in Park and reached for her.

And sure enough, when he let her up for air, her voice was very husky indeed.

After smoothing her hair, he said, "What do you need first? Dinner? Or would you rather head to your place so you can change and gather up whatever you need to spend the night while I check out your car?"

Whatever you need to spend the night. "Um…" Cherry licked her lips. "You're inviting me to stay over again?"

Pushing the sunglasses to the top of his head, he gave her a heated look that made her stomach flip-flop and her nipples tingle. "Given what I want to do to you, what I hope you'll do to me, it might be best to have the privacy."

What a terrific way to convince her. "Okay."

That slow smile came again. "I love an agreeable woman."

Again with the love word! "I…"

"You hungry?" he asked as he put the car in gear and pulled back out to the main roadway.

Bemused, she stared at him as she shook her head. "Not right now."

"Back to the house, then. I'll check out your ride while you get together enough for a few days."

Only a few days, she wondered? Damn, but he had her so confused. She had no idea where they stood, if he wanted her over often, or just for the short-term.

"Take a breath, girl."

She did, sucking in a shuddering lungful of air.

He reached for her hand. "One day at a time, okay?"

It no longer unnerved her, how easily he read her mind. She gave a sharp nod. "Okay."

During the rest of the drive, Denver asked about her day, about the kids she'd worked with. And he shared his day, telling her that he'd sparred with Leese, how Armie had been invited into the SBC, about the network Cannon had set up within the neighborhood.

"Unfortunately, they didn't find out anything last night. If anyone has been asking around about you, they've been really discreet."

"So everyone knows?" She shouldn't feel so embarrassed—what had happened was out of her control. She was a child at the time. Orphaned.

Mentally, she understood all that.

But emotionally, the shame of it left her devastated. Her pathetic past showed her lack of family morality even before her parents had died. And after their deaths, she'd been dropped right back into the same situation, only without any affection, without any concern for her well-being.

The past more than emphasized her lack of upbringing, extended family, friends.

Her lack of…everything.

"They know," Denver said gently, "and they're concerned. That's all, honey. No judgment, no pity. Just understanding."

Because Denver was now involved, too, she pushed the humiliation aside. She wanted him protected, and his friends were in a great position to offer that service. They were well-trained fighting machines with lethal ability, already spending a lot of time with him, and they were also the most moral men she'd ever met.

Denver probably thought he didn't need the added security. But then, he didn't know Carver, Gene and Mitty like she did.

DENVER KNEW SHE was trying to sound more upbeat and accepting than she felt when she said, "I need to thank the guys for their concern."

"Sure." None of them would expect that, but if it made her feel better he didn't see how it could hurt. He glanced her way, saw her chewing her bottom lip and wanted to say all sorts of things, most of them inappropriate to the moment. When he started declaring himself it'd damn well be in private so that as soon as the words were said he could take her to bed. He was better at showing than telling, and he wanted her to know every single thing he felt for her.

"We'll see them Friday night. That is, if you don't mind our date including a trip to Rowdy's bar." She'd been to the bar many times while he was also there, but they'd never gone together as a couple.

Pleased, she smiled at him. "That sounds like a perfect date."

"A movie first," he clarified, wanting her to know he'd taken to heart her request for a real date. "Then a casual dinner, and the bar last."

"Denver," she chided. "It doesn't have to be all that."

Hoping she'd understand, he said, "I think with you, with *us*, it has to be everything."

She opened her mouth, but nothing came out until she finally gave a strangled, "Okay."

And again he laughed. "By the way, I called in our RSVP to Dad's birthday party."

She went still in surprise. "You left a message?"

"Actually, no." He cleared his throat. "Dad answered."

Wincing, she asked, "How'd it go?"

His brows twitched together. "Better than I expected." Way better. He'd half expected his dad to kill the call—but he hadn't.

Tentatively, she asked, "That's good, right?"

"I could tell Dad was thrown by hearing from me." He scratched his chin. "I explained, told him that Pamela had invited me over. At first he didn't say anything."

"And then?"

Denver hesitated. He wasn't used to sharing, especially not with a woman. Damn, but it made him uncomfortable.

Cherry touched his arm. "I don't mean to pry. I know it's private."

That made him frown. "I want to tell you."

"You do?"

Strange as it seemed… "Yeah." Then he gave her a look. "I want you to share with me, too."

"I do."

Not everything, but hopefully he could lead by example. He went quiet as he recalled the details of his talk with his dad.

Sounding noncommittal, his father had asked, "So you'll be there?"

"If that's okay." Then to deflect some of the tension, Denver had added, "I'm bringing a date."

"A date," Lyle Lewis asked, "or someone special?"

That tone had been so familiar, so paternal, that Denver fell easily into the old camaraderie. "Very special."

"Then I look forward to meeting her."

Cherry nudged him. "Denver? Are you still with me?"

"Yeah." He was with her now, and if things went his way, he'd be with her always. "I told him about you."

"About me?" she squeaked.

"Yeah." Grinning, he said, "Hope you don't mind that I set you up as the buffer, a way for us both to give a little. I want to introduce you, he wants to meet you. You okay with that?"

She nodded fast. "Of course." And then with less confidence, "What did you tell him?"

"That you're special."

Her lips parted. "Really? I mean, I am?"

"Yeah," he said softly. "Very special."

Looking more than a little dazed, Cherry stayed quiet for the remainder of their ride to Merissa's house. Denver would have loved to know her thoughts, and usually he could sense them. But on occasion she could be so unreadable.

Her silence would have worried him, except for that small smile playing at her lips.

"Hey."

Brows up, she turned her head toward him. "Hmm?"

As he parked, he said, "How about you go grab your

keys and I can take a look at your car before we head to my place? That way I'll know if I need to pick up anything to fix it."

"Are you sure you want to bother with this? You have so much you're juggling already. I know your free time is precious."

Not as much so as his time with her. "It's not a problem." He drew her in for a soft kiss. "Grab enough clothes so you can stay the night again." Rather than give her a chance to question that, he said, "It'll save me time in the morning."

That's all it took to get her hustling. Denver went to her car and opened the hood to look inside, but nothing appeared amiss. When he heard voices he turned his head and saw Cherry exit the house with Merissa following her, both ladies chatting and happy.

Merissa wore shorts and an SBC T-shirt that, given its size, probably belonged to her brother, Cannon. She had a sandwich in one hand, a cola in the other.

She followed as Cherry stored a pile of her belongings in the backseat of Denver's ride. Seeing the two of them together always made him smile. Merissa was nearly as tall as her brother, but where Cannon was muscular, she was willowy. They shared the same light blue eyes.

In contrast, Cherry was shorter, rounder, her shoulder-length blond hair bouncy instead of straight.

They were both lookers but in very different ways.

Denver watched as they approached.

"Moving pretty fast, aren't you, Predator?"

He gave Merissa points for keeping her gaze on his face this time even as he grinned at her use of his fight name. "You think?"

Cherry snorted. "Seems pretty slow to me."

Giving her a hug, he said, "Then I'll see what I can do about making up for lost time."

"There you go," Merissa said, propping a slim hip against the fender and saluting him with the remainder of her cola.

Denver leaned back over the engine. "I don't see anything wrong. Turn the key a few times for me, will you?" If it was just a dead battery, that'd be easy enough.

Cherry walked around him to the driver's door, opened it—and screamed so loudly that Denver hit his head on the hood.

Cursing, feeling a trickle of blood run down his temple, he squared off for a threat only to see Cherry slapping at her clothes and hair, backpedaling in a high-pitched panic.

And no wonder. A dozen or more snakes spilled out of the car, writhing on the ground, mouths open, bodies coiled. Mixed with that horror, massive spiders, roaches, locusts and other creepy bugs fluttered and flew around the car.

"Ack!" Merissa dropped her cola and ran all the way to the house, darting inside.

After kicking the driver's door shut, Denver grabbed a wide-eyed, horrified Cherry, who continued to dance and screech while he shooed bugs away and ensured no snakes were near her.

"Shh. It's okay, baby." Holding her close, he pulled her around to the driveway. The snakes probably weren't poisonous, but he didn't know for sure. They didn't look like the little garter snakes he used to see as a kid, and since moving to the more urban setting of Warfield, well, he hadn't seen a snake.

"Ohmigod, ohmigod, ohmigod…"

"Are you okay?" He brushed Cherry's hair back and in the process dislodged an enormous praying mantis that took flight. Luckily she didn't seem to realize. "Cherry?"

Face pale with shock, she looked at the car—and screamed again. Denver turned to see a brown-and-black snake, probably four feet long, slithering across the street.

"Shit." He gave Cherry a squeeze. "Go get me a rake or something, and maybe a garbage can with a lid, or at least a garbage bag."

She blinked big dazed eyes at him. "Your head is bleeding!"

"It's fine."

"But…"

"Shh." Again he squeezed her shoulders. "I'm sorry, girl, but I don't know if those snakes are dangerous or not, so I need you to hustle up and get what I need."

Hand to her heart, Cherry closed her eyes as she nodded, sucked in a breath, then ran up the driveway to the garage.

From the front door Merissa yelled, "I called Cannon."

Great. Just freaking great. "Thanks," Denver called back to her. He searched the ground and found a small fallen branch that he used to corral the biggest snakes. There were maybe ten of them that were larger than the others, and they were testy and uncooperative. Denver barely kept them from getting away.

Some of the smaller ones made it into the grass and

down the street drain; nothing he could do about that. He didn't want to kill anything, not even a snake, if he didn't have to.

Looking like she faced the gallows, Cherry ventured forth with the requested items. She held the garbage can lid in front of her like a shield. She kept whispering, "Ohmigod, ohmigod, ohmigod," in a terrified litany.

"Leave everything right there," Denver told her, rather than have her come any closer.

"I...I should help."

"No, I've got it." He used his forearm to swipe the blood off his face.

Still, she gulped and inched toward him. "Here. I brought you a washcloth for your head. Are you sure you're not badly hurt?"

His heart swelled, both with love and pride. Clearly the girl had some issues when it came to creepy-crawlies, but she forced herself to be brave. "The bugs flew off," he promised her as he took the cloth and swabbed at his head. "And yeah, I'm fine. Just a split."

"I'm so sorry I startled you."

"You had good reason." He accepted the rake from her and worked to keep the snakes together. One particularly aggressive snake tried to come at them, sending Cherry scurrying back with a frantic gasp. Denver pinned it with the rake, then put the lid over it.

Luckily, Armie pulled up with Cannon. Both of them jumped from Armie's truck, looking at the twisting snakes with morbid awe. "Damn," Armie said after a peek in the car.

"You're okay?" Cannon asked when he saw the blood on Denver.

"Banged my head." He was so furious he could barely get the words out. "It's fine."

"And you?" he asked Cherry.

She gave a short nod. Denver didn't miss the fear in her eyes, the paleness of her face, or her determination to help.

With only a few more questions, both men got to work helping Denver get the snakes in the can.

Over his shoulder, wanting her away from the proof of Carver's obsession, Denver asked Cherry, "Would you have Merissa call the cops?"

From a safe distance away, Merissa said, "Already done. I called animal control, too. They're sending someone who's a rodent expert or something."

With the majority of the snakes in the can, Denver went to check out Cherry's car. Now that they'd been stirred up, bugs flew around inside, hitting the windows, clinging to the seats. The floorboards were alive with impatient, slithering snake bodies; he had no idea how many.

Had this happened while she'd been at his house?

Armie strode up beside him. "Totally fucked-up. They had to have brought in a shit-ton of snakes and insects."

"I'll tow it," Cannon said, and he looked more than pissed himself. "We can open it up along the river or something once we know if those snakes are poisonous."

"I recognized some of them," Armie said. "The big boy was a rat snake. Intimidating, but not all that harmful." Grim, he ran a wrist across his brow. "Pretty sure I saw a cottonmouth in there, though, and those suckers are scary."

Holding the lid on the can, Cannon frowned at the obvious movement inside. "Will they attack each other?"

Denver shrugged. "Better than having them loose." He wanted to rage. He wanted to find Carver and demolish him. But he saw Cherry standing back at the curb, Merissa beside her, huddled close.

"There's nothing else to do but wait. Why don't you two head inside? We'll be there in a minute."

Cherry nodded and started in. Merissa inched toward them.

Low, so neither of the girls would hear, Denver whispered, "This wasn't just a prank."

"No," Cannon agreed, and the fact that it had happened in front of his sister's house surely made it as personal for him as it was for Denver.

Suddenly, Merissa shrieked and they all jerked around to see a massive bug buzzing around her head. Like a giant flying cockroach, it terrorized her.

Cherry was already inside, thank God.

Slapping at herself and making crazy noises, Merissa ran for her brother. The bug stayed in pursuit—and landed on her shoulder.

"Ack!"

That really set her off, and Denver winced in sympathy when she caught the back of Cannon's shirt and almost jerked him off his feet.

Since Cannon held the lid on the can and no one wanted the snakes getting loose again, Armie intercepted Merissa, hugged her tight to still her chaotic movement, and swatted the bug away. It dropped to the ground, kicked its many legs, and subsided.

Clearly, Merissa didn't realize the bug was dead

given how she continued to yelp and high-step and flail her arms.

"Rissy," Armie said, drawing her away from Cannon again. "It's gone."

"Where? *Where?*" Now it was Armie she tried to crawl behind, twisting and jumping.

"Rissy," Cannon said, his tone controlled. "It's okay now, hon. It's dead."

"How do you know? Did you kill it?"

Armie grinned as he pulled her back around in front of him. "I think you screamed it to death."

She saw the bug, shuddered in squeamish distaste, and hid her face. Using the side of his shoe, Armie kicked it away.

Indulgent, he cupped her shoulder. "Now you can't even see it."

She peeked from between her fingers, saw it was true, and dropped her arms to glare at Armie. "Are you laughing at me?"

He smiled, smoothed her hair, and said in a soft, husky whisper, "Just a little."

In the next second, awareness sparked between them.

Denver saw it. Maybe Cannon did, too, given the way his brows slowly climbed up.

And suddenly Merissa smooshed her entire body up close to Armie and buried her face in his neck. "Thank you."

Holding his arms out to his sides, Armie said, "Uh…"

Cannon shook his head, gave Denver a look, and began dragging the can of snakes to the driveway. "I'm taking Rissy home with me tonight. I don't want her staying here alone."

Denver didn't want that, either. And since he was the one taking Cherry away, he offered, "I could stay here with both of them."

"No."

Understanding that Cannon wanted to ensure his sister's safety himself, Denver nodded. "I'm going in to check on Cherry."

"All right." They both looked back to see Armie slowly, cautiously, put his arms around Merissa. Cannon's expression seemed more thoughtful than anything else. "I've never seen Rissy freak out like that before."

"It was a gargantuan bug," Denver reasoned. "Most girls carry on over bugs."

"Rissy isn't like most girls." Cannon continued to watch his sister and Armie, especially now that Armie wasn't looking so uncomfortable, had in fact embraced her and was stroking her back. The arrival of a police car finally interrupted.

Cannon told Denver, "Go check on Cherry, maybe patch up your head, clean up the blood. I'll field this until you get back."

But it wasn't the officer he headed to. It was his sister.

And his best friend.

CHAPTER NINETEEN

DENVER FOUND HER just inside the front door, leaning back on the wall, her arms tight around herself, her eyes closed and her lashes damp.

Seeing her like that made the rage worse, turning it into a live thing inside him. He worked his jaw, sucked a slow breath in through his nose. Hoping to shield her from everything he felt, he kept a few feet between them. "I'll fix your car, but from here on out I'm driving you."

Her eyes opened and she swallowed hard. "Thank you. I know I should insist on driving myself—"

"Damn it—"

"—but truthfully, I don't know when I'll be able to get back in that car."

Not trusting himself to speak, he nodded.

"I have this...*thing* about bugs. Any bugs. But spiders..." She shuddered. "Things that *fly*..."

"And snakes," he agreed. "I'm sorry you were so scared. I should have checked the car first."

"You couldn't have known."

"I should have fucking checked anyway." He breathed harder, the anger blossoming no matter how he tried to tamp it down. "You're moving in with me."

She stared at him, her eyes flared.

Well, hell. He hadn't meant to blurt that out like

an order. What he said sounded…permanent, not a temporary solution to a bad situation. But fuck it. He wouldn't take it back.

Actually, now that he'd said it, he liked the idea. "Move in with me."

"I—" She stopped. Shook her head and strode to the kitchen. "I can't do this. I can't let Carver twist your arm and make you do things you don't want to do."

Still running on angry adrenaline, Denver followed close behind her. He wanted to deny that Carver had any influence, but they'd both see the lie in that. Instead he reiterated more harshly than he intended, *"You're moving in."*

Indignation stiffened her neck while she dampened paper towels in the sink. "I can barely afford this place. No way can I afford both."

Jesus, he wanted to shout. "What the hell does that mean?"

Going on tiptoe, she carefully cleaned the blood away from his face and temple, being especially gentle near the cut. "I split costs with Rissy, already."

He caught her wrist. "I don't want your money!"

Righteous with her own anger, she jerked free. "I don't freeload!"

From bad to worse. Denver ran a hand over his face. "I never said—"

She pushed his hand aside and went back to cleaning on him, this time not so gently. "I don't make enough to add anything else to my already strained budget. After being sick and missing work, things are tight already."

Now that really pissed him off. He stared at her, willing her to meet his gaze instead of focusing on a superficial injury. "If you need money, why didn't you tell me?"

She gasped so hard he felt it on his face. The wet towels got tossed at him. *"I would never come to you for money!"*

He drew back from her vehemence. They stared at each other, her heaving, him reevaluating. He had to get a grip. Fast.

It took an effort but he took charge of himself and the situation. "There are some facts we can't overlook, number one being that Carver is getting bolder. You're smart, Cherry. You know it's not safe for you to be alone."

She rubbed her forehead, saying nothing.

Denver drew her hand down, then held it. "I want you, not your money. Number two, staying with me doesn't obligate you to invest."

"I pay my own way."

The desperation in that statement helped him to relent. Her pride was important to her, and right now so many things were out of her control. She needed to know she still had the final say over her life. "If it makes you feel better, you could pitch in on groceries and stuff. Whatever it takes, I want you safe, with me."

When she continued to scrutinize him, he had to swallow back a growl.

"Call it temporary if that'll make you feel better. But stay with me." *Always.*

And still she waffled. Denver had the awful suspicion that she tried to think of alternatives.

"Should I go to my knees?"

At his tone, confusion filled her expression. "You're angry?"

Damn. He picked up the discarded towels, finished the cleaning himself, and strode to the trash can to throw them away. He took a second to collect himself, then faced her again. "I'm sorry. It's just…"

She nodded stiffly. "Me, too."

"I care for you, Cherry."

Her gaze shot up to his.

He drew a slow breath, wishing he could say more, but damn, given how she'd reacted to his invitation he didn't dare start declaring himself. "If you're not with me, I'll be distracted when I should be focusing on my training."

She covered her mouth.

He hated laying on the guilt when she already had too much of that, but he'd do whatever it took to see her secure. "So please, will you move in with me?"

She stared up at him so long he started to sweat.

Then she took his hands—and he realized he was shaking.

She realized it, too. "Okay. For a little while."

Forever, if he had his way. But for now that'd do. Drawing her into his chest, he carefully crushed her close. "I'm sorry I shouted." He held her back again. "You know I would never hurt you."

"Of course I do."

But she looked so emotionally brittle, so stoic. "I should be horsewhipped for losing my temper."

"Denver." She smoothed her hands over his chest, then hugged him tight. "You had reason to get angry."

"I wasn't angry with you."

She gave a shaky smile. "I know that."

He wasn't convinced. He'd already hurt her once,

shouting at the gym, embarrassing her. He was determined to never do it again.

"I screamed," she reminded him. "You yelled. Different reactions to the same upset."

Now he frowned. "I wasn't *upset*."

"Is that word somehow insulting?"

Damn straight. "I was pissed, girl. Not upset."

Patting his chest, she said, "Okay, sure."

Denver rolled his eyes in disbelief. "Now you're placating me."

"Yes. Because you're being silly."

"Silly?"

That made her outright laugh. And once she did, Denver's lips twitched, too. Seeing how quickly she regrouped again made him proud.

God, the things she made him feel, most of them nice, some of them disturbing as shit. But he wouldn't trade any of it. In fact, the feelings were growing on him.

In direct contrast to the humor, he said, "When I get hold of Carver, I'm going to rip him apart." He needed her to know that.

Instead of replying, she gestured at the door. "I can't go back out there just yet."

Denver held her to him. "You don't have to."

Merissa opened the door and stepped in with Armie right behind her, his arm around her shoulders, the two of them in low, intimate conversation.

Together, Denver and Cherry stared.

With a sigh, Merissa stepped away from Armie, but immediately wrapped her arms around herself. Her gaze sought Cherry's. "I am *soooo* creeped out."

Cherry nodded. "Me, too."

"I'm going to put on coffee." Merissa started for the kitchen. "Then I'm going to pack. Until that jerk is gone, I'll be staying somewhere else."

Denver leaned down to whisper to Cherry, "She'll be staying with Cannon. He insisted."

Looking even more shamefaced, she joined her friend. "Rissy, I am so sorry."

"Why?" Merissa got the coffee from the cabinet. "You didn't invite him here."

"But it's because of me—"

"No, it's because he's a certifiable lunatic." Merissa looked at Armie, then pulled Cherry close to whisper. The two women stayed like that, huddled in close conversation, occasionally glancing at the men.

Denver nudged a mesmerized Armie toward the door. "Let's go."

With a lagging step, Armie went. "I'm fucked," he muttered low enough that the women wouldn't hear.

"Or," Denver said, "you could just go with it."

But Armie wasn't listening. He was too busy trying to ignore what he felt. Denver could have told him that wouldn't work, but he figured it was something Armie would have to work out for himself—hopefully before it was too late.

HOURS LATER, DENVER and Cherry finally got to bed. Neither of them said anything for the longest time. The evening had been grueling. The animal control specialist agreed it'd be safer to have the car towed before inspecting it for other pests, especially since, as Armie had said, at least one of the snakes had been venomous. Given the ability to hide up under seats and other nooks and crannies, it was determined that the interior might need to be dismantled to some degree.

Denver had already decided she needed to replace it. Somehow he'd talk her into selling it, and letting him help with a new ride. That was a topic for another day, though.

The cop had tried suggesting an elaborate prank, but he didn't sound convinced, especially when they explained about Cherry's foster brothers being in town. It helped that Cannon gave Lieutenant Peterson a call.

Surprising Denver, the lieutenant showed up and then stuck around to talk to everyone. Cherry promised her that she'd let her know if any of them contacted her again.

They couldn't prove the brothers had anything to do with the latest harassment, but the lieutenant was more than willing to call it probable. Knowing she was on the case offered a little more reassurance. But since no one knew where to find the bastards, there was only so much the cops could do.

Once they were stretched out in the bed, Cherry asked, "How's your head?"

"Fine. Don't worry about it." He wanted her, but he also wanted her to know it wasn't just about sex. "You?"

She tipped her face up to see him. "I'm okay."

"You're beautiful."

A smile flickered over her lips. Lifting up to one elbow, she inadvertently left her bare breasts close enough for him to lick.

He fought temptation.

Stroking her fingers through his hair, she tortured him. "Thank you for asking me to stay with you."

What he'd asked was for her to move in. Big difference. But she looked too exhausted to argue semantics. "Thank you for agreeing."

Her gentle fingers moved down his jaw. "I'm relieved to be here, but I need to figure out a few things."

"Like?"

"It's not right to just leave Merissa alone there. I know she's staying with Cannon for a while. But that won't last. She's not the type to impose."

"How could she ever impose when he wants her there?" It was a message he wished Cherry would apply to herself.

"This is my fault. Carver is here because of me. The least I could do is—"

"No."

Denver tumbled her down in the bed and moved over her, pinning her in place. "You already agreed to stay."

She searched his face, and he saw so many questions reflected in her dark eyes. Questions about the future. Questions about them as a couple. He couldn't answer them all just yet, so instead he made a suggestion.

After he gently kissed her. "I know things are moving fast and we both have a lot on our plates already. I'm training, you're working."

"And my past is closing in, mucking it all up. I'm so sorry about that."

"I'm relieved that you're not dealing with those fucks on your own." When she started to speak, he touched a finger to her soft lips to quiet her. "I know you're independent, girl. It's one of the things I love about you."

Going utterly still, her eyes darkened and her face flushed.

Knowing he had her attention, Denver tried for a little leverage. "But being independent doesn't mean you have to do everything on your own. Trust me when I say that I want to be here for you." *Now and always.* "Trust Cannon to look out for his sister, and trust Merissa to understand the situation for what it is."

"It's—"

"*Not* your fault," he emphasized.

"Not directly because I would never, ever deliberately hurt my friends. But it's a fact that Carver is here because *I'm* here."

"I'm glad you're here—with me."

She relented enough to say, "I'm very glad about that, too."

To convince her, he gave her a different way of looking at it. "Blaming yourself because he's a psycho punk who needs to be committed is like blaming me because Pamela was an unhappy woman stuck in an unhappy marriage of her own making."

Her arms came around his neck and she held him to her, her hold...protective. "That was *not* your fault."

Touched, amused and loving her more by the minute, Denver eased her back. "And what Carver does isn't yours."

He felt her gearing up, knew he wouldn't like it, and leaned back to see her.

"I'm sorry, Denver, but I can't just wait to see what he'll do."

"Eventually he'll screw up and we'll have him. But no way in hell will I let him hurt you."

"I need to call him."

"No."

"I need to—"

"*I'll* call him.

She hugged him again, tighter this time, her face against his chest. "He doesn't want to talk to you."

"He'll fucking well talk to me all the same."

Resolve had her scooting away from him until she sat on the other side of the bed. "You need to understand something, Denver."

Damn, but he felt the loss of her warmth. Assuming they wouldn't be sleeping for a while, he sat up against the headboard and crossed his arms, his own resolve in place. "I'm listening."

"Carver isn't a man swayed by logic. You can't just warn him away. Threats will mean nothing to him. He thinks he's invincible. He thinks he can always do as he pleases because usually he can."

"Then he'll have to come to grips with the fact that this time he can't." *Because he can't have you.* "He needs to know you aren't alone."

She sucked in a breath. "If you do that, if you try to stress that you're here for me, then you become his target."

Good. "Better me than you."

"No!" Shoving a hand into her hair, she left the bed. "This is bad enough already without you getting—"

"Involved?" Though he tried, he couldn't remove the edge of disgust from his tone.

She whirled on him. "Hurt!"

Well hell, that was even worse. A slow pulsebeat of fury brought him forward with a building scowl. The disbelief emerged as a grated whisper. "You think that mewling punk could hurt me?"

Cherry threw up her hands. "He is not a fair fighter, damn it! He owns weapons. He skulks around in the shadows and…and…"

And he'd done terrible things. To Cherry. Choking on the awful mix of love and rage, Denver rose from the bed. Arms folded and expression shuttered, Cherry turned away from him.

He brought her back around. "Don't do that, Cherry. Don't ever shut me out."

It took her a second, but she got her chin up. "I don't want Carver and his insane brothers going after you full force. I know I'm responsible for a lot—but not that, Denver." She held his gaze, but her voice wavered when she said, "Please."

Carefully, he closed his hands over her shoulders and drew her closer. "What are you responsible for?"

Her lips firmed. "I need to tell you more about Carver. So you'll understand. So you'll know that it's not worth…"

"Fighting for you?" Was that what she thought?

She tried to push away from him, but Denver scooped her up and carried her to the bed, ignoring her struggles and excuses and all the reasons why he couldn't, shouldn't, know her in every way imaginable.

Getting comfortable with his back against the headboard again, but now with a disgruntled bouncy blonde on his lap, Denver said, "Settle down."

That really got her going and he laughed while subduing her. Laughter was the wrong move, apparently, given the killing glare she cut over him.

"We're not going to sit through this, huh? Have it your way." He stretched her out under him, pinning her legs with one of his, drawing her arms up high over her head. He took in the tantalizing sight of her, smiled and shook his head. "Damn, girl, no matter what, you do it for me."

"Damn it, Denver—"

He lightly bit her earlobe. "Shh. It'll be okay. You'll see."

"You don't know that! Carver is not a reasonable man."

"He's not a man at all." To tease her, he kissed a path from her ear to her throat. "Real men don't bully others. They sure as shit don't abuse women." He lifted up enough to see her eyes growing heavy.

Sweet Cherry. It always took so little from him to get her ready. That in itself was a blessing. To be wanted so much by a woman like her...

No way in hell would he ever give that up.

"Anyone who would terrorize a kid is the lowest scum on earth. Now, while I get that you'd rather deal with him on your own, it's not fair to ask that of me, so get over it."

The sensual fog cleared from her gaze. "It's not that easy!"

"It will be if you'll stop hiding from me. If you'll put a little of that effort into trusting me instead." Denver waited. When she said nothing, when her gaze darted away, he went back to nuzzling her fragrant skin. "I've got all night." Hell, he had a lifetime. With her. Sooner or later she'd get it.

He nibbled his way down her chest to the top of her breast.

Even as her breathing deepened, her mouth pinched. "Okay."

He saw the resignation in her gaze, and the belief

that things would somehow change between them. He smoothed back her hair, lightly touched his mouth to hers, and rose to one elbow, bracing his head on a fist. "Trust," he reminded her.

Tightly strung, quivering with tension, she met his gaze. "I told you that Carver stayed after me."

"Yes."

"He knows I'm afraid of bugs. I mean, really afraid."

Denver had to point out the obvious. "And yet today, because you knew I needed a hand, you stayed and helped."

Her eyes closed, her voice strained. "I was so scared."

"When someone faces their fears like that, it's called being brave."

She shook her head. "Not when the fear is—" she swallowed hard "—stupid insects."

"You're wrong. There are all kinds of fears, and people are all affected differently." When he released her wrists, she lowered her arms enough to put her palms on his chest. "I was so damned proud of you."

Her self-conscious laugh hurt him. "If I was brave, it's only because you were there and I knew you wouldn't let anything get me."

Progress. "I won't let anything or anyone ever hurt you."

Lashes lifted, showing him her beautiful dark eyes—and her stubborn pride. "I want to take care of myself."

"You do, girl. Given the foundation you started with, you're doing great. I'm proud of you, so I wish you'd be proud of yourself, too."

She did some of that sexy-bottom-lip-nibbling, then gave an uncertain nod.

"Good," he whispered, choking on his damn pride before steadying himself with a deep breath. "Now I need you to understand that relationships are all about taking care of each other."

"Right." Her mouth quirked. "Except I don't do anything for you."

She couldn't be more wrong. Thinking of everything she did for him, to him, made him desperate to taste her. Groaning, he took her mouth for a long, deep kiss then, keeping his forehead to hers, he admitted, "Seeing my dad again after all this time feels easier because I know you'll be there with me."

"Really?"

"Definitely." This time he pressed his mouth to her forehead.

"I suppose if you're determined to take on Carver, you need to know everything. You have to understand exactly how twisted and sick he is."

Denver already had a good idea, but he hoped that by telling him, by sharing the nightmare, it'd take some of the burden off her narrow shoulders.

She pushed him to his back and crawled atop him, then laid her head on his shoulder. "Once, before I could get away, Carver held me down and made me kiss him. He said if I didn't, he'd put this enormous cicada on me. It was screaming—" She lifted her head. "You know how those things do?"

His heart twisted. "Yes, I know. They scare a lot of people."

She hugged up against him again. "It was making that awful noise and he kept getting it closer to me just to see me go hysterical. I tried not to, but…" She took his hand and wedged it beneath her left breast. "Even talking about it now makes my heart race."

Carver had traumatized her. Deliberately. No wonder she was so afraid of bugs. If ever a man deserved a beat-down…

"He kissed me," she whispered, "but I was sobbing the whole time. And…and he liked it."

Motherfucker. Rage exploded, but with Cherry being his blanket, she'd feel it if he bunched up the way he wanted to. Determined to shield her from seeing his rage, Denver suppressed what he could and instead relaxed his hands so that they cupped her ass. It took him two tries before he managed to ask, "How old were you?"

"Not quite seventeen." Her fingers toyed with his chest hair. "Carver was twenty-three. Big and muscular." Again she lifted up to see him. "His brothers always watched. Carver enjoyed playing with me and they enjoyed seeing it. It was like he was showing off or something. Gene would go all intense and serious, practically drooling. Mitty would laugh like a kid watching a cartoon. Their reactions were so creepy. And they made me feel…" Her voice faded away. Cuddling down against him again, she whispered, "Helpless. They made me feel so damned helpless."

The reality of what she'd gone through was even more destructive than what he'd imagined. Physical abuse, yes. But also very emotionally disturbing. "I'm so damn sorry." He'd make them pay. All three of them.

"A few months after that, he caught me alone and he forced me to the woods." She sounded impassive, as if she were telling a dull story.

Denver felt the sharpening tension and stroked her from her behind to her shoulders and back again, even down and over her thighs. He wanted to touch every inch of her as if he could somehow heal the nightmare, maybe make the memory go away.

He turned them to their sides, tucking her close, protectively holding her. "Take your time, honey."

While he waited, he continued to stroke her, his brain in turmoil, his stomach sick.

After a shuddering breath, she started talking again. "He'd cleared a spot in the woods and he had a stake in the ground, with ropes tied to it."

Jesus.

"All around it, the locals waited, some looking uneasy, some anxious. He planned to make me the show and I knew it was going to be bad but I couldn't get free." Suddenly she sat up, but held his hand. "I'm going to rush through this, okay?"

Volatile emotion made a fist around his windpipe and he had to swallow twice before the restriction eased enough for him to speak. "Whatever you need." He sat up, too, and there, in the bed, they faced each other, him big and capable and her, whether she'd admit it or not, small and vulnerable.

"He stripped off my shirt and bra and tied my arms behind me to the stake. I thought he was going to rape me. I still think that was his plan."

With others to watch. To regain his composure, he closed his eyes, but only for a second. Cherry needed him. He'd asked for the whole truth so he'd damn well stick with her, body and soul, while she shared.

"Anyway," she said, her hand in his, "he'd wasted too much time for rape."

"Wasted how?"

"He… He had all these disgusting bugs and he kept throwing them at me. Some of the people watching laughed about it. Some just watched. No one helped me." Her hold on his hand tightened. "Every so often he'd come get a bug off me, but he'd use that as an excuse to cop a feel, too, and I was so hysterical I can't even remember what I said. I just remember…crying."

He'd tortured her. And some sick fucks had stayed to watch.

"There were maybe ten people there. Two of them girls who screamed each time one of the bugs took flight. I think I hated them the most, because they were just as scared of the bugs, but they stayed and watched anyway." She shook her head. "About the time Carver tired of that game and told me he was going to take off my shorts, Janet showed up."

"The stepmother?"

Cherry nodded. "I can still see it exactly as it happened. She stepped into the clearing wearing pajama pants and a man's T-shirt, her hair all ratty, a cigarette caught in her teeth and her shotgun aimed at Carver. She said she was looking for a reason to shoot him."

"Did she always look like that?"

"The cigarette, yes. The shotgun, often. But she usually cleaned up. I think she must've woken up after a late night of drinking and when we were all gone, she got suspicious."

"Thank God."

Cherry nodded. "She was like this crazy, mean avenger. She told one of the idiot girls there to cut me loose. Everyone was silent, unsure of what would happen. It was eerie quiet—except for the bugs. Bugs are never, ever quiet."

Using only his pinkie, Denver teased over her cheek, easing a tendril of hair away from her face.

Cherry didn't seem to notice.

"After I was free Janet backed us out of there and put me in her truck. It was so weird, but still no one said anything. Carver just stared after us like he hated us both—or like maybe he was planning…something." Her brows twitched as if even now, she couldn't understand his hostility. "Janet told me she'd had enough of worrying about Carver bringing the law down on them. She was so mad at him, saying he was too reckless." Cherry swallowed hard. "She also said she hated any man who'd rape a woman, and she knew that's where Carver was headed. So she'd brought some cash for me, my purse and papers and a few of my clothes in a bag. She drove me to the highway, told me to get out, to leave and never come back."

That was more than he could take, so Denver scooped her up to his lap again and squeezed the breath right out of her. She didn't complain, not even when he started to rock her.

Sliding her fingers into his hair, she whispered, "I'm okay."

She wanted to soothe him? Denver gave a low, gravelly laugh. "Better than okay. You're perfect." A thought occurred to him. "Did you ever consider reporting them? All of them?"

Shaking her head, she said, "It wouldn't have mattered. The local authorities covered for them. They came around and visited. Left with cash and sometimes drugs. Carver and his whole family had immunity in the town."

And she'd been stuck in the middle of it with nowhere to turn—except to escape on her own.

Cherry cupped a hand to his jaw. "Do you understand, Denver? I took *drug* money. They never discussed the business with me, but I knew. I'd have had to be a special kind of stupid not to know. Stupid and blind."

"And you're neither."

As if she didn't understand his nonchalant attitude, she searched his face. "They sold to dealers who ruined peoples' lives. There were beatings." Her gaze held desperately to his. "My own parents died because of a drug deal. Maybe even from trading with Carver's family. But at the time I didn't care. I just wanted out of there."

"You were a kid in survival mode, honey. And I'm so incredibly glad that you not only survived, you became you, someone who's now very important to me."

Her gaze searched his. "You don't think I was weak?"

"God, no. You were stronger than any kid should ever have to be."

Her bottom lip quivered, but only for a second, then she launched herself at him.

And to Denver's surprise, she started kissing him, not for comfort, but for so much more. "Cherry…"

She rushed into convincing arguments. "I can't do anything about Carver right now. He's out there, still a terrible human being, but he's not a problem I can solve tonight."

He wasn't a problem she had to solve on her own. But he'd already told her that.

"If we don't switch up the mood, I'm going to be an emotional mess."

God, he loved her. "You can be a mess with me."

A reluctant, only slightly sad smile teased her beautiful mouth. "I've been a mess with you too many times already. For tonight, I just want to forget Carver and the past. I want to enjoy you." Her heated gaze coerced him; her hands moved over him in irresistible ways. Lowering her voice, she whispered, "You can do that for me."

Given there was nothing he wouldn't do for her, how could he argue with that? He couldn't. Whether she was flirting, laughing, crying or sick, she was his. He'd show her that, and maybe by morning she'd believe it.

CHAPTER TWENTY

STRETCHING AWAKE ON the narrow, uncomfortable bed, Carver glanced at the clock. Nearly 7:00 a.m. He should go back to sleep but he knew he wouldn't. In the bed next to him, Mitty snored loud enough to rattle the windows and Gene muttered in his sleep.

But that wasn't what kept him awake.

Off and on all night Cherry had plagued his brain, leaving him edgy, too hot.

And angry.

Between dark, stirring dreams, he'd awakened a dozen times to ponder her reaction to the surprise he'd left in her car. Did she scream? Cry?

Did her fucking boyfriend console her?

Carver's hands fisted and his breathing deepened. Eventually, he knew, he'd make that guy pay. For interfering. For fucking her.

For having what Carver wanted.

Despite her hulking protector, it had been easy to pull the hoax. Too easy. He'd disabled the car to get her to leave it behind, and when she did, reacting exactly as he'd wanted, he, Gene and Mitty had slipped through the dead of night to dump in the snakes and various insects.

God, he wished he could have been there to watch her when she first opened that door. But even though he was a risk taker, he knew that'd be pushing the limits. On the quiet street filled with middle-class families, there'd be no place to hide, no place to wait and watch.

Staring up at the ceiling of the cheap motel room, Carver grinned. Cherry had always suffered a bone-deep fear of insects—a phobia he'd often used to taunt her. Once, when she'd been about fifteen, he'd dropped a big, juicy grasshopper down the back of her shirt.

Screaming as if he'd poured scalding water on her, she'd shed the shirt to free the hopper. Even then she'd had big tits. Didn't matter that she wore a plain white cotton bra. He'd gotten a boner, as had both his brothers. Janet had come running, bitched them all out, and taken Cherry inside.

But not before he'd stomped the bug, squishing guts everywhere—and almost making Cherry barf.

From that moment on, he'd taken perverse pleasure in putting a centipede in her bed, a cockroach in her cereal. Once he'd pinned her down beneath him, a cicada in his hand, and made her kiss him.

She'd cried the whole time, but damn, she'd tasted good.

Fuck. Carver sat up in a rush and ran both hands over his face. A crying, closemouthed kiss from a schoolgirl, and it still turned him on to think of it. When he got her again, he'd tie her down and do whatever he wanted to her. He knew her secrets.

As much as she feared snakes and bugs, she feared rape more.

Mitty raised his head. "What are you doin'?" Eyes squinted, he checked the clock. "You okay, Carver?"

Face half smashed in a pillow, Gene sneered, "He's thinking about *her* again."

"Go back to sleep. Both of you." Carver pulled out a cigarette, lit it, and sat back against the headboard. Yes, he was thinking of her. How could he not now that he was so close to getting her again?

"Let it go," Gene grumbled as he rolled to his back. Not a chance.

"The longer we stay here, the longer we're neglecting business."

"We need her to finish our business," Carver reminded him. "Or have you forgotten that Janet hid our cash?"

Mitty got up, scratched his crotch, and lumbered into the bathroom. He left the door open while he drained his pipe and said, "We could just make Janet tell us."

"We already tried that, idiot. With the security around her in the hospital, we can't get a private word." Gene looked at Carver. "But there's no reason we can't just shoot the damned fighter and grab the girl, then head home with her. She'll tell us what we need to know."

"No." Carver refused to have his plans spoiled. "I want the fighter to suffer."

Gene sat up, too. "If you keep dicking around, we're going to get caught."

Carver bolted forward. "Are you the brains now? You the one making the plans?"

"No. Just sayin'."

Mitty returned and dropped into the bed, almost launching Gene out of it. They argued for a minute before going quiet again. When Carver looked at them, he saw that Mitty was back to snoring, but Gene just stewed.

As long as Gene didn't interfere, he could mope all he wanted.

Quietly, Gene said, "I still remember that day in the woods as if it had just happened." He stacked his arms behind his head. "How she looked as you slowly stripped her, the scent of her fear." He glanced over at Carver. "How she pleaded with you."

Carver inhaled sharply. He wanted to hear her begging again. He wanted to see her naked, now with a lush woman's body.

"If Pops was here—" Gene began.

Carver cut him off. "He's not though, is he?" Carver was now the head of the family, and he wanted what had been promised to him so damned long ago. "We only have a few more days to torment her, and I plan to make the most of it. Then this weekend, I'll get her and we'll head home. Stop sweating it."

Gene considered him, but finally nodded. "All right."

Carver appreciated his acceptance, but he'd have done as he pleased anyway. And it would please him to make the fighter pay before he got his fill of little Cherry Peyton.

Yes, he needed her to tell him where Janet had stashed the cash. Cherry knew, he believed Janet about that. The old bitch wouldn't dare lie. If they didn't carry on business as usual, the ones who'd killed Pops and put her in a hospital would be back, and then they'd finish the job.

On all of them.

But settling business matters wasn't even close to everything he wanted from Cherry.

Thinking that, he checked the time again, then drew

out the card Pamela had given him and used the hotel phone to call her. That little bird was so desperate for a compliment he'd had her eating out of his hand in seconds. Getting an invite to her party had been a cinch. As Gene said, it kept them in town a little longer than he liked, but he couldn't pass up such a ripe opportunity to get revenge—and get his fill.

She answered with a brisk, "Hello?"

"Pamela? Hi. It's Carver, Denver's friend." Mitty and Gene both stirred themselves to stare at him. He shook his head so they'd know to keep quiet and smiled into the phone. "I hope I'm not calling too early."

"Carver," she said with pleasure. "It's fine. I've been up for hours."

"Somehow I knew you weren't a slug." He suffered through her twittering laugh before asking, "Denver confirm yet?"

"Yes, thank goodness. He spoke to my husband and agreed to attend."

"Good, good." Fucking fantastic. "Is he bringing the girl with him?" That would be the best scenario, an easy way for Carver to grab Cherry in front of him, to let him feel the helplessness while Carver manhandled her.

And then Cherry could watch while Gene gutted the bastard.

"Yes, he is. And it's actually a perfect situation."

Yeah, hadn't he just thought so? Carver laughed. "How's that?" He was pretty sure Pamela didn't have the same idea as him.

"There's so much bad blood, but with Cherry there, everyone will have to play nice. Plus befriending her gives us an avenue back into Denver's life. It's why I invited her."

"Good idea," Carver said. "Denver can be difficult. I told you that."

"Yes, and thank you again for offering your advice. It was very nice to discuss all this with one of his friends."

"Denver and I go way back," Carver lied. "I'm glad to help. It'll make him happy to reunite with his family."

From the opposite bed, Gene grunted.

"Just make sure you don't tell him that we talked. It'd piss him off big-time and you'd be back at square one."

"I won't say a word, I promise."

Breathing harder in anticipation, Carver bid her goodbye and disconnected the call. Thanks to Pamela, he knew exactly when and where to find Denver and Cherry. That gave him all the opportunity he needed.

He could hardly wait.

BEING WITH DENVER was amazing. After work, Cherry spent her time finding a good spot for some of her clothes. Easy enough, given his massive closet. Seeing her things arranged next to his gave her great satisfaction.

She loved him. She wanted to be with him forever.

For now, he wanted her to stay.

Remaining realistic, especially after he'd mentioned love, just wasn't possible. All problems aside, she beamed with optimism. Not that she'd pressure Denver by telling him her feelings. Never that. He had a fight to prepare for and more than enough of her emotional baggage already dumped on him. From here on out, she wanted to make their relationship easier.

About pleasure instead of the past.

Determined to make it work out, she talked with Yvette and Harper about good recipes for what the guys could eat during training. Denver informed her that he'd be helping in the kitchen and everywhere else. He was not a man to sit while a woman waited on him—unless he got his turn waiting on her, too.

She was still undecided what to do about Carver when he struck again.

After work, Denver had picked her up and they'd headed to the rec center. Stack was there, teaching a self-defense class that was attended by both Vanity and Merissa. Off to the side of that, Cannon and Miles worked with some high school boys on grappling moves. Yvette and her adorable dog, Muggles, watched from the sidelines.

It was a festive, busy group—until someone called in a fire that didn't exist. Fire trucks and police cars arrived with a lot of fanfare. Everyone was evacuated, and the only blaze found was a small one in the Dumpsters behind the center, easily put out and with no real damage done.

Yet hours were wasted as everyone milled on the curb out front, giving the firefighters a chance to do a more thorough search inside.

Unsmiling, his mood grave, Denver kept Cherry's hand locked in his while she spoke with an official, explaining that it was likely Carver who had made the call. That admission brought about a dozen questions. As she shared what information she could, Denver repeatedly scanned the area.

Cherry suddenly realized that Cannon, Stack, Armie, Miles, Brand and Leese all did the same. It disconcerted her to see that they'd formed a protective semicircle around the rest of the group. They each looked alert, incensed and…ready.

At least they were taking Carver's threats seriously, she decided, even while her worry expanded. She also noticed that Leese now appeared to be part of their group. Since she considered him a nice enough guy, she was glad.

The official took notes, including Carver's phone number. Through her repeated apologies for the bother, he reassured her that he understood.

And even though their time had been wasted, the firemen remained cordial, too, as they finished up their search.

In fact, not a single person looked at her with accusation, but no one needed to. She knew what had happened, and it devastated her. The rec center was not only special to the fighters, but also to much of the community. And it had now been violated—endangered—in a terrible way.

Because of her.

After the interview finally ended, Denver caught her chin. He tipped up her face and gave her a contemplative once-over. "Soon as they finish checking into things, we can head back in."

She nodded.

"You're all right?"

"Yes."

His thumb teased over her cheek. "Your face is hot."

"I'm…wrecked." And furious. "This should never have happened."

In contrast to his black scowl, Denver sounded gentle when he said, "No, it shouldn't have."

"I need to apologize to Cannon."

"No."

She looked around and knew the awful truth. "I need to apologize to all of them."

Now both of his big hands held her face. "You didn't do this, so you have nothing to apologize for."

She tried a reassuring smile. "You might think not, but everyone else—"

"Will agree with me." After a quick kiss that was so tender, it left her confused, Denver called over Armie and Stack. "I need a word with Cannon."

"Got it." Armie took her arm and stepped her back a little closer to the wall of the rec center.

Stack flanked her other side.

Then they both went back to surveying the crowd and surrounding area.

It was ludicrous how they shielded her while Denver strode over to Cannon. She could have told them that Carver was a coward at heart. Never would he step into the crowd of badass fighters.

No, when Carver came after her, he'd do so when she was alone. Only…Denver never left her alone anymore.

Sighing, she dropped back against the brick wall and closed her eyes. How long could her growing relationship with Denver last under the strain of Carver's dark shadow?

Seeing everyone outside the rec center, vulnerable, made her accept the truth: If Carver couldn't get to her, he would definitely go after someone else just to hurt her.

Everyone she knew and counted as a friend could be a potential target. She had to figure out what he wanted. And to do that, she'd have to talk with him again.

"Hey, chin up, doll." Since Armie had been in the middle of showering, he stood there on the sidewalk wrapped only in a towel. The females seemed to enjoy that. And why not? Armie was all muscles, sinew and cocky attitude wrapped up with sleek skin, sexy body hair and some intriguing tattoos. His deep brown eyes always held humor, and he didn't have a single modest bone in his body.

"You're making me feel naked," he told her with a grin.

Cherry started to apologize for staring at him, but Stack stated, "You are naked," forestalling any comment from her.

"I have a towel," Armie argued.

"You could have just as easily grabbed your boxers."

"Didn't have boxers today." He peered at Cherry, ensuring he had her attention, and she saw the wicked teasing in his eyes before he said, "See, I had these slinky little—"

Stack shoved him, making him laugh—and almost lose his towel.

There was some collective breath holding by all the females nearby, but Armie managed to keep the towel in place.

Without a care, he secured it again, then smiled down at Cherry. "Seriously, they'd have covered less."

Fighting a smile, Cherry shook her head. "You are so immodest."

"There you go," Armie murmured with satisfaction. "Much better than the long face."

"Not that you don't look cute when you're fretting," Stack said. "But the smile is a better look for you."

"You're *both* nuts."

They grinned at her.

Deciding they might make good confidantes, she whispered, "You know this was Carver."

Stack and Armie shared a look. Yes, she realized they'd been clowning around for her benefit, but how could she laugh when Cannon's business had just been interrupted? The firefighters had come out for nothing.

And she couldn't quit thinking about what Carver might pull next. She had to stop him—but how?

"Don't sweat it," Stack told her. "His bullshit petty games will end soon enough."

If only that were true. She nodded anyway, just to appease Stack.

Cherry realized then that he kept glancing over at Vanity. She looked, too, and realized why. Vanity had several admiring young men around her. When Vanity smiled, Stack frowned.

Taking pity on him, Cherry said, "You don't need to stand guard over me."

"What's that?" he asked without taking his attention off Vanity.

Armie gave Cherry a conspiratorial grin. "Go," he told Stack. "Cherry and I will entertain each other until we get the all clear. Looks like the firefighters are finally heading out, so it should be any minute now."

Without a word, Stack nodded and stalked away, leaving Armie and Cherry alone—or at least as alone as they could be on the crowded curb.

"So." Armie tipped his head to the side. "What's on your mind, Cherry Pie?"

She groaned.

Tugging a lock of her hair, Armie said, "It suits you, so stop the cow sounds."

"Cow sounds?"

"Mooing and groaning." He turned to lean on the wall beside her. "You know what? I'm disappointed in you."

Ouch. That hurt, but all she said was, "I understand."

"Doubtful. See, you're not only letting an asshole like Carver get to you, but you're really putting it to poor Denver, and that dude has a fight coming up."

Wincing, Cherry said, "I think that's called a one-two punch, right?"

He laughed. "Or maybe a body shot?" Playfully, he punched her ribs. "Really takes the wind out of you." Sobering, he blew out a frustrated breath. "If Carver is watching, do you really want him to see you looking all glum?"

She didn't want to think about Carver actually seeing her.

"Smile, Cherry."

She did.

"Better. And given you're madly in love with Denver…?" He waited.

Her smile faded and she gave a small nod. For the longest time after gaining her independence, all she'd wanted was stability. But Denver trumped that. He trumped…everything. "I've loved him almost from the day I met him."

Armie smiled. "Glad to hear it."

She noticed Armie didn't offer her any reassurance

on Denver's feelings. "The last thing I want is to inter-fere with his training."

"I doubt he'd let you. Denver is good. Really good. If I was a betting man, I'd put my money on him. The guy he's fighting though, he specializes in phone-booth warfare."

Cherry gave him a blank stare.

"Fighting close," Armie explained. "He stays right up in your grill, which is going to make it tough for Denver to get in much kicking, or to do a takedown. So he needs to do fine-tuning on some stuff."

"And I'm bothering him?"

Armie laughed. "Doll, you'll keep him bothered no matter what. But you could lighten the load a little by telling him how you feel."

She threw up her hands. "I *have*." Denver was the one who kept her guessing.

"*Pfft*. I ain't buying it." He shoulder-bumped her. "Know what I think you should do?"

"What?"

"First, quit letting Carver and his thug brothers get to you. You're not a stupid girl, so you're not going to go off on your own anywhere, which means he can't touch you."

No, maybe not. But what about everyone else?

"Second…" He paused for dramatic effect. "Drop the love bomb on Denver."

Tell Denver how she felt? Leave herself that ex-posed. And what if he rejected her?

She leaned into Armie's shoulder and whispered, "He might not feel the same."

"If you ignore the temporary insanity you've caused him, Denver is a real standup guy. He's got his shit together with this whole plan for the future and money in the bank and attainable goals. All that. If he wasn't figuring on fitting you in, he wouldn't still be with you. And he wouldn't want to fit you in if he didn't care an awful lot."

Wow, that made sense, didn't it? Happy to use Armie as a sounding board, she said, "Okay, let's say he cares, but—"

"He does."

"—what if he isn't sure about the whole lifetime-commitment route yet? If I tell him how I feel, wouldn't that pressure him?"

"The pressure was you not trusting him. I'm guessing he broke that barrier, though."

"What makes you think so?"

Glancing toward Denver, Armie rolled one bare shoulder. "He looks more relaxed today."

His statement so surprised her, she barked a laugh. Even from where she stood, she could see the angry set to Denver's muscled frame. "He's furious."

"Yeah, sure. This cowardly stuff enrages everyone. But there's still a difference. He's not as edgy." Armie eyed her. "I won't pry, but there was stuff in your background you didn't want to share?"

Turning her face away, she nodded. "Yes."

"I get it. I have my own tainted background, ya know?"

That got her gaze back on Armie. No, she hadn't known.

"I see where you're coming from. But I'm glad you opened up to Denver. That sort of thing is real important to him."

"But not to you?"

His rascal's grin returned. "Now, Cherry Pie, you know I don't do romantic relationships. And when it comes to one-night stands, no, I don't want to hear some chick's baggage any more than she wants to hear mine. Trust me, we have better ground to cover than history."

Cherry was still thinking about that, specifically how it might affect Merissa, when her pocket buzzed and she almost leaped out of her skin.

Armie caught her arm, unsure what had happened, but she laughed and withdrew her phone.

"Sorry. It just startled me." Feeling sheepish, she answered without thinking—and without checking the caller ID. "Hello?"

Carver said, "Little sister, how you doin'?"

Anger took her two steps away from Armie, before he caught her arm again. Ignoring him, she said, "Carver, what did you do?"

"No idea what you mean, sis."

"Are you dense? I am not and have never been your sister."

Suddenly Denver was beside her, too. She realized she was drawing attention and tried to turn her back on all of them.

Denver stopped her.

"Name-calling, Cherry? You're going to regret that."

"Another threat?"

"Now why would I threaten you? I just want you to come home."

"Not my home, Carver."

"But you'll return all the same, won't you?"

Denver's brows were down, his mouth flat, his chest expanding—and she realized Armie was right.

This hurt him, her insistence on trying to handle things herself. She'd been so intent on not imposing on him, she'd made matters worse.

Regret knotted her stomach, but she lifted her chin. "You want an answer, Carver, is that it?"

"You made me wait so long, darlin', I want a damn sight more than that now."

"All right." Her hand trembled, but she held the phone out to Denver.

Satisfaction altered his entire demeanor. His golden eyes glowed as he accepted the phone, bent to quickly kiss her, then clicked on the phone to check the number before putting it to his ear. In a near jovial tone, he said, "Damn, Carver, you must change out phones every day. That's got to be getting costly, you cowardly prick."

CHAPTER TWENTY-ONE

DENVER KEPT HIS gaze on Cherry while he listened to Carver's harsh breathing.

"Put Cherry back on."

"C'mon, Carver. You're not that stupid. You know you're never speaking to her again." Cherry hadn't agreed to that, but she'd trusted him this much so somehow he'd convince her. "Resign yourself."

Desperation escalated his rage. *"She'll tell you—"*

"What?" Denver touched her warm cheek, smoothed her soft blond curls. "That you're a twisted fuck who's too chicken-shit to talk to a man? That you get your rocks off tormenting little girls? I met you, man. I already knew what a weak fuck you are."

"I'll…"

"What?" Denver taunted. "What will you do?"

A lengthy pause showed Carver's reticence to implicate himself. Finally he said, "I heard there was some trouble at the gym today."

"Not that I've heard of."

Another tense pause. "Have you been there?"

"I'm there now. Why? You planning to visit?"

"But…I thought…"

"What?" Denver glanced at Armie and shook his head. Carver was nowhere around or he'd know the fuss his false alarm had caused. "What did you think?"

"I don't believe you."

"About what? You're not making any sense, man." He had Carver backed against the cage and they both knew it. "Maybe this conversation would be better in person. You man enough to meet with me, Carver?"

A faint, eerie laugh sounded. "Cherry knows what kind of man I am."

Knowing he had to stay calm to pull this off, Denver drew his gaze away from Cherry, popped his neck, worked his jaw. "Yeah, when she was a kid you were able to frighten her." Good, that sounded indifferent enough. "But she's a woman now, and she's with me. She knows there's no reason to be afraid."

"Goddamn you—"

"You see," Denver continued, still good-humored, "when compared to a real man, you're nothing, Carver. Nothing at all. Why would she even give you a thought?"

Armie snickered, but Cherry just stared at him, one hand over her mouth, her expression horrified.

Denver had already spoken to Cannon and made additional plans to keep Cherry safe, otherwise he might not have felt as comfortable provoking Carver's rage. He would never, under any circumstances, put her at risk.

Demented men could be unpredictable, especially when enraged. That's what he counted on. He needed Carver to act so he could get hold of him and end his bullshit.

Or just end him. Either way worked for Denver.

As long as the psycho hid away, Denver had no way to control things, so he'd do what he could to draw him out.

"Carver?" he asked quietly. "You still there, you lousy little puke?"

"She's mine."

The unnatural calm after near hysterics made the fine hairs on Denver's neck prickle. "If you believe that, you've lost your grip on reality."

"She'll *always* be mine."

It turned Denver's stomach to know Cherry had once had to deal with Carver on her own. "Tell me where you are, Carver. I'll be happy to meet up and prove to you just how wrong you are."

In a dead monotone, Carver said, "Tell her she can't hide anymore." And with that he disconnected the call.

God, Denver hoped Carver had cracked. He paused only a second to let his mind settle, to gather together his satisfaction, then he turned to Cherry. When he saw her standing alone with Armie, he realized everyone else had gone inside. And now that the call was over, Armie turned his back, giving them some privacy.

Denver couldn't seem to get a deep enough breath as he closed the narrow space between him and Cherry.

She said nothing, just stared up at him.

Talk about cracking... He hauled her up close and took her mouth, turning his head to part her lips, sinking his tongue in, tasting her deeply.

Cherry hung in his grip, shocked still...for about five seconds. Then she tunneled her fingers into his hair, pressed her body to his and returned the kiss full-force.

Denver backed her up to the brick wall, planted one hand flat on the wall beside her head, and deepened the kiss even more. He wanted her. So damn much.

All the time.

The significance of what she'd done today—

"This is getting way out of hand," Armie muttered. "Hell, I'm blushing, and I didn't think that was possible."

Denver lifted his head, dazed, astounded actually. He looked around and, thank God, no one else was in sight. But he had Cherry pinned to an outside wall of the rec center near a busy street and the rec center wouldn't close for a few more hours.

Cherry rested against the wall, her lips swollen and pink, her eyes misty, sucking in breast-enhancing breaths that made him even crazier.

"Damn."

"Yeah," Armie said. "If you want to take off, I can make your excuses inside."

"No," Cherry whispered, barely audible. She swallowed, filled her lungs, and pushed away from the wall. "He has to finish his training."

Armie grinned. "Hard to do with wood, doll."

"I'm fine," Denver lied. Hell, he was flattened. Completely leveled by the fact that Cherry had finally, 100 percent trusted him. He glanced at Armie. "I'm sure we're alone, but all the same—"

"I'll loiter," Armie told him, understanding that he wanted to remain cautious. He pointed near the front door. "Over there, okay? But keep in mind I'm bare-assed under this towel, okay?"

"I won't take long."

Nodding, Armie strolled away. He reached the door just as two women approached. "Ladies."

Instead of going inside, their gazes crawled all over Armie. He ended up starting his own conversation, and given the way the women giggled, he'd be hooking up again that night.

Denver shook his head. "He's a glutton."

"Look who's talking." With just her fingertips, Cherry touched her mouth. "I don't know what brought that on, but I liked it."

Yeah, she always liked it when he touched or kissed her.

And more.

From the inside out, Denver smiled. Primal satisfaction was a pulsebeat in his blood, making him feel like the luckiest man alive. He had her now, and he knew it. All he had to do was get things settled with her foster family and then he could cement the deal.

Late sunshine cast a rosy glow over her skin and made her blond hair brighter. "Thank you, Cherry."

She smiled up at him. "For?"

He handed her back her phone. "Giving over to me." Tugging at his ear didn't make the words come any easier. "Trusting me to handle things. But it's more than that."

Cherry smoothed a hand over his chest. "I trust you in every way there is."

Yeah, that about covered it. She was finally, really his, no holds barred, and damn, he loved it.

Until then she'd been holding strong, doling out the acceptance, mixing it with resistance. But not anymore.

No time like the present, Denver decided, to get a few things set up. "I want to get you a new phone."

Her big brown eyes turned wary.

"I don't want Carver to be able to reach you. He'll try," Denver explained. "And hopefully when he can't, he'll have to expose himself. Once he does, we can resolve things."

Slowly, she nodded. "Okay."

"You won't be in any danger. I'll see to that."

"I know." She moved away, but not far. "The contract for my phone plan won't be up for months, though."

Closing in on her again, Denver took her hands. "I'll take care of it." *I'll take care of you.* "I'll pick up a new phone and add you on my plan. Not a big deal, I promise."

Nibbling her bottom lip, she averted her eyes. "I want to do the right thing, Denver. It's just...it's not easy."

"I know. But it's me, not a stranger who's lending a hand." He bent his knees, lowering himself to meet her gaze. "It's me."

Worry kept her brows slightly pinched even as she gave a nod of agreement. Indicating the rec center, she said, "Everyone here could now be in danger. More so if I'm out of reach."

"I know. Cannon and I talked about it. He's going to add some additional security, guys who'll be at the doors seeing everyone to and from their cars."

"Our friends..."

The way she included herself when speaking about the others in their group further lightened his mood. Little by little, she came to realize she wasn't alone. Not anymore. "Got that covered, too. Cannon's already keeping a close watch on Yvette and Merissa." Nothing new in that. He was always extra vigilant when it came to his fiancée and sister. "Stack's happy to stick close to Vanity. Gage is with Harper."

"And you're with me."

A statement, not a question. He confirmed anyway. "I'm with you." Damn, but he loved her more every second of every day. "Miles, Brand and Leese will pitch in to help with door duty." He said again, "It's covered. No need for you to worry."

A wistful smile flickered over her mouth. "I'm not sure I can keep myself from it. Please don't take it as an insult."

He smiled, too. "All right. As long as you share your worry with me."

Now she laughed. "Like you give me a choice in that?" Going on tiptoe, she kissed him. "We should head in before one of those women steals Armie's towel. I swear, it looks like they're considering it."

Denver turned and saw the truth of that. One woman kept fingering the edge of the towel until Armie caught her wrist and laughingly reprimanded her. "Did I tell you he's advancing to the SBC?" While leading her in, Denver updated her on Armie's career. His friend deserved to be happy.

But Denver had a feeling it'd take more than the elite fight organization to accomplish that. And if Armie didn't stop dodging the truth, he just might miss his chance.

PLEASED WITH HOW things had rolled out, Armie made his excuses and escaped the bold women. Bold, ha! One had suggested he just lose the towel right there on the curb, for every passerby to see. When he'd refused, the other asked for just a peek.

To keep up his rep, he'd considered it, even pretended he might. They didn't bother hiding their disappointment when he laughed and only tightened the towel.

Crazy ladies, but man, he loved a bold chick. The bolder the better.

He smiled as he entered the rec center and headed for the hall leading to the locker room. With his thoughts occupied, he almost plowed into Rissy when she stepped out of the break room.

He stopped short. With her head down, she didn't. She bounced into his chest, then stumbled back.

She made an automatic grab for him—and got his towel.

Armie caught her shoulder to keep her from falling. "Easy, Stretch." At the same time, he turned her so her back was to his front.

His ass now faced the gym and he just knew someone was in the right position to take in his inadvertent show.

Rissy didn't say a single word. She just stood there, frozen stiff, her shoulders slightly raised as if caught in a wince.

Leaning around her, Armie took in her face. Eyes screwed tight. Lips caught in her teeth.

His towel clutched in one hand.

"Mind if I retrieve this?" He pried her fingers loose and quickly rewrapped his lower body. Amused—and oddly turned on—he asked, "You going to faint?"

"Maybe."

Grinning, he glanced back over his shoulder and got a titillated wave from Vanity, a wink from Harper. A second later Gage scooped up his wife like a football and, not even bothering to acknowledge Armie, disappeared from sight.

That left Vanity standing there, until Stack stepped in front of her, blocking her view.

Armie laughed. "Thanks to you, I just flashed the masses."

She said nothing.

Sighing, Armie bodily turned her to face him. He waited patiently until she'd peeked open one eye. "You okay?"

Seeing he was now decently covered, she released a breath and opened both eyes. "You may have stunted my growth."

"You're tall enough." While she was willowy slim, she stood only an inch or so shorter than his six feet, and every inch of her appealed to him. "If you grew much more, you'd tower over your brother."

"He's three inches taller than me."

"Doin' the math, huh? Still makes you tall, Stretch. Especially for a girl." While she grew disgruntled from his teasing—as he'd intended—Armie let his gaze drift over her again. She wore a simple, stretchy sleeveless cotton dress that showed the narrowness of her waist, the subtle swell of her breasts and hips. It ended several inches above her knees, showcasing those impossibly long, trim, shapely legs. No jewelry, very little makeup, flat sandals and her hair loose.

And God help him, she was so hot he had to sing a litany in his head to keep his body from reacting to her nearness. *Cannon's sister, Cannon's sister, Cannon's sister.* In his towel, he wouldn't be able to hide a rise.

"I heard you were signing with the SBC."

Her light blue eyes were the same as her brother's, but damn, they had a very different effect on him.

"Yeah." Discomfort had him rubbing the back of his neck.

With rapt focus, Rissy stared at his biceps, and then his underarm.

He scowled at her as he lowered his arm. "Heard that from your brother, I assume?"

"Was it a secret?"

"No." But it wasn't something he wanted to advertise yet. He needed time to get used to the idea.

Rissy took a step closer, making him catch and hold his breath. "You'll be away a lot now, won't you?"

Since he'd have to exhale to answer, he shrugged.

She stared into his eyes, and he felt her soft sigh on his mouth. "I'm thinking of relocating, too."

It hit him like a liver punch, stealing all his air. "Since when?" he wheezed.

Turning, she leaned on the wall, her arms folded behind her, one leg bent. Looking pensive, she kept her head down. "I got offered a promotion if I relocate to Indiana."

He'd half been hoping she'd say Kentucky, since that's where he'd be dividing his time going from the rec center to the camp where Cannon trained, with Havoc and Simon.

He wanted to say, *"Don't go,"* but instead he growled, "Congrats, then."

"I haven't accepted yet. I have a little time to think about it." Her gaze sought his. "You'll be in Kentucky, right?"

"Sometimes."

In a rush, she asked, "Why do you have to do that? Go away, I mean. What's wrong with training here?"

"Rissy." She already understood damn near as much

about MMA as he did. Every step of the way she'd been a dedicated supporter of her brother's career path. "Different camps make better rounded fighters."

"The variety, I know. But why can't those guys rotate here?"

"Havoc and Simon are a big deal." He choked out the words, saying, "It's an honor to be invited to their camp."

She made a rude sound. "You don't care about stuff like that."

His muscles tensed. "Honor?"

"Prestige."

"Oh." Yeah, he didn't much care about that.

"Armie?"

Wary, he said, "Yeah?"

"I would never question your honor." As she walked away, she trailed her fingertips over his right shoulder, across his chest, and off his left shoulder.

Stymied, he watched her go, specifically the gentle sway of her ass. Damn it, he had wood after all.

Then he remembered Cherry's sicko foster brothers and jogged to the end the hall in time to see Cannon walking her out.

If they both left Ohio, that could well solve his problem.

Then again, he had a feeling that particular long-legged, sassy-mouthed, tall temptation of a problem could only be solved by giving in.

And that was no real solution at all.

THANK GOD THE rest of their Friday went well.

Denver had been so entertaining through dinner and the action movie that Cherry almost forgot about the uproar Carver had caused. He treated their first official date very seriously and went out of his way to make it wonderful for her.

She had to think Armie was right—giving over to Denver 100 percent had made a marked difference.

It still wasn't easy for her. She'd gotten used to doing for herself, to making ends meet on her own and doing without when she couldn't. Having Denver take on some of her responsibilities left her uneasy.

For her, a new phone and additional bill would have been staggering. He treated it as no big deal. And she did understand the importance of cutting off all contact with Carver. In fact, Denver kept her phone in his pocket, and she carried his. First thing tomorrow, before they went to his father's party, he said they'd stop to get her a new number.

Repeatedly he thanked her for allowing him to do it. So ridiculous. Who thanked a person for letting them spend their hard-earned money on gifts?

In her heart, she knew it was a person who understood the importance of independence. In so many ways, Denver proved what a remarkable man he was.

Now they were at Rowdy's bar, as were most of their friends, and everyone seemed in a good mood. They took up two big tables and a booth toward the back corner of the bar. Denver had fans continually approach him. Cannon, too. The men took it in stride, laughing, signing autographs, always receptive.

When the women flirted a little too much, the guys were amazingly diplomatic, remaining polite and funny without encouraging.

At Rowdy's request, they moved to the side of the floor for a few photos with regular customers. The location would keep the crowd from jamming up the rest of the bar. Grinning, Denver stood between a woman and her boyfriend, his arms spread behind them. He was so big he towered over both of them, his shoulders broad enough to encompass them both.

So gorgeous, so sweet, so talented—and currently all hers.

"Young love," Armie quipped beside her with a dramatic sigh.

"Looks like Denver must be doing something right," Stack agreed while giving her a playfully critical appraisal. "She looks…satisfied."

Leese, now an accepted part of the group, laughed while nodding his head toward Denver. "So does he."

They all turned to look at Denver, who was now looking at Cherry.

She blushed at the heat in his eyes; Denver gave a slow, knowing smile.

At the table next to them, Vanity handed Cherry a magazine. "What do you think?"

The magazine showed a woman with a shoulder-length sleek hairdo. "You're getting your hair cut?" Cherry couldn't imagine it. Vanity's heavy, pale blond hair had just enough wave to always look amazing.

"Not me," Vanity said. "Merissa is thinking of changing her look."

Yvette crossed her arms on the table. "She wants to change things up a bit."

It was hilarious how all the men—all but Armie—started objecting to Merissa at the same time.

"But your hair is so pretty."

"It's downright sexy."

"Why would you want to cut it?"

Merissa went bright red at all the attention. "It's just…there. I wanted a style."

"Hell no," Stack said, and he reached out to run two fingers down a long tress. "Take it from me, dudes like your long hair, styled or not."

Leese smiled at her. "Hair that long is part of a dozen fantasies."

"Really?" Merissa didn't look convinced.

"At least," Stack said.

"I told you so," Vanity said, and then she seemed to remember her own hair was as long and she glanced at Stack.

He lifted a brow, and nodded.

Yvette and Cherry shared a look. They both realized that everyone had weighed in except Armie. And that was probably the person Rissy most wanted to hear from.

Vanity must've caught on, too, because she finally pulled her gaze away from Stack and leaned around Cherry to see Armie. "What do you think?"

"It's her hair," Armie said with bland indifference. He took a pull off his beer and shrugged. "She can do whatever she wants with it."

Merissa ducked her face, and damn, Cherry wanted to smack Armie. She was thinking of kicking him under the table when big hands settled on her shoulders. Standing behind her chair, Denver bent to whisper in her ear. "You doing okay?"

Happiness bubbled up. "I'm terrific."

He kissed her cheek, nuzzled her neck, then tipped her face back so he could put his mouth to hers.

After ending the kiss, he crouched down beside her chair. "I'm sorry about the fans."

"Don't be." Cherry cupped a hand to his jaw. "You're a very popular guy. I love it."

His golden eyes searched hers. "You're sure you don't mind?"

Of course she didn't. She'd fallen in love with a fighter; she accepted that his career would require a lot of training and many trips away from her. His success was important to him, and that made it important to her.

With a pat to his chest, she said, "Do what you need to do to keep your fans happy. It's not a problem." She leaned closer until her nose almost touched his. "But at the end of the day, you're all mine."

Funny, given they'd had sex many times now, but Denver's eyes flared with hot interest. "Damn, girl," he whispered low. "Much more of that and I won't be decent to talk to fans."

Giddy elation had her smiling like a sap. "Denver?"

"Yeah?"

"This is the best date ever."

He cupped the back of her neck and drew her in for another long kiss. "I'll wrap up soon."

"Don't rush. I'm enjoying myself." And after that display, not a single female in the bar had any doubts that Denver was taken. She especially loved him for that.

"You won't go anywhere, not even the restroom, alone?"

She crossed her heart. "You have my word."

After one more kiss that had Stack laughing and Armie rolling his eyes, Denver rejoined Cannon. The two men moved toward the pool tables with a small enthusiastic crowd.

"That'll be you soon," Cherry told Armie. "After your first match with the SBC, you're going to get mobbed."

In reply, he downed the rest of his beer.

When Merissa left her table, Cherry decided to go along just in case her roommate needed a friendly shoulder. Armie caught up to both of them right outside the women's restroom.

He took Rissy's arm. "Hold up."

Cherry started to go into the restroom to give them privacy, but Armie nixed that idea by blocking the door. He didn't look at Cherry, but kept his gaze focused entirely on Merissa.

She looked a little weak in the knees. "What—"

Jaw flexing, he watched her for several heart-stopping moments before finally grating out, "Don't cut it."

They stared at each other until Cherry started to feel like a voyeur.

Finally Merissa whispered, "Okay."

As if that broke a spell, Armie glanced back at Cherry. "See if anyone's in there."

"The john?"

"Yeah."

"Er…okay." She opened the door, poked her head in, and saw two empty stalls but three women at the sinks refreshing their makeup. "Just ladies."

Armie nodded. "I'll wait for the two of you right here."

Like a zombie, Rissy went in first, but as soon as the door closed behind Cherry, Rissy slumped against the wall and fanned her face.

"Good Lord," Cherry said, agreeing with her. "What was that all about?"

"No idea."

"He must like your hair long," Cherry said around a jaw-aching grin. She was happy and darn it, she wanted everyone else to be happy, too.

"I guess." Rissy covered her face, groaned, then dropped her hands and stared at Cherry. "It probably means nothing at all so please don't tell—"

Cherry launched to her tiptoes to hug her—and that was funny enough all on its own given the disparity in their heights. "My lips are sealed."

The three ladies exited the restroom, forcing Cherry and Rissy to separate.

Rissy went to the sink and smoothed her hair as if seeing it for the first time. "And to think I was ready to hide."

Watching her, Cherry asked, "What do you mean?"

"I was offered a promotion in Indiana. Branch manager at a smaller bank. It seemed the perfect way to… well, stay away from Armie. I mean, when I'm here, I see him everywhere and…" Though they were alone, she dropped her voice to a whisper. "Armie does it for me. Know what I mean?"

"I do." Because she'd always felt the same about Denver.

"Since he's not interested, it's always so uncomfortable for me."

Cherry gave her a look until Merissa started to grin. "Yeah," Cherry said. "I think he's interested."

Barely muffling a squeal, Rissy said, "So maybe I should put off hiding for a bit yet?"

"Yes, definitely." As someone who'd spent far too much of her life hiding, she would never recommend it. She'd hidden because she was more terrified of what

Carver and his brothers would do to her than she was of the bugs and snakes…in the woods…near the old rusted truck where *she always hid.*

Her eyes widened at the comprehension of her own stupidity. "Oh my God."

Smile fading, Rissy asked, "What?"

Cherry put a hand to her head while the puzzle pieces began clicking together. "How could I have not realized?" But of course she knew. *Fear.* Whenever Carver got close, it shook her so badly she couldn't think straight.

But no more.

She looked around the bathroom but found no answers. What to do? What to do?

Rissy frowned. "Cherry? You're scaring me."

The bathroom door cracked open, and Armie peeked in, looked at each woman and scowled. "What happened?"

Rissy gaped at him. "You can't come in here!"

He took another look at Cherry and pushed on in anyway. "Cherry?"

Awful comprehension kept her wide-eyed. "I know what Carver wants." Her own rushing heartbeat sounded loud in her ears. *"I know!"* Driven by urgency, she started out but Armie pulled her up short.

"Hang on, doll." He caught Rissy's hand and hauled her along with them as they walked. "What are we doing? Talk to me."

"I used to hide from Carver," she blurted while they were still in the small hallway with relative privacy and a little less noise. "He would…get after me." She shook her head, unwilling to spill her guts to Armie and Rissy. "I hid and that's what he wants to know.

Where I hid. It must be where Janet put the drugs or the money or both."

Confusion kept Armie's brows pulled together. "I'm not following, hon. Slow down and take a breath."

She stepped out to the floor and realized Denver was still surrounded by a group of admirers. She couldn't disturb him, not yet.

What to do?

She searched the room while trying to decide, and there at the bar she spotted Detective Riske and Detective Bareden. It looked as if they'd just come in together because they weren't yet seated, were only chatting with Rowdy and his wife. They were casually dressed, clearly off the clock.

She didn't know the men well but she'd met them through Cannon and Yvette. Lieutenant Peterson she did know, and hopefully the lieutenant would be joining them.

Cherry smiled at Rissy, patted Armie. "I'm going to talk to the detectives. No, Armie, I don't need you with me. It's…private. If you'll just go back to the table, I'd appreciate it."

Armie searched her face. "You're okay?"

Thinking she might finally be able to rid herself of Carver, she nodded. "Yes, I think I am." On impulse, she gave him a hug, then, because she felt so hopeful, she gave one to Rissy, also. "Don't disturb Denver, but if he finishes up, tell him I'm with the detectives."

Hoping to catch them before they got seated, she left Armie and charged up to the bar.

Carver's threats were about to end.

CHAPTER TWENTY-TWO

ACROSS THE ROOM, Cherry saw both Stack and Leese watching her, on alert. Since Armie stood guard nearby, neither of them bothered to intrude.

She had the most amazing friends. Yes, for a while there Carver's intrusion had rattled the very foundation of her newfound life. But not anymore. She'd do whatever she had to do to protect her independence, her friends and her growing relationship with Denver.

Her smile trembled, but she hoped it would be reassuring as she made a beeline for the bar, stepping up right between the two big cops.

Brows lifted, they looked down at her.

"I'm sorry to bother you, but..." She clasped her hands together to hide her nervousness. "Will Lieutenant Peterson be joining you?" *Please, please let her be part of their group.*

Detective Bareden, a hulk of a guy, shook his head. "Margaret and Dash are taking a three-day weekend away."

Well, damn. Cherry chewed her bottom lip.

The other cop, Detective Riske, said, "Something we can help you with?"

She stuck out her hand. "I'm Cherry Peyton."

"We've met, right?" Bareden asked her.

"Yes, briefly." She nodded at each of them. "Detective Riske and Detective Bareden. I'm surprised you remember, though."

Riske leaned on the bar and crossed his arms over his chest. "Margaret mentioned you before she took off. Asked me to keep an eye out. Snakes and bugs in your car, right?"

She shuddered in memory. "Yes, that's me."

"Has something else happened?" Bareden asked.

"No. Yes." She shook her head, a little hyper with the possibility of finally putting an end to Carver's reign of terror. "I'm so sorry to interrupt your evening, Detectives, but could I speak with you privately for just a minute?"

Rowdy braced his forearms on the top of the bar. "Problem, Cherry?"

She fashioned a stupid, unconvincing smile. "I don't think so. I just realized something…important."

Rowdy's stare took her apart, then he nodded and to the men said, "You can use my office."

"All right." Bareden took a sip of his drink, stood, and good Lord he was a big man. Even bigger than she'd remembered. "Call me Reese, by the way. I'm off-duty."

Close behind her, the other detective, who wasn't as big, which in no way made him small, said, "I'm Logan. We're both friends of Cannon's, and by extension, Denver."

"Did you need us to fetch Denver for this conversation, Cherry?"

It nearly put a crick in her neck to look up at Reese and once she did, she forgot to stop looking.

"Cherry?"

She nodded dumbly, then caught herself. "Denver is with fans. I don't want to bother him just yet."

The men shared a look.

Feeling guilty, she scowled at each of them. "I'll tell him. It's not like I'm keeping secrets. I just—"

"You've got me curious, I'll give you that," Logan said. "Come along, then." With a hand at the small of her back, he urged her forward, knowing exactly where to find the office.

Before they'd taken three steps, Denver was there. He didn't call a halt, just put his arm around her and kept pace.

When Cherry faltered, he said, "Armie got me."

"I told him not to!"

Denver bent and kissed her forehead. "He did the right thing." They entered the office. Denver held the door until the others were inside, then closed it. He watched Cherry until she started to fidget.

"I think I know what Carver wants."

"Other than you, you mean?" His gaze went to the detectives. "He enjoys threatening her."

Cherry rubbed her forehead. "I don't want to go into the whole thing, but the important part is that Carver and his family deal drugs."

Logan straightened. Reese frowned.

"I used to live with them. They were my foster family." She shared the town in Kentucky. "Everyone knew they were dealers but as far as I could tell the cops were part of it."

Going behind the desk, Logan rummaged over the surface until he found a pad and a pen. He scribbled some notes. "Go on."

Inhaling a shaky breath, she nodded. "Carver used to take liberties. With me."

"Cherry," Denver prompted.

Yes, she realized she had to own up to all of it. "He tried to…to molest me. Maybe rape me." She shook her head. "I'm not entirely sure what his intentions were, other than bad."

Denver pushed away from the door, came over to stand behind her, and put his arms around her. Very close to her ear, he asked, "Would it be okay if I summarized things for them?"

Grateful that she wouldn't have to, Cherry nodded.

Denver hugged her for agreeing, then in short, succinct sentences, he told of the trouble she'd had with Carver and his brothers, the threats that had been made since his return, and his own plays to cut the man out to force him out of hiding.

The sympathy she felt from Logan and Reese nearly choked her. She forced her chin up, her shoulders back, and met their gazes.

"Carver came after me for a reason. I knew he wanted something, but I didn't know what. I was never involved in any way with the family business. Other than taking the money when Janet sent me away, I was never told anything about it."

Reese took the paper from Logan. "We have the address. I can have local cops—those not from the area—check into things." Gently he added, "Not all cops are on the take."

"I know that," she assured him. "I trust the lieutenant, and I trust both of you."

"The cops you can trust," Logan said, "far outnumber those you can't. But I understand your reluctance to involve anyone in or around the area where you used to live."

"Thank you."

Reese studied her, his eyes narrowed and one side of his mouth kicked up in interest. "You've figured out what it is, haven't you?"

Denver's arms tightened. "Cherry?"

Lacing her hands over his where they crossed her waist, she nodded. "It finally just occurred to me."

Denver turned her, stared into her eyes, and let out a breath. "Let's hear it."

She never liked talking about her time with the Nelsons, especially not Carver's warped pursuit. But she wouldn't cower. Not anymore. Looking at Denver made it easier than looking at the cops. "I told you I would hide from Carver when he was in one of his moods."

"Yes."

"I didn't explain that I hid outside. Sometimes all night. I'd found this old rusted-out truck in the woods." Her hands started to shake—until Denver held them. "You could barely see it from all the weeds and vines growing over it. The inside was empty except for a seat. I'd crawled in there one night when Carver was looking for me. For over an hour I could hear him calling my name. Even after I figured he'd left, I was afraid to come out so I stayed there all night."

Looking pained, Denver nodded once to encourage her.

"Even with the bugs and a few snakes that I had to chase off, I decided it was a good place so I went back during the day and cleaned it out the best I could."

"You hate snakes and bugs," Denver said in a whisper.

Keeping her voice as low as his, she replied, "Not as much as I hated Carver." To stave off the lump of emotion crowding her throat, she turned to the detectives. "Carver said Janet hid something. I'm guessing either drugs or money. Maybe both. He said I would know where, which didn't make any sense at first. But Janet knew where I hid. That day she pulled the shotgun on Carver—"

"The day she sent you away," Denver clarified.

Cherry nodded. "She said she knew I hid in the old truck and that's where she was going to look for me, but she found me in the clearing instead."

"With Carver planning a public rape."

Because she didn't know what else to say, Cherry shrugged.

After pulling her up against his chest, Denver zeroed in on the detectives. "You have enough to check into it?"

"I'll make a few calls," Logan promised. "We know some cops in the area."

"Good cops," Reese clarified. "We can do a search, see what we come up with. But in the meantime, you need to be extra careful."

"Desperate people do terrible things," Logan agreed.

"He's psycho." Denver hugged her a little tighter. "Believe me, I won't let him get anywhere near her."

Logan and Reese shared a look, then Logan dug out a card and handed it to Denver. "If you hear from him again, and for damn sure if you see him, call me."

DENVER COULD BARELY credit the change in Cherry. Now that she assumed she knew what Carver wanted, she was more lighthearted. More open.

To him.

Last night, she'd initiated the lovemaking. Twice. She'd always been hot, but now she was also affectionate.

A potent combo.

Her smiles turned him on, and so did that breathy little catch in her voice when she said his name right before coming.

But it was more than that. It was her entire outlook. She looked free.

With the stereo playing, she danced around the bedroom, already dressed and patiently waiting for him to finish. Being reluctant to leave her, he'd done his workout at home that day. And now, as he watched the sway of her hips, he wondered if they had time to fit in a quickie before they needed to leave. He wasn't crazy about the trip back home, and Cherry—with her very sweet ass—could provide the perfect distraction.

When he reached for her, she laughed and danced out of reach.

"Tease."

"I'll make it up to you tonight, I promise."

She seemed to be settling in, and that gave him hope that when he told her he wanted her to stay forever, she wouldn't argue with him. "Come here." He caught her before she could get away again, then tugged her resisting body between his legs.

"Denver," she protested with a smile. "We have to leave here in less than five minutes and you haven't finished dressing yet."

All he needed was his shoes and a T-shirt. He'd told Cherry to dress casual, and while no one would call her outfit dressy, she looked amazing. Her white sundress with blue flowers fit tight to her waist with the top low enough to show off some tantalizing cleavage. The full skirt fell softly around her hips and thighs and ended at her knees. She wore heeled blue sandals that made her legs look incredible.

She laced her fingers into his hair, still damp from his shower. "I look okay?"

"You look so good, I could eat you up," he whispered, his hands now on the backs of her legs urging her closer.

"Denver."

He slid his palms up her bare thighs until he reached her bottom. His abs tightened as he explored her naked cheeks. "Damn, girl. What type of underwear are you wearing?"

"A thong."

He stepped her back. "Let me see."

Grinning, she slipped away from him. "You can see tonight."

Slowly, Denver rose from the edge of the bed. Yeah, this game would definitely ease any apprehension. "I don't want to wait."

Laughing again, the sound almost a giggle, she ducked to the other side of the dresser. "Now Denver…"

He gave her a wolfish smile. "Come here, Cherry."

Her face heated even as her mouth twitched. "No!" She turned to run but only got a few steps before he scooped her up high, making her screech in surprise.

Going to the bed, he sat down with her draped over his lap.

"Denver!"

"Hush, girl. You'll have the neighbors calling the

cops on us." While she alternately laughed and struggled, he flipped up the skirt of her dress. "Lord, you have a nice ass." He cupped one big hand over her. Her skin was so soft, her bottom firm and full.

Cherry stopped fighting him and instead covered her face. "I can't believe you're doing this."

"What about this?" he asked, slipping one finger under the seam of the thong and trailing it down, down, until he could touch her from behind.

"Or that!"

He stroked over her—and found her hot, damp and no longer protesting. He groaned as he carefully pressed into her.

Stiffening, she made a small sound in the back of her throat.

"Come on, Cherry," he crooned to her, his finger now teasing. "Tell me you want me."

Throaty, soft, she whispered, "I want you."

Hearing her say it broke his control. In one quick movement he turned her facedown bent over the end of the high bed. Her heels made it possible for her to plant her feet on the floor—raising up that sexy rump.

"Yeah." He opened his jeans as he strode to the nightstand to grab a condom, returning to her in less than twenty seconds. He pushed the dress up high and moved her miniscule panties to the side, groaning again at the ripe sight of her. With his foot he nudged her legs wider.

"Denver?"

"Stay like that."

Her hands knotted in the quilt.

So hot. "You're mine, Cherry." He planted one hand at the small of her back to keep her still and with the other, he guided himself to her, watching as he entered oh-so slowly, opening her, working his way in.

She shifted on a small moan.

"Okay?"

"Hurry it up."

Clasping her hips between his hands, he thrust into her.

Her legs stiffened and she cried out, but not in discomfort.

She called his name.

"You're mine," he said again, already rushing to the rhythm he knew she liked best.

"I'm yours," she agreed, clenching tight around him.

Neither of them lasted long at all. Denver waited for her, loving the way she moved, the sounds she made, how she strained toward her climax.

The second she tensed in release, he let himself go and joined her. When her legs gave out he dropped over her, crushing her into the bed.

Drowsily, she muttered, "My dress is going to be wrinkled."

"Sorry."

"Don't move just yet."

"No, I won't." He gave them each a full minute to recover before finally dragging himself back to his feet. Cherry didn't move, not even when he stroked her silky behind.

Sex with Cherry was the perfect cure—for everything. He was now so relaxed, he could barely feel his bones.

Smiling, he turned her over and kissed her parted lips. "Get a move on, girl, or we'll be late."

Her response was part laugh, part groan, but she

did get up and head to the restroom on wobbly legs. "We'll be late because of you," she complained. "You better start thinking up an excuse, because the truth won't do."

Denver barely held back his laugh. No way could he hide his satisfaction. He loved her. Tonight, no matter what, he had to tell her.

HE HELD HER hand as they went up the walkway to the front door of his family home. It felt familiar, yet strange. In the time he'd been away, the chairs on the front porch had changed, the shutters were a different color and flowers filled the window boxes.

"Are you nervous?" Cherry asked, sounding really nervous herself.

"No." He lifted her hand to his mouth to kiss her knuckles. "Thanks to you, I'm as mellow as can be."

She gave him a beautiful smile. "I'm glad."

The door opened before they reached it and both his dad and Pamela stood there. Denver didn't hesitate. Acting as if nothing had changed, he nodded. "Dad. Pamela."

Pamela looked flushed and anxious as she held the door wide. "I'm so glad you both made it."

Cherry shrugged off her nervousness and stepped forward. "Thank you again for including me." She went right up to his dad. "Hello, Mister Lewis." She held out her hand. "It's so nice to meet you."

A smile cracked, and then a full-fledged grin as Lyle Lewis pulled her in for a hug. "It's very nice to meet you, young lady. Cherry, right?"

"Yes, sir." She returned his embrace, then held him away. "Denver's right. You do look much alike."

Lyle's gaze shifted to Denver, and his expression went somber. "Son."

"Dad." He held out his hand, but he, too, got pulled into a hug, this time crushing.

It was the same type of hug he'd gotten after his mother died, when his father struggled so badly.

It surprised Denver, but he didn't mind. He clapped his dad on the back, gave him a second to compose himself, and stepped away.

Pamela flitted around, uncertain, looking like she thought Denver might accuse her at any moment. "Could I get either of you something to drink?"

Gaze averted, Lyle said, "He remembers where the fridge is, honey."

"I'm fine," Denver told her. "Cherry?"

"Maybe just water?"

Before Pamela could leave, his dad spoke up. "I'd like to talk to Denver alone a moment. Why don't you ladies go on out back and we'll be there shortly."

Worried, because Denver didn't want her out of his sight, he turned to Cherry but she was already agreeing. "I'd love to see your home, if that's okay."

As if someone had just given her a reprieve, Pamela jumped to agree. "I'll show you around. We can get to know each other better, then grab some drinks on the way out."

Cherry gave him one last smile before following Pamela from the entry.

"She's charming," Lyle said.

Denver nodded. "Smart, sexy, funny." He gave his dad a direct look. "I'm in love with her."

That brought another smile to Lyle's mouth. "She feels the same about you?"

"I think so. We haven't talked about it yet."

By tacit agreement, they headed for the office. "What's there to talk about? You haven't told her how you feel?"

"Not yet. There's been a lot going on. But we're getting there."

Once in the room, Lyle shut the door and walked to a small built-in fridge. "Can you have a beer?"

"Sure."

"You have a fight coming up, right?"

"Yeah, but one drink won't hurt." Denver accepted the bottle, went to the couch and sat down. The material was different, he realized. Then, looking more closely, he saw that the office had been painted, the large area rug changed.

Watching him, Lyle leaned back on the edge of his desk. "I know, it's all different. Pamela has changed so many things."

"Women like to make things their own." Denver shrugged. "She lives here now." His problem with his stepmother had never been her decorating choices.

No, the problems went a lot deeper than that.

"I still love her," Lyle announced.

Denver thought about shrugging again, but he didn't want to be that disrespectful so he did nothing at all.

"I've made many mistakes," his father added. "I'd just lost my wife, you were grown and didn't need me."

Denver barely kept from making a rude noise. A son always needed his father, but damned if he'd say so.

Lyle ran a hand through his graying hair. "I guess I had a stupid midlife crisis." His gaze met Denver's. "But I do love her—faults and all. I want to make it work with her. But first I need to make it work with you."

More uncomfortable by the moment, Denver shook his head. "You don't owe me anything."

"You're my son and I love you. These past years without you…" He paced away, came back, picked up his beer and put it down again. Finally he jerked around to face Denver. His shoulders were tight, his brows drawn in remorse. "Pride is a mean sonofabitch. I never should have doubted you. You're my son and I knew—*know*—you better than that. I shouldn't have believed Pamela's lies."

So he knew now they were lies? Had Pamela told him?

"But since I did," Lyle continued, "once I realized just how wrong I was, I should have called you. I just…" Helplessly he shook his head. "I never knew the words."

Denver's heart began to thunder. He cleared his throat. "That's understandable, Dad. I'm not great with words, either."

"I was an ass. Stubborn and stupid and I don't blame you if you're still angry at me."

"I'm not." Denver wasn't sure what he felt, but anger wasn't in the mix—not toward his dad. He tipped his head. "Did Pamela finally own up to the truth?"

"She came to me," Lyle said. "But I already knew. I think I've always known."

And he'd still chosen Pamela.

"I didn't want to believe it because I knew it'd crush me." He gave a sad smile. "But she insisted on telling me. She said she still loves me. That it was an unforgivable mistake but she wants my forgiveness anyway."

Nodding, Denver waited.

"I can more easily forgive her, if you'll forgive me."

"Nothing to forgive," Denver told him.

"That's not true. There's everything to forgive." Lyle drew a deep breath. "I know she loves me, just as I know you're the only indiscretion she had."

That made him laugh. Shit. Now he was an indiscretion.

"Denver…"

He scrubbed both hands over his face, then shot to his feet. "I never touched her except to push her away."

"I know." He held Denver's gaze. "She told me that, too."

"What do you want from me, then?"

"I know it's a lot to ask, that you hate her now for all the trouble, but that's more my fault than hers. I was older and should have used my head."

No way could Denver deny that.

"Will you give her another chance? Give *me* another chance?"

His mouth twisted with the sneer. "Start over like it never happened?" He strode to the window to look out at the backyard, hoping to see Cherry. She was nowhere in sight, and that worried him. He needed to wrap this up. "I don't hate her, Dad. I hate what she did. I hate how the situation rolled out. I hate that we lost so much time." He turned and saw his father's dejection, and it cut into him, into his heart. He moderated his tone, doing what he could to remove the edge. "But I love you. And if you love her, then sure, I can make nice."

Hope brought Lyle forward a step. "You mean that?"

Yeah, he did, and now that he'd said it, a weight lifted

off his shoulders. He grinned. "Cherry got me here. It's what she wants." Mostly because she knew it was important to him, and damn, but didn't that make her almost too special for words? "I don't ever want to disappoint her."

"The way I disappointed you."

Denver held out his hand. "We're moving forward, right? No more looking back. It's not necessary."

His dad looked at his hand, took it, and pulled Denver in for another big bear hug.

This time he returned it.

A second later his phone rang.

THEY TALKED ABOUT WEATHER, Pamela complimented her sandals, and Cherry admired her home. All superficial, easy chitchat. Until Pamela led her outside, and instead of going to the seating area, she started around to the side of the house.

"Where are we going?"

Smile strained, Pamela said, "Do you mind? I thought I'd show you the grounds." She halted, visibly wrestled with herself, and gave Cherry a direct look. "I also wanted to speak with you and I'd just as soon not be overheard by my husband or Denver."

"Oh." Thinking Denver might not like it if she got in the middle of things, Cherry said, "I'm not sure that's a good idea."

Pamela disregarded that. "I'm sure Denver talked with you?"

"About many things."

"You're in love," she said, as if that explained it.

Cherry prayed Denver felt the same, but rather than speak for him, she said only, "I am."

Clearly distressed, Pamela started walking again. "You must hate me."

"I barely know you." Seeing no choice, Cherry hurried to keep up.

"You know of me," Pamela persisted.

"I know you made mistakes, but then, we all do."

Stunned, Pamela stared at her.

In for a penny, Cherry thought. She took a breath. "I know Denver is here because he wants to be a part of his father's life. You're in that life." Cherry took her hand, drawing her to a halt. "And I know we can usually right the wrongs when we own up to them, apologize, and never, ever do them again."

Pamela closed her eyes, a tear squeezed out, and then she smiled. "I've kept the lie so long," she said brokenly. "I haven't had anyone to talk to. I know, boo-hoo for me. Denver's life was ruined and—"

"Not ruined at all," Cherry corrected her. "He's the strongest man I know. I doubt anyone or anything could ruin his life. But I believe it's affected him." Gently she added, "And it clearly affected you. Don't you think you'll feel better if you tell the whole truth?"

Pamela nodded. "Yes. I figured that out already. I was afraid…" She groaned. "God, I'm a coward on top of everything else. I wanted Denver to return because my husband isn't a happy man, not with his son gone. He deserves to be happy. But I was so afraid Denver would show up only to throw my lies out there again." She brushed the tears off her cheeks. "I talked with Lyle and told him everything."

For Denver's sake, Cherry hoped it worked out. "And?"

"It was difficult for both of us. He's… Well, he's

being kinder than I could have hoped. I think he's willing to keep the peace right now because he badly wants to mend things with his son." She let out a shuddering breath. "He said he'd already suspected much of it. The more he thought about it, the more he doubted his own initial reaction. He didn't want to believe it of me—I don't even want to believe it of me—but he *couldn't* believe it of Denver."

That was a good start, Cherry decided. So then why did she suddenly feel so uneasy? They were very near the pool house and the elaborate in-ground pool. Rubbing her upper arms to remove the gooseflesh, she looked back at the house. It seemed so far away even though, for convenience sake, the pool was located fairly closely to the back patio.

Turning a full circle, she searched while pretending to admire the beautiful grounds. "This is amazing."

"Thank you. The pool house was already here, but I changed the roof and added landscaping around it."

Absently, Cherry said, "You have very good taste." When the shrubbery behind the pool house trembled, her uneasiness escalated.

She took Pamela's hand, meaning to lead her away. "The men are probably waiting for us now." Heart pounding in unmistakable dread, she turned to go— and Carver stepped out, a gun drawn and aimed right at her. Mitty was beside him, laughing in that maniacal way of his.

"Hello, little sister."

Everything stopped for Cherry—her breath, her pulse, the air around her. "What are you doing here?" she rasped.

At the same time, Pamela said, "Carver?" Confused, she looked at the gun, then at Cherry. *"Sister?"*

Cherry gaped at her. "You know him?"

"He's Denver's friend."

Groaning, Cherry folded her arms around her stomach as it cramped with fear and misery.

"Yeah," Carver laughed. "Denver's sweet stepmama told me where and when to find you both."

"I…" Feeling the obvious tension, Pamela frowned with worry. "What are you doing, Carver?"

He laughed, the sound disturbed. "You're as gullible as she is. Denver's friend? Hell no. Right about now, Gene will be gutting the bastard."

"No!" Cherry started to run and with every step her fear spiraled. Wasn't this exactly what she'd expected? A surprise ambush. A cowardly attack when it was least expected.

She sensed Carver chasing her down and pushed harder, but her heels were sinking into the lush lawn and her lungs tightened, making it impossible to breathe.

Then a hand snatched at her hair, jerking her back forcefully. She cried out as Carver squeezed her against him.

Desperate, nearly hysterical, she fought him until he pressed the gun to her temple.

His hot breath in her ear, he whispered, "None of that now, sweet Cherry."

"What have you done?" She meant to shout it, but it came as only a squeak of sound. Gene was good with the knife, and just as Carver enjoyed tormenting, Gene enjoyed cutting. No, no, *no*. Not Denver. "Please," she pleaded. "Don't do this."

Carver twisted his hand in her hair, but spoke to Pamela. "Sorry babe, but I need you to stay put. Mitty, hang on to her. If either of you make a single sound, I'll start shooting."

He was worried about her screaming? Did that mean Gene hadn't gotten to Denver yet? Uncaring about her own peril, leaving Pamela to fend for herself, Cherry sucked in a great lungful of air and let loose a banshee cry that sent a flock of birds into flight.

"Jesus! *Shut the fuck up.*" Carver jerked her around and shook her hard until her knees gave out and she dropped to the ground, her head rattled and her limbs weak. He crouched beside her, his hand braced hard on her throat. "You used to hide."

"I had to."

His fingers tightened. "You always dodged out on me and no matter where I looked I couldn't find you."

"You wanted to rape me!"

"I wanted you, period. All kinds of want, Cherry." He breathed a little deeper while he looked at her body. "No place for you to hide now, is there?"

"You're going to be sorry." Somehow she'd make it so.

The threat didn't faze him, but his fingers squeezed more until she gasped and clawed at his hand. Smiling, he eased up the pressure. "It pisses me off to think of that long-haired Neanderthal fucking you night after night."

It took her a second to regain her breath, but she knew she had to defy him. She gave herself only a moment to brace for his reaction, then stared up at him. "Day after day," she taunted in a rough rasp. "Morning, noon and night."

His brows pulled down. "You mouthy little bitch. You think I'll take that crap from you?" Again his fingers squeezed, tighter and tighter.

She saw stars but at the moment she felt no pain, just a numb, pervading fear. Pamela stood frozen while Mitty smiled at her.

She listened for Denver. *Please let him be okay.*

Laughing, Carver again let up the pressure and moved his hand to the neckline of her dress, tracing a fingertip just above the material. "Maybe you need to learn another lesson, little sister. I had planned to get you back in the woods. You'd like that, wouldn't you? Communing with nature…and all the creepy crawlies?" He laughed at her automatic shiver. "But you know, maybe it'd be better if I take you right here while he's inside whining to his daddy. I'm betting that'd wipe the memory of him right out of your head."

"You can't," she told him, her voice now hoarse. "A pathetic worm like you wouldn't even put a dent into how I feel about him."

Before her eyes, his rage coalesced, growing brighter, hotter. When he drew back his fist, Cherry braced herself.

In the next instant, Carver literally flew away from her. Thinking only of getting to Denver, Cherry started to scramble up—but then he was already there, lifting her up against his chest and holding her close like he'd never let her go.

CHAPTER TWENTY-THREE

A LITTLE DAZED, Cherry touched his face to make sure he was real. "Denver?"

"I'm so sorry, honey." His mouth touched her forehead, her cheek. "So fucking sorry."

She looked beyond him and saw Armie holding the gun on Mitty, who knelt cradling his obviously broken arm. Carver sprawled on the ground, with Stack's boot on his throat.

That had to have happened fast—and she hadn't heard a thing. "What—"

"Gene caught me by surprise." Denver smoothed back her hair, cradled her face gently. "He managed to cut Dad before I could put him under."

Crying out, Pamela took off in a panicked run.

With her heartbeat just starting to return to normal, Cherry watched her go. "She's fast."

Denver squeezed her tighter, sort of laughing, mostly breathing hard. "God, girl, are you okay?"

Sensing he was on the edge, Cherry put her arms around him. "I'm okay. Are you okay?"

"I'll be better in a minute." Gently he set her down.

Struggling to get her wits back, Cherry grabbed for him. "Your father?"

"He's got a nasty cut on his shoulder, but he'll be

fine once he gets some stitches." He cupped her face, turned it this way and that. "He hit you?"

"No."

Denver tipped up her chin, examined her neck, and his expression went stony. "He *choked* you?"

Armie spoke up, asking, "Want me to kill him?"

Oh God. Cherry took in the look in Armie's eyes and believed him capable.

Denver shook his head. "Logan and Reese are on their way."

"Already?" With each second that passed, Cherry felt better, less frantic, less terrorized.

Less haunted by her past.

Denver had Carver and somehow he'd end it all today.

Swallowing hard, Denver closed his eyes a moment. "I told you I'd protect you."

"You have," she whispered.

"Not well enough. I knew Pamela had spoken with Carver, so I had the guys keeping an eye out. But I thought you were safe here or I'd never have let you out of my sight."

"You didn't know Carver had gotten details on the party." And then, hoping he wouldn't hate Pamela more, she rushed to say, "Pamela thought he was your friend. She was as stunned to see him as I was."

He nodded. "I hadn't thought of that, but I knew she'd talked with him, so I had someone tailing us, just in case."

"Armie and Stack?"

"Tonight. But Leese, Cannon, Gage, Brand and Miles have all agreed to help out, too." He tucked her hair behind her ears. "You have a lot of people who care about you."

It was more about those people being loyal to Denver, but she was happy to be included. "I need to thank them."

With a strangled laugh, he put his forehead to hers. "You're always wanting to thank someone." Just as quickly, he sobered again. "Leese will talk with the detectives tomorrow. He can verify that Carver drugged him, that they beat the shit out of him, all to get to you."

Carver struggled. *"That's a lie."*

Denver touched her one last time, then turned away. "Let him go, Stack."

The second Stack moved his foot away, Carver lunged up, heaving. "I'll fucking kill you."

Denver nodded. "Let's go."

With an ear-splitting war cry, Carver charged. Denver stood his ground until Carver had almost reached him. Then he moved so fast that Cherry saw it as a blur. She'd just sucked in a breath of fear when Denver halted Carver's rush with a massive fist to his face, followed by a kick that sent Carver sprawling back to the ground.

Impassive, Denver again waited.

More slowly, Carver stood, and this time he approached with caution, his fists up, his eyes narrowed. Carver swung and missed; Denver struck him on the chin. Carver swung and missed; Denver landed a blow to his temple.

Less steady, his fists dropping a little, Carver took another stance. Denver kicked out, catching Carver in the face. Blood sprayed, and Carver went flat, dead to the world. That wouldn't last, so he switched his gaze to Mitty.

When the big man snarled, Armie gave him a shove. "Get on with it, will you?"

"Fuck you." Mitty stalked forward, his hot, furious gaze a laser beam on Denver.

Watching him, Denver waited until his patience wore thin. When Mitty was still several feet away, Denver strode within range. Mitty threw a hook, but Denver caught him with a series of straight punches, backing him up with each combo of left-right, left-right, until he finished with a knee to the gut. As Mitty bent forward, Denver nailed him with a straight right that sent him flat to his back. He was so big that when he hit, Cherry thought she felt the ground shake.

Stack checked his watch. "I'm guessing you've got three minutes more, tops."

Nodding, Denver said, "Get her out of here."

Understanding what he planned, Cherry scrambled to her feet. "I want to stay."

He looked at her over his shoulder. "Cherry—"

She put up her chin. "I'm staying." With a flicker toward Carver, she admitted, "I want to watch."

Denver searched over her face, gave a slight smile, and turned back to Mitty. "You first." And so saying, he hit Mitty fifteen, maybe twenty times in a row, until the big man collapsed, choking on his own blood, curled in the fetal position.

Although the beat-down lasted less than a minute, it did the job. He wouldn't be getting back up.

Glad, Cherry clasped her hands together and resisted biting her lip.

Through it all, Carver just sat there on the ground, doing his best to regain his wits.

"Up."

Carver shook his head. "Where's Gene?"

"I left him unconscious. I broke his knife arm in two places, bad enough that he'll never play with sharp objects again."

Cherry smiled. So many times she'd seen Gene threaten and intimidate with that big hideous blade. But no more.

She couldn't wait to tell Denver how much she loved him.

"Broke his nose, too." Denver nodded at Carver. "Now get up, you sniveling puke, so I can give you some of the same."

Carver eyed his brother, the mangled condition of his face, and he shook his head. "I'll just wait for the cops."

Denver laughed. "Doesn't work like that." He reached for Carver, got slugged in the chin, and barely flinched. In fact, satisfaction shone in his predator's gaze. "There you go. Might as well give it a try, right?"

"You're insane."

"I love her." Denver shrugged his massive shoulder. "That means it's going to take all I have not to kill you."

Cherry gasped. With both hands she covered her mouth. *Denver loved her?* She frowned. Hell of a time to tell her!

Armie and Stack both grinned at her.

Carver made the mistake of sneering—and got his face bashed because of it. Denver had big fists and deadly accuracy. He hit Carver three times before Carver could even think of trying to defend himself.

Not that it would have done him much good.

Slumped on the ground, Carver shook his head.

Denver didn't give in. "Get up."

When Pamela and Lyle walked out together, Cherry pulled her gaze away from Denver long enough to peek at them. Lyle's right arm was wrapped in a white bandage. His left arm was around Pamela. The pretty redhead had makeup streaks down her cheeks and some of her husband's blood on her otherwise immaculate and stylish outfit. She clung to him as if she feared she might lose him if she loosened her hold.

Denver pulled Carver up and hit him time and time again.

"That's enough." Lyle Lewis stepped away from his wife. "Son, he's had enough."

"You have no idea," Denver told him without looking away from Carver.

Police sirens sounded.

Denver popped his neck. Carver hung limp in his grasp.

Cherry watched his back expand several times while he struggled with himself. She noticed that neither Stack nor Armie seemed inclined to put an end to things.

With a growl, Denver slugged him again. It amazed her that with each punch Denver seemed to get angrier, instead of shedding some of his rage.

Seeing the uneasiness on Lyle's face, the torment on Pamela's, Cherry took a step forward. "Denver?"

He went still, but didn't reply.

She didn't get too close when she said, "I don't want to interfere, but I need you. Right now."

Carver moaned, and Denver gave him another slug that shut him up.

"Denver?" She took another step closer. "I love you, too."

He started breathing harder, his broad back billowing, the pronounced muscles in his arms flexing and bunching.

"Way to drag out the suspense," Armie told her. He handed the gun to Stack and stepped in close, whispering something low to Denver.

Denver shook his head.

Armie whispered again, then pried Denver's clenched fist away from Carver's shirt. "There you go," he said as if soothing a wild animal. "A few more breaths. Maybe back up just a little? That's it. That'll work." He dropped Carver to the ground without concern for any additional injuries he might get.

The sirens grew louder.

Armie clapped him on the shoulder. "She's waiting for you, dude."

No, Cherry decided. She wasn't good at waiting; she'd already proven that. If she hadn't rushed Denver at the bar after Armie's fight, they might not be together right now.

Once again she'd have to act, to nudge him.

She'd taken only one step when he turned and stalked over to her, scooping her up without losing his stride.

Lyle said, "I'll go around front and fetch the cops."

"I'm going with you," Pamela told him, still sticking close.

Indicating the fallen men who were now unconscious, Stack assured Denver, "We've got this," as Denver walked away.

Armie added, "Take your time," and Cherry heard the suppressed laughter in his tone.

They were all nuts, but she loved each of them.

Ignoring everyone else, Denver left the yard with her held close to his heart.

DENVER WANTED TO take her all the way home, but he made it only as far as the back deck before emotion got a stranglehold on him and he had to sit down on the step. Never, not if he lived to be a hundred, would he forget the sight of Carver poised over her, a gun aimed at her head.

Thank God Armie called him when he did, that Armie and Stack had been close enough to disable Mitty without fanfare.

That Cherry hadn't been seriously hurt. *He couldn't lose her.*

Cherry tried to lift her head, but he hugged her tighter. "I love you." Saying it wasn't enough. Not near enough. "I love you so fucking much."

Her gentle fingers smoothed through his hair, over his shoulder. "I loved you first."

Laughing, he took a soft love bite of her neck, nuzzled his way over her cheek, and sealed his mouth over hers for a heart-stopping kiss. When he thought he might be able to talk normally, when some of the ragged tension making him shake had turned to lust instead of rage, he lifted his head and looked into her beautiful dark eyes. "I said it first."

"I knew it first."

God, he loved her. "It's not a competition, girl."

She settled in close to him and sighed. "If it was, you'd lose."

"Don't be so sure." Again he tipped up her chin to check her throat. A few of the red marks might turn to bruises, and it hurt him, physically and emotionally, to see them on her pale, soft skin. Back to trembling, he growled, "I should have killed him."

"I'm glad you didn't." She moved her fingertips over his bristly jaw. "I liked seeing you bloody him up some, though."

He'd bloodied him up a lot, but she'd seen and heard enough violence in her lifetime. "Carver is out of your life for good."

"I know."

"The detectives will bust up his drug trade, Lieutenant Peterson will make sure the dirty cops are exposed, and Leese is more than willing to testify. In fact, he's going to be pissed when he realizes he missed his chance to get even."

"He wanted to be here today?"

Denver shrugged. "He agreed to take his turn, but if he'd known things would break today, I know he'd have wanted to be here." It burned Leese's ass that Carver had gotten the better of him, never mind that he'd been drugged. Typical of trained fighters, Leese was cockier than most other men—and for him, this was now personal.

But not as personal as it was for Denver.

"I like the idea of Carver rotting in jail."

He just nodded.

"Pamela loves your dad."

"It would seem so."

"Will you be able to forgive her?"

Strange, but he enjoyed talking to her. Needed to talk to her. "He loves her, too, so I don't see any way around it."

Cherry hugged him tight. "You two talked?"

"Yeah." He cupped her face. "We're…getting there."

She pressed her cheek into his palm, then took his wrist and brought his hand around so she could examine his bruised knuckles. "You're really good, aren't you?"

"I got you, didn't I?" When she didn't laugh or even smile, he tipped up her face. "I do well enough, but you can't judge by any of this. Carver and his idiot brothers are thugs, not trained fighters."

He heard the shaky emotion when she whispered like a confession, "I was so worried."

"I know you were and I understand why. If Carver had fired that gun…" That thought made him feel it all over again, and he crushed her close. He wanted to hug her so tightly, hold her so long that she forgot about the past and everything she'd lived through.

"You saved me."

"You're here because of me." He looked around the yard. He'd grown up here. The conflict with Pamela hadn't tainted his impression of his childhood home, but what just happened to Cherry…he'd never again be here without remembering.

"Denver?"

"Hmm?"

"What now?"

Reese and Logan showed up in person, and they had a few uniformed cops with them, too. Armie was on his cell, probably talking to Cannon. Inside the house he could hear the paramedics and his father, likely fetching Gene from the wine cellar where Denver had locked him in for safekeeping.

"You don't mean now, today, do you?"

She shook her head. "I mean now, between you and me."

With everything that had just happened, she should have been in tears, not pondering their future together. The fact that she was proved her strength.

A match to his own.

"I have some options I'd like to offer up."

Her mouth twitched. "Go for it."

After a soft kiss, he said, "I think we should stay together."

"With you so far."

"You've been embarrassed about your past when there was no reason. I'm not the only one who looks at you and thinks it's amazing that you did so much with so little."

"So much?" Cherry shook her head. "I don't have any money. I barely have enough of my own funds to stay afloat."

Denver smiled at her. "Together, we have enough, girl. I already told you that."

"I live in the downstairs of Rissy's house."

"No, you live with me." He wanted no misunderstandings on that. He sucked in a breath, then bit the bullet. "Will you marry me?"

She went still, and *now* tears filled her eyes. "You mean it?"

"I love you." He saw everyone start toward them, Logan and Armie, his father and Pamela. "Say yes."

She nodded hard instead, swallowed audibly, and buried her face in his throat. *"Yes."*

Armie drew up short, his expression appalled. "She okay?" he asked in a whisper, as if Cherry couldn't hear him.

"Yeah." Denver cradled her close and ran his hand up and down her back.

"I could check her," his dad offered.

Cherry shook her head. *"No."*

The croak in her voice made Denver smile. "Girl, you need to say something to Armie before he starts crying, too."

Without showing herself, she wailed, "I'm just happy!"

Laughing, Denver stood with her in his arms. Insane after everything they'd just gone through, the threat to Cherry, the adrenaline dump and the damage to his knuckles, but he felt better than he had in years.

"You are so strong," she whispered.

"Not strong enough to resist you." He started toward Logan. "I'm guessing we need to answer some questions."

"I'm ready." She wiped her eyes on his shoulder, peeked up at Armie and his father, then nestled in tight again. "We should wait to get married until after Cannon and Yvette."

That made him pause. "Why?"

"We don't want to steal their thunder, and now that I have you, I don't mind waiting just a little bit. Maybe after your fight?"

Hell, he'd forgotten he had a fight right after Cannon's wedding. "Yeah, not a bad plan."

She hugged him again. "If you don't mind, I prefer a much smaller wedding."

"As long as your idea of small includes the guys."

"Of course it does." Tentatively, she asked, "And your father and Pamela. Is that okay?"

He was slowly coming to terms with it, but he said only, "Whatever you want."

"Oh, now a girl could do all kinds of things with a promise like that."

Denver grinned with her. "It's all good, as long as you know you're mine."

"I always have been." With her nose red, her eyes glassy, she kissed him. "And I always will be."

CANNON AND YVETTE'S wedding was a massive success, even though the best man had a very colorful black eye, and the maid of honor couldn't stop smiling.

Denver stood at the cash bar with Stack and Armie, watching the ladies dance. They'd shed their shoes and their fancy hairdos were starting to droop.

Armie, looking very slick in his tux despite his badly bruised face, had already danced with nearly every woman there. Now that he had a fight date set with the SBC, he was even more popular—and was working harder than ever.

When the music stopped, Denver cocked a brow.

Armie nudged Stack. "Yvette is going to throw the bouquet, and hate to break it to you, but Vanity looks determined to catch it."

Stack didn't take his gaze off Vanity. He stared at her with such heated intensity that Denver had a hard time not laughing.

"Dude," Armie said. "She's going to go up in flames if you don't cool it."

"I'm in a good mood, Armie, and nothing you say is going to change that."

Denver knew it was because today was the day he and Vanity had agreed to sleep together. He said nothing, of course, but few would miss the sparks between them.

Yvette, looking incredibly beautiful in her gown, sent the bouquet sailing—straight toward Vanity. At the last second, Vanity sidestepped, and it almost hit Cherry in the face.

Surprised, she managed to juggle it until it was secure in her arms. Denver grinned as she blew her blond curls out of her face.

Vanity peeked toward Stack, crooked her finger, and smiled.

"Later." Stack took off so fast he almost tripped up an older couple.

"He's got it bad," Armie noted, "and I don't think he realizes it."

"He thinks it's just sex." Denver shrugged. "And who knows. Maybe it is."

"Speaking of sexy women—"

"We weren't."

"Cherry is looking mighty happy."

"Shut up," Denver told him. 'Course, that didn't stop Armie.

"When are you two tying the knot?"

Denver smiled. "Not sure yet."

That got Armie's attention. "But it's on the table?"

Before he could answer, Cannon lifted Yvette up in his arms, turning a circle with her while everyone whistled and cheered and a few of the guys made bawdy comments.

Yvette waved, and together—as they were meant to be—they left the room. They could have taken a honeymoon, but neither of them were anxious to travel, so instead they'd just head home and begin their lives as a married couple.

Given Cannon's popularity in the sport, there'd be plenty of opportunity to travel.

Now that they were gone, Denver decided he could share. He turned to see Armie sipping yet another drink. "We're unofficially engaged."

Choking and coughing, Armie set his drink aside. "You sly dog!" He held out his fist and Denver bumped it.

"So what about you?"

Armie stared across the room. "Got my sights set on that lush brunette over there."

Not taking the bait, Denver shook his head. "You give yourself away by avoiding her. You know that, right?"

Rather than ask who he meant, Armie said, "No, I don't."

"Bullshit. You hit on every woman in sight, but refuse to even look at Merissa unless you think no one else is watching."

Just then Merissa shyly approached. That, too, was a dead giveaway because she flat-out wasn't shy. Only with Armie.

When she stopped in front of Armie, he froze, but only for a second.

"Hey, Stretch."

Rolling her eyes at the nickname, she held a hand out to Armie. "Dance with me."

"I—"

"You've danced with every other woman here."

"I—"

"My brother told me to make you dance."

Armie's brows shot up. "He did?"

"Right before he left." In an accusing tone, she muttered, "Something about you drinking too much and now he's worried about you and I'm supposed to be your babysitter."

Denver went a little wide-eyed. Hard to believe Cannon—on his way out the door—would have thrown the two of them together. But then again, maybe not. He trusted Armie more than anyone. They were as close as brothers. Who else would he have looking after his sister?

Not for a second did Denver believe that bit about Merissa looking out for Armie.

Armie laughed. "A baby bird keeping an eye on the hawk?"

"I'm well aware of your rep, Armie. No reason to throw it around." She snatched up his hand and began backing out to the floor.

"Rissy..."

"Don't be a coward," she mocked. "I promise not to bite. At least, no harder than you do."

His face flushed, but he went along and just as they got to the middle of the floor the music changed, going slow and sultry.

Armie tried to leave again but Merissa laughed, grabbed him by the back waistband of his tux pants, and refused to let go.

Amused, Denver watched them until Logan stopped at the bar for a refill. It was interesting, the variety of Cannon's friends. Locals young and old from the neighborhood, fighters from the rec center and beyond, including Havoc and Simon, cops, family… Everyone loved Cannon, and now they loved Yvette, too.

Logan nodded at Denver's sling. "Anything serious?"

"Just a tweaked muscle. Happens all the time in practice. I'll be back to full steam before the fight." It was almost comical how Cherry fussed each time he got hurt. But she was every bit as supportive as she was concerned, and he knew when he fought, she'd be cheering the loudest.

"Good to hear it." With a fresh drink in hand, he motioned for Denver to follow him to a quieter corner.

Denver did, but he also kept his gaze on Cherry. She'd just collapsed in a chair, her face dewy, her bouncy hair half tumbled to her shoulders, her eyes shining.

Men all around her.

He doubted she'd ever fully understand her appeal, but he did, and he counted himself damned lucky because no matter how many men admired her, or how she laughed with others, she saved all her love for him.

"I wanted to update you, if you don't mind getting news during a wedding."

Denver didn't mind at all. He already knew Janet had finally recovered, only to be arrested before leaving the hospital. In addition to Carver, Mitty and Gene, a dozen or more locals and a handful of cops had also been picked up. "I'm anxious to hear."

Logan looked at his drink, glanced out at Cherry, and smiled. "You already know they located nearly eighty grand in that old truck Cherry told us about."

The truck where she used to hide. Muscles going tight, he nodded.

"But drugs were also recovered from their residence. They'd had them hidden in the floorboards, the walls, damn near everywhere." He swirled his drink. "I heard it was a real hellhole. Hard to believe Cherry ever lived there."

They both heard her laugh when Brand pulled her back to the dance floor.

Speaking the truth, Denver said, "She's more of a fighter than any man I know."

"The Nelson boys won't be out of prison any time soon. You now have the ATF, Kentucky State Police, and two bordering sheriffs' departments working with the state and local police." Logan downed his drink. "Police corruption… I fucking hate it."

Denver got that. Thankfully, Reese and Logan had always been honorable men.

"You should know," Logan said, "they also found evidence to tie Carver, Gene and Mitty to a few murders."

"No shit?" Not that he was surprised. Every single day for the rest of his life he'd be thankful that Cherry hadn't given up on him.

Again Logan went quiet. "What you did to them…"

Denver raised a brow, waiting. He didn't regret mangling the bastards. Far as he was concerned, they got off light.

Logan hesitated, looked across the dance floor to his wife, Pepper, and shook his head. "I'd have done the same."

Denver held out his left hand. "I appreciate the update."

"Anytime."

"I think I'll go collect Cherry, now. I'm ready to

call it a night." More than ready to have her all to himself again.

He stole her away from Miles, who had just stolen her from Brand.

The life of the party—and the love of his life.

Her makeup now smudged and her hair completely loose, she smiled up at him. "It was a beautiful wedding."

In the middle of the dance floor, he kissed her. "You're beautiful."

"I love you."

"I love you more." He had to constantly up the ante on her because he had a feeling she'd never let him forget how he'd dragged his feet over idiotic assumptions and mistaken perceptions.

He carried her shoes for her as they headed out. Stack and Vanity were nowhere to be found, but Armie remained in the middle of the dance floor with Merissa. Other women tried to cut in, but both he and Merissa ignored them.

Denver was grinning when they stepped outside and got hit with a surprise mob. Apparently word of Cannon's wedding had gotten out and not only a few reporters hung out, but fans also. He groaned as three reporters started toward him.

Cherry started to fade back, but he didn't let her. "Not tonight," he whispered.

The first few questions were about Cannon, but Denver dodged them.

Cannon's business was his own.

After that, reporters and fans alike threw out casual queries about his training, his opponent and his odds.

Denver took the time to answer, letting them know

his opponent was good, his injury wasn't serious and that he was in the best shape of his life.

"So you think you'll win?" someone asked.

He stepped Cherry forward so that he could hug her from behind. "This is my future wife."

The men cheered and the women groaned.

Blushing, Cherry wiggled her fingers at the different camera phones flashing. "I'm his biggest fan," she announced.

So damn happy, Denver scooped her close, kissed her silly, and told the crowd what he already knew. "I'm a winner, and it doesn't have a damn thing to do with how I do at the next fight."

Cherry gave him an "aww" look and hugged him tight.

He headed to the car, but for the sake of the fans, Denver looked back. "But yeah, I'll beat Packer. Look for a knockout in the second round."

And right after that, he'd be marrying Cherry.

She'd gone through hell and come out swinging. And now she was all his.

"I'm so glad I didn't give up on you."

He laughed. No, she'd never let him live it down.

She was cute, sexy and voluptuous while still trim, adorably forgiving and wildly carnal. A survivor. A fighter.

Perfect for him.

He looked forward to her teasing for the rest of his life.

* * * * *

Look for Stack's book,
TOUGH LOVE,
coming soon from Lori Foster
and HQN Books!
Meanwhile, read on
for a special Cannon Colter bonus scene.

THE WEDDING

A Cannon Colter Bonus Scene

CANNON STOOD BACK, away from everyone else…just to take it all in. He'd already removed his tux jacket and tie and opened the top buttons of his dress shirt. Music played, the lights were low, people crowded the dance floor.

People who were a part of his life. Some for a long time, some more recent additions. All important to him. All there to celebrate with him.

He was now a married man. Yvette was his—forever. As he watched her dance with Armie, satisfaction kept a smile on his face. But what he felt was so much more than that.

It was love so strong that it made him stronger.

She excited and comforted him, challenged and encouraged him, made him feel powerful and left him weak.

What he felt for her was so rich that he knew no matter what the future brought, all he ever really needed to be happy was her at his side.

Well, and maybe a few kids at some point. Little girls with her smile and generous heart. Boys they'd raise to be good men.

Yeah, he'd like that a lot.

Busy as he stayed with his career, he and Yvette could still make parenthood work. They both loved the sport, and with so many other fighters as close friends, any kids they had would have a wealth of "uncles" looking out for them.

Thinking about pseudo uncles sent his gaze toward Armie. The best man had shown up in the requisite tux—and sporting a black eye. Damned if he hadn't grinned more than Cannon throughout the ceremony. Now that the vows were over and the partying well underway, Armie had already danced with nearly every woman in the place.

Everyone except Cannon's little sister, and that took his attention to Rissy. She looked beautiful in the bridesmaid dress, a fluffy, girly design his sister had never favored. Seeing her so dolled up made every guy in the place give her a second look—except Armie.

Little by little, Cannon realized that his best friend deliberately avoided Merissa whenever he could. And whenever he couldn't, there was so much naked emotion on his face that it left Cannon more than curious.

Merissa was his sister.

Armie was like a brother to him.

Maybe that's why he hadn't seen it before now. For him, they were both family. Apparently for them, the feelings were less…domestic.

For sure, Armie loved her. Cannon knew without a doubt that Armie would die to protect her. But more than that? More than dedication to a family member? Yeah, he did believe it was more.

A lot more.

The others knew. He remembered the jokes that he hadn't gotten, the different ways that both Stack and Denver had ribbed Armie.

He'd been blind, but no more. From here on out, he'd be vigilant where it concerned his sister.

And where it concerned Armie.

He really didn't want either of them hurt.

Just then, Cherry danced past his line of vision with Miles. They laughed together. Cherry had removed her shoes and her upswept hair wasn't quite so upswept anymore. Unlike Rissy, she appeared to love the frothy dress, twirling often. She filled it out, especially up top.

Cannon grinned. Used to be a time Denver would have scowled over her dancing with another fighter, but now, when he glanced at his friend, he saw that Denver's gaze blazed with an excess of emotions. No jealousy, just possessiveness, satisfaction—and love. It seemed the two of them had worked out the issues in their relationship. Cannon expected another wedding to be happening soon.

Next to Denver, Stack stared at Vanity so intently, it could have intimidated most people. But Vanity appeared to be having too much fun to let anyone spoil it for her. Unlike the others, she looked as perfect now as she had while being Yvette's maid of honor. Cannon liked her a lot, appreciated her friendship with his wife and was male enough to know Vanity was beyond just pretty. Well beyond.

Stack would have his work cut out for him with that one.

When Armie brought Yvette back, she announced it was time for her to throw the bouquet. It was nice, seeing her so relaxed and so happy. She'd rocked the traditional white dress, and she'd cried a little while reciting her vows. But beyond that, she didn't stand on formality. She wanted his friends and family to have a good time, period, which meant they'd done some things out of order.

No one seemed to notice or care.

As the men gathered toward the bar and the women crowded the floor, Cannon kissed her. "I love you."

"I love you, too. So much."

"You're beautiful," he told her. The requisite white dress, paired with her glossy dark hair and vivid green eyes, made her look almost ethereal. For the special day, she'd worn her long hair partially free, but with curling tresses pulled up and anchored with dainty flowers that also held her veil. Happiness, and a little more makeup than usual, made her eyes sparkle. "So beautiful," he said again, brushing his thumb over her warm cheek. "Inside and out."

Modest as always, she smiled, then lifted the bouquet. "Feel like taking bets on who gets it?"

Cannon swept another gaze over his friends. Armie avoided looking at him. Denver stared only at Cherry. And Stack looked ready to steal Vanity away. With a nod of his head, he indicated the other fighters. "No, but it'll be interesting to see how they react."

Yvette laughed, posed dramatically as she prepared to let the flowers fly, then sent them backward over her shoulder, her aim true as they sailed toward her best friend, Vanity.

Stack disappointed him by not changing expressions.

But Vanity, with a grin, dodged to the side at the last second and the bouquet hit Cherry in the cleavage. She barely held on to it in her surprise.

Everyone screamed and cheered, including Vanity and Merissa.

Cannon scooped his wife close. "Can we go now?"

She touched his face. "In a hurry?"

"Yes." He nuzzled her neck. "I want to show my wife how exciting marriage is going to be."

Yvette pretended to faint, but said with a laugh, "I never had a doubt."

Not true. She'd had so many doubts that she'd put him through the fight of his life. It had taken a while, but finally she was happy. He'd do what he could to ensure she stayed that way.

Waving for his sister to join him, he whispered to Yvette, "Give me just one second."

She studied him, glanced at Merissa, and smiled. "What are you up to?"

"Just laying some groundwork for the other people I love."

Wearing an "aww" face, Yvette said, "You are such a wonderful man. It's no wonder they call you Saint." She hugged him tight. "And it's definitely the reason I call you *mine*."

With Yvette as his wife, he couldn't imagine being more content. One way or another, he wanted everyone else to feel the same. It might lead to a few more conflicts—but for a bunch of fighters who knew how to win, he didn't see that as a problem.

In fact, with another glance at Denver, Stack and Armie, he thought it just might turn out to be fun.

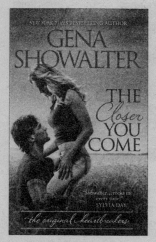

From the creator of *The Originals*, the hit spin-off television show of *The Vampire Diaries*, come three never-before-released prequel stories featuring the Original vampire family, set in 18th century New Orleans.

Available now!   Available now!   Coming May 26!

Family is power. The Original vampire family swore it to each other a thousand years ago. They pledged to remain together always and forever. But even when you're immortal, promises are hard to keep.

**Pick up your copies and visit
www.TheOriginalsBooks.com
to discover more!**

REQUEST YOUR FREE BOOKS!

2 FREE NOVELS
FROM THE ROMANCE COLLECTION
PLUS 2 FREE GIFTS!

YES! Please send me 2 FREE novels from the Romance Collection and my 2 FREE gifts (gifts are worth about $10). After receiving them, if I don't wish to receive any more books, I can return the shipping statement marked "cancel." If I don't cancel, I will receive 4 brand-new novels every month and be billed just $6.24 per book in the U.S. or $6.74 per book in Canada. That's a savings of at least 22% off the cover price. It's quite a bargain! Shipping and handling is just 50¢ per book in the U.S. and 75¢ per book in Canada.* I understand that accepting the 2 free books and gifts places me under no obligation to buy anything. I can always return a shipment and cancel at any time. Even if I never buy another book, the two free books and gifts are mine to keep forever.

194/394 MDN F4XY

Name _____ (PLEASE PRINT) _____

Address _____ Apt. # _____

City _____ State/Prov. _____ Zip/Postal Code _____

Signature (if under 18, a parent or guardian must sign)

Mail to the **Harlequin®** Reader Service:
IN U.S.A.: P.O. Box 1867, Buffalo, NY 14240-1867
IN CANADA: P.O. Box 609, Fort Erie, Ontario L2A 5X3

Want to try two free books from another line?
Call 1-800-873-8635 or visit www.ReaderService.com.

* Terms and prices subject to change without notice. Prices do not include applicable taxes. Sales tax applicable in N.Y. Canadian residents will be charged applicable taxes. Offer not valid in Quebec. This offer is limited to one order per household. Not valid for current subscribers to the Romance Collection or the Romance/Suspense Collection. All orders subject to credit approval. Credit or debit balances in a customer's account(s) may be offset by any other outstanding balance owed by or to the customer. Please allow 4 to 6 weeks for delivery. Offer available while quantities last.

Your Privacy—The Harlequin® Reader Service is committed to protecting your privacy. Our Privacy Policy is available online at www.ReaderService.com or upon request from the Harlequin Reader Service.

We make a portion of our mailing list available to reputable third parties that offer products we believe may interest you. If you prefer that we not exchange your name with third parties, or if you wish to clarify or modify your communication preferences, please visit us at www.ReaderService.com/consumerschoice or write to us at Harlequin Reader Service Preference Service, P.O. Box 9062, Buffalo, NY 14269. Include your complete name and address.

LORI FOSTER

77904	NO LIMITS	___ $7.99 U.S.	___ $9.99 CAN.
77857	DASH OF PERIL	___ $7.99 U.S.	___ $8.99 CAN.
77816	HOT IN HERE	___ $7.99 U.S.	___ $8.99 CAN.
77806	ALL RILED UP	___ $7.99 U.S.	___ $9.99 CAN.
77779	GETTING ROWDY	___ $7.99 U.S.	___ $8.99 CAN.
77761	BARE IT ALL	___ $7.99 U.S.	___ $9.99 CAN.
77708	THE BUCKHORN LEGACY	___ $7.99 U.S.	___ $9.99 CAN.
77695	RUN THE RISK	___ $7.99 U.S.	___ $9.99 CAN.
77656	A PERFECT STORM	___ $7.99 U.S.	___ $9.99 CAN.
77647	FOREVER BUCKHORN	___ $7.99 U.S.	___ $9.99 CAN.
77612	BUCKHORN BEGINNINGS	___ $7.99 U.S.	___ $9.99 CAN.
77582	SAVOR THE DANGER	___ $7.99 U.S.	___ $9.99 CAN.
77575	TRACE OF FEVER	___ $7.99 U.S.	___ $9.99 CAN.
77444	TEMPTED	___ $7.99 U.S.	___ $9.99 CAN.

(limited quantities available)

TOTAL AMOUNT	$ _____
POSTAGE & HANDLING	$ _____
($1.00 FOR 1 BOOK, 50¢ for each additional)	
APPLICABLE TAXES*	$ _____
TOTAL PAYABLE	$ _____

(check or money order—please do not send cash)

To order, complete this form and send it, along with a check or money order for the total above, payable to HQN Books, to: **In the U.S.:** 3010 Walden Avenue, P.O. Box 9077, Buffalo, NY 14269-9077; **In Canada:** P.O. Box 636, Fort Erie, Ontario, L2A 5X3.

Name: _____

Address: _____ City: _____

State/Prov.: _____ Zip/Postal Code: _____

Account Number (if applicable): _____

075 CSAS

*New York residents remit applicable sales taxes.
*Canadian residents remit applicable GST and provincial taxes.

HQN™

www.HQNBooks.com

PHLF0315BL